lapa
PUBLISHERS

CATALYST
PRESS

MARTIN STEYN

DARK TRACES

LAPA Publishers
Pretoria, South Africa
www.lapa.co.za

Catalyst Press
Livermore, California
www.catalystpress.org

Dark traces © 2017 by Martin Steyn

Martin Steyn, *Donker spoor* © 2014 by LAPA Publishers, Pretoria, South Africa

Published by LAPA Publishers (Pretoria, South Africa) and Catalyst Press (Livermore, California).

To order additional copies of the book, contact Catalyst Press at 2941 Kelly Street, Livermore CA 94551 or info@catalystbookpress.com.

Publisher's note: The body of a teenage girl sends Inspector Jan Magson on the trail of a serial killer.

Translation: *Martin Steyn*

Library of Congress Cataloging-in-Publication Data

Steyn, Martin, author and translator.

ISBN 978-1-946395-01-6 (paperback)
ISBN 978-1-946395-05-4 (ebook)
Library of Congress Control Number: 2016961581 September 2017

Printed and bound in the Republic of South Africa by Novus Print, a Novus Holdings-company

Serious Violent Crimes Unit
Bishop Lavis, Western Cape

Unit Commander
Lieutenant Colonel John Hattingh (46)

Group Leader
Captain Henz Kritzinger (37)

Detectives
Warrant Officer Jan Magson (54)
Warrant Officer Gys Burger (48)
Warrant Officer Colin Menck (40)
Warrant Officer Azhar Najeer (36)
Warrant Officer Patrick Zuzile Theko (31)
Warrant Officer Kayla Schulenburg (28)

Abbreviations

AFIS	Automated Fingerprint Identification System
SVC	Serious Violent Crimes Unit
FCS	Family Violence, Child Protection and Sexual Offenses Unit
LCRC	Local Criminal Record Center
SAPS	South African Police Service

Glossary

ag	ah, oh
bakkie	pickup truck
bleddie	slang, from the English "bloody," usually meaning "very" or "damned"
bliksem	literally "lightning," but used as a soft curse word to mean anything from "damnit" to "hit" or "strike," "bad person" to "very"
bloekom	eucalyptus or blue gum tree
boerewors	literally "farmers' sausage", usually made of beef
braai	barbecue
buk	bend over
dolosse	knucklebones used by sangomas to read the future
dominee	church minister
donner	literally "thunder," but used as a moderate curse word similar to bliksem
ja	yes
klagtebakkie	literally "complaints pickup truck," the vehicles typically used by uniformed police officers
koeksister	traditional sweet tea-time treat, of deep-fried dough soaked in syrup
lekker	tasty, but used to describe anything pleasant
meneer	mister
mevrou	missus
moer	versatile curse word similar to bliksem and donner in usage
nee	no
oom	uncle, but generally also used as a respectful form of addressing an older male
ouma	grandmother
poegie	motorized scooter
rottang	cane used for corporal punishment
sies	yuck, used to indicate disgust
slaptjips	French fries
soutie	a slightly derogatory term for an English-speaking person
vel	skin
worshond	literally "sausage dog," dachshund

One

March 9, 2014. Sunday.

"Yet another Sunday lunch with the family interrupted by blood and maggots," remarked Warrant Officer Colin Menck beside him. "What a great job we have, hey, Mags?"

Behind the wheel Warrant Officer Jan Magson did not respond. He simply continued along the meandering Vissershok Road out of Durbanville, looking for the murder scene.

"Casey has embarked on a grand campaign to get a horse for her birthday. Next year, when she turns ten. Because it's a special birthday."

Magson glanced at the horses looking out over the white wooden fence. Further on, on the opposite side of the road, a sign indicated the turn-off to the Meerendal Wine Estate. The rest was just vineyards, the green much too vivid. He didn't want a new docket.

"So I'm talking to myself again today."

Sometimes Menck was like a child whose mouth had to be in constant motion, opening and closing, emitting sound. "I didn't sleep well," said Magson.

"I don't ask a lot. 'Yes'. 'Oh'. Even a grunt will do."

The vineyards petered out, leaving only faded brown

grass. Magson glanced in the rear-view mirror. The road was empty, but his eyes lingered. The Corolla's dust-specked mirror turned his irises an even grayer green. There were lines etched in his forehead and cracks around his eyes. At his temples, the hair was receding. His moustache was edging away from brown towards gray.

He looked away.

There were two *klagtebakkies* at the side of the road, white pickups bearing the South African Police Service's logo and emergency number, blue lights on the roof and a holding area in the back. A few unmarked vehicles as well. No houses in the light brown surrounds. Magson parked the Corolla and turned off the ignition. As they got out, a uniformed officer came to meet them. They showed their identification cards.

The uniform nodded. "Warrant Officers. She's lying some distance in." He pointed with all five fingers extended.

"Were you first on the scene?" asked Menck.

"Yes, Warrant."

"Who found her?"

"A birdwatcher."

"Is he still here?" asked Magson.

"It was a woman, Warrant," said the uniform, now looking at him. "I kept her here until the first detective took her statement. He let her go when he was done. I have her details."

"That's good. Is Captain Kritzinger at the body?"

"Yes, Warrant." He removed his blue cap and scratched his black hair with the fingers of the same hand. It was glistening with sweat.

"All right. Take us to him."

"Wait," said Menck, "let me just fetch your bib."

"As long as you realize you'll have to carry it around the whole time," grumbled Magson. "Because I'm not putting it on in this heat." The temperature was only part of the reason—as Menck knew perfectly well. Magson loathed the stupid crime-scene vests. Besides, it said CRIME SCENE INVESTIGATOR on the ones meant for the detectives.

"The blue brings out your eyes, man," said Menck with a smile revealing his teeth.

"My eyes are green."

They walked up to the barbed-wire fence running all along the shoulder of the road. Magson noticed no signs of rust or disrepair, but here where most of the vehicles were parked, four of the posts had been overturned.

"I take it, it was like this?"

"Yes," said the uniform.

They followed him through the opening. No tire treads. And the gap was too small for a vehicle to fit through. Had the victim walked? Or had she been carried?

Everything in the hilly environment looked the same—brown and dead, like the tall grass brushing against the legs of his trousers. Except for the snake of reeds, most likely following a small stream. In the distance was a clump of blue gum trees. The air was dry and the smell reminded him of chili, the flakes Menck was always shoving under his nose. Sweat trickled down his neck and he wondered how much further it was to the body.

Reaching the top of a hill, Magson saw the people. Members of the Local Criminal Record Center had begun to document the scene. Captain Henz Kritzinger was in conversation with a small group of people, one of whom was the forensic pathologist—she stood out like a beacon in her white overalls and the bright orange vest with the words FORENSIC PATHOLOGY SERVICES on it.

Captain Kritzinger grimaced. "Well, do what you can."

The LCRC member nodded and walked off.

"Captain," greeted Magson.

"The doctor thinks we have a problem."

"She has already begun decomposing in this heat," said Doctor Sinette Killian, brushing an errant brown lock from her forehead, "but the indications are that she was hanged."

"*Hanged?*" asked Menck. "I can't remember us ever having a murder by hanging."

"I can."

"That is the problem," said Kritzinger.

"There was a girl, around September, October last year, I think, perhaps November," explained Doctor Killian. "There were signs of sexual assault. She was also dressed, but her panties were gone."

"But she wasn't one of ours," said Menck.

"I can't remember who the investigating officer was, but as far as I know, the docket is still open."

Two for the price of one, Magson thought. Fantastic.

The body looked like that of a teenage girl. She was clothed in a pair of shorts and a white top with spaghetti straps, but her feet were bare. Her abdomen was severely distended with gas and the exposed skin was a brownish yellow with dark green blotches. There was a lively presence of maggots, some quite large. Thick, dark fluid had seeped from her nostrils and mouth. The smell—something resembling rotten eggs and decaying meat coupled with that sweet smell unique to humans—was so strong that Magson could taste it at the back of his throat, and he knew it would be clinging to his clothes all the way home.

Doctor Killian knelt next to the body and gently turned the girl's head away from them. Her swollen face did not look good—the first wave of blowfly females had targeted her eyes, nose, mouth and ears to lay their eggs. But it was evident from the lush dark brown ponytail that she'd had beautiful hair. A discolored furrow was visible in areas around her throat and neck, despite the attentions of the maggots.

"The furrow is high here against the throat," indicated the pathologist. "Then it slants upward around the sides of the neck to the back." She looked up at Magson and squinted against the sun. "This is where the knot would've been."

He walked around the body and crouched on the other side. Blowflies buzzed around the girl, touching down, lifting off. The frenzied maggots were eating as if they knew their time was running out. The girl's clothes were not torn. Everything was where it should be. "And you say it looks like the previous one, Doc?"

"I'd like to do the post mortem first and have a look at my report on last year's case, but murder victims who were hanged are extremely rare, as you're well aware. Death by hanging is pretty much always suicide. So it would be quite a coincidence if we're looking at two different killers."

"Coincidence," said Magson. "Not likely. How long do you think she's been lying here?"

"Five to eight days maybe."

He placed his hands on his knees and pushed himself erect. All his hinges were in need of a few squirts of Q20. The left knee could do with some new parts.

Menck was looking around, rubbing his short dark brown hair, then stroking his moustache and goatee. "It's far to those *bloekom* trees. If she was hanged there, why drag her all the way over here?"

Doctor Killian rose as well. "There are indications that she had been bound."

"But he untied her," said Magson. "Probably after. No rope left with the body."

"Feels more like a dump site," said Menck.

"What's the birdwatcher's story?"

"She saw some or other bird and told her husband to stop," said Captain Kritzinger. "Got out and followed the thing to hell and gone, binoculars in one hand, bird guide in the other. Her husband says it's the story of his life."

"And then she found the girl."

"Hmm. I don't think the husband will be stopping for a bird again any time soon."

Menck chuckled.

Magson looked back towards the road, despite the hills hiding it from view. "I'm wondering about the fence."

"Did he break it," asked Menck, "or find it that way?"

"LCRC will have a look in any case," said Kritzinger.

"Hanging." Magson turned his attention back to the ugly furrow in the girl's neck. "It's not just a way to kill someone. It's also a form of execution."

March 10, 2014. Monday.

It was early morning when Magson signed the register at the Salt River Forensic Pathology Laboratory and followed the familiar path to the dressing room. He exchanged his shoes for gumboots, followed the kink to the passage and turned right. The air was cool, somewhat stuffy. The gumboots squeaked on the vinyl floor. He pushed the swing doors open and the rotten egg and meat smell hit him. And he still had to completely rid his dwindling hair of yesterday's assault. He greeted the pathologist and her assistant struggling to force open the fingers of a male body, and walked deeper into the dissection hall to the recess where Sinette Killian's station was located.

The murdered girl lay on the steel trolley, in the same condition as when Magson had seen her last, bar most of the maggots. Those that still remained were lethargic after their night in the fridge. The photographer was taking pictures.

"Morning, Doc."

"Morning," said Doctor Killian, dressed in deep green scrubs, with blue latex gloves. "I did some reading."

He looked up and found her blue eyes waiting for him. "And?"

"The rope marks look similar to the previous case." She picked up a photo.

He took it from her. A close-up of the same type of furrow in the neck as was evident on the girl in front of him. Comparing the two, he nodded. A dark lock of hair was visible next to the girl in the photo.

"Also a brunette?" he asked.

"Yes. And the same age group."

Magson sighed.

"There were a couple of other interesting findings with the previous victim. Abrasions and contusions on her wrists and ankles indicating she'd been bound. Bruises on her back consistent with blunt force trauma. Not perimortem."

"She was held captive for some time."

The pathologist nodded. "And she was found fully clothed, except for her panties."

"When was this?"

"She was discovered on October 24, last year."

"Where?"

"In the veld outside Brackenfell."

Doctor Killian opened a packet from the sexual assault kit and used the swab to collect any biological trace evidence, mainly semen, that might be inside the girl's mouth—and which had managed to survive the maggots.

"We have a possible identity," said Magson. "The clothes match. Hair, too. Teenage girl who disappeared on February 27."

"February 27. That's what …? About ten days." She nodded, placing the white swab in its special triangular box and sealing it. "That would be consistent. What were the circumstances?"

"She was walking home from a friend's house. Just disappeared."

Doctor Killian turned her attention to the lush hair, cutting matted locks and folding them into a piece of white paper. She pulled a number of strands from the scalp, sealing them in a second piece of paper. Her auxiliary service officer, Kennedy Zihlangu, lifted the girl's head when Doctor Killian gave a nod. She held a third piece of paper underneath the girl's head and drew a plastic comb through the long dark brown hair. She folded the comb along with any trace evidence into the piece of paper and sealed it.

Then she raised the girl's left wrist and cut the rubber band around the brown paper bag enclosing the hand. Carefully, she removed the bag and sealed it in an evidence bag. Having opened the next packet from the sexual assault kit, she moistened the swab with sterile water and rubbed the tip beneath every nail on the girl's left hand. Her nails were dirty due to the conditions her body had been exposed to during the previous several days, but otherwise short and neat.

"No clear defensive wounds."

Magson frowned.

The pathologist examined the girl's wrist. "Definite abrasions. Significantly worse on the outer sides. Indicative that she had been bound. Wrists against each other perhaps. There are signs of scab formation. Some yellow in the contusions. She was held captive for a period of time."

She completed the same ritual with the right hand and examined the wrist.

"Same?" asked Magson.

She nodded. "And similar to the previous victim. Her hands were probably tied while she was hanged as well. There are no scratch marks on her throat that would indicate that she tried to free herself."

Zihlangu helped her to remove the girl's clothes. The white top. Her bra. And the pair of shorts. It was all she was wearing.

Magson looked up, meeting Doctor Killian's eyes.

"No jewelry. Also the same as the previous victim."

While the pathologist was sealing and marking the clothes for the forensic laboratory, Magson thought out loud, "So he keeps their panties, jewelry ..." He looked at the tag tied to the girl's left big toe. WC/11/618/2014. "And shoes. Was the previous one barefoot, too?"

"No. She was wearing her hockey shoes."

"Hockey shoes?"

"She'd been on her way home after a hockey practice when she disappeared."

Doctor Killian looked over the body and more photos were taken.

Magson started wondering about Maryke Retief—the probable identity of the girl on the trolley. Fifteen years old, in Grade 10. After school she had gone home and a while later she had visited a friend. Later still she'd walked home again, never reaching her destination.

"Did the previous one also walk home?" he asked.

"I'm not sure."

Magson took out his notebook and jotted down a few thoughts. High-school girls on their way home. One from a sports practice. The other from a friend. Someone who was able to look for victims on weekday afternoons. Or at least some weekday afternoons.

Doctor Killian started taking swabs from areas where the killer might possibly have left biological evidence behind, like the breasts, stomach, thighs.

Magson watched the activities, distracted, thinking. Bound. Held captive. Dumped without panties. Which meant there had been some point at which she'd have been naked. Which meant sexual assault was probably a given.

Doctor Killian and Zihlangu each took hold of one of the girl's legs and moved them apart. She opened a new packet and combed through the girl's pubic hair.

Magson wondered whether the killer had had the girl dress prior to hanging her. Or had he hanged her naked and dressed her afterwards? Why had he left her with her clothes on? With this degree of decomposition, the suspicion that she was Maryke Retief was mainly due to the clothes in which she had been found.

Doctor Killian swabbed the girl's rectum and anal canal. "There are definite signs of sexual trauma here. Lacerations consistent with sodomy. Or penetration with an object. It was considerate of him to have her dress again. Her shorts were tight enough to keep the blowflies out. Otherwise, they'd have been here first." She sealed the final swab in a triangular box.

"Maryke Retief had exceptional eyes."

Doctor Killian looked up.

"On the missing persons photo," said Magson. He looked at the girl's face—what was left. "Bright green. It's what you notice first."

"Should I fetch the colposcope, Doctor?"

"Yes, please, Kennedy." The pathologist took swabs of the exterior vaginal area, and used a speculum to swab internally. Zihlangu returned with the colposcope. Doctor Killian positioned the special microscope and examined the interior of the vagina.

"There are tears in the inner lining. Quite deep inside. Whether due to rage or sadism—he was rough with her."

Magson turned his attention back to the girl's face. Taken. Held captive. Used and abused. For how long? A couple of days, at least. She would have cried. Pleaded. Begged.

But it hadn't made any difference.

And had there really been only one victim before her?

He rubbed his face. This was the last thing he needed right now.

March 11, 2014. Tuesday.

At the kitchen counter, Magson sat watching the early morning scene in the back garden. The day had barely begun and the sun was already poking around everywhere. Two turtle doves perched on the Vibracrete wall, one puffed up with its head tucked in while the other looked around jerkily. The grass on the lawn was too long.

He put a spoonful of Weet-Bix in his mouth. It was not particularly enjoyable, because the milk was a little off. He made a mental note to buy fresh milk.

The back of the barstool cut into his spine and he straightened away from it.

Another hot day was coming. It was supposed to be autumn.

The dove that had been looking around fluttered down to where the yesterday-today-and-tomorrow grew.

Magson doubted whether there could be much for the dove to eat—the summer had simply been too long, too hot.

He took another mouthful. On the cheap plastic clock above the door the thinnest hand ticked … ticked … ticked … The refrigerator started to groan.

The dove in the garden was still seeking something to eat, the other one had flown off.

Magson put the final spoonful in his mouth. When he was finished, he placed the bowl in the sink.

One last look out the window, and there, at last, Emma's little bird. The Cape robin perched on the edge of the wooden feeding tray, dapper in its gray-and-orange plumage. Below the white band across its head, the black eye glinted straight at him.

"I was beginning to think you weren't coming."

He carried the saucer with mince out the back door. The robin took wing for the white stinkwood tree. Magson scraped half of last night's leftovers onto the feeding tray. It was just an ordinary piece of timber with a rim. He'd varnished it and nailed a sawn-off branch onto the surface. The workmanship was decidedly rough, but Emma had been delighted, describing it as "rustic." The robin waited in the tree.

Back in the kitchen Magson paused to look out the window.

The little beak pecked, shook, swallowed.

A smile grazed his lips. Returning the saucer to the fridge, he left the kitchen to change for work.

Magson looked at the "murder mosaic" he had prepared on the wall. He was on the ground floor of the Western Cape Serious Violent Crimes Unit in Bishop Lavis, and this was what passed for decoration in the operational room: maps and photos of murder victims and crime scenes. Menck was sitting on one of the tables, feet dangling, playing with a cigarette—probably longing for the good old days when he'd still been allowed to light it inside.

Magson heard voices and turned around. Captain Kritzinger followed Warrant Officer Kayla Schulenburg into the room. Before this very wall, she'd one day launched into a monologue to no one in particular. *In primary school I made a mosaic with squares of paper. My art teacher liked it so much, she took me to the principal. They had it framed and hung it in the foyer at the entrance. She really wanted me to develop my artistic talent. I wonder what she'd say if she saw me today, using that talent to create murder mosaics …* It had made an impression on Magson, the melancholy look in her eyes as she'd stood staring at the wall, and the name "murder mosaic" had stuck.

"Missing Gys already?" asked Menck with a smile and raised eyebrows.

"I don't know why," Schulenburg grinned, pulling the curls of her ponytail through her fingers, "but since yesterday things just seem so peaceful."

"Enjoy it while you can."

Magson would gladly trade places with Warrant Officer Gys Burger. He would much rather be spending hours in court, testifying in the final throes of a docket—even answering nonsensical questions from the defense—than starting a new one. Especially one like this.

"Okay," said Kritzinger, "let's go over everything we know so far. Mags?"

"All right. We have two victims. Doc Killian is convinced that it's the same killer's handiwork. The first one was Brackenfell's docket, but we've taken it over now." He pointed to one of the photos affixed to the wall, a girl with dark hair, arched eyebrows and a somewhat mischievous smile. Next to the photo, her name was written in capital letters, a summary of her information below.

"Dominique Gould," said Magson. "Sixteen. She was on her way home from hockey practice at school when she just disappeared. That was on October 16 last year."

Magson pointed to the next photo. The slightly lopsided smile sucked dimples into her cheeks. One dark eyebrow was raised higher above the exceptional green eyes. "The second victim is Maryke Retief. Fifteen. She went to visit a friend after school on February 27, and on her way home just disappeared. Both girls were walking."

He strode over to the enormous map of Cape Town and surrounds. Pointed to one of the two markers. "This is where Dominique was found on October 24." A piece of string led away from the map to a color photograph of the crime scene, but Magson moved on to the next marker. "Maryke here, Sunday. Dominique went to Brackenfell High and she disappeared in Brackenfell. Her body was dumped near Brackenfell. Maryke lived in Bellville and disappeared in Bellville. Her body was dumped near Durbanville."

"Much further away," remarked Schulenburg.

Kritzinger nodded. "Maybe Dominique was discovered too quickly. So he put in more of an effort this time."

"But then a bird came along and ruined everything," remarked Menck. Magson noticed that he wasn't smiling.

"A birdwatcher found her," said Kritzinger when Schulenburg enquired with her eyebrows.

"Brackenfell, Bellville," said Magson. "That's his area."

"And serial killers find their victims in a comfort zone. An area they know."

"That's if he started in Brackenfell," said Menck. "If Dominique was the first."

Kritzinger nodded.

"If there were other victims and they were also hanged, it shouldn't be too difficult to find out," said Schulenburg.

"Sounds like you're volunteering." Kritzinger looked at her and she nodded.

"This hanging business is strange." Menck rolled the cigarette to and fro between his thumb and his index and middle fingers. "It has to mean something."

"Hanged. Strangled. Stabbed. Shot. Means nothing. Murder is murder," said Schulenburg in a gruff voice with an exaggerated scowl.

Menck smiled. "Even Gys would have to admit it's unusual."

"He hangs them somewhere else," said Magson. "And then he dumps them with their clothes on, but some articles are missing. They don't have any jewelry. Dominique always wore her watch. Maryke had a gold chain. And he keeps their panties ..."

"Personal things," said Kritzinger. "Mementoes."

"Maryke was dumped without her sandals. Dominique still had her hockey socks and shoes on, but her school and hockey bags were gone."

"Did he put her socks and shoes back on?" asked Schulenburg. "Or did he never take them off?"

"No, they had been off at some stage," said Magson. "There are marks on her ankles. She was tied barefoot."

"So ..." Schulenburg frowned, her head tilted to the left. "He dumps the one without her sandals, but he goes to all the trouble to put the other one's shoes back on?"

"Maybe he hangs them with their clothes on. Maybe Dominique put her shoes back on after he assaulted her. Maybe Maryke didn't, or they fell off during the hanging."

"What about their bras?"

"Both had their bras on."

Schulenburg's frown deepened. "Jewelry, panties, but bras he doesn't keep."

"He abducts them in the afternoon," said Magson, "while they're walking next to the road. He does it in such a way that there are no witnesses. Nobody saw anything. Nobody heard anything."

"Maybe they knew him," said Kritzinger. "They got in the car with him because he wasn't a stranger."

Schulenburg walked over to the map. She drew the nail of her index finger back and forth across her lower lip. "They were in different schools, different suburbs. A school friend or teacher doesn't seem likely."

"Unless it's a teacher that transferred from the one school to the other."

"He'd need a car to transport and dump the bodies," said Menck. "Which means he has to be able to drive and he needs access to a vehicle."

"It's too neat and sophisticated for a teenager anyway," said Magson. "And he keeps them captive somewhere for a couple of days."

"If it's in his home, he lives alone."

And Magson had recently learned that one who lived alone was more readily drawn to dark thoughts.

Two

March 12, 2014. Wednesday.

The church was filled almost to capacity. There were numerous rows of school children in uniform. The majority had long hair and many of the ponytails were dark brown.

Maryke Retief's family was seated in the front row. The friend she had visited, too. She and Maryke's brother weren't wearing their school uniforms.

Magson and Menck looked for seats at the back. They had come to observe the attendees.

Magson sat down.

The upholstery exhaled under his weight.

He looked up. His face felt too hot and his heart was racing and his palms were moist and cold. He glanced at Menck, but his attention was elsewhere. Magson was struggling to breathe.

"Bathroom," he whispered to Menck and got up.

He headed for the exit. His vision doubled. The floor was further away than it should've been. Cold sweat was dripping down the back of his neck.

The wall. Almost there. He could lean against it to keep upright. Follow it to the door. He pushed it open. It closed behind him. He lurched to the washbasin and planted his hands on the edge. He hung his head.

Just breathe …

At last he opened his eyes. Looked up. At his face. He looked away.

He will wipe away all tears from their eyes. There will be no more death … That was what the *dominee* had said. That day when Magson had sat in the front pew.

He opened the tap and let the cool water pool into his cupped hands. He dipped his face into it. And again.

He was beginning to feel better. His heart had slowed—it was no longer vibrating against his ribcage.

He wiped his face with his handkerchief and looked at the mirror.

… no more crying or pain.

He exited the bathroom. In the church the *dominee* had begun the service. Magson took a few deep breaths and went back to where Menck was sitting. His heart had picked up speed once more, but he couldn't get up again—which made it worse. Just breathe. He concentrated on inhaling and exhaling. And after a while, mercifully, it got better.

But his thoughts kept returning to that day when he had been sitting in the front pew of another church. Someone a few rows behind him had had too much deodorant or aftershave on. It had been a masculine fragrance, spicy, too strong. It had been hot in the church. His shirt had clung to him, his jacket locking all the heat inside. Someone had been coughing continually. Beautiful words had come from the minister's mouth, comforting words, but all he'd been able to think of …

Everyone was rising now. He realized the organ was playing. Menck held the booklet so he could read the hymn's lyrics.

Emma had chosen *"Ek sien 'n nuwe hemel kom."* I see a new heaven …

But he hadn't been able to put voice to the words.

Magson sighed and shook his head. "Houses everywhere you look and nobody saw or heard a thing."

Propped against the Corolla, Menck lit a John Rolfe and peered up and down the street again.

Magson became aware that he was staring at the house across the road. He couldn't stop thinking about Maryke Retief's funeral. He kept seeing her parents after the service, their red eyes, drained faces, how they accepted the hands offered, thanking another person for being sorry that their daughter had been murdered. Her younger brother standing around in the background like forgotten luggage.

He realized Menck was speaking, "… an explosion. You know how unobservant people are. They're so focused on their own thing—"

"That's the whole problem with today's society. People are just busy with their own lives. A teenage girl is grabbed in broad daylight along a road filled with houses and nobody sees or hears a thing."

"Well, maybe that's a clue in itself. Either he knows the victims, or he's able to gain their trust and lure them into the car willingly. So there *is* nothing to see or hear."

"And so they just go with him, without suspecting a thing …" Magson recalled all the schoolgirls in their navy blazers at the funeral. "Lambs to the slaughter."

"I don't know if I've told you this before, but Kathy's cousin studied to be a chef. He visited a factory where they slaughter chickens. He says they hang the chickens by their feet, and as soon as they do that, the chickens stop struggling. They just hang there. And then this conveyor-thing carries them off, upside down, to a V-shaped blade and it slices off their heads. And they just hang there. Calmly. They don't fight. They don't struggle." He took a drag of his cigarette. "It's rather disturbing. Not enough to stop eating chicken, but still …"

Magson was still looking at the house. It was the paint that was bothering him—there was too much yellow in the cream. "My mother caught chickens in the yard and chopped off their heads. Later my brother and I did it."

"Your mother? This is the same woman who taught you to speak such proper Afrikaans."

"Only mother I had."

"Hmm, that I would have liked to have seen. So do they really run around? After the head's off?"

He noticed Menck watching him. "No, man. The one takes hold of the body and the feet. And the other one grabs the head and chops it off."

"Just like that?"

"Ja. And then you let them bleed out. But you have to make sure to keep hold of the feet, because if they kick you, they can draw blood."

"But can they run around without a head?"

"They say so."

"But you never tested it?"

"No."

Menck sucked on his cigarette. "Jan Magson, chicken killer."

Magson shrugged. "That's how we grew up."

"I can't believe you've never told me this before."

"What does it matter? It was a different time anyway."

He peered up the street. Somewhere a dog started barking and a guinea fowl's panicked screams erupted from the same direction. If Maryke Retief had screamed, no one had heard her. Or paid any attention.

"Maryke disappeared on a Thursday. Dominique on a Wednesday. Weekdays. He has a house and a car. He gets them into his car without a struggle, so he must have a decent appearance. This all means he must have a job."

Menck nodded.

"So does he take leave to watch them while they're captive?"

"That, or he has a place where he can lock them up securely while he's away."

Magson pulled a face. "It will have to be very secure if he lives close to other people."

"If he ties them up properly, sticks some quality tape over their mouths, he can probably just leave them in his spare room."

Magson looked at him. "I'd be stressing the whole time, worrying she might get free."

Menck nodded. "I'd have trouble concentrating at work.

Keep watching the door for the police." He took a drag. "Maybe he's got a cage."

Chewing his lower lip, Magson mused, "Afternoons. You know who else has free afternoons, along with pupils?"

"Teachers."

"Teachers. They coach sports on some afternoons, but marking tests and homework, preparing lessons … All of that is done at home. It's not a problem to take a few afternoons to go look for a victim."

"No co-workers who'll know he took a day off or phoned in sick."

"No. And even if he does leave them alone at his house, it's just more than half a day."

"School comes out around two o'clock. Drive home quickly to make sure she's still nice and tied up."

"The Station Strangler was a teacher," said Magson. "And his victims were in different schools, too. Hell, different towns."

"A teacher knows children. He deals with them every day."

"Even if he doesn't know them from school, he'll know how to talk to children. How to make them feel comfortable. He can practice it every day."

Menck dropped his cigarette butt and crushed it under his shoe. "You know, hanging is actually not a bad option. It removes the entire blood problem from the equation, because that stuff always gets in somewhere. And with hanging you don't necessarily need to get rid of the body."

Magson closed his eyes and rubbed his face.

But Menck was surging along. "With the necessary planning you can even make it look like a suicide. Maybe slip her some downers a month or so beforehand, so people will notice her mood is low. Of course, you'll have to stop early enough not to have it show up in her system at autopsy. A convincing suicide. Best place to hide something is smack bang in the open."

"Don't you get tired of this! On and on with the perfect murder of your spouse. Why do you want to plan this so badly?"

Menck looked at him, one eyebrow raised. "Because it

keeps my brain sharp, Mags." He tapped his temple. "My criminal brain. You know, the one that helps me to catch murderers."

Magson turned away, but he could feel Menck's eyes studying him.

"What's eating you, anyway, Mags?"

"Nothing."

"You always used to plan along."

"Ja, well, it's different—" Movement in one of the gardens across the street caught Magson's attention. "Hey. There's a gardener over there. I didn't see him before." Magson didn't wait for a response. He crossed the road to where a man was pruning shrubs.

"Excuse me, we'd like to ask you some questions."

The man stopped pruning and looked at them. An older man, middle-aged perhaps. In blue overalls, despite the heat. He came closer.

"*Meneer*?"

"We're police." Magson raised his identification card. "On what days do you work here?"

"I work here for *Mevrou* Rauch on Wednesdays." He spoke somewhat slowly, carefully, with concentration.

"Where do you work on Thursdays?"

"I work for *Mevrou* Serfontein on Tuesdays and Thursdays. Her house is just a couple houses down the street."

"This same street?"

"Ja, *Meneer*."

Magson took out a photo of Maryke Retief and showed it to the man. "Have you seen this girl before?"

The man looked at the photo and nodded. "Ja, *Meneer*. She often walks past here. But for many days I didn't see her. I hope nothing happened to her."

"Can you remember the last time you saw her?"

The man's eyebrows drew closer together, his oil-black eyes staring down to his left. "I think I worked at *Mevrou* Serfontein, because I remember she came to talk to Butch."

"Who's Butch?" asked Menck.

"*Mevrou* Serfontein has a parrot. His name is Butch. We always put Butch's cage outside when I work there and the sun is out. If the girl walks past and Butch is outside, then she always comes and talks to him."

"Can you remember when this was?"

"It was not last week, *Meneer*, because last week I worked in the back garden on the Wendy house." He nodded a couple of times. "I sanded and I painted." He mimicked the movements with his hand. "It was maybe the week before."

"What's your name?" asked Magson.

"My name is Justus, *Meneer*."

"All right, Justus. This is very important. Can you remember which way the girl went?"

"I think ..." He looked down the road. In the opposite direction. Back the other way again. "I think she walked that way."

"Home," said Menck.

"All right, Justus," Magson said again. "That's very good. Did you see if anything happened to her after she left *Mevrou* Serfontein's yard?"

Justus looked down, the concentration evident on his face. He looked up. "A car stops. I can see. I work in the garden by the road. She comes say hello to Butch, then she says bye to me and she walks that way. The car stops and she gets in. But she knows the driver."

"How do you know?"

"She says hello and gets in."

"Did you see who drove the car?"

"*Nee, Meneer*, I don't see him."

Magson looked down the street. "Do you know what kind of car it was?"

"*Nee, Meneer*. I don't really know cars."

"All right, Justus. What do you remember about the car? What did it look like?"

"I think it is a white car. I just see it from behind."

Magson asked more questions about the car, but the man had no further information, except that it had been a car—not a *bakkie*, not a four-by-four, not particularly large.

"Thank you, Justus. We may need to talk to you again. I'm Warrant Officer Magson. Here's my card. If you remember anything, please ask the *Mevrou* to call me."

He nodded and took the card. He looked sad. "The girl, *Meneer*. Something happened to her."

"Ja. Something did."

"I'm sorry, *Meneer*. She had a good heart. People show their heart when they talk to an animal."

Magson sighed. The last thing he wanted to do was to knock on the Retiefs' front door on the day they had buried their daughter. But time was a luxury they couldn't afford. Tomorrow he would be visiting her school with Menck and then they would need as much information as they could get.

He rang the doorbell.

Maryke's father opened the door. He looked exhausted. There were dark, puffy crescents beneath his eyes and his shoulders sagged.

"Warrant Magson." The words came slowly, softly.

"Mr. Retief. I'm very sorry to bother you …"

"It's all right, Warrant. Anything to catch that …" The rest of the sentence failed to come, as if he lacked the energy to get the words out, and he just stepped aside.

"Thank you." Magson entered the house. He already knew from the cars parked in the street that the Retiefs were not alone, and now he could hear the muted voices. The aroma of food permeated the air. It smelled really nice. He wondered how much food would simply be thrown away. Everyone always brought food on such occasions. Too much.

"I'd like to see Maryke's room, if I may."

Her father nodded. "We went through it when … But it's still the way she left it."

"And then I'd like to ask your son a few questions, too."

"I'll go call him." He began to turn.

"Mr. Retief. I'd like to talk to him alone, if you don't mind. Sometimes it's easier for children to talk when their parents aren't there."

The man just nodded and went to fetch his son.

Magson knew what the father was feeling. Or perhaps no one could ever really know what another person was feeling. But he recognized what he was seeing. And he understood it. And he knew it never went away. After Emma died, many people said it would get better, he would get over his wife's death. They had probably meant well, but only one person had told him the truth. He had said you never really got over the death of someone you love, but you did learn to live with it. Magson was a slow learner.

He sensed someone's presence and saw the boy watching him.

"Hello. Your name is Wynand, too, like your dad, right?"

The boy nodded.

"We didn't get a chance to talk the other day."

The boy just looked at him.

"Your dad said it's all right if I look around Maryke's room. Will you show me?"

The boy turned around and Magson followed him down the hallway. The other voices faded out behind them.

"It's here." The boy opened the door.

Magson entered the room. Looked around. The boy remained outside, looking like he wanted to leave.

"How old are you?"

"Fourteen." One year younger than Maryke.

"Grade 9?"

The boy nodded.

Magson looked around again. Posters of pop stars he had never heard of. The bed was made up in light orange. A rag-doll with a dark violet dress lay against the pillow. The eyes were shimmering buttons, bright green like Maryke's. Pine desk in the other corner, a neat pile of school books, stationery, two small speakers on top. She had kept her work area surrounded by photographs on the two walls—her family, always everyone together, bunches of friends. She was laughing in every photo.

He turned around. The boy was still hovering in the doorway, his feet just outside the room. His right hand held the fingers of his left.

"Brothers and sisters sometimes know things about each other that their parents don't. Do you know if Maryke knew someone older than her? Someone who's not in school anymore. Someone with a car. Someone your parents don't know about?"

The boy shook his head. "All Rykie's friends were in her grade."

"Did she go to clubs?"

He shook his head.

"Did she ever say something about someone watching her, someone who made her uncomfortable, anything like that?"

Another shake of his head.

"Did she complain about a teacher at school?"

The boy looked at him. "Do you think a teacher did it?"

"To be honest, Wynand, we know very little at this stage. That's why anything you might know could be important."

He looked at the carpet. "Rykie was a good girl. She didn't hang out at weird places. She played on her keyboard, hung out with friends, listened to music and read. During winter she played netball. She didn't smoke or drink, and she didn't have any weird friends. And she never said anything about a teacher bothering her."

"All right. Someone saw her getting into a white car one afternoon while she was walking home. She knew the driver. Do you have any idea who that might be?"

Yet another headshake. "Was it … *him*?"

"I don't know."

It seemed like he wanted to say something.

"What is it, Wynand?"

"The newspapers are saying there was another girl."

"It looks that way."

"So a serial killer killed my sister."

Magson didn't answer.

The boy stared at the floor, squeezing and rubbing his left hand's fingers with his right thumb. "Everyone looks at me funny. At school. When I walk past, everyone stops talking. I wish things could just be the way they were."

Maryke Retief's diary lay in his lap, but Magson was staring at a spot somewhere on the opposite wall. The house was silent. His thoughts had drifted aimlessly until it had found Hannes. Hannes far away in England. Another world. Another life. He so desperately wanted to hear his son's voice again. Sometimes he stared at the phone. Sometimes he picked it up and dialed the number, but dropped it back in its cradle before it could start ringing. Even before his mother's death their conversations over the phone had usually only consisted of a couple of short sentences. But they had been good. And then Emma would speak to him. She had been the glue keeping them together. She had been the glue keeping him together. Why did she have to get sick? If only it were possible for things to be the way they had been.

March 13, 2014. Thursday.

Magson stopped the Corolla in the parking area next to the school and eyed the green rugby fields behind the thick black iron fence. They got out and walked over to the building. Red tile roofs and neatly painted walls. Menck glanced at the light-colored emblem on a dark blue background above the door as he entered.

"It's hit us all very hard," the principal said in her office. "Many of the children are afraid. If it could happen to Maryke, it can happen to anyone. She was a good girl."

"We'd like to talk to her teachers," said Magson.

The principal nodded. "Of course. We want to do whatever we can to help."

"We'd be grateful if we could use an office or a classroom. We'll try to cause as little disruption as possible."

"I would appreciate that. We're trying to keep the environment as normal as we can for the learners."

"We understand."

One teacher after another painted a very similar picture of Maryke Retief. The theme was that of an above-average child, but not exceptional. Academically in the seventies. Second best netball team in her age group. No complaints or problems in the classroom, on the playground or the sports field. Well adjusted. Fit in well. Part of a close group of friends. Disbelief, shock and/or anger that such a thing could have happened to someone like her. Condemnation of the crime situation in South Africa.

"That one reminds me of Miss Banner," said Menck, wearing a rather tortured expression. "Standard 8 English First Language. She once had me memorize and recite ten minutes of Shakespeare just because I'd forgotten my book at home. I think a man hurt her badly somewhere along the way, because she *loathed* boys. And I don't use 'loathed' lightly. I'm telling you, that one had that same look in her eyes."

Which reminded Magson of old Spaais, who had always cracked a crooked smile when one of the female teachers sent a boy his way for the purpose of receiving some discipline. Then he'd take out his *rottang* and walk in a circle around you, all the while caressing the thin cane. Usually there would be a classroom full of pupils—all boys because Spaais was the woodwork teacher and only boys were allowed to do woodwork—but you couldn't hear a single one of them. Only Spaais's footsteps on the floorboards. And then those would fall silent, too. He'd be right behind you. *Buk!* That meant bending forward with your hands on the edge of a worktable, so that your back was horizontal. After you had unbuttoned your trousers, dropping them to your ankles. In Magson's Standard-9 year, old Spaais had assaulted a Standard-6 boy who had done something stupid with the woodwork equipment. Spaais had not been seen again and a new woodwork teacher had arrived to take his place. This one hadn't looked like he enjoyed hitting a child, but he had not allowed it to hold him back, either. Magson shook his head. "Can't say I've ever really missed school."

"No." Menck frowned. "I was always in trouble, too."

"And just look at you today, a policeman of all things." His cellphone rang. "Magson."

"Warrant Officer Jan Magson?" asked a female voice. Middle-aged or older. Cultivated.

"That's right."

"My name is Helena Serfontein. I'm phoning on behalf of my gardener, Justus."

"Oh, hello, Mrs. Serfontein. Did Justus remember something?"

"Yes. But first there is something I want clarity on."

"Ja?"

"What exactly are your intentions with regards to Justus?"

"I'm not sure what you mean," said Magson.

"Warrant Officer, Justus is a good man and a good worker. He is a bit mentally retarded and as a result somewhat naive. I won't have you involving him in something."

"We don't want to involve him in anything, Mrs. Serfontein. Justus may have important information about a crime. He's not under suspicion himself."

There was a moment's silence. "Fine then, Warrant Officer. Justus remembered something about the white car you were discussing."

"Ja?"

"There was a sticker on the back. It was oval in shape and dark in color. That is all he remembers."

"Does he know on which side of the car it was—left or right?"

"Hold on a moment, please."

While waiting, Magson shared the new information with Menck.

"Warrant Officer?"

"Ja?"

"He says he thinks it was on the same side that the girl got in."

"Left side. Thank you very much, Mrs. Serfontein. Please thank Justus, too."

"Could be helpful," said Menck.

"Ja. You never know."

"Well, let's get these interviews over with. My nicotine reserves should've been replenished a long time ago."

"Shall we take a stroll through the parking area?"

"Yes." Menck whipped out his pack of cigarettes.

Magson shook his head. "On the schoolgrounds. Is that the kind of example you want to be?"

"Believe me, if you have a child at school these days, you'd be only too happy if he's only smoking instead of all the other things."

"Who's worrying you now: Ben or Casey?"

"Casey is still in her angelic phase. She still believes her mom and I know everything. Ben is convinced we know nothing. And I'm not too sure about a couple of his friends."

"Did you check them out?"

"They're clean. So far."

Magson raised his eyebrows—he hadn't been serious. "Casey's boyfriends are going to have a hard time."

"No, man. Don't say 'Casey' and 'boyfriends' in the same sentence. Please. I need my sleep."

"I think it might be a good thing that I never had a daughter."

"How is Hannes? You haven't said anything in a long time."

Because there was nothing to say. "He's well. We spoke the other day."

"It's bad that so many children have to live so far from their parents these days."

Magson nodded. If only the distance between them could be measured in kilometers alone.

"When is he coming for a visit again?"

"He's busy. He can't just drop everything and fly over here."

Menck looked at him. It had come out too sharply.

"Work is keeping him busy."

Menck took a deep drag. "Well, what about you? Why don't you go visit him? When was the last time you went on holiday?"

"With two murdered teenage girls and the colonel already giving me the look?"

"When it's over. When we get him."

"Ja, we'll catch him just like that," said Magson, snapping his fingers. "We have so many fantastic leads."

"You have to be positive, man."

About what?

The cars were parked between the buildings on one side of the school. Magson started looking. "All right … white cars …"

"Toyota … Volkswagen … Hyundai … another Toyota—hey, here's something."

"What?" Magson followed Menck's gaze.

"Dark oval sticker."

Magson looked at the blue Stormers sticker on the back of a red Toyota. Could it have been the local rugby team's sticker the gardener had seen?

"There are more cars around the corner."

They walked around the building to another parking area. Magson noticed two more stickers, but one was on a *bakkie* and the other was melting away on a blue Opel Corsa.

"Here," said Menck. "White Honda Civic. Blue Stormers sticker on the left side."

Magson joined his partner.

"I'm so glad they stopped putting this red reflector across the back. *Sies*, man."

Magson had no interest in the styling. He walked around the car. The Civic was not particularly dirty, but it could use a wash. Tires were a bit deflated. He peered through the window. The ashtray was pulled out and half filled with coins, mostly copper in color. There was a flyer on the passenger seat. Furniture at discount prices in massive green digits. Most likely received at a traffic light. Other than that, there was only an empty can of Stoney ginger beer.

"All right," said Magson, writing down the registration number in his notebook. "Let's go find out whose it is."

Three

Cornelius Delport. Born in 1985. Unmarried. Not only a teacher at Maryke Retief's school for the past three years, but one of her teachers as well. And owner of a white Honda Civic with a Stormers sticker on the back.

It didn't even qualify as circumstantial evidence, Magson reflected, turning his eyes up to the ceiling of his office. Delport had no criminal record, either.

He was one of the teachers they had spoken to, but Magson couldn't recall much about him. Which meant he hadn't made much of an impression. Always useful if that person aspired to being a successful murderer.

It wasn't much, but it was something. And no clue was too weak to follow up on.

He took his jacket and left the office.

A large part of police work consisted of phone calls, but Magson had always felt that face-to-face conversations were rather more productive. People were more likely to divulge information, particularly of the sensitive kind. And it was easier to see if they were hiding something or lying. Thus, whenever possible and when the potential information could prove to be important, he always tried to go to the person. Cornelius Delport had previously taught at a different school, and Magson was curious about his reasons for leaving. Maybe it had been nothing, but maybe it had been something.

And if it had been something, his former principal might just be more inclined to talk about it with Magson sitting right there in his office.

"Thank you for your trouble." The principal had already been home when Magson phoned and had come back to school.

"As I said, I live nearby. And it is truly awful about that girl. But, Warrant, I still don't understand how I could be of help." He had his elbows on the armrests of his chair, his fingers forming a tent in front of him.

"Well, obviously we have to take a look at everyone who had contact with Maryke Retief, including her teachers. One of them taught here in the past."

"Oh? Who's that?"

"I just want to state that we're not talking about suspects here. It's just routine."

The principal nodded, but his bushy eyebrows rose. "And yet you drove all the way here, Warrant."

"I had to come in this direction anyway. But it is a sensitive case."

"What is the individual's name?"

"Cornelius Delport."

"Neels? Oh." It was obvious the name didn't leave a pleasant taste in the principal's mouth. He lowered his hands and shifted in his chair.

"Why did he leave?"

The principal rubbed the tip of his nose and straightened a book on his desk. "People do sometimes change employers, Warrant."

"That is true," said Magson. "But usually they have a reason."

"It was years ago …" He wiped along the edge of the desk, as if he'd noticed some dust.

"Is there someone else who might remember?"

The principal looked up quickly. "There was never—they were only ever allegations …"

"What 'allegations'?"

The man's shoulders sagged. He stared at the book on his desk. "There was a rumor that Neels Delport had had a … re-

lationship with one of the girls in Grade 11." He looked up at
Magson. "But there was never any concrete evidence, and the
girl denied it. Still, the rumors persisted. The learners circulat-
ed it as fact. Some of the parents got wind of it and eventually
the situation became unsavory. The governing body decided
it would be best if Neels … resigned."

"And Delport just accepted it?"

"Well, he denied the allegations, but the situation was unpleasant for him as well. He offered to leave if we … supported
his applications at other schools."

"Do you think he was involved with the girl?"

"As I said, there was never any concrete evidence. But I
had the feeling there was …" He paused. "… something going
on. I'm not sure how serious it was. Children have a tendency
to embellish a story and that was where most of the details
had come from. Neither Neels nor the girl admitted to anything." He looked at Magson. "But, Warrant, surely you don't
think that he …"

"What happened to the girl?"

"She transferred to a different school. The learners made
it impossible for her to stay."

Magson nodded. "Was she a loose girl?"

"That wasn't the impression she gave. She wasn't the
type of learner teachers really talk about among themselves.
There were no complaints about her, but she didn't excel."

The principal might just as well have described Maryke
Retief. "Was Delport involved in any other incidents?"

"None before the rumors started circulating. After that
there was … an episode involving Neels and one of the other
teachers."

"What kind of 'episode'?"

"Well, they had words, a confrontation, I suppose. When it
got physical, other teachers intervened."

"Other than these incidents, what was your opinion of
Neels Delport during the time he was here?"

The principal was silent for a moment. After a while he
sat back and rebuilt his finger tent. "Warrant, I have been in
education for a long time. There are always some children
who are troublemakers. Usually, it derives from a lack of

attention and love at home. Children fight it for all they're worth, but they like discipline. It means they are being protected because they're precious. Of course they would never admit it—and I doubt whether many even realize it on a conscious level—but that's what these troublemakers are really seeking with their behavior. But then, Warrant, there is another type of child. He isn't conspicuous, he doesn't really cause any problems. You barely remember him after he's gone. And then, one day, you read about him in the papers. Perhaps he swindled some elderly people out of their pensions. Perhaps he murdered his wife. Neels Delport reminds me of that kind of child. Prior to the story with the girl, he was here without being noticeable." He stroked his chin. "Of course, some of these … 'invisible' children simply become 'invisible' adults."

March 14, 2014. Friday.

Lieutenant Colonel John Hattingh walked to the front of the operational room. He looked at the photographs and information on the wall, and turned around. "Right. Where are we with Gould and Retief? It's Friday. My phone doesn't stop ringing. Tell me the beautiful words I can convey to the brigadier and the general. So they can gaze upon me and my specialist unit with joy in their hearts."

How Magson wished he had beautiful words to offer. "There is a teacher at Maryke's school, Colonel. Neels Delport. Bit early to talk of 'suspect', but there are some interesting things."

"I don't hear anything that will inspire joy yet. How interesting?"

Magson went over the details.

"How good is this gardener's description?"

"Good enough to lead us to Delport's car. Too vague to say it's definitely the car that picked up Maryke."

The unit commander nodded. "Any connection between Delport and Gould?"

"Nothing yet, Colonel."

"There's no connection between the two schools in terms of personnel," added Menck.

"There are no other homicidal hangings, Colonel," said Schulenburg. "But there are a couple of open dockets with similar victims. One of which is quite interesting."

Lieutenant Colonel Hattingh turned his head and cupped his left hand behind his ear.

"Schoolgirl. Strangled with rope. She was found in the veld. Clothed, except for her panties."

At the last part, Magson looked up at Schulenburg. "When was this?"

"April 2013. She'd been with her boyfriend, they'd had an argument and she walked home alone. It was a Friday night."

"Where did she disappear?"

"Durbanville."

Magson walked over to the map. "Brackenfell." He pressed the tip of his index finger against the name. "Bellville. The area where Maryke was dumped. And right in the middle is Durbanville." He looked at Schulenburg. "But you said it was at night?"

She nodded. "Ja. But her photo will not look out of place with those two. Her hair was also dark brown."

"What's her name?"

"Lauren Romburgh."

"Okay," said Captain Kritzinger. "Schulenburg, dig deeper into the Romburgh girl's story. I want to know if she could be part of the series or not. Mags, what is your plan for today?"

"Delport's old girlfriend from school. I want to talk to Maryke's friends again, too. And get around to Dominique's friends."

"Okay. Also, send everything you have to Pretoria for a profile. It might help with Delport or if we have to look further."

Denise Pont was now a student at the University of Cape Town. Like many of the female students on campus, she was dressed in jeans and a top. Emma had been wearing a dress when he'd met her, he barely a year in uniform and she an eyewitness ... Magson shoved the memory away and looked beyond Denise Pont's heart-shaped face and deep brown eyes to the long dark brown hair tied back in an unruly ponytail.

"We'd like to talk to you about your relationship with Neels Delport."

A shadow passed briefly across her face, leaving a frown in its wake. "He was one of my teachers at school. What is this about?"

"As we understand, he was more than just your teacher."

She rolled her eyes. "That old story again. It was years ago. What—"

"Miss Pont, we're busy with an important investigation. We would appreciate your honesty in the matter. Did you and Neels Delport have a relationship?"

"It's ancient history. What's it got to do with the police now?"

"I would prefer to just have a conversation here. Rather than have to take you to the station for a formal interview."

She glanced around, fidgeting. "Okay, fine, we had a relationship. But it really is ancient history. What does it matter now?"

"Do you still have contact with him?"

"No. After it came out, I went to a different school. Neels as well. And he moved. He didn't want to tell me where. Now I don't care anymore."

"How did the relationship start?" asked Menck.

"He was my hockey coach."

Magson caught Menck's quick glance at him.

"One afternoon after practice we started talking. Just about stuff. He was nice. He listened, cared, and I was flattered by the attention. It started like a normal relationship. It wasn't some wild, sordid affair."

"But it was a romantic relationship?" asked Magson.

She nodded.

"A sexual relationship?"

She looked away and there was a brief twitch at one corner of her mouth. Her right hand moved across her body, holding her left arm. "If you want to ask such personal questions, I want to know what's going on. Because I really don't understand why it matters after all this time."

"Miss Pont," said Magson, "we are investigating the murder of a schoolgirl."

"Murder?" Now she was holding both her arms, looking from Magson to Menck and back again, her forehead creased.

"Neels Delport was one of the murdered girl's teachers. It is routine to investigate everyone who had contact with her."

"Did Neels … Was he in a relationship with her?"

"The investigation is still at an early stage."

"Neels wouldn't …" She looked down, her frown etched deeper, and shook her head. "I can't believe that Neels had anything to do with her death."

"Was your relationship sexual, Miss Pont?"

She nodded.

"Was the sex ever rough?"

She looked away. "I wouldn't use the word 'rough'."

"What word would you use?"

She looked at Magson. "Is this really necessary?"

"I'm not asking for my enjoyment."

She sighed. "Passionate."

"What about sodomy?"

She frowned. "Sodomy?"

"Anal sex," offered Menck.

"I know what 'sodomy' is. No. It was just normal sex."

"Last night Kathy made ostrich and cabbage for supper."

The traffic had ground to a halt yet again. On the sidewalk the wind swept a white plastic bag up against a post, where it wrapped around, just above the garbage bin.

"It means something, but I can't figure out what."

Magson sighed. The bag flapped loose and gusted past the Corolla's windshield. "Why does it have to mean something? It's food."

"Ostrich?"

"What's wrong with it?"

"I don't like it."

"There is nothing wrong with ostrich," said Magson. "Tastes almost like beef." Couldn't the traffic just start moving?

"It's not right."

He rolled down the window. The din of cars and people flooded in. The stench of the diesel *bakkie* smoking diagonally in front of them. He rolled the window back up. "What do you mean, 'it's not right'?"

"An ostrich is a stupid bird."

He turned to Menck. "An ostrich is a stupid bird?"

"The thing's brain fits into a teaspoon. That's five milliliters. An ostrich is quite large."

"Maybe a teaspoon is all it needs."

"All it needs? We're talking about a bird that sticks its head in the sand when it's scared or confused or whatever."

"That's a myth, man."

"Most myths sprout from the seed of truth."

"In any case, it's just meat," said Magson. "Who cares how clever it was? Don't tell me you believe those pork-fat-makes-you-stupid stories?"

"No, man."

"Well, what does it matter then?" At least the traffic was in motion again.

"It bothers me."

Magson shook his head. "If that is your reason for not eating something, you're more stupid than the ostrich."

"Well, that was uncalled for. Anyway, Kathy doesn't like cabbage herself. She went out and bought food she does not really like, and cooked it."

He should instead be glad to *have* a wife who cooked for him, thought Magson.

Within a few meters they left Parow and entered Bellville. Voortrekker Road was bustling as usual. And as soon as they started moving, they had to stop at one of the pedestrian crossings. Everyone wanted to be on the other side of the road today.

He glanced at Menck beside him. The gray was catching up to him at the temples. Magson looked away, grimacing. "Maybe it was on special," he said in a gentler tone.

"Just because it's cheap is no reason to buy something you don't really want."

"Millions of people do it every day."

"Kathy's not an impulse buyer."

Magson began looking for the street where he had to turn right.

"No, it means something," insisted Menck. "I did something … Or I *didn't* do something. Ten to one, that's what it is—I failed to do something. Again."

"Why don't you just *ask* her?" Magson noticed the movement on his left and could feel Menck studying him.

"Are you just pissed off in general today, or is there something in particular?"

Magson sighed and turned right.

"It's a test," said Menck. "Like Purgatory. If I can figure it out on my own, I can still redeem myself. If I have to ask her, my sin gets multiplied by a secret number, and who knows what she's going to cook up then. The cabbage didn't even have a sauce or anything. It was just boiled. Or microwaved. Or whatever she did to it."

"You can always kill the taste with one of your chili powders."

"It's useless talking to you when you're in this kind of mood. Where are we going?"

"To Delport's house," said Magson.

"Aah … Are we going for a visit? Because he is probably at school at the moment."

"I just want to see what the place looks like."

"Hmm. So the hockey thing is interesting?"

"Ja. It is."

"So we know he likes teenage girls. He has no problem getting involved in physical altercations. The car. And now hockey. The coincidences are coming together rather nicely."

Magson parked next to the sidewalk. "Number sixteen. There it is."

The wall on the sidewalk was probably about hip height to Magson, who had stopped growing just short of 1.8 meters. Someone had made an attempt to paint the gate the same orange brown as the bricks' natural color, but hadn't been particularly successful. It didn't seem to have a lock. The garden consisted of some trees and shrubs, and a lawn struggling after a difficult summer that was refusing to end. The house didn't create much of an impression, either—white walls, tiled roof, big enough for two bedrooms, burglar bars in front of the windows. Like Delport, his property melted away into its surroundings.

Beside him Menck sighed. "Sure wouldn't mind having a look inside."

"I would be satisfied to let LCRC take his car apart. If it is him, everything we need could be in the boot."

"And the car didn't look particularly clean."

"No, but for how long?" Magson noticed dog feces on Delport's sidewalk. Near the mailbox. Someone had stepped in it. "Do you think she was truthful about the sex? Denise Pont?"

"Difficult to say. Her reaction seemed genuine enough. Or the question might have caught her off guard."

"It's a pity. A taste for sodomy would've helped. With the warrant. At the moment things are a bit thin."

Menck was toying with his goatee. "Yip. But I did get the sense that he might have been a bit rough. Maybe not as much as with Dominique and Maryke ..."

"Well, he didn't need to hold back with them."

"No. That is the benefit of a victim who won't be surviving. No rules."

She held the black-and-brown dachshund against her chest, her arms a protective circle around the small body, her legs tucked underneath her. The sadness that had been close to the surface earlier in the week had now settled in her eyes. The skin beneath was the color of day-old bruises. Magson recalled her photos on Maryke Retief's bedroom wall, laughing and bright. Now she looked tired and gray, someone who could not find rest. The little dog nibbled on the hair hanging onto her shoulder. Blonde hair.

"I couldn't think of anything else. I want to help, but ..."

"It's all right," said Magson. "You and Maryke had the same subjects, didn't you?"

"Yes."

"Was there a teacher who was interested in Maryke, who maybe paid more attention to her?"

"What?" She tilted her head and stared at him with intense eyes. "A teacher? Do you think it was a teacher?"

"At this stage we are still investigating every possibility," said Magson. "We are looking at everyone who had contact with Maryke. Was there a teacher?"

"I don't know."

Magson scanned the page containing a list of Maryke Retief's teachers. "Mr. Rutherson? Mr. Duvenhage?"

She blinked. "Doempie? He's as gay as Christmas."

"What about Mr. Delport?"

"I don't know." She looked past him, her forehead scrunched up.

"Think. It could be important."

"I don't know. Sometimes he is a bit flirty with some of the girls."

"With Maryke?"

She pushed the dog's muzzle away from her hair. "I don't know. Maybe."

"Did she say anything?"

"I don't think so." She stared back at him. The intensity didn't suit the soft features of her face. "Do you really think it was a teacher?"

Magson's cellphone rang. "Excuse me."

"We're just investigating all the possibilities," he heard Menck assuring her as he got up.

"I always took her for a walk in the afternoon," the girl said, stroking the dog's head. "Rykie, too, if she was here. She loved animals. But now I'm too scared. Rykie was just walking down this street. We've walked to one another's houses a thousand times."

He left the sitting room before he pressed the phone's answer button. "Magson."

"Er … Warrant Officer Magson?" A boy's voice. Soft. "It's Wynand Retief. Rykie's brother?"

"Hello, Wynand. How is it going?"

"Okay … I found something."

"What?"

"In Rykie's room. I was thinking. About teachers and so on. One of Rykie's teachers gave her a book. One of those little gift books. I don't know if it means anything, but …"

"Do you know which teacher it was?"

"Mr. Delport. There is a message."

"Mr. Delport?" Well, well.

"Yes. I have the book, but I don't want my parents to know. They're not really coping."

"All right. But I would like to see the book."

"Give me a time, and I'll wait for you on the corner."

It was a small hardcover book. Dark blue with a yellow stick figure surrounded by speech bubbles. Above it, *Hearing Voices* was scrawled in an arc. Magson opened the book. Read the message.

> Rykie,
> Listen to the voices—
> some of them make sense
> remember—you are special
> Neels Delport

He paged through the book. It was a collection of quotes and sayings—some familiar, some clever, some humorous.

Magson rubbed his face. "It's not really incriminating." He stared at the three words, read them aloud, "You are special."

"It's a bit too overfamiliar, as well," said Menck. "It sounds innocent, but with his history … It's open to interpretation."

"And it is evidence of personal contact with Maryke in particular. Maybe together with Denise Pont's statement, the other things …"

"It could be enough. With a bit of luck we catch the right magistrate on call."

Magson reflected on the phone call from Maryke's brother. A detective could never hand out too many contact cards. He had once had a breakthrough that solved an entire case because a woman had repurposed one of his cards as a bookmark.

Menck groaned and pressed his fingers against his eyelids. "I know why I'm eating ostrich and cabbage. It's because I'm an idiot." He shook his head. "It's the garage door."

Magson didn't care to listen to any more of Menck's domestic problems. But he glanced at Menck just long enough to serve as an invitation to continue.

"The wooden frame on Kathy's side, the section where the latch is, has come loose. So now the door can't close properly, because it pushes it away. She has to wrestle the thing closed every time. I promised I would fix it on the weekend. And I didn't. She's been asking me for weeks."

A garage door. And ostrich meat. These things were Problems.

Until cancer's hand came to rest on your shoulder.

Magson was sitting at the dinner table, the docket open in front of him. On a Friday evening. Everything they knew about the case so far was here—the autopsy reports and everything they had learned about the victims, the sketches of the scenes, statements, information about potential suspects. His focal point was Neels Delport—the search warrant for his house and the Civic was ready and waiting for tomorrow morning.

But maintaining concentration was a struggle. And it wasn't because of the pounding music next door—a party or something had steadily been picking up speed, and volume, for hours over there. He was thinking about ostrich and cabbage. About how he would devour an entire plate of Brussels sprouts boiled to mush, with a beaming smile, if only Emma could prepare it for him.

Thumping drums outside, but the house was so silent. He longed for her sounds. Her voice. Her presence.

How many late nights had he spent sitting here, the contents of dockets spread across the table, and then she would bring him a mug of Milo. A stroke of the hair. Or a kiss on the cheek. Before returning to watch something on TV or to read a book.

All the time he had wasted on dead people while the most important one had been alive and right here. All the hours he'd sat at this table, staring at photos of corpses while she had been only a few steps away. And for what? For what? There were always more. And more. And more. It never stopped. He could have sat next to her. Talked to her. Listened to her. Touched her. Just been with her.

He shot to his feet and wiped the docket from the table. The chair toppled backwards. Reports and statements and photographs whipped through the air and scattered all over the floor.

He turned away, to the buffet against the wall. The turquoise glass bowl of glazed clay fruit Emma had bought at a craft market, apples and pears and purple plums. The two watercolor paintings on the wall, aloes with bright orange flowers in rocky landscapes. He had never asked her where she had bought them.

His shoulders drooped, he hung his head.

He turned back and started collecting the papers. The photo of Maryke Retief. It was the school photo. Her thick dark hair tied back. Her smile, the dimples in her dusky cheeks. And, of course, the bright green eyes.

He placed the photo on the table, returned the chair to its feet, and went to the kitchen. Switched on the kettle. Washed the bowl containing the remnants of his microwave-Knorr-pasta-and-sauce while he waited for the kettle to boil.

Emma had fought with so much courage. Until the wheelchair had become her sole method of mobility.

He added two spoonfuls of Milo to a coffee mug. Mixed it with a bit of boiling water. That was the secret, she would always say. Mix it well before adding the milk. Put it in the microwave oven.

The walker hadn't bothered her so much. It had helped with the tiredness. But the wheelchair …

The microwave emitted its shrill beep.

He removed the steaming mug. It was important to heat it for the correct amount of time. It had to be hot, but the milk should not reach boiling point. Because then it left a *vel*, and Emma had despised it when hot milk formed a skin on top, which was why she had never taken warm milk with her coffee or tea. He stirred the mixture, looking at the froth swirling round and round. It looked almost exactly like Emma's.

The wheelchair had been the sign that she had lost. That she would not recover. She had no longer fought like before.

But his wife had been brave to the end.

Especially at the end.

He looked at the Milo and poured it out into the sink. Dropped his face in his hands. And cried.

Four

March 15, 2014. Saturday.

"The date is March 15, 2014. The time is twenty-one minutes past eight a.m., at the Serious Violent Crimes Unit in Bishop Lavis. Present are Warrant Officer Jan Magson, Warrant Officer Colin Menck and Mr. Cornelius Delport."

Magson studied the man sitting across him in the interrogation room. Uncombed. Unshaven. Uncomfortable. He had been properly shaken when they had came knocking on his door in the early hours, shoving a search warrant in his face.

The table was situated diagonally opposite the door, with Magson seated in the corner. Menck sat on his left. Two cameras recorded the session, one behind Delport's back, in the corner above the door, and the other above Magson.

"Mr. Delport," Magson began, "you are not under arrest at this time, but you do have the following rights. You have the right to remain silent. You have the right to have an attorney present. If you cannot afford a private attorney, you can apply to the court for a legal aid attorney. Do you understand these rights?"

"Yes, but I didn't do anything! I had nothing to do with Rykie's death!"

"Maryke Retief didn't just die, Mr. Delport. She was murdered."

"I know. I know she was murdered." Delport's hands pressed on the glass top of the table as he leaned forward. "But I had nothing to do with it."

"You were Maryke Retief's teacher, is that true?"

"You know I was."

"Everyone we've talked to said she was a good person." Magson turned to Menck. "Didn't they?"

Menck nodded. "Yes, everyone said she was a good girl."

"Do you agree, Mr. Delport?"

"Yes," said Delport.

"Did you enjoy having her in your classroom?"

"She never caused any problems. She was a good learner."

"'Learner,'" said Magson, looking at Menck. "It's such an ugly word."

"Yes," said Menck, "I don't know why they had to go and change it."

"What was wrong with 'pupil'?"

"Nothing. I don't even think there was a word like 'learner' while I was at school."

"How do you feel about it, Mr. Delport?"

Delport shrugged. "It's the terminology. We are educators."

"Educators?"

Delport nodded. He wiped his left eyebrow with the back of his hand.

"I'm glad I was never a 'learner,'" said Menck.

"Educators and learners," said Magson. "Do you take your role of educator seriously, Mr. Delport?"

"Yes."

"But my children are 'learners,'" said Menck.

"There are so many areas where children need to be educated," said Magson. "Would you say it's more difficult to educate children nowadays, Mr. Delport?"

"I only know the children of nowadays." Both hands were in his lap now. He was slumped, shoulders drooping.

"What is wrong with 'teacher'?" asked Menck.

Delport looked at him. "I don't know."

"But is it difficult?" asked Magson. "To educate them?"

"There are challenges. It's not always easy to maintain discipline."

"If someone speaks of 'teacher' and 'pupil,' everyone knows what is going on," said Menck. "A 'learner' and an 'educator' can mean anything."

"It's been this way for many years now," said Delport.

"Is discipline important to you, Mr. Delport?" asked Magson.

"Well, it's difficult to explain the work when there is chaos in the classroom."

"When I was at school, discipline was very good. Otherwise the *rottang* sang."

"Yes," said Menck. "I was chronically *bliksemed*."

"We were just talking about this the other day," said Magson. "Warrant Menck who was always in trouble at school and now he's a policeman. Maybe all those beatings brought him onto the right path."

"I don't know, I was often hit without proper justification." Menck placed his left elbow on the table, leaned forward with his chin on his fist, and glared at Delport. "I don't really like teachers." Delport shrank back in his chair. "They never wanted to listen to my side of the story. Just skipped directly to the hitting part."

There was a twitch at the left side of Delport's mouth. "We can't do that sort of thing anymore."

"But you'd like to. Wouldn't you? You'd like to."

"No. I ..."

"Some children need discipline," said Magson. "A good smack at the right time can perform miracles."

Menck shoved his index finger in Delport's face. "You would like that. I can see it in your eyes."

"No—"

"You would've been one of those teachers with a special cane or a strap with a name and everything."

"No, I've never—"

"What about Maryke?" asked Magson. "Did she need discipline?"

"No. No. Like I said, she was a good learner."

"Learner," said Menck. "Educator. Educator my arse, man!" He shoved his chair backwards and got up. Delport recoiled.

"She was special," said Magson.

Delport looked over his shoulder at Menck, who was standing against the wall behind Delport's back.

"Did you like her, Mr. Delport?"

Delport looked back at Magson, but his attention was divided. "Everyone liked her."

Menck paced up and down. Delport turned his head to look over his shoulder again.

"You too?"

"Yes, me too. But …"

"But …?"

Delport looked at Magson and then at his hands in his lap. "… as a teacher."

Menck bent with his mouth right next to Delport's ear. "I thought you're an *educator*."

Delport shifted in his chair, away from Menck.

"Is that the way you felt about Denise Pont, too?" asked Magson.

Delport looked at him sharply. "What?"

"Denise Pont, Mr. Delport. I'm sure you remember her."

"I …"

"We had a long conversation with her. She told us everything about your relationship."

"Nice girl," said Menck, sitting back down at the table. He leaned back comfortably in his chair and looked at Delport. "Quite chatty."

"We …" Delport dropped his head in his hand. He looked up at Menck and then at Magson. "Listen—" He swallowed. "It was long ago. I have never again …"

Magson looked at him. "Never again …?"

"It was wrong. Denise Pont. Okay? It was wrong, and I have never again done anything inappropriate with a learner."

Magson just looked at him. Silence could be very powerful during an interrogation. Menck got up again, this time without any drama.

"I never hurt Denise! And my relationship with Rykie was

completely professional. There was nothing inappropriate about it."

"'Remember—you are special.'"

"What?"

Magson just looked at the man opposite him.

Menck dropped the dark blue book on the table.

Delport flinched and looked at the little book. "This?"

Magson said nothing.

"It was a gift because she did well in her exam last year. I gave it to her at the beginning of the quarter."

Still Magson only looked at him.

"I gave the same book with the same message to about ten other learners as well."

"Ten others as well."

"So you're also a hockey coach," said Menck, taking his seat again.

Delport looked at him for a moment. "Yes."

"For girls," said Magson.

"Warrant Officer … Magson, right? Warrant Officer Magson, I had nothing to do with Maryke Retief's death. I made a mistake with Denise Pont, but I learned my lesson. I've never crossed the line again. I swear."

Menck placed his left elbow on the table and rested his chin in his hand. He was inside Delport's space, staring at him. Delport shifted uneasily.

"Do you have a girlfriend, Mr. Delport?" asked Magson.

"Not …" He looked away. "Not at the moment."

"Not? But you're an attractive man. Athletic. I wouldn't think you would struggle. Hey, Warrant Menck?"

"I have never been able to understand what women see in men," said Menck. "Every single day I am amazed that they aren't all lesbians."

Delport leaned to his left and stared at Menck. His mouth was slightly open.

"Why don't you have a girlfriend, Mr. Delport?" asked Magson.

"I …" He looked down. "I just haven't found the right woman yet."

"Have you had a girlfriend before?"

"One that isn't still in school," added Menck.

"Yes," said Delport. "Of course."

"Of course, Mr. Delport?" asked Magson. "Because it looks to me like you prefer girls. Teenage girls."

Menck nodded. "That is how it looks."

"The first school where you applied for work was a school for girls. Two schools for girls, in fact. Isn't it because they didn't want you that you settled for a mixed school?"

"I applied at many schools." Delport said this softly, looking at his hands.

"And you're a hockey coach," said Magson, "for the girls' team."

Delport dropped his head into his hand. "It's not how it looks."

"Why don't you explain it to us then."

"I …" He licked his lips. "I'm just more comfortable with the girls."

"Girls like Maryke Retief."

"I didn't do anything to her."

"An eyewitness saw her getting into your car before she disappeared."

"What? No, that's not—She was not in my car on the day she disappeared."

"Mr. Delport, at this very moment a forensics team is searching through every centimeter of your car. They are extremely thorough. If Maryke Retief was in your car, they will find something. She had lovely, thick hair. Did you know that you lose more than one hundred hairs every day. We only need one."

"She has been in my car."

Magson nodded.

"But *not* on the day she disappeared. I know, because the police came to the school the next day. The last time I saw her was in class."

"I thought you said there was nothing inappropriate about your relationship."

"I drove past her and gave her a lift home. That's all."

"I see."

"That's *all*. I dropped her at her home and that was all."

"And when would this have been, Mr. Delport?"

"Earlier that week."

"Earlier in the same week that Maryke Retief disappeared, you gave her a lift."

"That's right." Delport nodded repeatedly.

Magson sighed.

"That is quite a coincidence," remarked Menck.

"And your houses aren't even in the same area," added Magson.

"Miss Bosch was ill," said Delport. "Melanie Bosch. One of her classes had an assignment they had to hand in that day. She asked me to collect them. I went to drop them off at her house that afternoon. On the way back I drove past Rykie and offered her a lift."

"And that was when you saw your opportunity."

"Don't you listen? It was just a lift. To her home. It probably wasn't even three blocks."

"Why would she accept a lift for such a short distance?"

"I don't know. It was hot."

"Wasn't it because you had a relationship with her?"

"*No*. I told you, I didn't have an inappropriate relationship with Rykie." Delport sighed and shook his head. He was hunched over even more than earlier. "But it doesn't matter how many times I say it, does it?"

Magson just looked at him.

"I think I want an attorney now."

Magson picked up the phone and dialed. "Captain? How is it going over there?"

"Except for some porn," said Captain Kritzinger from Neels Delport's house, "not much."

Fantastic. "What kind of porn?"

"The computer was on, so we looked around a bit. A couple of teen sex sites, according to his favorites. Typical barely legal type of stuff. Girls that look young for their age. But he's got a bunch of photos in his collection of women who definitely aren't teens. It's the usual type of stuff. Nothing violent."

"Nothing with rope?"

"No. And none of the models look uncomfortable or as if they're being forced or anything."

"What about sodomy?" asked Magson.

"Nothing that he kept. We don't want to dig around too much. How is the interrogation going?"

"He has all kinds of stories, Captain. Claims he gave Maryke a lift earlier the week that she disappeared."

"That would mean nothing if we find evidence in the boot."

"He's asked for an attorney now, anyway."

Kritzinger clicked his tongue. "Pity."

"What about panties?"

"We're still searching, but so far there's nothing. No sandals or jewelry, either. We have found a bunch of hockey sticks, but they're all large, adult-sized. And no rope at all."

"Maybe the primary scene is somewhere else."

Magson made several phone calls. He learned that Delport had indeed given the *Hearing Voices* book to other pupils, three of them in Maryke's class. They were pupils who had improved significantly in their exams at the end of the previous year, and each one bore the exact same message on the first page. Melanie Bosch confirmed that she had been ill and had asked Delport to collect the assignments on her behalf. He had brought them to her house that afternoon and she was even able to tell Magson which afternoon it had been. Tuesday, February 25th. Two days before Maryke Retief had disappeared. Delport's parents were both still alive and living on the only property they owned. His older sister was married to a businessman in Johannesburg. Not much in terms of other family, and no indication of any other location where he could have held the girls captive.

In the end, Delport walked out of the SVC building with his attorney. Magson watched him leave. A false lead? Or a sharp pencil ...

The search of his house yielded nothing. Captain Kritzinger reported that they hadn't even found a suitable place to tie a rope in order to hang someone. No rafters or anything in the garage that might contain scuff marks or rope fibers. One long strand of dark brown hair had been recovered from the back of the Civic's front passenger seat, but nothing from the boot. Even if the hair did turn out to have come from Maryke Retief's head, all that would prove was that she had probably sat there at some point in time. Delport had already admitted to offering her a lift the Tuesday afternoon and they couldn't prove exactly when the hair had ended up on the seat. The team had collected fingerprints and a host of trace evidence, but it would be weeks before the results were known.

All of which left Magson chewing his lower lip and shrugging. "Maybe he is telling the truth. Maybe ... I don't know. He bothers me."

Menck shook a John Rolfe from his pack and started playing with it. "Do you want to go for a beer? I'll sponsor the first one."

"I have a headache. I'm going home."

Magson stopped in front of the gate, unlocked the Viro and removed the chain. Pushed the gate wide open. Walked over to the garage and unlocked that. The hinges whined as he lifted the door. Everything was in need of lubrication—the garage door, the gate, his knees. He walked back to the old white Jetta. The car could probably use some oil, as well—when was the last time he'd checked? The paint was dull in the late afternoon sun. His entire life he had washed his car every week, usually on Saturdays. He glanced at the patch of bird droppings on the roof that had begun to flake from weeks of dehydration and got in. Turned the key. Parked the Jetta in the garage. Got out. Shut the garage door and locked it. Walked over to the gate and closed it. It had to take ten minutes just to arrive at home, he thought, locking the Viro.

Glass shattered somewhere to his right. He turned to look, but saw nothing. He walked to the corner of the house, his right hand touching the pistol on his hip. A soccer ball was nestled in the tall grass. Had the two Koertzen brothers from next door finally kicked hard enough to shatter a window? No small faces peeking over the Vibracrete wall. The ball was a bit too far away from the house. He peered around the corner, down the side of the house, but saw nothing.

More glass breaking—behind him—and he whipped around,

heart thumping. Nothing. Must have been at the neighbors, the Bradleys.

He walked over to the wall separating the yards, stood on his toes to peek over the top.

A rifle against a shoulder. The finger pulled the trigger. Glass shattered.

The last brown shards of the beer bottle settled on the ground. The Bradley boy lowered the airgun and sauntered over to the plastic crate to replace the broken bottle.

Magson turned around, walked to the soccer ball and tossed it back over the wall to the Koertzen side.

After Emma's condition had worsened, he had sometimes gone to the shooting range. He had pumped bullets into black-and-white targets. Sometimes he had even felt better for a few minutes.

These days the front door was just another door. He missed the smell of food when he came home. Onions frying. Chicken in the oven. Something that roused his appetite. Finding Emma in the kitchen, kissing her, telling her it smelled wonderful. He wished he'd appreciated that daily routine more.

After locking his service pistol in the safe, he fetched two Adco-dols in the bathroom. Cupping his hand beneath the tap, he swallowed the bitter yellow tablets.

In the kitchen he took a plate from the cupboard and eyed the bread. Not exactly soft, but still edible. Emma's little bird would have to be satisfied with cheese tomorrow morning. He stacked three slices of bread atop one another and opened the fridge. Margarine and … apricot jam. He carried his one-and-a-half sandwich and a glass of milk to the dinner table.

Five

"I believe Lauren Romburgh is part of the series." Kayla Schulenburg untied her ponytail and crumpled the curls into a kind of wild bun. "She may have been the first one."

Once again Magson caught himself glancing at Warrant Officer Azhar Najeer, studying his own murder mosaic in the operational room. Prostitutes, Magson knew. He also knew that Najeer had a very strong suspect. Unlike him. Instead, Magson would soon be sticking a third photo of a girl to the wall. She would probably be smiling, too.

"Unfortunately, there hasn't been a great deal of progress made in the investigation."

"Because the investigating officer is a fucking idiot," said Gys Burger, having returned following several days of questioning and cross-examination in the High Court. He had to be just a few years shy of fifty. Magson had always thought of Burger as something hewn from a solid block of wood, but never sanded. That applied to both his appearance and personality.

"There was a scene." Schulenburg smiled.

Burger pulled a face. "I hurt his feelings. Shame, because nothing hits harder than the truth." There had been fervent speculation, wagers even, when the temperamental old South African policeman and the female detective not much older than his daughter were paired together. Nobody placing wagers had won.

"Lauren Romburgh was sixteen," said Schulenburg. "Grade 11 at Durbanville High. She was out for the evening with her boyfriend. He is eighteen. They went to Tyger Valley. On the way back from the mall they got into an argument. She told him to stop, got out and walked home. That's the boyfriend's version. And that was how he told it to us, as well, but then Gys ... had a more intimate chat with him, and he eventually admitted things actually happened somewhat differently."

"He was sick of her bitching, so he just stopped by the side of the road and kicked her out. Real gentleman."

"Children from Bloekombos found her body the following Thursday." Schulenburg flipped open her notebook. "She was wearing: black top, black bra, blue jeans, black socks, black shoes, but no panties and no jewelry."

"That sounds very familiar," said Captain Kritzinger.

"She had been wearing a silver chain, silver earrings, silver bracelet and a silver ring before she disappeared. And she had a little black handbag, which is also still missing."

"But she wasn't hanged," said Magson.

"No," said Schulenburg. "She was strangled. But a rope was used. Her wrists and ankles were bound. Signs of sexual assault, including sodomy, but no semen. Doc Killian didn't perform the autopsy, but she looked at the report and, except for the fact that Lauren Romburgh wasn't hanged, it is very similar." She produced a photograph. "And that's not all."

Magson took the photo. A pretty face, thin, oval, perhaps a hint of shyness. Dark brown eyes. Long dark brown hair. "Did the investigating officer find anything?"

Burger laughed through his nose and shook his head.

"First he tried to nail the boyfriend," said Schulenburg, "but when it turned out that he had an alibi ..."

"After he left the girl by the side of the road," said Burger, "he went drinking with his buddies. Other people saw him there, too."

"So then he shifted his investigation to Bloekombos, and

well, he hasn't really made any progress since then." Schulenburg raised her eyebrows.

"He is developing informants," said Burger, mimicking quotation marks with his fingers around the last two words. "He should go babysit cars at Tyger Valley. Not that I'd park my car in his block."

"Is there a reason why she didn't phone her parents?" asked Menck.

"Her phone was broken," said Schulenburg, "so she didn't even have it with her."

"Didn't her parents complain about this detective?" asked Kritzinger.

"Her dad is a computer programmer—the stereotype—and he doesn't appear to be too comfortable around people. His wife isn't Lauren's biological mother—who is dead—and she seems quite timid also."

"Where exactly was she found?" asked Magson.

Schulenburg pointed with a finger on the map. Beside the R101, on Bloekombos's side, diagonally across from Kraaifontein.

"Same type of place as the others. But she was abducted in the evening."

"She was obviously a victim of opportunity," said Menck.

Schulenburg nodded and lifted her bun, which had sprouted several tentacles, away from her neck. "I think he just happened to drive past her, saw her walking alone and exploited the situation."

Menck fiddled with his goatee. "He could've offered to take her home."

Magson stuck the photo to the wall. "If the boyfriend had just dropped her off at home, she would have been alive today."

"All right then," said Burger, "it's been fun and everything, but we have our own dockets to close."

"Pretoria sent us a profile," said Magson.

"And there is our cue."

"I'm sure you can spare another half-hour, Gys," said Kritzinger. "More heads and all."

"*Ag*, come on, Captain. These profiles are just a load of

shit. We might as well get ourselves some *dolosse* and throw them here on the floor."

"And who will be reading the bones for us, Gys?" asked Menck, grinning. "You?"

"Might as well." He scratched behind his ear, eyeing the door.

"Just because you don't believe in it, doesn't make it nonsense." Najeer had joined them, rather surreptitiously.

Burger glared at him. "And just because you believe it, doesn't make it true."

Najeer had a thin face with high cheekbones, a long straight nose and a short beard he maintained with great care—or so Magson believed, because it was short and neat without fail. His clothes received the same meticulous attention as his beard. He had arrived here from Durban a couple of years ago, and although he understood Afrikaans reasonably well, he only spoke English. "Why do you always have to be so stubborn?"

"Tell me, Azhar, do you also believe in the Tooth Fairy?"

Najeer rolled his jet-black eyes. "It's like arguing with a child. Profiling is based on scientific research."

"Are you finished?" asked Kritzinger. Arguments between these two could go on for a while.

Burger sighed, took a seat and crossed his arms.

Magson scanned the first couple of paragraphs of the report, summarizing it as, "White male. Twenty to thirty years old." He read on, "The victims are middle to higher middle class and the killer probably is too. He fits in the communities where the victims are abducted and he feels comfortable there. The first murder in a series, in particular, is frequently committed close to the killer's home or place of work, in an area he knows well. Dominique Gould was abducted in the Brackenfell area and her body was left there. If she was the first victim, it is highly probable that this is where the killer lives and/or works."

"We now think that Lauren Romburgh is part of the series," said Kritzinger. "So that changes things."

"She was abducted in Durbanville," said Schulenburg. "In the evening, so …"

"She was a victim of opportunity," said Menck once again.

"Exactly. If he usually looks for victims in the afternoon, why did he just happen to be in Durbanville in the evening? Maybe he was on his way home. Maybe he lives in Durbanville."

"Makes sense," said Kritzinger.

"And then Brackenfell and Bellville," said Najeer. "He's getting more comfortable moving around."

"Both victims were teenage girls," read Magson, "approximately the same age. The killer targets teenage girls specifically and is probably a hebephile, someone who is sexually attracted to teens."

"They have names for every bloody thing these days," grumbled Burger. "Just another thing to hide behind. I can't help that I did it. See, this clever doctor says I have this problem. It's not my fault." He leaned back in his chair and stared up at the ceiling.

Magson continued. "The victims share a number of physical similarities, particularly the fact that both were brunettes who wore their hair long. It could be important, but since there are only two known victims at this point, it could be coincidental. Physical appearance often plays an important role in how serial killers choose their victims, but not always."

"Three known victims now," said Menck. "Three with long dark brown hair."

Magson read on. "The nature of the sexual acts, particularly the sodomy, and the severity of the injuries inflicted while performing these acts, coupled with the fact that the victims were held captive for a period of time, point towards a sadistic killer, who derives pleasure from torturing his victims. This type of murder is the result of fantasies developed over many years. It is about the victim's suffering, rather than the acts being performed. The killer acts out a ritual where he has complete control over his powerless victim, who cannot do anything to stop him, and that, together with the suffering she experiences, provide him with sexual gratification. He has no remorse for his acts. On the contrary, he does not perceive his victims as human beings, but merely as objects, props, to use in acting out his fantasy."

"Used and thrown away," said Schulenburg. "Like an empty can of Coke."

"That's all these bloody profiles ever do," sighed Burger. "Makes everyone somber and depressed. Without bringing us any closer to catching the bastard."

Magson continued with the report. "The killer enjoys, and probably prefers, sodomy because it is degrading. He will probably also use objects to penetrate his victims. In addition, there will be psychological and emotional torture—verbal abuse, crude references to the victim and her sexual organs, forcing her to refer to herself in crude and degrading ways."

Magson recalled the ragdoll with her dark violet dress and large bright green eyes on Maryke Retief's bed. For a moment he just looked at the photos of the three girls on the wall. Three smiles. One somewhat shy. One with a hint of mischief. One bright, like her exceptional eyes. All three of them looked happy. Unblemished. As his colonel at the old Peninsula Murder and Robbery Unit had once said, *investigate murders for a few months and it becomes a job like any other. And then you find yourself at a scene and it's a child. Suddenly, it's not just another victim anymore.*

He turned his attention back to the profile. "The killer is intelligent," he read. "He plans the murders carefully and leaves very little evidence behind. He is probably quite charming and would rather employ some kind of ruse to manipulate the victim into a situation where he can control her with a weapon instead of overpowering her with violence in a blitz-style attack. He transports her to a location where he knows he will be safe and can act out his fantasies without any disturbance. After the murder he is able to remove the body without being seen. If he holds the victims captive in his home, he would be living alone in a neighborhood where the houses are not too close together."

"He may have access to a second location," said Najeer. "Somewhere more private. Remote."

"Hanging victims, as the method of murder, is rare among serial killers," read Magson. "It is unique and probably has some special significance for the killer. Perhaps there is a sexual connotation that derives from his childhood and it was incorporated into his fantasies. He will take photographs and/or videos of the victims. He keeps the victims' panties and jewelry. These are possessions with personal rather than monetary value, and he employs the items as props while reliving the torture and murder, and also while fantasizing. If he is married or in a relationship, he probably gives some of the jewelry to this woman. Such a woman would be young and she would look and act like a teenager. She would behave submissively towards him. Their sexual relationship would include sadistic aspects."

"Just what I'm looking for in a man," said Schulenburg.

"Too bad you're too old for him," said Burger. Rather curtly, Magson felt, and he noticed the look in Schulenburg's eyes.

"You know just how to make a woman feel good," she said.

"What?" Burger turned to face her. "Do you want to look like a teenager?"

She raised her hands and gave him an exasperated look.

But Magson noticed that Burger was glaring at him. "How much longer is that thing, Mags?"

"It will go faster if you stop interrupting me."

Burger "locked" his lips with his right hand and tossed the "key" away while pulling a face.

Magson read. "It might be useful to contact prostitutes in the area, since he may act out his fantasies on them. He will have a pornographic collection and it will reflect his fantasies. In this killer's case, the models will be teenage girls and/or young girls who look like teens. They will be tied up and appear to be uncomfortable. Sexual acts will have a strong focus on anal sex and penetration with objects. He will also keep photos and/or videos of his victims, possibly hidden in a special place."

"Now that would be nice to find," said Menck.

"This type of killer tends to have many victims," read Magson. "Now that he has started acting out his fantasies, he will be thinking about them even more. He will not stop of his own volition."

March 20, 2014. Thursday.

Magson lay in bed, staring at the ceiling. White, with the scattered desiccated remains of mosquitoes he had assisted in exiting this world during summer. He closed his eyes, pressing his thumb and index finger into their corners.

Mornings and evenings. That was when it gnawed at him. While he lay waiting for the alarm to ring or sleep to take him away. That was when he replayed the final days of Emma's life, over and over. When his thoughts found Hannes. The last time they had spoken, the disbelief in his son's eyes, the hurt in his voice … They had stood there, in the TV room, Hannes with his mother's eyes, glistening …

Finally, the alarm went off. He reached over, pressing the button on the clock to silence it. And there was the photo in the golden frame, Hannes in his black robe, degree in his hand, Emma on his left, and him on the right. He'd been so proud that day. All three of them were smiling. His hand rested on Hannes's shoulder.

He looked away, swung his feet onto the floor, rubbed his face. After a visit to the bathroom, he plopped down on the edge of the bed, sliding his feet into his slippers. His right big toe protruded from a hole, a worm in a dark blue fruit. On his way out, he unhooked his dressing robe from the door, pulling it on as he made his way to the kitchen. He inserted a filter in the percolator. Added coffee and water. Set his mug on the counter.

The newspaper was lying in the flowerbed alongside the driveway again, where the delivery boy had simply tossed it over the gate. What had happened to the days when he would open the front door to find it lying on the rug, neatly rolled? Of course the boy could no longer reach the doormat, but was it really asking so much to slide it between the bars of the gate? Then again, he should probably be grateful that the paper had been placed inside a plastic bag. Magson sighed, bent down to retrieve it—a motion accompanied by a strange sensation in his left knee—and returned to the kitchen.

The percolator was still dripping, so he sat down at the table, spreading *Die Burger*. Almost the entire front page was black. Reeva Steenkamp at the top. Another half a page on the Nkandla scandal after the Public Protector's report had been released yesterday. He shook his head. And it didn't get any better inside the paper. At least he was not confronted by the lack of progress in his case this morning. But when he turned the page, he found it lying in wait, in between more Zuma on the left and the permanent page-five-Oscar-Pistorius report. *Maryke's mother writes to killer*, read the headline.

Maryke Retief's mother had written a heart-wrenching letter to her daughter's murderer and sent it to *Die Burger*:

> To the person who murdered my daughter,
>
> I don't know who you are or what went wrong in your life that you would do such a thing. But I want to tell you about the human being whose life you took.
>
> Her name was Maryke, but we called her Rykie. She was born on 14 June 1998. She was my first pregnancy and I was a little scared. She was such a tiny little thing when she came, but so beautiful. Just a little patch of hair on the back of her head. I loved her on the spot.
>
> Rykie was never a difficult child, although she could throw a tantrum when she was little. Something fierce. But she has always had a good heart, especially when it came to animals. She was probably about five when she picked up a dove beside the road. A car must have hit it. Her eyes were filled with tears. We had to bury the dove and pray and everything.
>
> When guinea fowl chicks hatched in our garden, one remained in the nest. Its head hung to the side and there was no hope that it would survive. It kept on cheeping until Rykie picked it up. Then it was silent and content in the warmth of her hands. The chick was weak and would not eat, but Rykie held it and spoke to it until it died.
>
> That was the kind of person she was. Full of love, especially towards those who were weak or hurt.

She knew early on that she wanted to be a veterinarian. She would have been such a good one.

Rykie was with us for only fifteen years. The time went by so incredibly quickly. I miss her so much. I wish I had just held her that morning as tightly as I could and never let her go.

I don't know what happened to you. I don't know why you chose Rykie. But she did not deserve what you did to her. She was a good person. She was my precious daughter.

Sonja Retief

After he was finished reading the paper, he rose and opened the cupboard to get a porridge bowl. But he just closed the door again. He had nothing for Emma's little bird. Last night he'd actually prepared something without INSTANT written on the box, but it had been crumbed chicken out of a packet, with mashed potato. The last sliver of cheese he had given the robin yesterday morning.

He opened the fridge. Margarine. Jam. Cucumber. A few tomatoes, a bit mushy by the looks of it. An egg carton. He was unsure when he'd bought it. He removed it from the fridge. Still a few days from the expiration date.

He boiled two eggs. Left them to cool in cold water. Placed two slices of bread in the toaster while he shelled the eggs. On the other side of the window the feeding table was deserted. A male sparrow hopped around on the lawn in the company of two females, but of the robin there was no sign.

He diced one of the eggs. The other one he sliced and arranged on a piece of toast. Added some salt and pepper.

Emma's little bird glided onto the branch attached to the corner of the feeding table and gazed straight into the kitchen.

Magson smiled and opened the back door. He spooned the egg onto the table and looked up at the robin, now waiting in his usual spot in the white stinkwood.

Emma had regularly bought bird seed and scattered it on the grass. For the turtle doves and laughing doves, sparrows. But it had been the Cape robin that had burrowed its way into her heart. It had started with bits of fat from the previous night's pork chops, chicken skin, sometimes bacon. Fine egg or grated cheese. It hadn't been long before the bird began appearing as soon as Emma had gone outside. Often he had sung to her. Even when she had been having a particularly bad day, she had made sure that Magson set out something for the robin.

The bird watched him with his shiny black eyes.

Emma's little bird.

"You miss her, too, don't you?"

Back inside the house he sat at the counter to have breakfast with the robin.

Having finished, he looked at the newspaper. And went searching through the drawers until he found an old marker.

On the way to work, he stopped at a café and bought another newspaper. Across Neels Delport's house he opened the paper at the letter Sonja Retief had written and drew a red rectangle around it. He left the paper on the doormat.

Six

Magson slammed the Corolla's door, turned the key and stomped on the petrol pedal.

"Don't you feel better?" asked Menck.

High-profile cases, particularly those enjoying decent media coverage, always yielded numerous tips from the public. The majority of them led to nothing, but Magson didn't mind the odd wild goose chase, because it might just prove to be the breakthrough. It was the attention seekers and clowns that bothered him. And those who deliberately provided false information to further some personal agenda.

"I thought it would've been quite cathartic for you to rip into her," said Menck.

"I'd rather have the time back I wasted on her false accusations."

"Sadly, time is one thing we can never get back."

"What are you? A fortune cookie?" Magson pulled away, engine growling. "I can't understand people. How do you give your neighbor's name to the police as a murder suspect just because you have a feud over your pets?"

"Ah, forget about it and rather help me think of something for April Fool's for Casey. The older she gets, the harder it is."

"That is the most stupid day anyone has thought of." Magson had never understood the appeal. His tongue was back to prodding the cavity he'd discovered between his molars.

"You, Jan Magson, are like the scent of spring blossoms."

While he gave Menck a look, his phone started ringing. "Magson."

"Warrant. It's Sonja Retief." Her voice was high, pinched.

"Mrs. Retief, did something happen?"

"A letter—a letter came today. It's … from him. The one who …"

"Are you at home?"

"Yes."

"We're on our way. Don't touch the letter anymore."

"All right."

Wynand Retief opened the door. "Thank you for coming so quickly. Come in."

Magson and Menck greeted and walked past him into the foyer.

"Did the letter come in the post?" asked Magson.

"Yes. It's here in the dining room. My wife dropped it when she began reading and you said we shouldn't touch it. So I didn't pick it up when I came."

"That's good."

They followed him into the dining room. A few envelopes were lying on the table, some open. A light green sheet of paper was lying on the carpet.

Magson pulled on latex gloves and picked it up. The paper was somewhat rough with an uneven texture. It contained a short message, in a solid black typeface, the letters tall, narrow and angular.

> Maryke you were so beautiful
> So beautiful
> The most beautiful eyes
> I had to have you
> Now you are mine for Always

Menck opened one of the evidence bags he'd brought along from the Corolla. As Magson slid the sheet of paper inside, he caught a scent. He raised it to his nose. Yes.

"It's scented paper." He pulled the yellow strip from the evidence bag, pressed along the length of the seal, and marked it.

Sonja Retief had come into the dining room and was now staring at the letter with an expression that looked a bit vacant to Magson.

"It was just in the mail," she said, her voice lacking emotion. "Together with the other letters and bills and junk mail."

"Do you still have the envelope?" asked Magson.

Her eyes shifted rigidly in the direction of the table. "It is there."

Magson turned to the opened envelopes. The top one was white and plain. It contained the Retiefs' address, in the same black letters.

"Is it this one?"

She nodded slowly.

"Is there something else you want to ask my wife?"

"Not at the moment," said Magson.

Wynand Retief went to his wife and put his arm around her shoulders. "Come, Sonja, come and sit." He led her out of the dining room.

The envelope went into a second evidence bag. While sealing and marking the bag, Magson said softly, "He put effort into this. Special, scented paper."

"Not printed," said Menck, taking a closer look at the letter. "It looks like those letters you rub off. Can't remember what it's called. I used it for a few of my projects in high school."

"Time and effort. It's almost …"

"Like a love letter."

"Ja." Magson read the message again. "Neat. No spelling mistakes."

"No name …"

"Why put all this effort into the letters? Doesn't he have a printer? Or is there some other reason?"

"What are you thinking, Mags?"

"A love letter is personal. Why didn't he write it? Just because he's careful? Or maybe because we know what his handwriting looks like?"

Menck's eyes, narrowing, turned to Magson. "You're thinking of Delport."

"It's a possibility. I … left a newspaper with the letter Maryke's mother wrote at his door."

Menck chuckled. "And you think this was his response?"

"I don't know. But I would like to know if they found paper like this during the search of his house."

Wynand Retief returned. "The doctor prescribed some tranquilizers," he said in a muted voice. "It's quite strong. I gave her some when I got here. This thing …"

It wasn't only Sonja Retief who was struggling. Her husband's face looked as if all the muscles were slack and his eyes were dull. It always seemed as if a light were extinguished in a parent's eyes when a child was murdered.

"We'll send the letter and envelope for forensic analysis," said Magson. "If another envelope like this comes in the post, don't open it at all. Phone me immediately."

"Do you think he'll write again, Warrant?"

"I know it's difficult, Mr. Retief, but I hope so, because every time he does, there's a chance he'll give something away about himself."

They took their leave.

Back in the Corolla Magson hesitated. "There is nothing in the letter that proves it came from Maryke's killer. But let's say it did. Why did he write?"

"He's sadistic," said Menck. "He wants to torment her parents."

"That's what the profile would say. But why like this? Why write to Maryke? Why a love letter?"

"Instead of something cruel to her parents. Like describing what he did to her."

"Why only Maryke? Why didn't he write to Dominique?"

"Maybe he didn't think of it. Maybe it's the publicity. Or maybe it *is* because of her mother's letter in the newspaper."

Magson gazed down the street. A girl jogged past. Her

dark brown ponytail swayed from side to side with each stride. "Or Maryke was different. Special. He wanted to have a relationship with her, but he couldn't."

"So he punished her."

Magson nodded. "So he took her and made her his."

"For 'Always'."

March 28, 2014. Friday.

The letter was back in Magson's possession. LCRC had found several fingerprints, mostly partials along the sides of the paper. The prints had been scanned into the Automated Fingerprint Identification System, but the database had failed to identify any, which meant whoever had left the prints had no criminal record. The envelope was currently at the Forensic Science Laboratory in Plattekloof. Perhaps he had licked the envelope or the stamp, enabling the Biology Section to retrieve DNA from it. Of course this would only be of any real help once they had a suspect's DNA to compare it to.

Magson knew very little about paper, but it was clearly a special kind. And anything that was special held promise. Thus he had gone through the Yellow Pages yesterday and below PAPER MERCHANTS he'd found a shop that might be able to assist: Paper Paradise in Tyger Valley.

They got out at the shopping center and were immediately greeted by a car guard. Magson nodded and showed his identification card.

"Oh, I keep a good eye, Captain."

"You just can't park anywhere without being accosted by someone who wants money," grumbled Magson once they had walked some distance away.

"Fortunately, you have mastered your badge action," said Menck, demonstrating the move.

"Can you think what it will cost per month if you have to hand out a couple of rands every time you get back in your car?"

"It's like drugs, Mags. Just say no."

They entered the shopping center and started looking for the nearest information board. Magson scanned the list of shops for the number and located it on the map.

Paper Paradise was in one of the side corridors on the upper floor. In the window was a display of invitations, menus and a photo album, everything of handmade paper, for a bride favoring an apricot-themed wedding. The ribbons were light violet. Maryke Retief's colors. Her bed. And the ragdoll. Inside, the shoulder-high shelves and limited floor space gave the shop a cramped feeling. The shelves were filled with A4 sheets of paper in a variety of colors.

The girl behind the counter had long, straight black hair and dark make-up around her eyes. "It's handmade paper," she said after Magson explained the purpose of their visit. She took another, closer look at the green sheet inside the evidence bag. The fingerprints were fine dark pink patterns. "Looks like Kleider."

"Do you sell it here?" asked Magson.

"Yes."

"Does it come in a packet?"

"When we buy it?"

"When you sell it."

She shook her head. "No. All our paper is sold uncovered as single sheets on the shelves."

Fantastic. That made a significant dent in the evidential value of the fingerprints.

"You said it's handmade," said Menck. "Who manufactures it?"

"Kleider Paper. It's a place in Milnerton. They make paper for fine art and also handmade paper."

"Is it sold in many shops?

"Most shops that sell handmade paper would probably stock it."

"This color, does it all have the same scent?" asked Magson.

"Scent?" she asked, her black eyebrows arched.

"It's scented paper."

The right eyebrow lowered and she shook her head. "No, it's not."

"You can't smell it anymore, after the ninhydrin, but I promise you it had a scent."

The girl shrugged. "Well, it's not scented when we sell it. Ours just smells like … it smells papery."

"Are you sure?"

"Come smell for yourself." She walked out from behind the counter and led them to one of the shelves, where she removed a sheet exactly like the one in the evidence bag. She watched him as he sniffed.

That meant he had scented the paper himself. "This paper, this color, is it something that sells well?"

"Fairly."

Magson sighed. They wouldn't be able to trace it.

"The letters look like Letraset," said the girl.

Menck snapped his fingers. "Letraset. That's the name."

Seven

April 17, 2014. Thursday.

The tires squealed as Magson took the corner, the Corolla careening to the point where he received a fresh squirt of adrenaline. The rear wheels lost grip and slid, but he kept the car under control. He floored the petrol pedal. The girl had been missing less than two hours. Seventeen years old. Every minute could make a difference.

In his mind, he saw Maryke Retief's bloated body in the veld.

The magnetized blue light flashed on the roof and the siren wailed, but the Fiat in front of them was slow to yield. Now the brake lights were glowing. He slammed the heel of his hand onto the hooter and forced his way past, turned just as the orange traffic light switched to red, narrowly missing a Berco delivery van.

"Shit," said Menck, "one more coat of paint on this Corolla and we'd have hit him."

"They said something about a number plate. I hope they've found something by now."

Careering down Van Riebeeck Road, Magson weaved through the traffic trying to make way within the confines of the street, brushed one side mirror, hurtled across a red light past Kuils River Police Station, forced the Corolla into the right lane, making good progress with two wheels on the island while it lasted, and finally turned right into Energy Street. The Detective Branch was on the next corner. He stopped across two parking spaces and shoved the door open.

They jogged into the light brown brick building, up the stairs, and turned right down the narrow corridor. They enquired at the first open door and the detective took them to another office a few doors down.

"Specs? SVC about the missing girl." The detective motioned for Magson and Menck to enter.

A short, slight woman beckoned them closer while talking on the phone. "Okay. Phone me as soon as you know." She ended the call and looked at them with black, almond-shaped eyes, a tight smile on her wide mouth. "Niquita Brill."

Magson took the proffered hand and introduced himself and Menck. "Have you found anything yet?"

"Well, the girlfriend took a photo of the car with her phone. So we got the number plate. It's an Avis car. Hired by an Allan Norton. Paid with a credit card."

"Have you found the car?"

"Won't be long now. Norton is from Gauteng. His record is clean." She took a photograph from the desk and handed it to Magson. "Anja Heyns. Seventeen."

"New hair color," remarked Menck. It had been the first thing to catch Magson's eye, too. She was not a brunette.

"Her friend and Anja's mother are in the colonel's office. Come. I'll take you through."

They walked further down the narrow corridor, around the corner to the end. Brill knocked on the door and they followed her inside, greeting the unit commander.

He turned to the woman sitting on one of the chairs, kneading her hands. "Mrs. Heyns, these are Warrant Officers Magson and Menck of the Serious Violent Crimes Unit."

Next to the mother a teenage girl was seated, her hands locked between her knees. She was still wearing her green school tunic.

Magson pulled a chair closer. "Mrs. Heyns, please tell us everything that happened."

"You have to talk to René. She saw everything."

He turned to the girl. "What happened, René?"

She took a shaky breath and looked at him. "We were walking home. Anja and I always walked together, because we live close to each other, but at the beginning of the year we had a ..." she looked down and folded a stray lock of hair behind her ear "... a fight. So she was walking on her own and I was behind. A car stopped next to her and she went over and spoke to him."

"Did she know the man?"

"I don't know. He got out and they argued about something."

"Could you hear what they said?"

"No. I was too far away. And then he grabbed her wrist." She demonstrated on her own. "And he pulled her to the car. He opened the door. That was when I called to her. I don't know if she heard me. She got in and he closed the door. I ran and kept on calling. He saw me and quickly got in the car and drove off."

Magson's heart was beating quickly, because this was exactly what could have happened to Maryke Retief and Dominique Gould.

"That was when I thought I should take a photo."

"That was very clever," said Menck.

A fleeting smile touched the girl's lips.

"Did Anja look scared?" asked Magson.

"Yes. She didn't want to go with him."

"Have you seen the man before?"

She shook her head. "No."

"Did he have a weapon?"

Anja Heyns's mother made a sound.

"I couldn't see," answered the girl. "I was too far away. I phoned her. It rang and then it went dead. When I redialed, it went to voicemail."

The phones of Dominique Gould and Maryke Retief had been shut off quickly as well.

"Her phone is still off." Anja's mother was wringing her hands so hard the knuckles had turned white. There was no wedding ring on her finger. Her eyes filled up again.

"Mrs. Heyns," asked Magson, "does the name Allan Norton mean anything to you?"

"The other detective already asked me. I've never heard of him."

"All right." He started to get up, but two hands shot out, grabbing his fingers.

The woman's eyes were pleading. "Please bring my daughter back."

"We'll do everything we can to get Anja back safely, Mrs. Heyns." Magson left the office.

Menck followed him into the corridor. "Serial killer tourism?" he asked softly.

"Right now I don't care where he lives. It fits."

Menck nodded. "But if his home is in Gauteng and his work is there, it shouldn't be too difficult to find out if he's been here—" He glanced over Magson's shoulder.

The girl was standing there. She was holding herself as if she were cold. "I should've yelled louder. Started running sooner."

"You did what you could, René," said Menck. "If you hadn't had the presence of mind to take that photo, we wouldn't know what car to look for."

"But what if it's already too late? What if Anja … like Maryke Retief …" She swallowed and looked down.

Maryke Retief was turning into one of those names. Like Leigh Matthews and Inge Lotz.

"Warrant Magson?"

They turned around, saw the female detective approaching, and went to meet her.

"We've found the car," said Niquita Brill.

"Where?" asked Magson, as they continued on towards the exit.

"Bloubergstrand. The Blue Ocean Apartments."

"Who's at the scene?"

"We have two uniforms there."

"Have they done anything?"

She shook her head. "Just made sure the vehicle is there."

"All right. Make sure they keep their distance. And stay

out of sight. Unless Norton leaves, they must do nothing. We're on our way."

She frowned. "It's a long way to Blouberg. If it's the same killer—"

"Anja Heyns still has a lot of time. We don't want to be too hasty."

"Warrant Magson—"

"Warrant Brill, we have no idea what the situation is inside that flat. We don't know what weapons Norton has with him. We don't even know what position Anja Heyns is in. Do you really want to have two uniforms storm in there and hope for the best?"

The black eyes turned away and she shook her head.

"I don't want her to be alone in there, with him, until we get there, either. But it's more important to me that we get her out alive."

Brill did not look happy, but she nodded, before turning around.

"Warrant? Good work finding Norton."

She looked back over her shoulder. "Just make sure Anja is okay."

Magson and Menck ran out, got in the Corolla, and Magson pulled away with screeching tires.

The Blue Ocean Apartments were on the beach front with a view of Table Mountain, Robben Island and the hazy arc where the Atlantic Ocean disappeared on the horizon. Large, white, modern, angular. No need for Magson to go any closer to know it was well beyond his price bracket. He parked in the street.

Getting out, he shook his head. "Is that what they call 'out of sight'? We can just be grateful there are almost no windows on this side."

They walked over to the *klagtebakkie* and the two uniformed officers inside. One was staring in the wrong direction, visibly bored, the other was eating something greasy-looking. The latter glanced up, noticed Magson and Menck approaching, and apparently recognized them as detectives, because he shoved the packet somewhere. The first officer realized something was happening. They clambered out.

Magson said nothing, merely looked at them pointedly with raised eyebrows. Menck studied the building and the parking area.

"The suspect is still inside." The officer rubbed his greasy fingers on his uniform.

"Which one is his?" asked Magson.

"Number four. That's where his car is parked."

"That doesn't mean *he* is in number four."

The uniform stammered, but Magson had already lost interest. "I'm going to reception, to make sure they are in number four, and to get a key."

Menck nodded. "I'll wait for Gys and the others and keep an eye out."

Magson watched the apartment as he walked across the parking area. What was going on inside? A girl on an autopsy trolley seeped into his thoughts and he forced the image away. It was only when he grasped the handle to open the door marked RECEPTION that he became aware of the rumble of the ocean.

The reception area was modern, spacious and obviously expensive. The walls were white, the furniture a combination of brushed metal and glass. Large, frameless paintings of Table Mountain and Bloubergstrand in light blues and violets. Behind the counter was a stylish young woman, black suit seemingly designed for her, black hair tightly tied back.

The slight lift of the eyebrow as she looked at him did not escape Magson. "May I help you, sir?"

"Warrant Officer Magson," he replied, showing her his identification card. "There is a suspect in one of your apartments."

"A sus—" She shook her head. "I'm sure that can't be."

"Have you seen this girl?" He showed her a photo of Anja Heyns.

"Yes. She came in earlier this afternoon."

"Was she with an older man?"

"Yes, she was with a man. What is going on?"

"In what room are they?"

"We don't have rooms, sir, we have apartments, and our guests place a premium on their privacy."

"The man is a suspect in a serious crime."

"Yes, I understand, but we have a strict policy …"

Magson glanced at the name tag, ANN VILJOEN engraved in the silver metal, and switched to Afrikaans, "No, Miss Viljoen, you do not understand. There is a teenage girl in one of your apartments with a murder suspect. I couldn't care less about your policy. I want to know what apartment they are in and I want a key."

She blinked and it took her a moment to recover enough to speak. "They're in … apartment four. What are you going to do? Our guests …" She gesticulated with her left hand.

"Where is the key?"

"You can't just … These are premium apartments!"

"Miss Viljoen, that girl is most likely in serious danger. If you give us the key, we can unlock the door. Otherwise we'll have to break it down."

"You can't do that!"

"It's your choice," said Magson. "And I can also tell you this, Miss Viljoen, you are on the verge of obstructing the course of justice."

She glanced around, picked up the phone. "Let me phone my—"

"Then we'll break down the door." He started turning around.

"Wait!"

"Miss Viljoen, you're wasting my time."

"Okay. Okay." She raised both hands, indicating he should wait, reached for a keycard and, with some hesitancy, handed it to him.

"Thank you. Can you describe the layout of the apartment, please?"

Her face took on a pained expression, but she did as he asked.

Gys Burger and Kayla Schulenburg were waiting with Menck when Magson exited the reception area. They had already put on their bulletproof vests and Menck handed him his.

"Thanks." He pulled it on. The breeze was clammy against his skin. He could smell the salt of the ocean in the air.

"Norton is in number four. There are two entrances, the one here and a glass sliding door on the other side. The sliding door opens onto a balcony with stairs down to the beach. Gys, Schulenburg, you go around and cover the sliding door, but keep out of sight. There's a lot of glass on that side for the view."

They nodded.

"Colin and I will enter through the front door. It's an open plan—only the bedroom and bathroom have doors. We'll go in silently, but things can change quickly. Remember, the girl is inside and we don't know what kind of weapons Norton's got with him."

Burger and Schulenburg left to go around the complex and cover the balcony. Magson and Menck took their positions outside the front door to number four.

Magson flicked his pistol's safety off and folded the fingers of his left hand around the doorknob. His tongue was probing the hole between his molars and there was a sharp sting as it got nicked.

Menck held the keycard next to the sensor. He looked at Magson and nodded.

From somewhere came a seagull's lamenting cry.

Magson nodded back.

Menck pressed the card against the sensor.

The lock clicked open.

A wave broke on the other side of the building.

Magson turned the knob and slowly pushed the door inward. He peered through the growing opening. Everything was bright and white. The kitchen section came into view, a metal table and chairs, then a couple of pillars, a white couch and chairs. No people.

He moved in, pistol at the ready. On the other side a passage led to the bedrooms. Quietly, he made his way across the tiled floor to the corner.

A girl giggled.

He frowned and glanced at Menck at the opposite corner. Nodded.

He moved around the corner and into the main bedroom. Two naked bodies, a man on top of a girl.

"Allan Norton! Police! You're under arrest! Get off her and put your hands in the air!"

The man jolted and began to swing around. The girl screamed and jerked in the opposite direction. She kicked a tub of ice cream off the bed and it tumbled to the floor. Light brown ice cream plopped onto the tiles. She snatched at the sheet—arms, blonde hair and huge eyes. Magson recognized Anja Heyns from the photo.

Norton had rolled off the bed and was sitting against the wall, his legs drawn up, his arms raised in the air. He looked quickly from Magson to Menck.

"Allan Norton?"

Anja Heyns turned to the man. "Who? Brian, what's going on?"

He did not answer her.

She clutched the sheet to her breasts. A wet spot was seeping through the white sheet, the same color as the ice cream on the floor. Next to a bottle of Moët & Chandon on the night table were half-filled champagne flutes.

"Anja, get your clothes, go to the bathroom and put them on. Your mother is worried about you."

They searched the apartment. Norton's weekend suitcase had only clothes in it. His toiletry bag contained a toothbrush, toothpaste, soap, shampoo, aftershave and a host of skincare products.

"Check out all the labels," said Menck.

Magson opened the closets, only to find empty coat hangers.

"Sometimes I think weapons and greed are the only reasons we're at the top of the food chain. We pay four times as much for the same blue T-shirt because it's got Levi's or Jeep or something written on the front. What we're really doing is paying four times as much so we can walk around advertising Levi's. It doesn't say an awful lot about our intelligence."

Magson shut the closet door. "And everything is Made in China."

"But, hey, if my T-shirt's got Levi's printed on it and there's nothing on yours, then I'm a better person than you are. So it's cheap at the price."

Magson really couldn't care less at this moment about how much people spent on clothes with brand names. He was more concerned about the bottle of champagne and tub of ice cream next to the bed instead of a length of rope.

"People are like crows," observed Menck. "We work ourselves *moer toe* so we can collect shiny things we actually have no real use for."

They moved on to the living area. All they found was the key on the Avis fob, lying abandoned on the kitchen counter.

Menck opened the fridge and whistled. "Four more bottles of French champagne. Do you know what these things cost?"

"Doesn't look like they were planning on eating."

"Just a bit of ice cream. There's nothing here, Mags."

Magson sighed. "Let's have a look in the car."

He grabbed the key on the counter and they went outside to the parking area. He pressed the button to unlock the car and opened the boot. Inside was a medium-sized camera bag. Menck zipped it open.

"Video camera. Tripod."

"So Norton was planning on making a movie."

Menck switched on the video camera and pressed a couple of buttons. "Memory card is empty."

Magson lifted the carpet. Only a spare wheel and tool bag. No rope. No weapon.

Menck slipped a John Rolfe between his lips. "I get the feeling we broke up a different kind of party here."

Magson shook his head. "Let's go and hear what Anja's story is." He shut the boot.

Anja Heyns was sitting on a chair in Magson's office, her legs pressed together in the short black dress, her school shirt on top to cover the revealing low cut and straps, her school dress folded in her lap. Her mother was sitting on the second chair, her eyes cast down at the floor. The chairs were little more than a meter apart, but the distance seemed much further.

"Anja." Magson waited until she looked up with a flip of her head. "How do you know Allan Norton?"

"He said his name is Brian, so I probably don't know him at all." She looked at his desk.

"When did you meet?"

"Today."

"That is, this afternoon after school."

"Yes."

"You've never seen him before?"

"No."

"Why did you get into his car?"

She shrugged.

"Did he force you? Threaten you?"

No reaction.

"Anja," said her mother, "he just wants to help you."

Anja shot a glance at her mother, rolling her eyes as she turned away.

Magson wondered what was going on in their relationship.

"Yes. He threatened me."

"How?" asked Magson. "What did he say?"

"He said he had a knife."

"What kind of knife? What did it look like?"

"He said it was in his pocket."

"What happened when you got in the car?"

"We drove."

There was something hard about her, someone who had learned to form a scab when she got hurt and keep everyone out.

"Where did you get that dress?"

"From him."

It was what she had chosen to put on, not her school dress.

"Anja, are you sure you didn't know Mr. Norton before to-day?"

"She already said so."

Magson ignored the mother and maintained his focus on

the daughter. "The thing is, Anja, it didn't look like you were there against your will."

"How can you say that to my daughter?"

Anja snapped towards her. "Why not? Isn't that what a woman does, Mom?"

Her mother turned away. "That's unfair."

Magson could barely discern the words.

"This is a strange police station." Allan Norton looked around the interrogation room.

"Have you been to many police stations, Mr. Norton?" asked Menck.

"No." Norton seemed very relaxed. "It's just a strange building. It doesn't look like a police station."

"It's not a normal station," said Magson. "This is the SVC Headquarters in the Western Cape."

"What's SVC?"

"Serious Violent Crimes."

Norton's eyes widened and he raised his hands, palms to the front. "Hey. There was no violence involved. She was there because she wanted to be there. If she—"

Magson raised his own hand. "Wait, wait, Mr. Norton. Let me first read you your rights, then we can talk." He went through the recitation. "Do you understand these rights?"

"Yes, and I'm telling you if she's saying I forced her to do anything she didn't want to, she is lying."

"She's still at school, Mr. Norton."

"She told me she's at college."

"She was wearing her school uniform when you picked her up."

Norton's eyes didn't waver. "We all have our fantasies. She told me she still had her uniform, she would wear it."

"You're thirty-six, aren't you?"

He sat back, interlocking his fingers on the table, rubbing his thumbs. "What about it?"

"Why did you pick up a schoolgirl and take her all the way to Bloubergstrand?"

"I wanted to have sex with her. And I told you I didn't know she was still at school."

"But you wanted her to wear her school uniform."

"So what? Besides, she's older than sixteen, isn't she?" Norton's smirk and the challenge in his eyes annoyed Magson.

"So you came all the way from Joburg?" asked Menck.

"Broke away for the Easter weekend."

"It's a nice time in the Cape. Just before the cold and the rains come. What kind of work do you do?"

"I'm a manager. Marketing."

"Is it a good job? Do you like it?"

"Yes." Norton's smile was beaming and smug. "In a couple of years I'll be a director. The board deems me the natural successor of one of the members who'll be retiring." He straightened his fingers and pressed the tips together. "I'll be the youngest director in the firm's history."

Menck whistled.

"When did you ask Anja to wear her school uniform?"

Norton's eyes shifted to Magson. "When did I ask Anja to wear her school uniform?"

"Ja. When?"

Norton looked to the right and touched his earlobe. "Yesterday."

"What were you talking about when you asked her?"

"About the weekend."

"How did you meet?"

Norton's fingers interlocked again, tighter than before. "Online."

"How?"

He glanced at the wall. "A social website. I can't remember which one."

"When was this?"

"February."

"February," said Magson. "How many times have you seen each other now?"

"This weekend was the first time."

"Oh." Menck was nodding. "You had one of those online relationships. How does it work? My wife sometimes has to go away on business for a month at a time and I'd like to try it."

Kathy was a pharmacist who, as far as Magson was aware, had never gone on a trip on account of her job.

"I mean, you and Anja probably did some stuff over the internet?"

"There are websites where you can meet someone," said Norton.

"Any you can recommend?"

"Google is your friend."

"So you've had a relationship with Anja since February?" asked Magson.

"It developed over a period of time."

"Why would she say she didn't know you before today?"

"Because she's lying." There was a twitch at the left side of Norton's mouth. "And I can prove it. Look on my phone."

The elevator's doors clattered open on the ground floor, and Magson walked to the right. He opened the door to the tea room. Anja Heyns and her mother were sitting at the table, several chairs apart.

"When can we go home?"

"Soon, Mrs. Heyns. Thank you for staying. Can I get you something else to drink?"

"No, thank you. We just want to go home."

"I understand. There are just a few more questions."

A cellphone started ringing. It was Anja's. As she looked at the screen, her eyes widened, her lips got thinner and it seemed as if her skin was stretching tighter over her face.

"You're welcome to answer it," said Magson.

She looked at him, quickly, and declined the call. "No, it's okay."

"All right. We have spoken to Mr. Norton and there are a few—"

Her phone started ringing again, startling her.

"Maybe you should just answer," said Magson. "It might be important."

"It's not." She grabbed the phone, but it stopped ringing.

The door opened and Menck entered. "So what did she say? He's lying, isn't he?"

"I haven't had a chance to ask yet," said Magson.

Anja's head was bowed, but she was watching him from beneath her eyebrows.

"Ask what?" her mother wanted to know.

Menck took a seat at the table. "I'm sure he's lying."

"About what?"

"Mr. Norton claims you met on the internet," Magson told Anja. "He claims you've been in a relationship for a couple of months now. But you told us you didn't know him before today. Is it like you told us?"

She nodded slowly.

"The problem is, how do we know who is telling the truth?"

"My daughter is telling the truth! That man forced her into his car—"

Anja's phone started ringing and this time she jumped.

"Who's phoning you the whole time?" asked Magson.

"Nobody," said Anja. "Just a friend. It's not important."

Menck raised his hands from his lap and placed a cellphone on the table. He pressed the screen and Anja's phone fell silent. She stared with wide eyes at the phone in front of Menck.

"What is going on?" asked her mother. "Whose phone is that?"

"That is Mr. Norton's phone," said Magson.

She looked at her daughter. "Why is your number on his phone?"

"He took my phone in the car—" the girl began.

"Anja." Magson raised his hands. "It's time for the truth now."

"It is the truth."

"No, it's not. There are messages on his phone that were sent by you. Photos you sent him. We can get a warrant for your phone records and see exactly when it began."

Anja glared at him, her mouth tight, and turned her head away.

"He didn't force you, did he?"

She was still looking the other way, but shook her head slightly.

"Why?" asked her mother. "Why would you do something like this with a man in his thirties?"

Anja snapped around. "Because he said he would take me away."

"But he was only using you. He didn't even give you his real name."

"But at least I got something in return this time."

Her mother recoiled as if she had been slapped. Her mouth hung open.

"This dress isn't the only thing he gave me."

"Anja …"

"It was okay to keep quiet when your boss touched me."

"Because it was your word against his. You know I can't afford to lose my job. Where will I find work again? How will I take care of us?"

"Yes, well, now I'm taking care of myself. I don't care what his name is. He's going to take me away from this dump and I'm never coming back."

"Teen logic, hey?" said Menck, his back against the outer wall of the conference hall. He blew a cloud of smoke into the air. "One moment she's saying he abducted her, the next she wants him to take her away to Joburg. And she believes he'll still do it."

"If he ever would have," said Magson.

"People's lives are so messy."

Yes.

"And it happens so quickly," Menck continued.

Too quickly. And afterwards nothing is the same again.

The smoke was acrid in Magson's nostrils. "The question is, where does this put Norton in terms of the murders?"

"We have him. I say we keep digging until we don't need to ask that question anymore."

Magson rubbed his mouth. "There are no signs of any internet relationships with the other two. Maryke would've written something in her diary. She wrote about a boy in her class; she wanted him to ask her out. And Dominique was happy with her boyfriend."

"His usual MO may be to drive around in school areas, looking for a girl walking alone. Anja may be the exception. Or an evolution."

"He was working on Anja before Maryke."

"Grooming takes time. Maybe Anja wasn't ready yet."

"And where is the rope? Where is the sadism?"

"Just like my friend JR here," Menck blew on the cigarette, making the tip glow brighter, "you can buy rope at any Pick n Pay. The entire Easter weekend lay ahead. He hadn't even taken out the video camera yet." Menck dropped the butt onto the ground and crushed it under his shoe. "Let's go shake him and see if anything falls out."

"Good news, Mr. Norton." Magson took a seat at the table. "Anja admitted that you know each other and that she went with you of her own free will."

"Good. So I can finally go." He got up.

"Sit, Mr. Norton. There are a few matters that have to be resolved first."

"Like what? You just said she was there of her own free will. And she is older than sixteen. So what is there to be resolved?"

"Do you often travel for your work?" asked Menck.

"What does that have to do with anything?"

"Nothing. But we have to wait for the paperwork and that can take a while." Sometimes Magson wondered about the lies that slipped so easily from Menck's lips.

"How long?" asked Norton.

Menck shrugged. "It's a pain in the arse, really, but what can you do? You know, I can see myself in marketing."

Norton looked at him, but said nothing.

"It's basically about convincing people that they need a product, hey?"

Norton nodded. "If you're really good, you can get someone to believe they have to own a product they don't actually want."

Menck smiled. "You can do that, hey? That's why you're going to be the youngest director."

Norton smiled back. "Well."

"So the secret to being a good marketer is being good at manipulating people."

Norton grimaced. "'Manipulate' is such an ugly word." He brushed it away with his hand. "It's more about creating a desire, a need if you will, that previously did not exist."

"Creating a desire that previously did not exist."

"Are you going to see Anja again, Mr. Norton?" asked Magson.

Norton raised his chin. "Why would I want to see her again?"

"You've put in such a lot of effort."

"She said she didn't know me. She said I kidnapped her."

"I just thought, all that time you've invested, all that work to get her to this point ..."

"She wanted it."

"A desire that previously did not exist," said Menck.

Norton's eyes narrowed to slits, his eyebrows drawing closer together. "What are you really doing? When is the paperwork coming? When can I go?"

Menck turned to Magson. "You know, it's almost like those other schoolgirls."

Magson nodded slowly. "Ja. It is."

"What 'other schoolgirls'?" asked Norton.

Menck ignored him. "They were also walking home."

"Ja. They were."

"What are you talking about?"

Magson stared at the man on the other side of the table. "Mr. Norton, you said Anja told you she was in college. And you asked her to wear her school uniform, because it's your fantasy."

"What about it?"

"Why did you stop on the way to buy her a different dress? If she had to wear the school uniform when you picked her up, because it is your fantasy, why did she wear the new dress after you bought it?"

Norton's mouth opened and closed again. "I ... What 'other schoolgirls'?"

"You knew very well Anja was still in school. Your fantasy is not a school uniform. It is a schoolgirl."

"Who are the 'other schoolgirls'? Answer me!"

"Anja Heyns wasn't the first schoolgirl who disappeared while she was walking home. But we weren't so lucky to find the others. Not safely."

"What? What are you talking about?"

Magson leaned forward, placing his elbows on the table. "I'm talking about two schoolgirls who were murdered, Mr. Norton."

"What does that have to do with me?"

"At this point, you're a suspect."

"What? A suspect? You can't be serious."

"I am always serious when children are murdered."

"I didn't murder anyone! It was just sex! At the end of the weekend I would've taken her home."

Magson regarded him for a moment. "I have noticed that you haven't once used her name."

"What?"

"Anja, Mr. Norton. Her name is Anja Heyns."

"I want a lawyer."

April 18, 2014. Friday.

Captain Henz Kritzinger entered the operational room. "Sorry to drag you into the office on Good Friday. I'd love to say the SAPS will make it up to you, but at least I can show my appreciation." He upended a bag and Easter eggs spilled onto the table—red, yellow, blue and green.

Menck, sitting on one of the other tables, clapped. "Behold! The Easter Bunny has arrived!"

"And they're halaal, Azhar, so you can just enjoy it for the marshmallow and chocolate."

"What?" Menck hopped off the table. "They're Easter eggs. How can they be halaal?"

Warrant Officer Patrick Theko picked up one of the eggs. "They're actually called marshmallow eggs. Look." Theko had a round face with a wide mouth that smiled effortlessly, sucking dimples into his cheeks. He unwrapped the chocolate and took a bite. "Thanks, Captain."

Menck reached for an egg, turned it over and shook his head. "Halaal. There's the sign and everything. What color do you want, Azhar?"

"Yellow." Azhar Najeer caught the egg lobbed in his direction. "When I was little, my cousin told me I was hatched from an egg. He said my father brought a duck home to do it."

Menck burst into laughter.

"He said that was why I had such a funny walk. Because the duck had taught me." Najeer seemed to ponder the memory for a moment. "I was rather upset." He bit into the egg.

"If Gys should hear about this …"

Captain Kritzinger clapped his hands and rubbed his palms together. "Okay, now that everyone is on a sugar rush, let's get to work."

"Norton didn't stay at the Blue Ocean Apartments earlier this year," said Menck. "He booked using his own name and paid by credit card. They have no record of him prior to this weekend, and the receptionist said it was the first time she's seen him."

"So," said Theko, "if he abducted the other girls, he didn't take them there."

"No."

"The most important thing is to find out if we can tie Norton to the murders," said Kritzinger. "Otherwise I want to know he had nothing to do with it, so we can eliminate him. Concentrate on Maryke Retief and Dominique Gould. Forget about the Romburgh girl for now and focus on Maryke—she disappeared less than two months ago and her case should be easier. We need to find out where Norton was at the end of February. It's Easter weekend, it won't be easy."

At eight minutes past two Allan Norton's name was crossed off the list of suspects. There was no way that he could have been involved in Maryke Retief's abduction or murder—he had been in Johannesburg at the time.

As Norton had told them, it was just sex. One thing he hadn't lied about.

Magson locked the front door, dropped the keys on the small table, walked down the short passage and around to the TV room, where he collapsed onto the sofa.

He didn't want this case.

Neels Delport's name remained on the list. There were a number of things that fit. Like the letter that had been posted to the Retiefs. Perhaps Delport was just intelligent. Informed. Thorough. These days everyone with a television knew about forensic evidence, thanks to the American police series. There were hundreds of books explaining everything. Not to mention the internet. The advantage had long since shifted away from the detective.

But there was a very real possibility that there was absolutely no connection between the killer and any of the girls. For all he knew, that afternoon in February had been the very first time the killer had laid eyes on Maryke Retief. Without eyewitnesses, without evidence at the scene—and they didn't even have the primary scene—where did you search with any degree of certainty? He didn't even know whether the letter had really come from the killer. It might just as well have been sent by a fellow pupil with a twisted sense of humor, a wannabe seeking to share in the "glory," or a mentally disturbed individual.

This docket might simply go on and on, growing thicker and thicker without him making any progress towards solving it. Three girls murdered. That they knew of. How long before he found himself once again standing in the veld somewhere, looking down at a teenage girl being devoured by maggots? The stench in his nostrils. That wet sound, like spaghetti being stirred.

Serial murders could continue for years.

He felt trapped. Why did Maryke Retief have to come to him? Why couldn't it have been Najeer's case?

Easter eggs on a table. Blue and yellow and red and green.

Emma had always hidden Easter eggs in the garden for Hannes to find. They would follow him while he looked for them, saying, "Warm ... Warmer ... No, colder ... I'm actually getting goose bumps ... Your hair is starting to burn ..." And the little face when he had found one. It was so easy to make children happy when they were small, so easy to fix things when they broke.

Then they got older and all of a sudden it was impossible to fix something you had broken. You couldn't simply go and fetch the superglue in the fridge. Even if you tried, your child couldn't fail to see the ugly joint. Anja Heyns's mother knew this.

If only Emma hadn't become ill.

He rose and walked to the bookshelf against the left wall. Emma's books. A few on birds. A few on gardening. Some on health. An atlas. The black spines of the *Wêreldspektrum* encyclopedias they had bought when Hannes had been in primary school. All the love stories Emma so adored. She used to read her favorites over and over again.

But you know what's going to happen. Why don't you rather read a new one?

She had looked at him with that soft expression of hers. *Because sometimes it's nice to know everything will end well and—*

"—not simply hope it will," he said out loud.

He smiled, and had to bite down on his lip.

The photo albums were on the bottom shelf. He pulled out the second one and returned to the sofa. Hannes's birth. It had been the happiest day of his life. That tiny body. In his arms. Little, puffy face. Eyes closed. Tiny mouth yawning. Nine months had been insufficient to prepare him for the moment he had held his son in his arms for the first time. And even had he known every word in the Afrikaans language, he would not have been able to describe how he felt right then. On the next page Hannes was lying on his mother's chest in the hospital bed, a white baby beanie on his head, eyes closed. And then one of his favorite photos. His hand. The fingers, somewhat short, somewhat thick. And the tiny hand. The stubby fingers holding his thumb. So small. The folds in the skin where the fingers bent. A little nail on each end. His index finger stroked the small hand on the photo.

If Emma did have to get sick, why couldn't the treatment have worked? If only she could have gone into remission …

When Hannes had learned to walk, to run actually, he'd had this way of jumping unexpectedly. He wouldn't say anything or give any warning; he would simply leap, without any doubt that his father would catch him. From the bed. From the stairs at the end of the corridor in the old house. He was convinced his son had never even considered the possibility that the hands wouldn't be there to catch him.

That was what was broken.

He had been relieved to finally get away after Emma's funeral. To finally just get home. Away from all the people and their condolences and good intentions. He had walked into this very TV room, his hands over his face.

Mom didn't die on her own. Never before had he heard Hannes's voice sound like it had on that day. *I didn't want to believe it, but it is the truth. That's why she held me like that. Why she told me how proud she was of me. How much she loved me. She said that several times.*

Magson had just stood there, mute and motionless, his hands covering his face.

She knew. She knew it was the last time. That's why it was so important that I come and visit. You planned everything for weeks.

Something had been missing from Hannes's voice, like a photo that had faded.

How could you, Dad? You gave me a list and sent me to Tyger Valley—

Magson just stood there now, mute and motionless, his hands covering his face.

—and while I'm doing shopping, you're killing Mom ...

Magson took his hands away. Looked at them. The hands that had done it.

I wish I had just held her. I wish I never let her go. Now it was Sonja Retief's voice.

She had said it the first time he had spoken to her. And had repeated it in the letter to the newspaper. The refrain of a parent of a murdered child.

When he had turned around, that day after Emma's funeral, his son had gone. He had had to let him go, because he no longer had the right to hold him.

He picked up the photo album off the floor and returned it to the shelf. In the bedroom he removed his holster. Turned it over in his hands.

His fingers curled around the grip and he pulled out his service pistol.

He looked down at the dull black metal.

Eight

April 22, 2014. Tuesday.

Magson sat in his office, the three dockets open in front of him. Almost all of the forensic reports had been completed—the one benefit of a high-profile case. No semen, which meant the killer had either used a condom or an object. Or he hadn't ejaculated—perhaps he had difficulty completing the act and that was why he tortured the girls. Or maybe he withdrew in time. Similar fibers on the clothes of both Maryke and Dominique, probably originating from a shag carpet. And then the thing that bothered Magson: a single long blonde hair. It had been found on Maryke's clothing. Whose hair was it? Was there another victim somewhere?

The clock on the wall kept on ticking. It had been a present from Hannes, when he was still at primary school, for Father's Day.

Daddy, you can also move these black things for the date.

He looked at the sliding bars. Tuesday, April 22.

Captain Kritzinger entered the office. Magson watched the group leader shutting the door behind him and felt even more exhausted.

"Anything?"

"Nothing helpful."

Kritzinger sat on the corner of the desk. "*You* magazine is doing a story. It's about parents who can't cope with the murders of their children, and also that the killers haven't been caught. That they haven't received justice."

Magson said nothing. He wanted to close his eyes and bury his face in his hands, but instead he turned his eyes to the small cactus, still green in spite of a lack of attention, water and natural sunlight. It was even producing more thorns.

"They're focusing on two in particular, Liesl-Marie Goosen from the late nineties and Maryke Retief. The question, of course, is whether the Retiefs will also still be waiting to see their daughter's killer brought to justice in fifteen years' time."

Magson rubbed his face before throwing both hands in the air. "What do you think I'm doing, Captain? I've been through the notes, the statements, the reports, the photos over and over and over again. Colin and I have walked up and down that street. We have spoken to everyone. Several times. If there is something else I can do, tell me, Captain, and I'll go out and do it."

Kritzinger watched him for a few moments. "Mags. I know."

"So what then, Captain? Why come in here and close the door if it's not to tell me I'm not doing my job?"

"How long has it been since Emma passed?"

He could only stare at Kritzinger. "What does that have to do with anything?"

"I know you're struggling. I know it's a process you have to go through and it takes time. And it's fine, Mags. But I want you to be honest with me. Are you in a place where you can deal with a case like this?"

"Captain, if I can't do my job anymore ..." He raised his hands. Let them drop on the desk.

Kritzinger regarded him for a while. "Okay." He got up. "Who knows, maybe someone reads the story and comes forward." His voice didn't sound particularly optimistic.

Magson sat at his desk and watched the captain leave his office. He shook his head. This was all he needed.

He didn't want the case. He would much rather investigate a normal murder, and spend more time on his other open dockets. But if he did that ... They were already keeping an eye on him, they already had doubts.

His eyes settled on the small cactus again.

"Kathy's car is still not fixed." Menck followed his words into the office and plopped down in the chair. "They promised me it would be done by last Monday. Then it was 'definitely before Easter weekend'. And now the guy I need to talk to is supposedly not there. *Bliksem* is probably hiding in the toilet." He shook out a cigarette, stuck it between his lips, pulled it out again. "I miss the nineties. You could smoke in the nineties."

Magson didn't answer.

"If he doesn't call me back within an hour, I'm going to go over there and drag his arse out of that stall. I'm in the mood for a good fight." Menck coaxed the cigarette back into the pack and nodded in the direction of the open dockets. "Find anything?"

"A hair and fibers without owners. The captain was here. There's going to be an article in *You* about unsolved murders of children, Maryke Retief in particular. Focus is on the parents."

Menck rolled his eyes. "Shit, what, wasn't there a soap star or a rugby player involved in some kind of scandal this week? Did you receive the hurry-up?"

Magson nodded.

"Well, you know how it goes. The brigadier kicks the colonel. Colonel kicks the captain. Captain comes and kicks us."

"The problem is we don't have anyone to go and kick." Magson looked at the reports in front of him. "I wish we also had databases for all these things. I could do with a computer that can simply tell me this fiber is from a 2010 Mazda 6. Or a specially imported carpet only sold by two shops in the country."

"Is it a specially imported carpet?"

"How should I know? I had to buy every carpet in my house with a policeman's salary."

"I've found my way to the dog box thanks to *CSI*," said Menck. "Ben never misses an episode. And then I tell him, you know, how it really is. But it usually turns into an argument and now Kathy is pissed because I can't just watch it for the story."

"Why do you *want* to watch it? *CSI* makes it look like detectives are only there to put cuffs on the suspects."

Once again Menck shook out a cigarette and started playing with it. "That's my point. I can't just sit there. I have to defend my profession. They don't understand."

"Why don't you rather watch *Law & Order*? If you really want to see more murders in your free time."

"Because Ben doesn't watch *Law & Order*. Ben watches *CSI*. And I watch it to spend time with him. The older he gets, the more difficult it becomes." Menck studied the cigarette while rolling it between his thumb and index finger. "Sometimes it feels like he's drifting away. So slowly, you don't realize it until one day when you stop and look …"

Magson said nothing.

Menck rose. "Anyway. Want to go for a drive?"

"Depends. Why and where?"

"Johnson phoned. He says he's got something."

"Johnson?" Menck's longtime informant had his fingers in all kinds of pies, several of which Magson would rather not know about. "What would Johnson know about our case?"

Menck shrugged. "Let's go and find out."

Johnson's Bistro was part café, part restaurant. Not Johnson's primary business, it was the only one completely legit. Magson was glad to see few patrons when he entered behind Menck. He had never particularly cared for the red-and-black interior, and the plastic tablecloths tended to be either sticky or greasy. The aroma of the place, on the other hand … At present the predominant smell was that of dough frying in oil. And spices. His stomach groaned.

"Misters M 'n M!" said Johnson with his customary hospitality. "Welcome to my bistro. You're very scarce these days."

"Honest work keeps one busy," said Menck.

"Jaaa, but your pockets stay empty. Come closer so I can introduce you to my niece here. This is Shamia, my sister's daughter."

They greeted the slender girl. Large black eyes, shy smile.

"First you must taste these chicken samoosas. New recipe. Much improved. Shamia, find us two nice ones there."

Magson and Menck each received a samoosa on a white plate with a serviette. Golden brown. The steam ferried the promise of curry, coriander and other pungent spices. Magson took a bite. The crunch of the outer layer of the pastry came first, followed by the chewy inner layer and finally the meat, hot and spicy, but not so much that it overpowered the flavor of the meat and onions.

"This is a *bleddie lekker* samoosa, Johnson," said Menck.

"Of course. Johnson is in the *bleddie lekker* business. And, as always, special price for you. Get it sorted with Shamia, then we'll go to my office and discuss our business."

Menck smiled, taking out his wallet.

Johnson's office smelled of smoke, the consequence of his love of cigars. He shut the door behind them.

"Look, I don't know if this will help you. But I had a chat with a joygirl. She had a hook-up with a couple. Man wanted to tie her up first. Paid extra. Then she and the woman played round the world. Then the man tied her up again, strangled her with rope and worked her over with a tool of some sort. Via the back road."

"When was this?" asked Magson.

"About two weeks ago."

"And you only phoned today?" asked Menck, annoyed.

Johnson pressed his fingertips against his chest. "Shocked am I, that you would think Johnson holds back. I only chatted to her yesterday. When she dropped the rent."

"I apologize," said Menck, bowing his head.

Johnson spread his arms. "Apology accepted. If you're interested, a meeting can be organized. But her time costs, whether you get joy or not."

"Even for the police?"

"A joygirl must eat, too, pay rent. She had to take time off already because he damaged her."

Magson received a raised-eyebrow look from Menck. "Ja, let's hear what she has to say."

"Right," said Johnson. "Let me make a call. With luck she's

between joyrides. Why don't you go ask Shamia for a menu while I get things sorted."

Johnson had told them she was nineteen, but to Magson she looked like a schoolgirl. Her hair was draped long and dark across her shoulders and the white top clung to her breasts. She hid a pretty face beneath thick base and lipstick the color of fresh blood. Whatever her age, she had been doing this work long enough to harden her eyes.

"I'm Lola. Come in."

She turned to the side, her belly-ring glinting, and ushered them inside. There was a noticeable fragrance—perfume, a decent kind, fresh and with a hint of apples. Magson wondered whether the idea was to excite or to conceal the smells of the previous encounter. A bedroom with a double bed, a chair and a cupboard. Another door to a bathroom. Not much in the way of decoration, but everything looked clean.

"I like to get paid up front."

Magson turned around, removed his wallet and paid her fee, hoping her information would be worth it.

She took it with a smile which, like the long nails lightly trailing his skin, did not seem real. "Thanks."

"Okay," said Menck. "Tell us about the couple with the rope. What happened?"

"The wife said he liked to tie her up and he wanted to tie me up. He'd pay extra. He went through this whole thing—it took at least half an hour. Tied me up in different positions. The rope had to be perfectly aligned or something, symmetrical. Then he took it off and he watched while I did the wife. She told me what she wanted. Then he told her what to do to me. He spoke to her as if she was the whore. But he wasn't very excited about it. I mean, the whole thing was for him, but he sounded bored. While she was busy, he had me turn on my stomach and tied my hands to the bed. Next thing I knew, he had a rope around my throat and I couldn't breathe. He stuck something up my arse and it hurt a lot. He was very violent. Finally he pulled the thing out, untied me and they left."

"Did you report it?" asked Menck.

She laughed without humor.

"How did they contact you?"

"I have ads in the papers. He phoned. Asked if I'm really nineteen and if I did couples."

"Age was important?"

"He asked more than once."

"Can you describe them?"

"The wife was smallish, pretty. Had blonde hair …"

"Blonde?" asked Magson, thinking of the hair on Maryke Retief's clothes.

"Natural blonde."

"How long was her hair?"

The girl pursed her lips. "Bit longer than shoulder length."

"What about the man?" asked Menck.

"He was strong. Well-built. I'm sure he gyms a lot. Not a body builder, but strong. Not unattractive, but not wow, either." She looked up, to the left. "Brown hair, I think. They wore nice clothes, not cheap stuff. I'd say they've got money. Or debt."

"And they were married."

"They had wedding rings."

"Was it this man?" Magson showed her a photo of Neels Delport.

She shook her head. "No."

"Would you be willing to work with a sketch artist?"

"Do you know how many faces I see? Except for the regulars, they all blend together. I don't remember details. I don't want to."

"What about the wife?"

Again she shook her head. "I don't want to get involved."

"But would you be able to describe her?"

She looked away.

"Please," said Magson. "It would help a lot."

"I'll think about it."

"Thanks. Here is my card."

She took it.

"Thanks for your time."

"Well, you paid for it."

At the door, Menck turned around. "I'm sorry this happened to you."

A faint smile touched her lips, a real one. "You live, you

learn. I won't lower my guard again just because there's a woman present."

"It does sound a lot like the way Lauren Romburgh was killed," said Menck as they walked to the Corolla. "Plus the sodomy. The violence."

"Hmm, but I don't know about the man and woman thing."

"It happens. Fred and Rose West, for example."

"Not often. But it would explain the blonde hair." Magson looked up at the gray sky. All the clouds appeared shapeless. "I'm not convinced I got my money's worth."

"At least she didn't charge you for a full house. But Lola did say one very interesting thing."

"What?"

"'I won't lower my guard just because there's a woman present.' It could explain why the girls so readily get into the car. Because a woman feels safer when there is another woman with a man."

April 23, 2014. Wednesday.

They were back at the Retiefs' house. Sonja Retief had retrieved a second white envelope, identical to the first and similarly addressed, from the mailbox. She'd recognized it immediately, placed it unopened inside the house, and phoned Magson. He, in turned, had phoned the Local Criminal Record Center.

They watched as the crime-scene technician carefully handled the envelope with his latex gloves. He photographed it and turned to them. "I still think I should just seal it and take it to the lab so they can open it there."

"I want to know whether Mrs. Retief recognizes the scent," said Magson. "It can't wait. But I take full responsibility. Just make sure you document the whole process."

The technician shook his head one more time, slit the envelope open with a blade and took another photo. He sniffed, nodded and held it so the detectives could have a smell.

"I think it's the same," said Magson. "Must be some kind of perfume."

"It's something nice," remarked Menck. "It doesn't have that sharp, sickly smell of the cheap stuff."

"Mrs. Retief, do you recognize it?"

She approached, reluctantly, dread etched into her features. No tranquilizers today. Her eyes were green as well, but lacked the impact her daughter's had had. She stooped and sniffed. Shook her head.

"Are you sure?"

"Yes."

"It's not something Maryke wore?"

"No." She shuddered and returned to her husband's side.

"You know," said Menck, "Edgars has quite a collection of perfumes. Maybe they'll know what it is."

"That's a good idea," said Magson.

In the meantime the technician had removed the letter with tweezers. The same light green handmade paper. He folded it open. The same black letters.

> Maryke
> I made you a part of me
> You are now tied to me
> For All Time

"How can anyone be so cruel?" asked Sonja Retief. Her cheeks were wet with tears. "Isn't it enough that he killed her? Isn't it *enough*?"

She left the dining room.

While more photos were taken, Magson opened his notebook and wrote the message beneath the previous one.

The technician placed an evidence bag beside the envelope and took a photo, the unique number clearly visible. He sealed it, marked it and proceeded to do the same with the letter.

"I'll see what prints I can lift and let you know."

"Thanks," said Magson, "but we want to try to identify the scent first."

"Okay. So I should first send it to Pretoria for chemical analysis?"

"That will take weeks. Months. We'll just take it to Edgars."

The technician looked at him. "I have to go and book this stuff into the SAP459."

"We'll follow you. Then you can book it in and book it out for us. And we'll bring it back as soon as we're done."

The wound left by the Inge Lotz fiasco still hadn't healed. The LCRC members employed at the time of Fred van der Vyver's trial were especially testy. Magson preferred it that way, since there were few things more pathetic than a defense attorney ripping holes in your chain of custody.

"Another outing to Tyger Valley," said Menck as they entered the shopping center.

"I don't know why you're so excited about it," muttered Magson.

"What? No decomposing bodies. No crying relatives. No lying suspects. No court appearances. It's fun."

"You know, you've been too cheery all day."

"What can I say? My day started with a climax."

They walked down the shiny corridor. Magson never ceased to be amazed by the host of people wandering around in a shopping center at this time on a weekday. Didn't they have jobs where they were supposed to be? The place was practically teeming.

"While we're here, we should get something for you, too," said Menck with a smile as they turned towards Edgars.

"What?"

"Aftershave."

"Why? There is nothing wrong with Shield."

"Does Shield make aftershave?"

"I don't use aftershave," said Magson. "I use deodorant."

"How long have you been using Shield?"

"Since … Who cares? I like Shield."

"Don't you feel like using something different?"

Magson sighed. "Do you have a problem with my Shield?"

"No, probably not. But there's nothing wrong with a little bit of change now and again."

"Oh. So after all these years, now you have a problem with my deodorant."

"I'm just saying change isn't always bad. But you Afrikaners are so stubborn."

"We Afrikaners. Now you're insulting my heritage, too."

Menck laughed. "I thought you Afrikaners considered stubbornness to be a compliment."

Magson gave him a look and Menck laughed harder. "What's with the 'you' anyway?" asked Magson. "You're half an Afrikaner yourself."

"Hmm. Looks like it's my dark half."

Magson sighed.

They went to the nearest perfume counter and the woman behind it greeted them with a friendly smile. Her coffee-colored skin was smooth, her hair and make-up immaculate, as if she had been carefully prepared for a magazine photo shoot. Magson didn't like it—she looked unnatural. He had always felt that the "flaws" were what actually made a woman beautiful and different. Like Emma, who had frequently bemoaned her large mouth, while he loved it. Especially when she'd smiled. He used to joke that he was the only man whose wife complained about her big mouth.

"Can I help you?"

Magson presented his identification card. "I'm Warrant Officer Magson and this is Warrant Officer Menck. We're hoping you can help us with something."

The woman turned serious. "Should I call the manager?"

"No, no, that won't be necessary. We just want to know if you can identify a perfume for us."

"Oh."

"It's evidence, so it has to be handled with care." He cut the evidence bag along the broken line at the bottom, and held it out to her. "If you could just smell it, please?"

The woman bent over, sniffed carefully at first, then deeper. She closed her eyes and smelled again. Nodded. "Yes. I think …" She turned around and retrieved a bottle from the shelf, sprayed some of the scent on the inside of her wrist, smelled. "Yes." She held her wrist for Magson. "It's Tommy Girl."

Magson sniffed the letter. "Hmm," he said, pleased. "That's quite impressive."

She smiled and looked down, shrugging. "That's what happens when you work behind a perfume counter for six years."

Hy placed the bag containing the letter inside a new evidence bag and sealed it. "Who usually buys Tommy Girl?"

"Mostly the younger girls, sixteen and older. But I've got a lady in her sixties who likes it, too."

"What about men?"

"There's a Tommy for men—"

"No, I mean, do men also buy Tommy Girl?"

"Oh. Yes, for their girlfriends, wives, daughters."

"Does it sell well?"

"Yes. It's quite popular."

Magson clicked his tongue. "Can I see the box, please?"

The woman took one of the white boxes off the shelf and handed it to him.

He looked at it, noticed the price, and handed it back. "Thank you very much for your help." Magson began to turn.

"Sir? We also have lovely fragrances for men. Eau de toilette, perhaps? Or an aftershave?"

Menck erupted into laughter. "A Shield refill, hey, Mags?"

"I have enough, thanks," Magson told the woman and gave Menck a look. "I've got some Stetson aftershave at home." Most likely scentless from age. "I'll put it on tomorrow, all right?"

"Stetson. I should get you a hat for your birthday," said Menck as they left the store. "Sheriff Magson."

"You know, it's because of clowns like you that people complain about the police."

"And some chewing tobacco."

Magson sighed and glanced at the ceiling.

"Listen, since we're here, I just want to pop into Secrets of India for some chili powder," said Menck.

"I need to use the bathroom. See you at the car."

No sign of Menck at the Corolla when he got there. The car guard scurried over. "Here's your car, sir."

Magson glared at him. "I'm a policeman. I can find my own bloody car." He unlocked the door, got behind the wheel and yanked the door shut.

The guard walked off.

Magson opened the window and sat back. Looked at his watch. He took out his notebook and leafed through the pages. Until he reached the messages from the two letters.

The passenger door opened and Menck slid in. He leaned over, holding a brown paper bag under Magson's nose. "Just smell this."

Magson could feel the burning promise in his nostrils.

"Specially mixed," said Menck, practically beaming, and took a deep whiff.

"It's a miracle you haven't burnt a hole straight through your intestines."

"Chili is good for you. It keeps all sorts of bad things at bay." He rubbed the curve of his belly. "You know, I could really do with one of Johnson's samoosas. It worries me a bit to think what he might be putting in them, but damn, they're good."

Magson was still staring at the two messages:

> Maryke you were so beautiful
> So beautiful
> The most beautiful eyes
> I had to have you
> Now you are mine for Always
>
> Maryke
> I made you a part of me
> You are now tied to me
> For All Time

He tongued the cavity in his tooth.

Menck was frowning. "Won't be surprised if it's cat or something."

Magson shook his head. "I don't understand it."

"I heard somewhere cat kind of tastes like chicken. Those samoosas were chicken … Supposedly."

"How do you do that to a girl and then write letters on special paper, which you spray with perfume that costs almost six hundred rand, going on about how she's yours 'for Always'? With a capital letter."

"Maybe it's better not knowing."

Magson sighed and shook his head. "Unless LCRC finds something, these letters won't mean shit." He snapped the notebook closed. From dead end to dead end. How long before Captain Kritzinger was no longer simply inquiring behind a closed door?

"Let's take the letter back and go get a samoosa. Hey?"

"A samoosa. I'm trying to find something so I don't get thrown off the case, and all you can think about is samoosas."

Menck looked at him. "Why would you get thrown off the case?"

"Because what have I just learned? That this letter was sprayed with Tommy Girl. That helps us fuck all. I don't even know that this letter was actually written by the killer. I'm not investigating a suspect's background. I'm not on my way to go and interrogate a suspect. Because I don't have a suspect."

"Mags, you know there's always more pressure with these kinds of cases. But you can still only work with what you've got."

Magson stared out the windshield. Menck didn't understand. He didn't come home to a dark, silent house. He had not failed his wife, his son, and now had to hear he was failing his job as well. He had not lost everything yet.

Nine

April 24, 2014. Thursday.

Well, even the devil's luck can't last forever, Magson thought. One fingerprint, a thumb, on one of the corners of the latest letter. There were other fingerprints as well, but this one was in the AFIS database. The owner had a criminal record. A sexual offence in 2011. He had exposed himself to a teenage girl.

"She was on her way home after school," said Magson. "On foot."

"That sounds familiar," said Menck.

"When she crossed the veld, he accosted her."

"Did he try anything with her?"

"No. When she saw what he was doing, she ran. There was a surveyor and he asked her what was wrong. She told him, and he and his assistant went looking for the guy. They found him still in the veld, busy."

Menck cast his eyes downward, lowering his head. "Caught with the redheaded monster in his hand."

"Ja."

Menck looked up again. "So surveyors actually have a use. They don't just stand in the middle of the road with their weird binoculars."

"The flasher is twenty-four. It's his first offence on record, but …"

"We know offenders learn from their mistakes. And they tend to begin with lesser crimes."

Magson nodded. "The pieces fit so far."

"What's the flasher's name?"

"Roelof Kirstein."

"Okay. So how do you want to do this?"

The house was rather old, white and dark green. It seemed to be kept in good condition and the garden was tidy. The yard didn't look particularly large. A low white wall had been built higher at some stage. White columns with black metal bars in between. Magson wondered how many walls in South Africa had changed from decorative to defensive during the last two decades.

He pressed the button on the intercom.

A female voice answered. She sounded elderly.

"It's the police. Can we speak with you a moment, please?"

"Is there a problem?"

"We're looking for someone. Maybe you can help us?"

"Just wait a while. I'm coming."

She was indeed an elderly woman, Magson noticed when she arrived at the gate. Probably late sixties, early seventies. Short and somewhat portly, her straight gray hair just reaching below her jaw. She favored her left leg.

"I'm Warrant Officer Magson. This is Warrant Officer Menck."

She took his identification card with one hand, put on the spectacles dangling around her neck, and studied it down her nose.

"We are looking for Roelof Kirstein. Does he live here?"

She handed the card back and looked at him over the top of her spectacles. "He does, but he's not here at the moment. What do you want with him?"

"He might be able to help us with an investigation."

She frowned, staring at Magson. "What investigation? Roelf is a good boy. He isn't involved in the wrong kind of things."

"Mr. Kirstein may have information that could help us. Are you sure he's not here?"

"No. I told you. He's at work."

"May I ask who you are?"

"Bets Lennard."

"How do you know Mr. Kirstein?"

"This is my house. Roelf rents the outside room."

Magson nodded. "Do you know where Mr. Kirstein works?"

"Of course I do. He works at Kirstein Pool Services."

"Is he the owner?"

"No. He works for his uncle."

"Thank you for your time, Mrs. Lennard."

Kirstein Pool Services had two premises. One in the industrial area—presumably where the fiberglass swimming pools and equipment were stored—and the other was a combination office/service shop in Bellville. The store was not large, but the shelves were neatly packed with Kreepy Kraulies and pipes, nets, brushes and miscellaneous products that supposedly kept water clean and clear. As always, the smell of chlorine transported Magson to the old municipal swimming pool of his childhood, the baking Transvaal sun …

The woman behind the counter was watching him. Something about her looked wrong. He walked closer and realized it was the light brown eyes—clear as glass—in the brown face that gave the strange appearance. He took out his identification card.

"Warrant Officers Magson and Menck. Is the owner here?"

"Mr. Kirstein is in his office." Her eyebrows scrunched together. "Is there a problem?"

"We'd like to talk to him, please."

She picked up the phone and pressed a couple of buttons. "Mr. Kirstein? The police are here to see you." She listened, said, "Yes, sir," and replaced the receiver. "He says he'll be here now."

Menck took a chlorinator from the shelf. On top of it was a plastic shark wearing reflective sunglasses and he started fiddling with it.

"Did you know a person produces enough spit in a life-time to fill two swimming pools?"

"No," said Magson. "And I could've gone through the rest of my life without that knowledge."

"My son told me the other day," said the woman behind the counter, "that if you take all the arteries in your body and put it in a line, it can go around the earth, not once but twice."

"Ah," smiled Menck. "Someone who appreciates the wonders of the human body." He returned the chlorinator to the shelf.

"I still can't believe it," she said.

"Did you know your entire skin is replaced every month?" asked Menck.

Magson sighed.

The door behind the counter opened and a man with a bit of a paunch and a round face appeared. He seemed to be compensating for the deficit of hair on the top of his head in the lower half of his face.

"Boy Kirstein. How can I help?"

Magson accepted his strong handshake and introduced himself and Menck. "Can we talk in your office?"

"Sure. Come through."

Like the store, the office wasn't large but neat—desk, computer, framed photos of vehicles and workers installing swimming pools on the walls, framed photos of wife and children on the shelf.

"Sit." He swept an arm at the chairs and walked around the desk. He sat down, propping his arms on the desk. "What do you want to talk to me about?"

"Do you know where Roelof Kirstein is?" asked Magson.

The man's face froze for a moment. "He's on his rounds. Did something happen to him? Was he in an accident or something?"

"Not as far as we know. What rounds, Mr. Kirstein?"

"We offer several services. One is pool maintenance. That's what Roelf does."

"Do you know where he is now?"

"I can phone and find out. Why are you looking for him?"

"It's possible that he might have information that could help us with an investigation."

Boy Kirstein hadn't moved since he sat down. A groove had steadily deepened between his eyebrows. "What information?"

"I'm afraid I can't discuss it," said Magson.

"Look." Boy Kirstein crossed his arms. "I'm not stupid. You could've asked this out there in the shop, but you wanted to come to my office. Did Roelf do something?"

"Mr. Kirstein, what do you know of Roelof's private life? His habits, comings and goings, that sort of thing?"

He placed his hands in his lap and shifted in the chair. "To be honest, not much. I often see him on workdays, of course, and sometimes he comes over for Sunday lunch, but I don't really know what he does in his free time. Roelf is my brother's son. After my brother's death, I've tried to take care of Roelf as best I can. I gave him this job, organized a place to live. But he keeps to himself."

"We understand he rents an outside room from a Mrs. Lennard?"

"That's right."

"Does Roelf have access to a vehicle?"

"He does. It's not a wonderful car, but it takes him where he needs to be. And of course he uses the *bakkie* for work. Won't you tell me what's going on?"

Magson considered his options, and followed his instinct that the man presented good potential as an ally. "All right, Mr. Kirstein. The truth is that Roelof might be in some trouble."

Boy Kirstein closed his eyes for a few seconds. "Roelf has been in trouble before."

Magson nodded. "We know."

"Is it … the same thing?"

"I'm afraid it's worse."

"Worse?" Boy Kirstein looked down at his desk calendar. His shoulders sagged.

"It's obvious you care about Roelof. We don't want to arrest him at this stage, but we do want to talk to him. You can help make sure that happens without incident."

"It's really serious?"

Magson nodded.

Boy Kirstein shook his head. "I'm just glad my brother isn't here to witness this day. What must I do?"

In the morning, Roelof Kirstein drove to Kirstein Pool Services' other premises, where he loaded the necessary pool-cleaning equipment into the back of the business's *bakkie* and went out on his rounds. Only on rare occasions did he come around to the store.

Magson had listened to Boy Kirstein's explanation of his nephew's routine and decided it would be least suspicious if they went to the premises in the industrial area, from where the phone call would be made, and Magson and Menck would await his arrival.

They followed Boy Kirstein in his double-cab Toyota Hilux. Magson sympathized with the man—it couldn't be easy for him.

"This story fits particularly well," remarked Menck. "Kirstein can easily drive around between pool jobs, looking for schoolgirls."

"He can use his job, too. He can stop next to them and say he's looking for an address. The business's name is painted on the side—she would have no reason to suspect anything."

Menck nodded. "He could even convince her to get in and show him. Otherwise, the canopy is painted white. He can force her into the back, tie her up or something, tape her mouth shut, and no one would know she was inside."

"Ja, so far so good, but where does he take her? He can't take the girls to his room at old Mrs. Lennard's house."

"I don't know. But it wouldn't be the first time horrific things happen right underneath someone's nose."

"Hmm. But he'd have to get them in there in broad daylight without her noticing anything."

"Perhaps he takes them on days he knows Mrs. Lennard has some engagement."

"Still," said Magson, "he's got to leave the girls there the next day while he goes to work. I wonder what this outside room looks like."

"Well, we can deal with the details later. The uncle just has to do his part when he phones."

That was what worried Magson.

Boy Kirstein turned in at the gate and Magson followed. A sign proclaimed KIRSTEIN POOL SERVICES in large letters. On one side of the premises were a few fiberglass swimming-pool shells. Magson had never owned a swimming pool and had never had much of a desire to, either. When Hannes had been small, he'd sometimes turned on the sprinkler so his son could run through the water. The skinny body, just legs and arms and the open-mouthed laugh of a child's easy delight. Had Hannes ever asked for a pool? He tried to remember, but could not. He did recall when Hannes had first learned how to swim. They had been on holiday somewhere, a resort in KwaZulu-Natal, and he'd had Hannes lie on top of his outstretched arms so he could learn how to kick and put his face in the water and breathe the proper way. By the time the vacation had drawn to a close, Hannes had been able to swim.

He pushed the memory away and got out of the Corolla. Boy Kirstein led them to another office, very similar to the first one. The same photos of his family in the same frames. Again Roelof Kirstein was absent.

"Sit."

Magson took a seat, but Menck walked over to the window and peered outside.

Boy Kirstein stared at his cellphone and sighed. He pressed a button and held it to his ear.

"Roelf. Where are you?" He nodded. "Okay. Listen, when you're done, come over here. Mr. Theron phoned. They have a crisis. Sounds like the pump's motor has burnt out and they have a party on Saturday, so … Okay." He ended the call and let his head hang.

"That was very good, Mr. Kirstein," said Magson. "I know it wasn't easy."

The man shook his head. "How do you get to the point where you have to deceive your own brother's son …"

Almost three quarters of an hour later, the *bakkie* finally turned in at the gate and parked next to the building. Magson watched Roelof Kirstein through the dusty window of Boy Kirstein's office. He was rather scrawny. Hair shaggy and unkempt. As arranged, one of the workers passed on the message to come see his uncle in his office. As soon as he entered, Magson and Menck were at his side.

"Roelof Kirstein, I'm Warrant Officer Magson and this is Warrant Officer Menck of the Serious Violent Crimes Unit."

The young man did not even bother with the identification card. He only stared at his uncle. "*Oom* Boy?"

Magson hesitated. It was the empty sound in his voice. The disbelief. The hurt. Exactly how Hannes had sounded that afternoon after Emma's funeral.

"We want to talk to you about Maryke Retief." Menck's voice.

"*Oom* Boy?"

Hannes. Betrayed by his own father.

"You can come with us freely," said Menck, "otherwise we will arrest you."

Roelof Kirstein was still staring at his uncle. "I'll come," he murmured. He turned around, head down, and started walking out the door.

Magson became aware of Menck looking at him. "Okay?"

He nodded.

They escorted Roelof Kirstein to the Corolla. Magson looked at the *bakkie*, then at Boy Kirstein. "Would you give us permission to search the *bakkie*?"

"Yes."

Roelof Kirstein turned his eyes back to his uncle and the older man looked away.

Menck stayed with him while Magson retrieved latex gloves from the Corolla and walked over to the *bakkie*. He opened the door. He wouldn't perform a thorough search, that was for LCRC to conduct later on. But if there was something conspicuous inside the vehicle, he would rather get it now, before Boy Kirstein's guilt got the better of his judgment.

The cabin was not messy, but it was dusty, with a fair amount of sand and dirt and pieces of plant material around the pedals. A Crunchie wrapper was crumpled halfway into the ashtray. On the left side of the seat was a clipboard containing names and addresses. One off-white sock lay bunched up on the floor. He opened the glove compartment. There was a camera inside. Looked like a digital one. With a decent zoom lens.

He retrieved the camera and pressed the power button. The lens extended and the *bakkie's* interior appeared on the screen. He scanned the other buttons and pressed the one to show the photos on the memory card. The lens retreated and a girl appeared on the screen. Her brown hair was tied back in a ponytail and she was wearing a white shirt and tie—a school uniform. She wasn't looking at the camera. He pressed the triangle pointing to the left. Another photo of the same girl, from further away. Now he could see her skirt as well. She was sitting on the ground. Legs crossed. With a book in her lap. He pressed left. A close-up of her legs. He glanced at the white numbers: *23-04-14*. Yesterday. Left. Another close-up of her legs. Left. Left. Eventually there was another girl in a different school uniform. She was standing, a cellphone against her ear, her back to the camera. In the corner the photo counter read *0749*.

Magson got out, raising the camera. "Is this your camera?"

Roelof Kirstein looked down.

"The date is April 24, 2014. The time is twelve minutes past two in the afternoon, at the Serious Violent Crimes Unit in Bishop Lavis. Present are Mr. Roelof Kirstein and Warrant Officer Jan Magson."

Kirstein was looking down through the glass table, shadows in his eye sockets and grooves in his cheeks. He had not spoken a single word since they left his uncle's office.

"Mr. Kirstein," proceeded Magson, "you have the following rights. You have the right to remain silent. You have the right to have an attorney present. If you can't afford a private attorney, you can apply to the court for a legal aid attorney. Do you understand these rights?"

He was still looking down. "Yes."

Magson slid the first letter, inside its evidence bag, across the table in front of Kirstein.

The young man looked at it. There was a tiny twitch at his mouth, but nothing further.

"Do you recognize it?"

"No." Softly.

"What about this one?" Magson placed the latest letter next to the other one.

"No."

"No? Never seen it before?"

"No."

Magson nodded. "So how do you explain your fingerprint in the corner here?" He tapped his index finger on the dirty pink pattern.

"My fingerprint?" Kirstein's eyebrows rose and drew closer together.

"Ja. Your right thumb. You weren't as careful as you thought."

Kirstein said nothing, just looked at the letter.

There was a knock on the door. Menck peered around the corner and nodded. That meant the search warrant was ready.

"We'll talk again later, Mr. Kirstein."

They took him down to one of the holding cells on the ground floor. Where he could sit and brood on the evidence against him.

Bets Lennard first looked at Magson, then at the LCRC technicians in their dark blue overalls, back at Magson, finally put on her spectacles and took her copy of the J51.

"The warrant only covers Mr. Kirstein's room," said Magson. "We won't search the rest of the house."

She looked at him across the top of the spectacles and the wrinkles at the corners of her mouth sank deeper towards her chin. "All you're doing is upsetting an innocent child's life."

"Will you please open the gate for us, Mrs. Lennard?"

Her lips pursed into a tight little circle and she shook her head, but she opened the gate.

"I don't know what you think Roelf has done." She led them down the side of the house. "He eats supper at my table."

"Do you ever go into his room?"

"No." She came to a halt at a dark brown door. "This used to be the domestic's room. When I still had one living in."

"Thanks, Mrs. Lennard," said Magson. "We'll let you know if there's anything more."

She gave him a look, turned and walked off.

Magson pulled on his latex gloves, inserted the key into the lock and turned. The door swung open.

The room was about four by five meters. Its main contents were a bed, single, with blue sheets and duvet, not particularly neatly made, and a dressing table with a computer on top. A door led to a bathroom. Magson was especially interested in the newspaper clippings on the dressing table, but he stood clear so that LCRC could take their photographs first.

"Mags."

He turned around.

Menck pointed to a frame on the bedside table. Inside was a photo he had seen far too often—in the papers and on the wall in the operational room. A girl with dark brown hair tied back, a lopsided smile and dimples in her cheeks. But it was always the bright green eyes that grabbed the attention.

Maryke Retief.

"Make sure you get this," Magson told the photographer.

The clippings were from *Die Burger*. Every one about Maryke Retief. The letter her mother had written was here as well. In the left drawer of the dressing table was an assortment of items, from a couple of screwdrivers to batteries, a calculator, notebooks and a few Crunchies. Also a knife, black rubber grip, with a blade measuring about ten centimeters, sharp at the tip, teeth at the hilt. He opened the drawer on the right. And called for the photographer.

Several sheets containing an alphabet, many of the black letters missing, LETRASET printed in the corner. Three pages of the same green handmade paper as those of the letters sent to the Retiefs. A pack of white envelopes. An examination pad. Two latex gloves, the semi-translucent cream-colored kind for sale at pharmacies.

"Well," said Menck, "that's the end of any benefit of the doubt then."

"No, he's definitely our letter writer."

Magson leafed through the exam pad, pointing to where the content of the letters had been composed. It had taken several attempts before Kirstein had been satisfied.

Menck shook his head. "So much effort and that was the best he could do."

"Now if we can just find the panties or jewelry, we've got the *donner*."

Menck opened a closet door. Clothes were hanging on the left. On the right were shelves. More clothes. Some folded, others stuffed in.

"Not exactly neat," remarked Magson.

Menck looked through the clothes. "All men's clothes … Hey, what do we have here?"

"What?"

Magazines. Looked like teen magazines: *seventeen*.

"Just the kind of thing I'd expect to find in a grown man's closet," said Menck. "Aah, and also …"

"Tommy Girl," said Magson. "But I would be much happier if we could find the panties."

They scoured the entire room and the bathroom, but there was neither female underwear nor jewelry, nor any of the victims' belongings. No rope, either.

Magson's tongue found the cavity in his tooth. The letters by themselves were not worth an awful lot. There was nothing on those green pages that proved Maryke's killer had written it. Nor did the attempts on the exam pad include intimate details. Of course, there was still Kirstein's car.

An LCRC technician was dusting the bathroom's doorframe. Another one started with a wall. If the girls had been here, a fingerprint could be waiting somewhere.

They would also investigate the computer. There had been no photos of Maryke or Dominique on Kirstein's camera, but if he was the killer and he had taken photos of them, these might well be on the hard drive.

Back at the SVC office they fetched Roelof Kirstein from his cell and escorted him to the interrogation room. Magson sat down opposite Kirstein and explained his rights once again, while Menck took up position behind Kirstein.

"Mr. Kirstein, earlier we talked about these two letters that were sent to Maryke Retief's house." Again he placed the two evidence bags containing the letters on the table. "Do you still deny that you wrote these letters?"

Kirstein looked at the light green pages, but didn't answer.

Menck put a box on the table.

"We searched your room," said Magson.

"And just look at all the goodies we found there," said Menck, lifting the lid. "Let me show you, Warrant Magson." He began removing evidence bags one by one.

"Green paper," said Magson. "Handmade." He slid the evidence bag containing the sheets next to the letters. "Hmm … looks exactly the same."

Menck placed the Letraset alphabet sheets on the table.

"Also the same."

"And look which letters are missing," said Menck.

Magson compared the sheets to the letters. Through the glass he noticed Kirstein's hands fidgeting in his lap.

"And perfume," said Magson, lifting the evidence bag containing the Tommy Girl.

"I hear the girls quite like it. Especially the teenage girls."

"Oh."

"Yes. It's a fresh, free, energetic, lively fragrance." Menck looked at Kirstein. "Do you agree?"

Kirstein's hands stopped moving. His eyes were large. His mouth opened, but no words were formed.

Menck turned to Magson. "I think it's because they're constantly sniffing the stuff that they come up with these stupid descriptions."

"Hmm," nodded Magson. "Same with wine."

"What else have we got? An exam pad. And …" Menck removed an evidence bag and dangled it in front of Kirstein. It was the one containing the latex gloves. "Do you also hate the powder inside these things? We have to wear them when we're searching for evidence—we've got blue ones—but, man, the powder. The gloves make you sweat and then it mixes with the powder and you end up with this mess underneath your nails."

"That's why you were surprised by the fingerprint," said Magson.

Kirstein's eyes skipped to his and fled again. He was sweating.

"You did write these letters, didn't you?"

Kirstein slowly nodded. "Yes," he murmured.

"When was the first time you saw Maryke Retief?"

"In the paper. After ..."

"Did you take photos of her at her school?

"No."

"You like taking photos of schoolgirls."

Kirstein didn't answer.

Menck moved the box to the floor, pulled out the chair and sat down. He took a deep breath. "There's just something about schoolgirls. Young and pretty and they look so innocent in their school uniform. But then you notice the short dress. The legs perfectly tanned. The skin so smooth."

Magson watched as Kirstein swallowed, the tip of his tongue slipping across his lower lip.

"A white shirt. And these days they wear it as tightly as they can get away with. Sometimes you can just about make out the bra. Dark brown ponytail down her back, maybe a braid."

Kirstein sat very still. He stared at the evidence bags on the table, but he was listening.

"I can understand that you enjoy looking. All fathers look when they pick up their children at school."

"And if you take photos," said Magson, "you can look for longer."

"The problem is," Menck grimaced, "how long is looking enough? A man wants to touch as well. Feel that soft skin. Smell the perfume."

"But they don't want to."

Kirstein's lips pressed more tightly together.

"They don't want to," Magson repeated.

"They tempt you," said Menck. "Tease you with their short dresses. Their tanned legs. Their dark hair. They sit and smile, but they won't let you touch them."

Kirstein opened his mouth. "I only take photos."

"How long can photos be enough? How long can the sock in the *bakkie* be enough?"

"I … only take photos."

"What about 2011, Mr. Kirstein?" asked Magson. "When you exposed yourself to a schoolgirl?"

Kirstein dropped his head further, slipped the tip of his left index finger between his lips. "It was one time."

"One time. I'd like to believe you, but that's what people always say when they get caught."

Menck nodded. "It's true. It was always the first time. Even when we have his record and we know he's done it four times already."

Magson watched Kirstein for a while. With his weak chin and drooping shoulders he didn't look particularly intimidating, but when you took a look at photos of serial killers there were few who appeared anything but average. Besides, this might very well be why he had the urge to control and torture his victims.

"But maybe you are telling the truth," said Magson.

Kirstein looked at him.

"Maybe it *was* only that one time. But then you saw Maryke Retief." He placed a color photograph of her on top of the evidence bag containing one of the letters.

Kirstein looked at the photo. He scratched his cheek, then his eyebrow, his forehead.

"Maryke, you were so beautiful," said Magson, watching Kirstein. "So beautiful."

"She was," said Menck.

"The most beautiful eyes."

"You could barely look away."

"I had to have you."

"I can understand that," said Menck. "A girl like that. You see her and you just want her. You look at her. You look at her photos. And you just want her."

"I had to have you."

"You can't help it. Look at her. Of course you had to have her. But she didn't want to. Maybe she thought she was too good for you. Maybe she looked right through you. So what else could you do?"

"You watched her," said Magson. "You saw her walking alone."

"You couldn't help it. She refused to understand. And you had to have her."

"So you took her."

"I didn't," said Kirstein, softly. He was still scratching above his temple, looking at the photo.

"You just wanted to have her," said Menck.

"I didn't."

"Oh, come on, Mr. Kirstein!" Magson grabbed the letter. "Here it is! 'I made you a part of me'! 'Now you are mine for Always'!"

"I just wanted to—"

The door opened.

At first Magson just stared at Captain Kritzinger. A man pushed past him. Fine suit and tie. Curly brown hair. Dark eyes with a hard look.

"I'm Adolf Bressler, Roelof Kirstein's attorney. This interrogation is over until I have consulted with my client."

"Mr. Kirstein didn't ask for an attorney," said Magson.

"Robert Kirstein hired me. Come, Roelf."

Kirstein looked at him, rose and left the interrogation room with the attorney.

Magson watched him leave and hit the wall. "What the hell was that, Captain! He was on the verge of saying something!"

"I delayed as long as I could, Mags. He threatened and insisted on coming along."

Magson placed his hand over his eyes. What would the rest of that sentence have been?

April 25, 2014. Friday.

Adolf Bressler had cut off all communication with Roelof Kirstein. He had the right to remain silent and that was the extent of what he would be doing in the presence of the police. Magson was still embittered about yesterday's interrogation, but while he had been brooding last night, he'd come up with a new strategy. Perhaps Roelof Kirstein was simply a pervert who photographed schoolgirls and who had developed an obsession with Maryke Retief following her murder, but perhaps he was the one who had tortured and hanged her. While he was hiding behind his attorney, getting to the truth was substantially more difficult.

Magson walked into Kirstein Pool Services, the cardboard box under his arm, and went straight to the counter, Menck behind him. It was the same woman as yesterday. "Is Mr. Kirstein in his office?"

"Yes, I—" She reached for the phone.

"That's all right, we know the way."

He walked past her to the office, knocked on the door and opened it.

Boy Kirstein looked up. "What—?"

"Sorry to barge in here like this, Mr. Kirstein."

"Warrant Magson. The attorney said I shouldn't talk to you."

"That's all right. You don't have to say a word, just listen."

Menck shut the door.

Magson put the box on the desk and removed the lid. The first item he took out was a photo of Maryke Retief, the one always appearing in the papers.

"This is Maryke Retief. She was fifteen years old. She loved animals."

"What?" Boy Kirstein looked at the photo, then at Magson.

"This is a copy of the letter her mother wrote to the newspaper. Read it, Mr. Kirstein."

"Warrant—"

"All right. I'll read it for you." While reading the words aloud, Magson didn't look up from the photocopy, but from the corner of his eye he noticed Boy Kirstein shifting in his chair.

Magson made eye contact and retrieved an evidence bag from the box. He placed it on the table. "This letter was delivered to Maryke Retief's home."

Boy Kirstein looked at it and Magson waited until he'd read the words.

"And a while later, this one." He placed the evidence bag containing the second letter on the desk.

"I don't understand. Why are you showing these things to me?"

Magson took a third evidence bag from the box, this one containing the examination pad. "These are photocopies of the pages inside this exam pad." He placed the two pages on top. "Do you recognize the handwriting?"

Boy Kirstein frowned. He looked at the copies of the exam pad, to the letters and back again. Back and forth. Back and forth.

"We also found these items in Roelof's room yesterday."

Magson unpacked more evidence bags: the green paper, the alphabet sheets, the gloves. Boy Kirstein's face was pale, the skin tight. He had ceased shifting in his chair.

"This is how Maryke Retief looked when we found her."

Magson put a crime-scene photo of Maryke's body in the man's hand. A close-up of her chest and face, the furrow around her throat clearly visible.

Boy Kirstein's free hand covered his mouth. "What do you want, Warrant Magson?"

"I don't want this to happen to another girl."

About two hours after they had arrived back at the SVC office, Magson received a phone call that Adolf Bressler was waiting for him at reception. He sighed and took the elevator down to the ground floor.

The attorney was standing next to the reception desk in another fine suit, a black leather briefcase in his hand. He approached the moment Magson exited the elevator.

"Mr. Bressler," said Magson, extending his hand.

The attorney didn't take it. "There have been many occasions that I've dealt with police who believe that, because they suspect someone, that person does not have rights, but this is the first time I've met a policeman who manipulated someone into firing a legal representative."

Magson only looked back at him.

"It was a reprehensible misuse of your position."

"It's a shame the victims of crime don't have lawyers who are so concerned about *their* rights. But in any case, Mr. Bressler, I simply provided Mr. Kirstein with information. He does have the right to know, doesn't he—after all, it is his money."

"Very cute, Warrant. But we both know your only goal

was to deprive Roelof Kirstein of proper legal representation. So that you can intimidate him."

"You should be careful with your accusations, Mr. Bressler."

"No, Warrant, you're the one who should be careful. Roelof Kirstein does have problems, but he did not kill that girl. If you'd done your work properly, you would've known that."

"What are you talking about?"

The attorney opened his briefcase and removed a sheet of paper and a book. "This is the service log of February 27. The names and addresses where Roelof Kirstein had and kept appointments."

Magson took the sheet. "It's almost two months ago. It's not difficult to fill out a piece of paper and people's memories are not that reliable after so much time has passed."

"Here is the logbook of the vehicle Roelof Kirstein uses. Each time he stops at a petrol station, he has to note it here. Look at February 27."

Magson took the notebook and turned to the relevant date. He read the entry.

"And here is the receipt."

Both the date and time corresponded with the entry in the logbook. February 27. 16:32. The Stellenberg Engen. Quite a distance from Boston, the area in Bellville where Maryke Retief had disappeared. The distance and …

"If you take note of the time, you'll find that it is impossible that Roelof Kirstein could've had anything to do with Maryke Retief's disappearance."

"We'll investigate it, Mr. Bressler. Thank you. But Roelof Kirstein is not out of trouble yet. Even if he wasn't involved in Maryke Retief's disappearance and murder, there is still the matter of the letters he sent her mother. And the photos of the schoolgirls."

But the attorney had already landed the hard punch. They both knew it.

Magson locked the front door, dropped the keys onto the small table and walked to the TV room. Plopped down on the sofa with his elbows on his knees, head bowed.

On the plastic clock in the kitchen, time ticked by in relentless angry jerks, but in here it happened so gradually that he simply realized at some point that all the light had drained away.

He should probably get up and eat something. In the bedroom he pulled off his jacket and opened the closet. Emma's clothes were still on her side—they had shared this one. He hung the jacket in the closet and shut the door.

He took off his holster, heading to the safe, but sat down on the edge of the bed instead. On the side where he had always slept.

How many years had they shared this bed? It was not their first bed, the one where they had made Hannes. But later Hannes would often crawl into this bed when he awoke in the night, afraid of the dark or something in his mind. And on birthday mornings he'd sat in the middle, opening his gifts with bright eyes.

This was also the bed where Emma had chosen to spend her final days. Where she had asked him to help her. Where he …

Since that day he had not been able to sleep in this bed. His clothes were still here. He dressed here. He used the bathroom. But he slept in Hannes's bed.

He looked down at the pistol and drew it from the holster.

Emma had never liked firearms. After they had been married, when he'd come home that first day back at work, she had accepted a peck on the lips and told him to go put the weapon in the closet and then come back and greet her properly. It had become their homecoming ritual.

He looked at the pistol in his right hand.

Was she waiting for him?

April 26, 2014. Saturday.

He woke up.

He stared at the ceiling.

It was gray and out of focus in the dusk.

The birds had not started singing yet.

He wondered what time it was.

But if he looked at the alarm clock, he might see it was still the middle of the night.

The dusk was not dark enough; morning must be approaching.

He sighed.

He was tired.

He closed his eyes.

From months of experience he knew he would not fall asleep again.

It was Saturday.

He opened his eyes.

He shook his head.

What was the point?

The motorcycle's engine always reminded Magson of a high-school boy's voice, one that had broken but hadn't quite found itself yet. At least it meant he now had something to do.

The alarm clock's digits glimmered in the dusk: *6:21*.

He got out of bed. Spent a long moment pushing his spine back into place. Groaned and walked to the main bedroom. Stepped over yesterday's vest, underpants and socks to get to the bathroom. While the toilet was whooshing and he was washing his hands, his reflection in the mirror caught his eyes. Cracks in his forehead. Shadows beneath his eyes. Hollow cheeks. He looked away. He put on his slippers and dressing gown, and went to switch on the percolator in the kitchen. He went out the front door to go and find where the boy had tossed the newspaper this morning.

Back in the kitchen he read a few of the reports, drinking his first cup of coffee. Emma's little bird had not made its appearance yet. He shook some chocolate ProNutro into a bowl, added milk and stirred, and carried on reading while he ate. Every once in a while he looked up, but there was still no sign of the Cape robin. Strange. Meanwhile, the ProNutro had turned to cement. He got up to fetch more milk. The bottle was close to empty again.

It was almost half past seven when he swallowed the last

of his second mug of coffee. A lone laughing dove roamed beneath the yesterday-today-and-tomorrow. But the feeding tray was deserted. The white stinkwood's branch was empty. He dragged the saucer containing the last piece of the *boerewors* he had cooked two nights ago closer, peeled the skin off the sausage and crumbled the meat.

Just after nine he returned to the kitchen—shaved, showered, dressed. He was not in the mood to go and buy bread and milk, but he wanted to do it before the masses descended on the shops. The robin still hadn't put in an appearance.

He frowned and went outside, scraped the meat crumbs onto the feeding tray. The chances were excellent that one of the olive thrushes would come and devour it—they were such greedy, self-serving birds—but this was not a restaurant.

One final look at the branches of the white stinkwood and around. And he went back inside.

Magson turned into his street, grateful to be done with the shops. The elderly lady two houses from the corner was on the sidewalk, hat on, weeding fork in hand, red bucket beside her. Three houses further on, Jeffries, in his usual oil-smeared T-shirt and backwards cap, was halfway into a Ford Focus's engine. There had been a time when Magson had had some suspicions regarding the mechanic, more specifically the succession of cars he was always tinkering with in his driveway, had even had a look at his record and done some detective work, but hadn't found anything. He drove to the end of the cul-de-sac. The boy next door was performing tricks on his skateboard.

As he stopped the Jetta in front of the gate, Magson reminisced that they had made most of their childhood toys themselves. Like the go-cart he and Robbie du Toit had built. Old Robbie, all red hair and freckles. They had spent most of a week's worth of afternoons building that car, in between rugby practices and homework. The Saturday morning, the first full-blown test, he remembered well, because on that day he had brushed past death—or at the very least serious disfigurement—by less than a meter. He'd gone first, and Robbie had given him a running push down the long slope, shouting encouragement when his legs could no longer keep up with the accelerating cart. It had gone well until old Drunken Bart had come careering out of a side road in his rusted Ford *bakkie*. A panicky tug on the rope had made the cart swerve to the right, enough to send him over the angled curb—instead of underneath the Ford's wheels—where he had tumbled down the embankment and broken his left arm. That sickening crack had stayed with him long after the pain had subsided and the bone had grown back together.

Times had changed irrevocably.

He pulled the Jetta into the garage and went to lock the gate. As he turned around, he noticed the soccer ball. Black and white in the lush grass. They simply could not play with that ball without kicking it over the wall.

He really should mow the lawn again. The grass had never been this long. Not even half this long.

He had to mow the lawn. He had to wash his clothes. He had to polish his shoes. He had to clean the house. He had to wash the dishes. He had to. Had to. Had to.

Each "had to" felt like another weight pushing down on him until everything was just too heavy to lift.

Hannes had had a rugby ball. It had been made of real leather, laced up, not like these plastic things they used nowadays. He'd taught Hannes to polish the ball with Dubbin, so the leather would remain healthy and waterproof. One Saturday afternoon, after he had mown the lawn, they'd kicked the rugby ball to and fro. The vibration of the lawnmower had still lingered in his hands and the fragrance of freshly cut grass had been everywhere. Hannes had to have been around Grade 5 or 6, those final years a boy still enjoyed playing with his dad. He had kicked the ball, too hard, too far from Hannes's outstretched hands, and it had sliced to the side, bouncing once and into the yucca's needle-like leaves. The ball was beginning to sough when they'd reached it. He had immediately started apologizing, but Hannes had only looked up at him and said that it didn't matter, because they could just fix it like they did when his bicycle tire got a puncture. And then they could continue playing.

He tried to blink the memory away along with the wetness in his eyes. He stooped, the bag containing the bread and bottle of milk in his left hand, and picked up the soccer ball with his right.

As he straightened, he saw it. In the garden. The tiny bundle. Orange and gray and black.

He walked closer.

There was the white stripe above the eye. Except that there was no longer an eye, because the teeming ants had already eaten it away.

At first he could only stare.

He dropped the ball and the bag with the bread and milk. Sank to his knees in front of the dead bird and started to wipe away the ants. Somewhere he heard his voice, but he didn't know what he was saying. He turned the Cape robin over. This side was even worse. The little head that had always tilted when the bright black eye had peered into the kitchen window looking for the bringer of food had been eaten away so that the bone was exposed. The ants were everywhere. He wiped and wiped, but they seemed to be multiplying ...

There was a hole in the skull. Round. About four millimeters in diameter. Fissures spreading outwards. An entry wound.

A loud smacking sound came from the direction of the street, followed by a grating noise. The boy next door on his skateboard. Empty beer bottles had no longer been enough. Live prey was always better. The robin had sat on the branch, probably in the Cape chestnut, here on his property ...

He was only a few strides from the gate. The boy kicked down hard on the tail of the skateboard and bounced into the air. Smack. He ripped off the chain and yanked the gate open. The boy pushed with his back foot and the skateboard grinded in an arc across the tar.

He strode to the boy. He did not think.

The boy stomped down with his back foot and kicked out with his front as he jumped.

He only saw the boy, the rest of the world was out of focus.

The skateboard rotated around an invisible axis and the boy landed on top.

His fingers seized the boy's shoulders, wrenched him from the skateboard and hurled him to the ground.

The boy stared at him. "What the hell, man?"

"What did you do!" he yelled. "What did you do!"

He moved closer to grab the boy again.

The boy pushed with his feet, scraping backwards on his buttocks and elbows. "What are you talking about, man?"

The boy kicked at him, but he grabbed the feet, tugging him closer, swatting away the hands, yanking him to his feet by his shirt. Fabric tore somewhere. The boy's face was centimeters from him.

"Why! Why! Why!"

"Don't hurt my brother!" The little voice cut shrilly through the air. She came running—knees, arms, pigtails, eyes. "Let my brother go!"

He heard more voices, but it was the little girl's that stopped him.

"Let him go! Let him go!" yelled a man.

Hands grabbed him from behind, pulled him back. The boy slipped from his fingers and he was thrown backwards. He fell on the tar. A woman, his neighbor, folded her arms around her son, stroked his hair. The little girl was standing in front of her brother, her head barely higher than his hip.

The woman turned to him, keeping her son behind her, pulling the girl back, too. "What the hell is wrong with you?" she screamed. She glared at him before taking her children inside.

A man—he saw it was Jeffries, his hands black with grease or oil—stared at him, breathing hard. "What's going on, oke? What did he do to work you up like that?"

The little girl paused at the gate and looked back. She frowned, her mouth tight. "You're a bad man!" she yelled and ran after her mother.

Magson rested his head on the tar. The girl's bicycle was lying in the street. The back wheel spun slowly.

"Mags. What happened?"

Lieutenant Colonel John Hattingh sat in the chair in the

sitting room. He leaned forward and Magson knew that he was looking at him. Magson sat on the sofa. His hands hung between his knees, his head bowed.

"It's a charge of assault."

He did not reply.

"I was sure it must be a mistake—Gys maybe—because it can't be the Jan Magson I know. So what happened, Mags?"

He just sat.

"All right, then." The chair creaked as Hattingh got up. "Then you're on leave."

Leave. He looked up. He couldn't sit around here every day. "What about the investigation?"

"Menck will take over."

"But it's my docket."

"Not anymore."

"Colonel. Don't take my job away."

Hattingh paused at the short corridor leading to the front door. He did not turn around.

"Please."

Hattingh turned to look at him. "Then help yourself, Mags. How do you think this looks? Month and a half after Maryke Retief's murder, not to mention the other two, and we have nothing. *You* magazine is already casting doubt around whether we'll catch the killer, and now they have their next chapter: investigating officer assaults teenage boy in the street."

Magson dropped his head in his left hand. "I'm sorry, Colonel."

"I don't want to hear 'sorry'. I want to know what the fuck happened."

He sighed. "It won't happen again."

"That's not good enough, Mags."

When he finally started talking, he spoke to the carpet. "He shot the robin."

"He did what?"

"Emma." Magson had to take a deep breath to get his voice back. "Emma loved birds. She always set out food for them. The robin wasn't like the doves and sparrows. He was different. He came looking for her. She always made sure

there was something for him. Pieces of fat or meat. Cheese …
I promised her I would look after him when she died."

Hattingh sat back down on the chair. "And the boy killed
the bird."

"With a pellet gun. When I saw that, Emma's little bird,
and when I heard him in the street …" He looked up. "I didn't
think, Colonel."

Hattingh took a slow breath. "Okay. You wait here, let me
see what I can do."

Almost forty minutes had crawled by when Lieutenant
Colonel Hattingh returned. Magson had passed the time
cleaning the kitchen.

"Fortunately for you, the Bradleys are sensible people.
And the boy wasn't really damaged. So they will drop the
charge. This is what you will be doing: You will apologize to
them, under no circumstances get involved in anything like
that again, and you will make an appointment to go and talk
to someone."

Magson had nodded all the way until this last part. "Talk
to someone?"

"Yes. And the *dominee* is not good enough."

"Colonel. That's not—"

"We're not negotiating, Mags. I'm giving you a chance to
do it on your own, but I want this person's name and number
so I can find out whether you actually went. If you want to
remain the investigating officer, this is what you'll have to do
for me."

He rubbed his face. "All right."

"This week, Mags."

He nodded.

After Lieutenant Colonel Hattingh had left, he walked over to
the Bradleys' home. He pressed the button at the gate.

"Yes?"

"It's … Jan Magson. May I speak with you, please?"

The father opened the gate from inside and he walked up
to the front door.

"Mr. and Mrs. Bradley, would you call your children, too,
please?"

The boy—Magson thought his name was James or Jason or something like that—took his position between his parents, his mother's arm around him. The girl twined around her father's leg.

"I am sorry," he told the boy. "Are you hurt?"

The boy shook his head.

"Mr. and Mrs. Bradley, I am sorry about what happened. I have no excuse. Thank you for understanding. It won't happen again."

The girl was staring at him with huge eyes.

"I'm sorry I frightened you," he told her, and to the parents, "Please replace the shirt and send me the receipt." He nodded and left.

He was almost at the gate when a voice spoke up behind him. "I'm sorry, too."

It was the boy.

"I didn't know. She always called me over to taste the cookies and *koeksisters* she baked to send to your son." He smiled faintly and looked down. "I wouldn't've shot the bird had I known. I liked her."

Magson nodded. "Thank you."

Emma had never sent cookies or *koeksisters* to Hannes after his years at university. Had she continued baking for her son in England, giving it to the boy next door?

At some stage Hannes had had a hamster. He'd been light brown and white and happiest while running on his wheel. Magson couldn't remember his name. Emma had explained to their son that it was his pet and his responsibility to take care of the animal. Hannes had not taken this responsibility lightly. Every afternoon after school he would remove the seed husks from the food bowl and add fresh seed if necessary. On Saturdays he would clean the cage. And whenever he'd carry the hamster, it would always be with both hands against his chest.

One morning before school Hannes had come into the kitchen. He had stood in the doorway, his too-long pyjama pants bunched at his feet, his pillow-hair at an angle to the left. He hadn't said anything, had just looked at Emma while tears had streaked down his wrinkled cheeks. His hands had formed a bowl in front of him, and inside had lain the hamster.

Hannes had spent the majority of that afternoon fixing the hamster's coffin. It had been a shoebox. His son had painted it light blue. Emma had had to go and buy paint. Two layers, as his dad had done when he'd painted the cupboards in the bathroom—Hannes had watched him. The bottom had been covered with wood shavings. Sunflower seed and peanuts had been sprinkled on top of the shavings. All the things the hamster had loved.

When everything had been ready, he had waited for his dad to come home, because they all had to be present. The hole had been dug. Hannes had placed the shoebox inside, stood on the edge and looked down at it. His shoulders had dropped and his lower lip had quivered. More than once, Magson had wondered why a person's heart ached when they were sad. It was merely an organ like a liver or a lung. But that was exactly where the slow, dull ache had been when he'd looked at his son.

Why couldn't he remember the hamster's name?

In a trembling voice, Hannes had said he'd been a good hamster and he would never forget him. He had said a prayer, taken the small black spade with the yellow handle, and shoveled dirt into the grave.

Emma had caressed Hannes's head and said the hamster had been fortunate to have had someone who loved him so much.

Magson looked down at the hole he had dug beneath the white stinkwood. He had not painted the shoebox after he'd removed a pair of Emma's shoes. But he had taken some of her cotton wool from the glass jar in the bathroom and padded its base. He'd wanted to put some flowers on top of the cotton wool, but nothing in the garden was in bloom this time of the year. The fern leaves looked nice, though.

For a moment he stared at the Cape robin on the fine green leaves. He closed the lid and placed the shoebox in the hole.

"Emma's little bird."

He took the same yellow-and-black Lasher spade his son had used so many years ago to bury his hamster, and began filling in the grave. The clatter on the cardboard sounded too loud.

What was really worse? Being the one who died? Or the one who kept on living?

Ten

Magson raised the pages once more. He had taken down some strange statements in his time, but this one had been a first. The girl had asked for his pen, sat down and wrote it like a scene from a movie. In the third person. Her mother had told him she was always writing stories, that was her way. Of course Magson had had to rework it with her, with additions and adjustments, for the docket. But he'd kept the original pages:

The girl with the long, brown hair was walking home. Today her hair was in a braid, hanging down the middle of her back. She had pulled the sleeves of her school jersey over her hands and crossed her arms against the cold. Autumn. The best time of the year. The smell of the air changed and the leaves fell and danced in the wind. She thought about the party to-morrow evening—

The man grabbed her and shoved a knife against her stomach. She had been aware, but only vaguely, of the car stopping next to the sidewalk, the man getting out.

"Scream and I'll cut your throat."

She went cold. She struggled to breathe. She wanted to run, but she was too scared. The man's eyes were without emotion, without life. She had never been this afraid in her sixteen years.

"Get in the car, bitch."

The man's left hand was a clamp around her upper arm. The fingers were strong and hard. He began tugging her, the knife still against her stomach.

Why didn't anybody see? she thought, panicky. Was there nobody who could help her?

"Please." It felt as if her voice was gone, she couldn't breathe. "Let me go. I won't tell anyone."

The man laughed. It was a cold laugh. It didn't reach his eyes. "Do you get together in the afternoons to practice these sentences. You're so pathetic."

What did he mean, "you," as in plural? she wondered, now even more scared.

"I won't. I promise." She tried to pull away from him.

He yanked her towards him and held the knife to her throat. The blade burned her skin, but it had to be from cold-ness. His face almost touched hers. His breath was warm and bitter. "Shut up, bitch, and get in the fucking car. Or do you want to bleed to death here in the street?"

She cried. The tears were hot against her cold cheeks.

He almost had her at the car. The knife was back against her stomach. She looked around. Where was everyone? Why had they all turned away in this moment?

They were at the back of the car. His right hand, the one with the knife, went away from her stomach. He opened the boot. Once he had her in there, once he shut her inside …

She remembered. Her uncle had shown her how to do it. She raised her right foot and thrust it down on top of his. The boys' shoes she wore to school had thick heels, and it must've hurt, because he yelled. At first his fingers bore deeper into her flesh, but then the grip loosened.

She tore herself from him. Her school bag slipped and dropped to the ground. She just ran.

The man yelled something at her, but she just ran. She didn't know where, because her house was several blocks in the opposite direction. It didn't matter, she just had to get away, get away, away from HIM.

Her eyes flitted from side to side, searching for a person, someone, rescue. She looked back and saw him limping after her.

The ground was suddenly lower beneath her right foot and she stumbled. Her ankle gave way with a sharp pain and she tumbled down. The tar tore through her pantyhose into her knee. She stuck out her hands to break her fall, losing more skin from her palms. But she pushed herself back up and started running again, grimacing against the pain in her ankle.

The man had almost caught up. She could hear his foot-steps, his heavy breathing. The fear drove her forward, faster, but he was close, close enough to—

"Hey!"

The girl looked in the direction of the voice and saw an elderly woman a couple of houses down on the opposite side of the street. She was standing at the low wall, staring.

"Help!" the girl screamed. "Help me! He's got a knife!" She ran straight to the woman, across the street.

"Hey!" the woman yelled again. She was looking past the girl.

Was he still coming?

She only dared look back once she had made it to the wall, filled with fear that he would be right behind her. But he wasn't. He picked up her school bag, got into his car and drove off.

"Good heavens, child."

The girl was breathing hard, her heart thudding. Her ankle hurt and her knees and hands were burning. Tears streaked down her cheeks.

"Come in, child," the woman said. "Let's phone your people and tend to your knee."

She looked down at the blood crawling down her shin, soaking into the torn pantyhose. She held her scraped palms for the woman to see. She struggled to keep her hands still.

"I'll fetch you some sugar water for the shock." The woman put an arm around her shoulders and led her to the front door. "Who was that man?"

"I don't know," she whispered, looking down the street.

He'd taken her bag. Before he drove off, he'd picked up her bag. But she got away.

The girl with the long, brown hair got away.

Karlien Pretorius. Another teenage girl with long, brown hair. Magson still couldn't get over the irony that that had been how she'd chosen to identify herself in the statement. If it had indeed been the killer, that made it four out of four. The likelihood of coincidence was diminishing.

Once again a schoolgirl walking home. Stellenberg High this time. Magson studied the large map on the wall.

"It's almost exactly the midpoint between Durbanville, Bellville and Brackenfell."

Menck nodded. "In other words, exactly our killer's area."

"Ja. And the MO fits, too. It would've worked with all three. Stop next to them, threaten them with a knife, force them into the boot."

"Probably sticks some tape over their mouths to keep them quiet. Won't do to have them screaming all the way home."

"Hmm," said Magson. "Probably ties them up, too. At least their hands."

"It's an MO carrying a lot of risk."

"Ja. Anyone can drive by at any time and see what he's doing. Or someone coming out of a house."

"And yet we have not a single description from a witness except now with the Pretorius girl."

Magson nodded. "But we have one now."

Light brown hair, longish, straight. Gray-blue eyes. Cleanly shaven. More or less 1.8 meters tall. Neither scrawny nor overweight, but strong. Karlien Pretorius had looked at Neels Delport's photo and without hesitation said it hadn't been him.

"He does sound quite a bit like the man in Lola's couple," said Menck.

"Hmm, he does. We can have Lola look at the identikit when Karlien is done. If she recognizes him, we can probably get a warrant for her phone records … Hope it doesn't cost me more money."

Regarding the vehicle, the girl hadn't been able to remember much more than the color. Silver. Magson had asked about the licence plate, but she'd just shaken her head.

The woman had not been of much help with any kind of description. Since she had only been on her way to the postbox, she hadn't been wearing her spectacles and consequently hadn't been able to make out any details.

Menck came closer and looked at the photos of the victims on the wall. "She's lucky," he said quietly. "We could very well be sticking her photo up here next to the others right now."

"It's just a damn shame she didn't break his bloody foot. Then we might've been able to track him down through a hospital."

Magson arrived at home, dropped the keys on the small table at the front door, switched on some lights and lowered himself onto the sofa. For a moment he just stared at the dark TV screen, then closed his eyes and dropped his head back.

How close had they come today, how close to adding a fourth victim to the series. But the real question was, how would the killer deal with this failure? Would he keep a low profile for a while? Or would he simply go in search of another victim? And do worse things to her …

And if he was the man who had visited Lola, where did the woman fit into the picture? Was she aware of what he was doing? Was she involved? Were they a killer couple? Or were they merely a husband and wife with a twisted sex life?

Perhaps the identikit would provide the breakthrough. It should be in the newspapers on Monday, if things went according to plan. Someone had to know him, after all. If Karlien's description was good enough …

He rose and walked to the kitchen. He got the bowl of mince from the refrigerator, and grabbed a fork on his way to the dining-room table. The prescription was still there. What a waste of time and money that had been, he thought, taking a mouthful. The cold grease stuck to the roof of his mouth, but he couldn't be bothered to heat it in the microwave. Antidepressants. As if pills could fill the void Emma had left behind.

The psychiatrist was a woman with a serene voice, who nodded often and never looked away. He had told her about Emma and the cancer, but not what his wife had asked of him. She had wanted to know about children and he had told her about Hannes, but not when he'd last spoken to his son, nor why. She had wanted to know about his work and pretended to understand how difficult it was. He'd been able to tell she tried, but it was just not who he was. Finally, the time had passed and she'd let him go with a prescription and a follow-up appointment for next week.

He shook his head and took another bite. A layer had formed along the roof of his mouth. There was no need to leave some meat anymore …

His cellphone rang. He removed the thing from his pocket. "Magson."

"Warrant Magson. It's Karlien Pretorius."

"Hello, Karlien. How are you?"

"Not so good. I'm stressing about my bag. He knows who I am, where I live, what school I go to. There's such a lot of stuff in my homework book. My friends … It freaks me out just thinking about it."

"I understand. Are the uniforms there?"

"Excuse me?"

"The police officers."

"Oh. Yes. Shame, I feel bad that they have to sit outside in the cold. I made them some hot chocolate."

"Don't feel bad. It's their job. Those *bakkies* aren't so uncomfortable. The important thing is you're safe."

"They can't protect me every day."

"No. But I'll make sure they drive past regularly. And you have my number."

"I'm just so scared."

"I know," he said softly. "But you were very brave. To step on his foot like that—it took guts."

"My uncle showed me. My mom's brother. He was in the army, but now he's in private security. Actually, I only played along when he showed me the self-defense stuff. The last time he visited. Now I wish I'd taken it more seriously."

"You remembered what you needed to."

She didn't reply.

"Maybe you should go and talk to someone," said Magson. "It helps." He glanced at the prescription, got up and walked away.

"I remembered something."

He stopped walking. "What?"

"When he opened the boot. There was stuff inside."

"What, Karlien?"

"I don't know if it means anything, but you said anything could be important."

"You'd be surprised how often it is something small that helps catch someone. What did you remember?"

"There was a bunch of video-game boxes in the boot. Xbox games. But they were wrong."

"What do you mean, 'wrong'?"

"Xbox games come in green boxes, but these were all clear."

Magson was not sure what to make of this information. He knew nothing about video games.

"The whole thing keeps churning around in my head. I can't shut it down. My mom wants me to take a sleeping pill, but …"

"Maybe that's not a bad idea," said Magson. "So you can get some rest. You need rest."

"Maybe I'll take one. But the games. My friend Gerhard has an Xbox. He told me many guys at school buy pirate copies, for much cheaper. But he prefers to buy games at the shop, even if it means he has fewer, because he says pirate copies are stealing. Maybe that's why the boxes weren't green. Maybe they were pirate copies."

"Maybe."

"Could it help?" She sounded so full of hope.

"It's definitely something to look at. I can't make any promises, but I'm glad you told me. Really, anything you remember, Karlien, phone me."

"Thank you, Warrant Magson. You make me feel better."

He looked at the phone for a moment, before he slid it back into his pocket.

May 3, 2014. Saturday.

Magson took his seat at the counter, a bowl of Weet-Bix in front of him. His eyes still automatically turned to the white stinkwood, searching for the Cape robin. To the sawn-off branch on the feeding tray where he'd always perched, casting mournful glances in the kitchen's direction when there was nothing for him.

At first Magson had been skeptical about these "wrongly colored" video-game boxes, but his mind had kept on turning the idea around. Even if Karlien Pretorius was correct, and the games were pirate copies, why would a serial killer busy himself with such things? For the money? How much money could be made from selling pirate video games? Magson couldn't believe it would be a particularly profitable venture. Or was it a way in which to make contact with schoolchildren? Perhaps a "valid" reason to be close enough to watch high-school girls, depending on where the transactions took place.

Perhaps it was just the thread he needed to pull in order to make the whole thing come undone. He wanted to speak to Karlien's friend this morning. If he didn't know where the children bought the pirate copies, he would at least know someone who had bought them in the past. Why hadn't he asked for this friend's details last night? He didn't want to phone too early and wake her.

It was just after half past nine when Magson was sitting across from the boy in his parents' sitting room. Gerhard Cronjé had shy, but intelligent, eyes.

"Karlien told me about the video games at school," said Magson. "The pirate copies."

The boy frowned.

"I'd like to know where they get them from. The children at school."

"A man tried to kidnap Karlien and you're worried about pirate Xbox games?"

The boy might be shy, but he obviously liked Karlien.

"No, Gerhard, I'm a detective with the Serious Violent

Crimes Unit. I don't care about pirate Xbox games, but it might be important."

The boy was still frowning. "Okay. I haven't bought any myself, so I don't know all the details, but I know they buy it from a guy in Grade 11. I don't know where he gets it."

"Do you know his name?"

"Wayne. Wayne Guthrie."

"What do you know about him?"

The boy shrugged. "Not much. He's English. If you're not one of his customers, it's best to stay out of his way." It seemed like he had more to say.

"What else?"

"Look. I want to help Karlien. And I'm no fan of Wayne Guthrie. But I still have to go to school there."

"Gerhard. I have no reason to mention your name. But the more you tell me, the more I can do."

The boy cast his eyes down towards the carpet. After a while he looked up. "Well, pirate copies aren't the only thing he sells."

"Drugs?"

"There's a rumor. Everyone knows about the games, but the drugs could just be a story."

"But you believe it."

The boy's silence was answer enough.

May 5, 2014. Monday.

"The guy who can get you stuff," said Menck. "A couple of buddies and I once washed a shitload of cars to buy a *Scope* from this guy. Brand new."

"And was it worth the effort?" asked Magson.

"Oh yes. Not one of our dads bought the *Scope*. After school we used to drool over the covers in the café. Until the old Greek chased us away." Menck shook his head. "He sold us cigarettes without a word, but we weren't allowed to look at his naughty books."

"What was it with old Greeks and cafés? We had one in town, too. Extremely hairy—and oily—but he made the best bloody chips. *Slaptjips*, salt and vinegar, wrapped in newspaper." Magson's stomach actually groaned as he recalled the sharp smell of the vinegar rising from his memory. "I wonder what happened to all those Greeks."

"Ruined by supermarkets and Seven-Elevens. But that was a different time, hey? When the female body was still this mysterious thing. Nowadays you don't even need to wonder or invest any effort at all. Hell, you can just leaf through your mom's *Fair Lady* or *Cosmopolitan*. And they don't even bother with stars."

"Not to mention the internet and cellphones," said Magson. "The thing is, we had to use our imagination with everything, not just girls. My dad made me a toy gun from wood. When you see a child with a gun today, it's a plastic AK that looks exactly like the real thing."

"Sometimes it *is* the real thing."

"Hmm."

Menck sighed. "Yip, children today have all this stuff. Clothes with labels, TVs in their rooms, cellphones and iPads, internet, don't have to work for pocket money. But I think we had the better deal."

Magson nodded and pressed against his cheek. "Ja. Won't change it."

"I hope you're not trying to self-medicate that thing with Sensodyne or something. You know those ads lie."

"I use plain common Aquafresh, if you must know."

"Well, no wonder your tooth is falling apart. Everyone knows Colgate is the number one toothpaste, according to dentists."

"I like Aquafresh."

"They got you with the different layers, hey?"

Magson sighed.

"I'll make an appointment for you."

"I can make my own bloody appointments, thank you. I don't need you to be my secretary."

"Ve-ry sensitive. So what's the plan with Guthrie?"

"Let's hear what he has to say first," said Magson, relieved to move on to a new subject.

The address was only a block further. The gate was open

and they followed the driveway. The same bricks swept up some steps, twisting upwards to the front door. Small trees in pots, the trunks entwined, marked every fifth step.

As Magson rang the doorbell, he hoped they would have more success than they'd had with Lola earlier. Her reaction to the identikit had been a shrug and a "could be." More than that she had not been able—or had not wanted—to say, despite his best efforts.

A tall boy with wild hair and a pointed chin opened the door. Loud music poured out around him. The boy looked annoyed. "My parents aren't home." He started closing the door, but Magson held it open.

"Are you Wayne Guthrie?"

"Why do you want to know?"

Magson could understand why Gerhard Cronjé would rather not end up on the wrong side of this boy. His attitude made it clear he had a fair amount of power at school and was used to getting his way, by force if necessary. Self-assured. Arrogant. Not afraid of confrontation. The teachers must love him.

Magson shoved his identification card into the boy's face. "We're from the police." Quick and loud. "SVC. Are you Wayne Guthrie?"

The boy flinched, a nervous look washing over his features, but he regained control. "Yes, I'm Wayne Guthrie. What do you want?"

"Can we come in?"

"No. What do you want?"

"Your supplier," said Magson. "Where do you get your pirate copies?"

"My what?"

"The Xbox games you're selling at school."

"I don't know what you're talking about." He started closing the door again.

Once more Magson held it open. "Do we really have to turn this house upside down before you'll become a good citizen?"

"You can't just do that. You need a search warrant."

"Aah, someone watches the cop shows and thinks he's

getting clever," said Menck. "You shouldn't believe everything you see on TV, Wayne. Besides, this isn't America."

"We have enough for a warrant, anyway," said Magson. "Meanwhile, Warrant Officer Menck here will take you to the station and store you in a cell until I come back. We don't want you to accidentally pervert the course of justice."

"What? You can't just lock me in a cell."

"Actually, we can." Menck produced his handcuffs.

The boy's eyes flitted between them.

Menck stepped forward.

"Wait! You can't just arrest me!"

Menck hesitated, seemed to contemplate the situation, turned to Magson. "If he cooperates, it can save us a lot of time and effort."

"*Ag*, I don't know," said Magson. "Let's just lock him up, shake the house and see what falls out. Where are your parents?"

Guthrie, who had followed their discussion like a tennis match, opened his mouth, but Menck interrupted him. "What kind of toothpaste do you use?"

"What?" asked Guthrie.

"Toothpaste, Wayne. You do brush your teeth, don't you? Hey?"

"Yes …" The confusion on Guthrie's face diluted the irritation that had risen in Magson.

"So? What brand do you use?"

"Colgate, I think."

Menck nodded. "So then you don't have any dental problems."

"No."

"You see, my partner here chooses not to use the number one toothpaste as recommended by dentists. As a result, he has a sore tooth. This makes him extremely irritable. In fact, at present the man has no patience whatsoever. So you can imagine what effect your attitude is having." Menck had built up speed and was rollicking along now.

Guthrie only looked at him.

"But here's the thing, Wayne. You see, you're just a little peanut. We're really interested in the big nut. The Brazil nut.

The guy you get your pirate copies from. But if you're going to continue down this path, we'll have to take you in and call your parents and it's going to turn into an extremely unpleasant situation. For you, that is."

"No." Magson shook his head. "It's too late. He'll sing soon enough once he's in a cell. Especially after he's met the gangsters. We don't have any empty cells, so you'll have to share."

"No," said Guthrie to Magson, licking his lips. "Wait." He looked at Menck. "I don't know who he is."

"Please tell me you're trying to be funny," said Menck, "because if you're going to treat us like idiots …"

"I'm not. I don't even know his name. I don't know anything about him."

"You don't know anything. So you've never seen him, never spoken to him. Are you a Red Indian, Wayne?"

"What?"

"Well, you must be communicating through smoke signals."

"We use email."

Menck made a rolling movement with his hand. "Go on. How does it work?"

"It works like email. He sends me a list of games. I let him know which ones the kids want."

"How do you get them?" asked Magson.

"On my phone. I use gmail and I get it on my phone."

"The games. How do you get the games?"

"Oh. He … drops them off."

"Here?"

"No," said Guthrie.

"Then where?"

"He lets me know."

"And then you meet him?"

Guthrie nodded.

"But then you *have* seen him," said Menck, his voice loud and angry.

Guthrie stared at his shoes.

"What's he look like? And be specific."

"I don't know. I'm not into guys."

"*Ag*, enough of this," said Magson. "He's just wasting our bloody time. Cuff him and let's go." He started turning.

"Brown hair. He's got brown hair and he's about your height."

Menck threw his hands in the air. "That's it? I'm trying my best to keep your arse out of a cell and you tell me he's got brown hair?"

"I don't know," said Guthrie. "I don't look at him that way."

Menck sighed. "Does he have a beard? Is he fat? Does he speak with an accent? Does he have a scar or a tattoo? Is one of his fingers crooked?"

Guthrie's eyes had brightened. "He does have a beard. And he's Afrikaans, but his English is good. He doesn't have any tattoos on his arms, but I don't know about the rest of his body. And he's always got a cap on."

"What kind of cap?"

"Different ones. But he's always wearing one."

Magson unfolded the identikit. "Is it this man?"

Guthrie looked for a long while. "I don't know. He's got a beard."

"If this man had a beard?"

"Maybe. It's difficult. He's got a beard and cap. It could be."

Fantastic. Another "could be." "What kind of car does he drive?"

"Usually a BMW, sometimes a … I thinks it's a Hyundai, maybe an i20."

"Color?"

"The BMW is silver." Right color. Pity Karlien Pretorius had not been able to identify the manufacturer.

"Give me your phone." Magson held out his hand.

Guthrie stared at the open palm as if it held a poison capsule. "Why?"

"Because that's where you get his emails."

"I deleted them."

"Surely his address is still there," said Menck.

"Yes … I don't have it with me."

"So go fetch it."

"You can't tell him you got it from me."

Menck clapped his hands. "You could've been back already."

Magson watched Guthrie disappear into the house. Of course, he would have wanted to go along, but they were already talking to him without his parents' knowledge or presence.

"I hope that was the last of your Colgate campaign."

Menck smiled as if he were an actor in one of their adverts. "Come on, that was classic. I should write it down for my memoirs."

"Memoirs." Magson shook his head.

"Don't worry, you'll be in there, as well. Mags, my moody sidekick."

"Sidekick." Magson sighed. Loudly.

Menck found it hilarious.

Magson peered into the house. Guthrie appeared around a corner and dragged his feet all the way to the front door, a small black phone in his hand.

"What took you so long?" asked Magson.

"I had to use the bathroom."

"What's his address?"

The boy went through a sequence of taps and swipes on the screen. "Here." He turned the phone, but Magson took it from him.

"What does 'CJ' stand for?"

"I don't know. I don't think it's his real name."

"Why email?" asked Menck. "Why doesn't he just phone you?"

"He says the government tracks you and listens in." Guthrie shrugged.

"When was the last time you had contact with him?" asked Magson.

"Last week."

"All right." Magson handed the phone back to the boy. "This is what we're going to do. You're going to contact your buddy CJ and order some games. And then we're going to wait for him when he comes to deliver them."

Guthrie shook his head. "No. Do you know what he'll do to me if …"

Menck held up his hands. "Wayne, Wayne, Wayne, listen to me. You're selling pirate video games. That's a crime. And once we start investigating you, we'll be digging around everywhere in your life. We'll find the other stuff you're into as well. Your future is screwed. This plan is your chance to help yourself."

"You don't know what he's like."

"You won't be in any danger. You're just going to arrange it and point him out to us."

"We'll need to talk to your parents," said Magson.

Guthrie looked at him, annoyed rather than nervous. "Why?"

"Because you're not eighteen yet."

"My dad's in Germany on business."

"When is he coming back?"

Guthrie shrugged. "He's never here."

"What about your mom?" asked Menck.

"She's at her charity. So many black tummies to fill."

"We'll need the address and her number."

Guthrie tapped a few times on his phone's screen and handed it to Menck, who wrote down the information in his notebook. "We don't need to tell you not to contact CJ before we've spoken to you again, hey?"

"And if CJ contacts you, phone me immediately," added Magson, presenting the boy with a contact card.

Guthrie sighed and nodded.

"In the meantime, I'd advise you to cease all your criminal activities before we come back."

"When are you coming back?"

"Anytime. It's like the Second Coming, Wayne. You should always be ready."

May 6, 2014. Tuesday.

The identikit drawn up from Karlien Pretorius's description was in the newspapers.

Wayne Guthrie had sent an email to CJ's gmail account.

The lines had been cast. Now Magson had to sit on the bank, waiting to see if something bit.

In the meantime, the process had been initiated to obtain the identity of the gmail account's owner, which would be neither quick nor easy. And even with the company's co-operation, Menck had delivered the happy news that any-one could create a gmail account by typing in any informa-tion, since it wasn't verified. Apparently there were methods by which a user's computer could be traced, but to Magson Guthrie sounded like the only option holding any real prom-ise.

Back in his office, Magson sat down behind his desk. Among the phone calls yielded by the identikit, three callers had of-fered the same name. A consultant at the Standard Bank branch in N1 City. An alibi made it impossible for him to be the man who had attempted to abduct Karlien Pretorius on Friday, but the resemblance was uncanny. Had his alibi not been so ironclad, Magson would have been arranging an identity parade.

He answered his cellphone. And went to Menck's office.

"Guthrie just phoned. CJ is apparently busy at the mo-ment, but he'll try for Thursday. CJ, that is."

"Thursday." Menck pulled a face. "I need to do something about my blood sugar."

Magson watched his partner retrieving a box of Cracker-bread, a jar of peanut butter and a bottle of syrup from his drawer.

"Sooner would have been better. Can I offer you some?"

"No, thanks," said Magson.

Menck was setting about the task like a bricklayer, apply-ing the peanut butter in a thick layer on two of the wafers, squeezing a gooey blob of syrup on top.

"Guthrie must just keep cooperating."

With each bite Menck took, the smell of peanut butter grew stronger. Magson tongued his steadily deteriorating tooth. Funny how the tongue just couldn't leave it alone. Fun-ny how toothache came and went.

"*Ag*, shame, I don't think Wayne has it too easy. Dad's nev-er there. Mom's a crusader for everyone except her own child …"

"You're making a mess," said Magson.

Menck looked down. "Shit!" He forced the rest of the wafer into his mouth and tried to rub the syrup off his tie.

"You're just making it worse."

May 7, 2014. Wednesday.

Magson tried to identify the cause of the traffic jam, but all he could see was a line of cars. What a way to drive home after a long day at work. At least he had been able to cancel his appointment with the psychiatrist, since there was a "possible breakthrough" in the case. He'd said he would make another appointment, but that had been a lie. Sitting in that room and telling a woman how he felt didn't change anything. Emma was dead.

Movement again and he crawled another car length along.

The identikit had not delivered a breakthrough as yet. But tomorrow was Thursday. If luck would take their side for once, CJ would meet with Guthrie and they could grab him right there. And perhaps this whole thing could come to an end.

He switched on the radio. A few seconds later, he switched it off again. These days the only choices were doof-doof-doof, men talking instead of singing, and women who sounded as if they were practicing scales. Magson's taste in music had not changed with the times. To him, the stuff the young people listened to nowadays was just noise. When he and Emma had started dating, you could still dance. When he looked at the young people "dancing" in clubs, their writhing bodies reminded him of maggots in the flashes of police cameras.

His cellphone rang and he sighed. "Magson."

"Warrant Magson. It's Karlien Pretorius. Something happened."

Her voice made him think of a wild bird in a cage, and he closed his eyes. "What?"

"When my mom came home from work, there was a parcel at the front door. It's from *him*. He was here! Right at the door! And I was inside the house the whole afternoon. While he was here—"

"All right. Slow down, Karlien. Take a breath. Are you at home now?"

"Yes."

"Is your mom with you?"

"Yes."

"All right. Make sure all the doors are locked and the windows are closed. Don't touch the parcel or do anything with it. I'm stuck in traffic, but I'm coming as soon as I can."

Eleven

He studied the wine box. Graça. The cardboard was shiny, ostensibly a good surface for fingerprints, but also easier to wipe clean of prints. Carefully, using one latex-covered finger, he folded the flap open. School books. And on top: one long-stem rose that appeared to have been crushed underfoot.

Was this what CJ had been busy with?

He looked at mother and daughter, close together a few steps away, watching him with large eyes. "There was no message or anything?"

"No," said the mother. "Just this."

Magson nodded and let go of the flap. It folded back on its own. He didn't want to handle the box or its contents further before LCRC arrived.

"Are you sure you heard nothing, Karlien?"

"No." Her head shook from side to side, her face a white mask. "I was listening to music. Why—" Her mouth closed and he saw her throat move. "Why did he bring it back?"

"To scare you."

"Well, I am scared."

"Is there no one you can stay with for a while?"

"Our only family is my brother," said her mother, "but he's in the Congo. It's really only Karlien and I." She pulled her daughter even closer.

"Well, there will be uniforms outside throughout the night."

"It was my first afternoon on my own," said Karlien, staring at the floor.

"On Monday and yesterday I took the afternoons off," said her mother, "picked up Karlien at school and stayed with her. But I can't take every afternoon off."

Magson nodded, and also stared at the floor, because he didn't know what to say.

"I'll phone Chantal's mom."

"He's got my homework book, Mom! Chantal's name and her address—all my friends …"

"Okay." Her mother wrapped her in her arms, kissed her forehead and her temple and her hair. "It's okay. We'll figure something out."

"They won't want me to be with them." Her voice cracked as the tears came. "Especially after today."

May 8, 2014. Thursday.

"You don't understand what he's like." Wayne Guthrie had been fidgeting since he'd gotten in. "This one time, when he brought the stuff, this black guy was walking past. He'd looked at us and CJ just lost it. He grabbed the guy and beat the shit out of him."

Magson watched him in the rear-view mirror as he scratched at his lip with his thumb.

"Nothing is going to happen to you," said Menck, not for the first time.

"He broke that guy's ribs just for looking at us. What do you think he's going to do to me?"

"He's going to do nothing to you, because there's going to be a shitload of detectives to protect you."

"And next week? When he gets bail, because you give out bail like flyers at the traffic lights. He will know it was me."

"We're going to arrest you, as well."

"What?"

"For the show, Wayne. For the show."

Guthrie gnawed on his thumbnail.

"Maybe you should go now and wait there," said Magson.

"Don't worry," said Menck.

Guthrie opened the door, muttering, "I'm so screwed," as he got out. He walked down the street, head down.

The meeting place was a piece of open ground near Stellenberg High. Mowed grass. A fair number of trees, mostly smaller kinds, but there was a clump of tall eucalyptus in one area. The park hugged the street, with houses on the other side of the road.

Guthrie sat down on the bench, his motorbike next to it. It was a convenient spot—CJ could simply park by the side of the road and they could conduct their business without attracting much attention.

Magson and Menck got out to take up their positions.

"It's a shame these people aren't here," said Menck, nodding towards the house opposite Guthrie's bench. "I'd like to see what they look like."

Since their arrival, Menck had been fascinated by the lack of a wall or fence at the house. It only saddened Magson. Twenty-five years ago this had been the case for almost every property in South Africa.

The front garden consisted of islands of shrubs in an ocean of lawn. Magson and Menck concealed themselves behind one of the larger shrubs, less than thirty meters from the bench. Kayla Schulenburg sat on one of the swings on the other side of Guthrie, her back to him.

The street next to the park was a very shallow and misshapen U, with both ends forming T-junctions. Patrick Theko and Azhar Najeer waited in their Mazda at the one nearest the meeting place, Captain Kritzinger at the other end. An irritated Gys Burger was in the sole side street next to the house where Magson and Menck were hiding.

Magson scanned the area one last time. The clouds hung light gray and motionless in the sky. Two hadedas sauntered along the grass, stabbing their long beaks into the ground. Guthrie sat on the bench, his right leg bouncing.

Magson moved back into their hiding spot and fiddled with the earpiece and microphone. "We're in position."

The time of the meeting crawled closer. And ticked past. Five minutes. Ten. Two cars drove past, a white Kia Sportage and a red Toyota RunX, both from Captain Kritzinger's direction, both without slowing or stopping.

"The *worshond* is getting anxious," remarked Schulenburg. Burger referred to a reluctant informant as a dachshund—sausage dog—and it had seemingly rubbed off on her. "And I have run out of things to tell my imaginary friend for the second time." She was walking up and down, "talking" on her cellphone.

"Where the hell is he?" asked Menck, again glancing at his watch. "It's almost twenty minutes."

"Someone's coming," said Theko. "He's walking, Blue cap on his head. Backpack."

"What does he look like?" asked Magson.

"I can't see his face. Brown hair. The length is right. A bit scrawny. He's crossing the road. He's coming in your direction. Across the grass."

"I see him," said Schulenburg.

Magson could not. They had to rely on the other detectives. "How far is he from Guthrie?"

"Hundred meters."

"Why is he walking?" asked Menck next to him. "Guthrie said he always comes with a car."

"Has Guthrie seen him yet?" asked Magson.

"He's looking in the other direction," said Schulenburg.

Was it CJ? Or just a man with a blue cap?

"Fifty meters."

"It's your call, Mags," said Captain Kritzinger. "But either we grab him before he gets to Guthrie, or we wait until he leaves. I don't want a hostage situation."

"Guthrie's too jumpy," said Menck. "I don't think he'll be able to keep it together."

"Thirty meters," said Schulenburg. "Guthrie sees him. He keeps on looking. He's gripping the bench."

"Go," said Magson and ran out behind the shrub, Menck alongside him, across the street, pistols raised. The man with the blue cap froze as they started shouting, "Police! Hands in the air!"

Schulenburg was running from the other side. "Hands in the air! Do it!" The man's head whipped from side to side and he raised his hands.

Menck stood in front of the man, pistol aimed at him. "On your knees! Down! Down! On the ground!"

The man fell to his knees, arms straight above his head. "I didn't do anything."

"Shut up!"

Magson removed the backpack, cuffed his hands behind his back and searched him. Meanwhile Guthrie had run in the opposite direction, Schulenburg giving chase. Najeer and Theko screeched to a halt in the street. Magson discovered a set of keys, a cellphone and a wallet on the handcuffed man. The driver's licence belonged to M. Ellwood, born in 1991.

"What's your name?" asked Menck, ripping off the cap.

"Mark," said the kneeling man. "Mark Ellwood."

Magson walked around to his front and compared his face to the photo on the licence. It was the same. He bore no real resemblance to the identikit, though.

"What are you doing here?" asked Magson.

"Nothing. I just went to the Spar."

"What did you buy?"

"Chips and lemonade. They're in my bag."

Magson opened the backpack. A bottle of Sparletta, a bag of Lay's and a Bar-One. No video games.

Captain Kritzinger arrived with Schulenburg and a hand-cuffed Wayne Guthrie. Magson went to meet them, gripped Guthrie's upper arm. "Is that CJ?" he asked softly.

Guthrie shook his head. "No. I don't know who this guy is."

"Are you sure?"

"Yes."

Magson sighed, glanced at Kritzinger, and returned to Mark Ellwood. "Where are you going?"

"Home," said Ellwood.

"Where is your home?"

Ellwood nodded in the direction he had come from. "In Haarlem Drive."

"Well, if your house is that way," said Menck, "what are you doing here?"

He lowered his head. "A guy at the Spar said he'd give me two hundred bucks if I'd come get a key."

"What key?"

"A key for his car. He said his brother Wayne is waiting for him here, but he hurt his foot and it's too far for him to walk."

"What did this man look like?" asked Magson.

Ellwood shrugged. "He had a black Ecko Unltd. cap on."

"Where are you supposed to meet him again?"

"Next to the Spar. I think he stays in one of the townhouses there."

"Come. Come and show us."

They spent two hours scouring the area around the Spar, asking people whether they had seen a man wearing a black Ecko Unltd. cap, knocking on every door in Eike Close, and finally met in the parking area in front of the supermarket.

"Okay," said Captain Kritzinger, "I'll get us some Cokes."

Menck lit a cigarette. "How did he know?"

Mark Ellwood was employed at a place printing signs, labels and designs on T-shirts. Captain Kritzinger had gone there and two people were prepared to make affidavits that Ellwood had been there the entire Friday. And consequently could not have tried to abduct Karlien Pretorius. So far there was nothing contradicting Ellwood's story. And if Ellwood was not CJ, it meant that CJ had become suspicious.

Magson shook his head.

"It's because you're not on top of this case," said Burger.

"What?"

"Gys," said Menck.

"*Ag*, man, don't 'Gys' me," said Burger. "You can cover for your partner as much as you like—good for you—but we both know he's never grabbed this thing by the balls."

Menck turned towards him. "And of course you've been part of the investigation this whole time to see what's going on. But it's nice to stand on the sideline and judge, hey? And don't decide for me what I do or don't know."

"Well, then you can continue to play blind man and stumble from one dead end to another. I've wasted enough of my time here. Come, Kayla. If we hurry, we might just still drag Jafta from his hole." Burger walked off.

"Cheers." Menck waved his hand as if he were chasing away an annoying fly.

"Gys," said Schulenburg.

"Come or stay, Kayla."

She glanced at Magson, raised her eyebrows and her hands. "I can't let him go in there alone."

Car doors slammed and an engine roared.

"Forget about Gys," said Menck, "he's just—"

"Right," said Magson, and turned around.

Magson scanned the latest entry in the C section of the docket, basically a diary of the investigation. He glanced at his watch. During the day, time slipped away but the evenings crawled by. Burger's words kept gnawing at him, like that dull kind of toothache that wouldn't go away. He closed the docket and went to the kitchen to throw the empty KFC packet, which had contained his chicken burger supper, in the rubbish bin. They used to call it Kentucky's, when Kentucky Fried Chicken had still been the brand name. Nowadays the children probably didn't even know what KFC was short for.

Back at the table he pushed the docket away. He placed his elbows on the table, rested his temples against his palms and stared at the grain of the wood. Emma had bought this yellowwood table with her inheritance. It was meant to become an heirloom, Hannes's, before South Africa had turned into a country young people wanted to leave.

In England, Hannes had met Christine. Her name had begun popping up with increasing frequency during phone calls. One evening Emma had remarked with a smile, "Now it's always 'Christine-and-I'." When Hannes had finally visited, he'd brought Christine along. Emma had immediately liked the dark-haired girl. Magson had, too. At the end of the first week, Hannes had taken them to Cattle Baron and announced that he and Christine were engaged. Emma had been delighted at the prospect of gaining the daughter she'd never had. Magson had been glad to see Hannes so happy, but he had still held onto the hope that his son would someday return to his country of birth. After that visit, they had only seen Christine once more, when they'd gone overseas for the wedding.

He picked up his cellphone, typed in the international code for England, followed by the number. He stared at the little green telephone icon. One button away.

How did you ask forgiveness for such a thing? How did you earn the right to ask for forgiveness?

And what if you asked and it was not granted?

Like so many times before, he pressed the red telephone and watched the number disappear in an instant.

In the end, the only way to help Emma, had been to break everything.

He placed the phone on the table, pushed it away and folded the cloth open in front of him.

He picked up his service pistol. Z88. South African version of a Beretta design. The standard pistol of the South African Police Service since the late 1980s. A good, dependable firearm, but important to keep clean.

He removed the magazine, pulled and locked the slide, checked that the pistol was safe. His old fingers knew the movements to take the weapon apart so well: remove the slide, place the pistol grip on the cloth, remove the recoil spring and rod from the slide, finally the barrel. And there all the components were spread out on the cloth.

The cleaning always started at the barrel. Until it was bright silver on the inside, the grooves clearly visible. Then a touch of oil. He wiped the other components clean and re-assembled the pistol.

He slid the magazine into the grip and smacked it home against his palm. Cocked the slide.

He had never taken a life with this pistol.

His work phone rang next to him, startling him. He put the weapon down and answered. "Magson."

"Warrant Magson. It's Karlien Pretorius … Am I bothering you?"

"No, Karlien. Did something happen?"

"No. I just …"

"Did you remember something else?"

"No. I wanted to know if maybe … I made batter, for pancakes, and I wanted to invite you. For coffee and pancakes. It's my granny's recipe. They're the best pancakes ever."

It was so unexpected that Magson had no response. Why would she invite him?

"I'm sorry. You must be busy. I shouldn't've called."

"Pancakes would be very nice," Magson heard the words coming from his mouth.

"Awesome!"

She sounded so genuinely pleased that he smiled.

Of course the smile was replaced by closed eyes and a shake of the head as soon as the call ended. What did she want? A progress report? He rubbed his face. Or did she and her mother want to ensure the investigation remained a priority? Why had he said yes? What did he have to tell them?

He rose with a sigh. Washed his face, brushed his teeth and put on a clean shirt.

In his car he turned the key and immediately shut the engine off again. What had he been thinking? He would just have to phone back and say that something had come up.

But she'd sounded so pleased …

He couldn't do that to her. Especially not with a lie.

He shook his head, turned the key once more and pumped the petrol pedal. Reversed all the way out to the edge of the street. Got out and shut the garage door and the gate. Put on the chain. He missed with the lock and it dropped to the ground.

"*Ag, donner, man!*" He had to remove the chain again to open the gate. "Because you have to lock everything and you have to do it on the inside so it looks as if you're actually at home." What had happened to this country? There had been a time when he would sometimes drive into town without bothering to close the garage door.

With the gate finally locked, he got back into the Jetta. He drove more slowly than usual. Why did she have to phone?

He parked in front the Pretorius home. Gazed down the street. He really did not want to go inside. But he got out and locked the door.

A Vibracrete wall separated the property from the street.

There was a wooden gate for vehicles at the driveway and another one for pedestrians. All of it was about the height of his shoulders and both gates were kept locked. Karlien's attacker must have climbed over when he'd brought the box containing her school books, but LCRC had been unable to lift any fingerprints. He didn't hesitate to take risks and yet he remained careful.

Magson pressed the button beside the smaller gate. A few moments passed before he heard the front door open and light footsteps approaching.

"Who is it?"

"It's Warrant Magson."

The lock clicked and the gate opened, revealing a smiling Karlien Pretorius. This was the first time he had seen her not looking traumatized or terrified. Of course it was merely lurking beneath the surface, but still, he was glad.

"Sorry. I had to make sure."

"You'd be in trouble if you didn't."

She smiled again. "Come in."

He noticed her mother standing at the front door, watching them. It had to be hell for her to have her daughter out of her sight for just a second.

Karlien locked the gate and they walked to the house.

"Evening, Warrant."

"Mrs. Pretorius. Thank you for the invitation." She was wearing jeans with a cream-colored jersey. The same color hair as Karlien, but a different face, rounder and fuller.

"Come in."

"We always eat pancakes in the kitchen," said Karlien. "I hope you don't mind. But it's best to eat pancakes hot out of the pan."

"I don't mind."

The kitchen walls were painted white, but the rest of the color scheme consisted of blue and yellow with a touch of green. A blind made of fabric covered the window—yellow and blue flowers, green leaves—blue oven mittens, blue-and-yellow dishtowels. It rendered the space cheerful, even in the unnatural glow of the fluorescents.

They sat at the table next to one of the walls. Karlien

took up position at the stove. Magson glanced at the woman across the table, smiled and looked at his hands.

"I hope you didn't have to leave your wife alone at home."

"No. My wife has passed away. I just still wear the ring."

"I'm sorry."

"Thank you."

She smiled. "It says a lot about her. That you're still wearing her ring."

He nodded. "She was very special."

"The first pancake is now going in," announced Karlien from the stove.

The batter sizzled in the pan.

"Can I pour you some coffee?" asked her mother.

"Please. That would be nice."

He remained at the table. Hannes had always loved pancakes. Emma would mix the batter, after which she would leave it to rest—to Hannes's exasperation—and only then would she start baking, one after the other, sprinkled with cinnamon sugar, rolled and packed close together on an oval plate. The plate would go into the oven with additional pancakes added in groups of three. Hannes would watch his mother throughout—naturally devouring a few along the way—until she was done. Then they would feast. Magson had always liked the ones that had been in the oven for a while, the sugar melted to a cinnamony syrup.

Karlien's mother put a mug of black coffee in front of him, along with a sugar bowl and some milk. There were hand-painted flowers on all the crockery.

"Thank you." He added milk and sugar and stirred. It was percolated coffee. "It smells very good."

"Karlien is a coffee pot. When we do our shopping, half the time is spent in front of the coffee shelf."

"This is House of Coffees' Java Seduction," said Karlien. She placed a plate with a neatly rolled pancake and a fork in front of him. "It's my favorite."

"Thank you."

"Please don't be all proper and wait. Cold pancake is not on." She returned to the stove. There was a lightness to the way she moved.

He picked up his fork and took a bite. Hot, spongy, and despite the crunch of the sugar between his teeth, it was indeed
a particularly delicious pancake. He told her so.

She looked at him and smiled.

Magson took another bite and fumbled for something to
say. He felt uncomfortable eating alone. "Have you been living here a long time, Mrs. Pretorius?"

"Oh, no, you can't be so formal while eating pancake. I'm
Marina."

"… Jan. But everyone just calls me Mags."

"That's much better. To answer your question, Jan, about
seven or eight years."

When last had a woman called him "Jan"? Probably his
sister-in-law, at Emma's funeral.

"I was in Grade 3," said Karlien. She placed a plate in front
of her mother. "So it's seven."

"Thanks, Kars." Using the side of the fork, she sliced the
pancake into squares. "But we're putting the house on the
market."

Magson looked up. "Where will you go?"

"Just somewhere temporary at first, while we decide. I
like my job and Karlien has good friends, but maybe …" She
looked at her daughter rolling a pancake. "Maybe we need a
complete change." Her eyes turned back to him. "Unless you
can guarantee that you'll catch him soon?" she asked, her
voice low.

He looked down. "I wish I could."

She opened her mouth to say something, but Karlien delivered a fresh pancake to Magson's plate.

"Why are you talking so softly?"

"We're just enjoying your pancake. It really is delicious."

"*Ouma* Lien's recipe is the best."

After the sixth pancake, Magson declined any more.

Karlien started brewing a fresh pot of coffee and sat down
with them, three pancakes on her plate.

"Do you want to write?" he asked. "Or is it just a hobby?"

"I'd like to write. It would be awesome to see my book on
the shelf at Exclusive Books. But I simply enjoy writing stories, even if no one reads them."

"Karlien is very creative," said her mother, looking at her daughter with a smile. "She draws as well."

"I like making things."

"I think the coffee's almost done. Why don't you go in the TV room and show some of your drawings."

"Mom."

"I'd like to see them," said Magson.

"I'll bring the coffee," said her mother.

Karlien led him to the TV room, left and reappeared a short while later with a black portfolio bag, about A2 in size. She opened the zip all the way round and folded it open. She removed a sheet of paper and held it for him to look.

It was a landscape, a green valley nestled between two mountains, blue sky overhead. Although the colors were quite intense, the style was wispy, giving the scene a dream-like quality. Magson knew little about art, but he liked it.

"How did you do this?"

"It's pastels," she said. "You get oil pastels, kind of like a good-quality version of wax crayons, and soft pastels. That's what this is. Soft pastel is more like chalk. Powdery. Serious artists would freak out if they heard what I'm comparing it to."

"The colors are very rich." He had no idea what the correct word was.

She smiled. "It's so vivid. It's one of the reasons I'm so fond of soft pastels. And you can easily rub and blend it with your fingers. It gets really messy."

"I like it. I wanted to say you should open a coffee shop, but it looks like you should rather do exhibitions in art galleries. Do you have more?"

Karlien showed him more drawings. More landscapes and also flowers in vases with that same dreamy quality. Emma would have liked the flowers, but one of the landscapes ... He stopped her when she wanted to move on to the next one. It was a forest scene, darker greens and brown trunks, the light shimmering through in a few areas onto simple yellow flowers. It looked as if someone had walked through the foliage.

"Do you sell them?"

"No." She shrugged.

"I'd like to buy this one. If you're willing to sell it."

"Oh." She smiled. "You can have it."

"Thanks, but I want to buy it. It's too beautiful to be free. And besides, a policeman is not allowed to accept gifts."

"Oh. Okay."

He finally managed to convince her to accept five hundred rand.

After their coffee was finished, he stood. Karlien rolled the drawing into a tube and tied it with a piece of string.

"Just untie it and put it down on a flat surface, then the curl will go away."

"I will. Thank you."

Karlien walked him out, to open the gate, while her mother remained in the doorway.

"Thanks for coming, Warrant Magson." Karlien hesitated, as if making a decision. "I was able to feel safe for a while."

"I enjoyed it. I haven't had pancakes in a long time. You're a brave girl, Karlien. You'll be all right."

She nodded.

"Good night."

"Good night."

At home Magson locked the front door and switched on a few lights as he made his way to the dining room. He unrolled the drawing on the table and stared at it. His. This was the first time he had bought a piece of art. He realized he'd never asked Karlien whether it was a place that actually existed. It was as if he could peer into the scene, follow the bruised leaves, where the feet had stepped … It would look really beautiful once it was framed and hung.

Hung.

Was that why he hanged the girls? To watch them while the life drained from their bodies. To watch the *life* draining from them? With rapt attention from a distance, rather than in the struggle of throttling …

He shoved the thought away. He didn't want to lose the feeling inside. Instead, he wanted to remember Karlien's smile when he'd told her he wanted to buy one of her drawings.

Without thinking, he picked up the phone and pressed the number.

It started ringing.

What was he doing?

And ringing.

His heart thumped and his chest tightened. But he was frozen, the phone pressed hard against his ear.

It felt like a weight hitting his chest. "You have reached John and Christine Magson. We're not in at present, but please leave a message and we'll ring you back."

His son's voice, but strange. He sounded like an Englishman.

It was just a recording. He realized he was not breathing and had to consciously begin again.

His son was not Hannes anymore.

Now he was John.

Magson put the phone down.

May 9, 2014. Friday.

Mark Ellwood had been quite positive about the identikit. Except that the man wearing the Ecko Unltd. cap had had a beard. A brown beard, which Ellwood said had definitely been more than a week old.

So it seemed like Guthrie's CJ and Ellwood's Ecko were the same person. But where did that leave Karlien's clean-shaven attacker? Guthrie and Ellwood had both described his hair as longer than depicted on the identikit. Moderately curly, as well.

The only fingerprints on the Graça wine box belonged to Karlien and her mother. Which meant he must have wiped the box down. The results of the contents were not back yet.

Magson stared at the wall in the operational room. Three photos. Three girls. Three smiles. They deserved better. Karlien, too. She didn't deserve having to leave her home, her school, her friends, perhaps even this province, behind.

Once again the voice, simultaneously strange and familiar, echoed in his head.

You have reached John and Christine Magson.

He turned away from the wall.

It was almost half past eight. He was sitting on the sofa, a glass of KWV brandy in his hand, the bottle on the coffee table. He had never been much of a drinker. His uncle had taken care of that as he'd been growing up, each time Magson had witnessed him stumbling around, trying to pronounce the nonsense spewing from his mouth. The sickly sweet stench clinging to him had been the worst, which was why Magson never drank his brandy with Coke as the other detectives did.

After supper Emma had usually retired to this sofa to watch some TV. She had loved her stories, speaking about—and to—many of the people on the screen as if they were family friends. On some evenings, particularly after the country had changed, he would bring dockets home and so he had stayed at the dining table. Otherwise, he would join her here on the sofa, usually falling asleep with her against his shoulder. Such a lot of time with her that he had wasted by sleeping.

He gulped down the remaining brandy and poured more into the glass.

Detective work used to be different. The police had commanded respect, had made a difference. There had been time to investigate every docket. There had been a braai grid in the boot of every unmarked vehicle and time to use it for the odd impromptu braai. Nowadays a person's life was often worth fifty rand. A policeman was a means to obtain a pistol. You tried to catch the stupid and inexperienced criminals as quickly as possible so you had more time to spend on the clever, cunning ones. You managed to close one docket, only to receive two new ones in its place. They received a prison sentence, only to be released after serving a fraction of it. Meanwhile, you were working overtime, without the remuneration you deserved, instead of spending time with your wife. You thought there would be time later. Your retirement was not so far off and then there would be time. But then she got sick and there was nothing the doctors could do and you watched her slowly being eaten from the inside while there was no longer a death penalty for those who deserved it. She asked you to help her, because she was but a shell and all she felt was pain or medication and she couldn't anymore.

You helped her, even though it was terrible, because you had looked into her eyes when she'd asked you, when after three decades of marriage she'd had enough trust in you to drop all her defenses to the ground, to stand before you with nothing left to reveal. Because you had seen she knew what she was asking. Because you loved her. But neither of you realized that there would be a hidden cost. Like regret, it arrived too late, when your son stood behind you after the funeral, telling you he knew what you had done. And then you were alone. Everywhere there were holes that would never be filled and you learned that you had never really been sad before. All that remained was your job. Because there would always be another senseless murder.

He swallowed the last of the brandy, took the glass to the kitchen, and sat down at the dining table. On the buffet, Karlien's drawing was perched against the wall. He would have liked to have seen it framed. The tree trunks. The rays of light filtering down. The disturbance among the flowers and leaves as if someone had passed through it. It changed the entire scene.

The revolver was already in his hand. He and Emma had had a bitter argument the day he'd brought it home, an argument he'd finally won by claiming it was for her, and particularly for Hannes's, safety. Because a mother's instinct to protect her child was stronger than anything else. Twice she had allowed him to take her to the shooting range, to learn how to use the revolver, and thereafter she would not touch it.

He looked at her photo. She was standing in front of the low wall on Signal Hill, an orange scarf wrapped around her head, the Atlantic Ocean bright and blue and endless behind her. The crutches she had used to get to the wall were not in the photo, and he'd had to run to support her after the camera had clicked.

She smiled.

His eyes burned and he stroked her face with his thumb.

"I want to be with you, Em."

She would have looked at him, placed her hands on his cheeks and nodded, told him she knew. And then she would have said, "But …"

But Emma was not here to complete the sentence.

"Two for me," he said, removing two bullets from the box. He placed them upright on the table, swung open the revolver and fed them into opposite chambers.

"Two for you." Two chambers remaining empty.

"And one joker." Because the Smith & Wesson had five chambers.

He removed another bullet from the box, placed it flat on the table between him and the photo in the frame, looked at Emma's eyes, and spun it. The metal scraped against the wood. The light bounced off in copper flashes onto Emma's face. It spun more slowly. And stopped.

The tip was pointing just past him.

He picked up the bullet and fed it into one of the open chambers.

Spun the cylinder.

Raised the revolver and pressed the barrel against his temple.

He looked at Karlien's drawing. All he wanted was to follow Emma's path through the flowers.

He pulled the hammer back with his thumb.

Took one last breath.

Closed his eyes.

Sometimes at a crime scene in the veld there was this quiet, a stillness. There was just a light stirring of the air, just enough to feel it against your skin. It was as if the life that had expired at this place had taken everything with it.

His index finger curled around the trigger.

Emma was propped against the pillows on their bed. Everything had been said. She looked at him. He looked at her. This was the last time they would look at each other. He held her hand. Her fingers were cool. His were warm and sweaty. "I'm sorry," she said. A single tear spilled from the corner of her left eye, slipped down her cheek, seeping into the white pillow. His throat was constricted. He kissed her for the last time. "Blow out all the air." She emptied her lungs and waited while he opened the cylinder's valve, pulled the Glad roasting bag over her face, down below her chin past the rubber hose. He positioned the elastic band around the bag against her neck, just the correct length to leave a small gap so the carbon dioxide could escape. Her eyes waited for him. He nodded and she started breathing again. He held her hand in both of his, the fingers he knew so well, the bones that had become so prominent. The helium sighed softly. Her head lowered completely to the left. He kept looking into her eyes, even though she didn't see him anymore. Her arms and legs contracted and relaxed a few times. Her breathing stopped. Her pulse was still. He held her hand and waited. He shut the valve and removed the bag from her head. Rested his face against her chest and, for the first time since she'd become ill, he cried in front of her without restraint.

The hammer snapped down. There was only a metallic click. Behind him the refrigerator started groaning.

He opened his eyes. Emma was standing in front of the low wall. Her dress hung loosely on her withered frame. Her thin strands of hair were hidden beneath the scarf. Her cheeks were hollow. But she smiled.

"Why, Em? Why!"

He started pulling the trigger. The next chamber contained what he wanted.

Pressure against his index finger as the hammer lifted.

The bang echoed against the walls. There was a dent in the table where he had slammed down the pistol.

I know it hurts. I know it feels as if something inside you has been broken forever. As if you'll never feel better again. But you will. Not tonight. Not tomorrow. Not next week. Maybe not even next month. Nothing hurts like losing someone you love. You're bleeding now. But it will form a scab. You will pick at it—you always do. You'll tear it off, or it will catch on something, and it will start bleeding again. But it will form another scab, because the body can't help it. And eventually it will heal. You'll have a scar, because the heart always forms a scar. But you will heal.

He had stood outside in the passage in silence while Emma had spoken softly with Hannes in his room. Hannes had been in Grade 11. He had had his first girlfriend and they had been together for four or five months. Hannes had fallen for her like a dove that had been shot, the way you probably always fall for your first real love. And then she had broken up with him.

How long will it hurt so much, Mom?

I wish I had an answer. The heart has its own time. And it doesn't follow instruction. But it doesn't give up easily, either. Your dad told me if you cut out a person's heart and put it in a certain solution, it will continue beating for a long time.

Magson had heard that from a pathologist, who'd been holding a victim's heart in the palm of his left hand at the time.

That's gross, Mom.

When he had told Emma, she'd grimaced and thanked him for sharing this grisly image.

It is. But it is also an amazing display of spirit.

Actually, it was a pathetic image. An organ lying in a bucket filled with fluid, continuing to beat simply because it was receiving the requisite nourishment. Without the insight to realize it was no longer serving any purpose.

I was able to feel safe for a while. Karlien Pretorius. Standing at the gate, looking up at him in the dark. As the taste of coffee and pancake still lingered in his mouth.

While the heart kept on beating, a doctor could remove it from the bucket and transplant it to a new body.

He looked at the revolver on the table, Emma's photo, and behind her, the prescription for the antidepressants.

"All right, Em. I'll give the psychiatrist a chance."

Twelve

The girl lay on her back. She was wearing dark blue denim jeans, a black top and jacket, all of it soaked from the rain that had started falling during the night. Discarded bubble-gum was stuck to the bottom of her left shoe. Her long hair was a mess of untied, wet tangles, her head turned to the right. Her eyes were open halfway, her tongue dark and pro-truding from her lips. A deep furrow went around her throat.

Magson looked up at the sky. The rain had been a con-stant drizzle all morning. The drops fell softly onto his face. Onto the girl's as well, but she hadn't been able to feel it for quite some time.

Who was she?

Two boys had found her. Children of the area's farm work-ers. Who'd come to try their luck fishing despite the light rain, and had discovered the girl among the reeds instead.

"She looks fresh, Doc."

"Body and environmental temperature are the same," said Doctor Sinette Killian. "At least twenty-four hours, depending on how long she's been lying here. That's if it rained throughout the night, otherwise I'll add a couple of hours. Rigor mortis is still present. In this weather it could take anything between thirty-six and forty-eight hours until it disappears."

"So yesterday morning or Saturday, then."

The pathologist nodded. "But between you and me, I don't think she's been lying here that long."

"She's pretty close to the road," said Menck. "He didn't put in the same amount of effort this time."

"Why would he? He probably thinks we're a bunch of arses." This kind of killer would follow the newspaper reports. He would have seen the identikit, and still he'd snatched another girl. And had dumped her next to the Vissershok Road some distance from Durbanville. Just like Maryke Retief. As if he was mocking them.

Magson glanced at the police tape that had been tied here and there to whatever the uniforms could find to tie it to, the yellow bright against the green background. He looked around. With Maryke everything had been brown and dead. Now the hills were green. And the rain had washed the tall grass in vivid hues, almost like one of Karlien's pastel drawings. Above, everything was gray and nebulous, as if the color had seeped from the sky, pooling on the earth below.

The air was cool against his wet skin, heavy with the earthy smell of rain. He was still waiting for the antidepressants to take effect—Doctor Hurter had told him it could be a couple of weeks—but he did seem to be a bit more ... "switched on." Had to be his imagination.

He looked down at the girl.

"Why don't we know about her?" he asked. "She didn't come off the streets. Someone has to wonder where she is."

"Well," said Menck, "either they have no reason to wonder yet because they think she is safe somewhere, or it simply hasn't reached us."

"If there was a gap in communication ... shit, man, all the stations *know* we want to hear about every teenage girl that goes missing."

"I'm phoning right now to find out." Captain Henz Kritzinger had just joined them. "We have to identify her as soon as possible." He dug out his cellphone. "And don't worry," he told Mags. "If someone at a station was remiss, there will be hell to pay." He walked off, the phone against his ear.

"She doesn't have dark brown hair," Menck finally said out loud.

"No." The stringy wet locks were likely to be dark blonde when dry. "Maybe hair color was never important."

Two forensic pathology officers crouched next to the girl. They unfolded a cream-colored body bag and lifted the stiff body on top. One tore off the strip to expose the glue; they folded the bag over and sealed her inside.

May 20, 2014. Tuesday.

Magson parked in the first open bay in Durham Avenue and jogged to the guard at the gate, then along the stretch of tar and into the Salt River Forensic Pathology Laboratory, signed the register and bounded down the corridor to the cloak-room. A few curses were required to get the temperamental rubber boots onto his feet, but then he was out and around the corner into the dissection hall. The floor was covered with a layer of bloody water.

Doctor Killian was bent over the wooden table she always used when dissecting organs and intestines. Magson sighed. She had already started cutting, then. But then he noticed the dark skin of the person on the trolley.

"Morning, Doc. Sorry I'm so late."

"It's all right. I skipped her, because I knew you'd want to observe."

"I appreciate that." He watched her studying the second lung on the cutting table. "I must've driven over a nail yesterday. So this morning I had to change the tire."

"Not the way you want to start your day." She placed the lung, its twin and the heart into the bucket.

"Especially not on such a cold winter's morning. My knuckles still feel as if they need some grease."

She weighed the organs and wrote each one's weight on the greenboard. Meanwhile, her assistant, Lungelo Saphetha, had removed the next block of organs, placing it between the man's legs on the trolley.

Doctor Killian returned and started with the stomach. She slit it open and a mass of rice spilled onto the cutting table. It seemed the man had eaten his last meal not long before his death, because the kernels had barely been digested.

"Hmm, last night I tried an extremely tasty chicken jambalaya recipe."

"What is jambalaya?" asked Magson.

"It's a lot like paella. This recipe is rice with chicken chunks and chorizo sausages and tomato, everything sort of cooked together. Nice and spicy." She raised the table to let the stomach contents flow onto the trolley.

"Sounds nice. My wife used to make a great chicken paella."

"I can give you the recipe. It's not difficult to cook."

Doctor Hurter had told him to start with the small pleasures. And she had specifically mentioned food. And then he would have something to say when he slunk back on Thursday. "Maybe I should try it."

Once the autopsy had been completed, Kennedy Zihlangu wheeled the next body to the pathologist's station.

Photos were taken and Doctor Killian studied the furrow in the girl's throat. The rope's twisting pattern was clearly discernable on the skin. "In each case, the knot is at the back, in the center. Everything has to be just right."

She opened a sexual assault kit and went through the process of collecting swabs and samples. After removing the paper bag from the girl's hand, she turned the wrist to the side. "The abrasions and contusions to her wrists are more severe than those on the previous victims. They also go all the way round. Each hand was tied individually."

"Why the change?" wondered Magson.

"In the previous victims, the abrasions were on the outside, as if the insides were tied firmly together, the rope going around both wrists." Doctor Killian demonstrated with her own hands. "Here there are abrasions on the insides of the wrists as well. It may be that he simply tied her hands together in a different manner, or each hand could've been tied to something separately. But what is clear is that she strained against it. She fought to free herself."

Zihlangu assisted in removing the girl's clothes.

As they turned the girl onto her side, Doctor Killian's eyebrows drew closer together, her eyes narrowing. "Here's something."

Magson walked around to her side of the trolley. The pathologist indicated a mark, although it really wasn't necessary. A rather large triangle, the two longer sides of equal length and convex.

"Burned," she said.

"Looks like an iron," said Magson. "Shit."

"It was in contact with the skin for quite some time."

"The rest isn't enough. He had to torture her, too."

"Okay, Kennedy."

The auxiliary service officer nodded and they removed the rest of the girl's clothes. There were no other burns. And no underwear beneath her jeans. Doctor Killian resumed collecting evidence for the sexual assault kit.

"The damage to her rectum is more severe. Her perineum is torn. I wouldn't be surprised if he used an object. But someone washed her. Or she did it herself."

"Maybe he forces them to wash before he hangs them," said Magson.

Once the sexual assault kit was done, they washed her and started documenting all her injuries. With the girl now on her stomach, Doctor Killian pointed to bruises on the left buttock. "Five oval-shaped contusions." She turned her left hand around, holding it beside the girl's buttock, thumb to the outside, the other four fingers in a semicircle to the inside. "Fingermarks."

"To pull her buttocks apart," said Magson. "While he sodomized her."

Doctor Killian nodded.

"The marks are very …"

"Pronounced?"

"Ja."

"It was done with considerable force."

"He's becoming more sadistic."

Doctor Killian measured the fingermarks with a ruler—a white one with SHATTERPROOF on it. They had been using the thing for years and it had always bothered Magson a bit. One of the pathology officers was very interested in photography and consequently took all the pathologists' photos. The close-ups always included the Shatterproof ruler. It just seemed a bit tactless.

Next was the burn on the girl's back. "Two hundred and twenty by one hundred and fifteen millimeters."

"He burned her with a fucking iron," said Magson.

The photographer took more photos.

Meanwhile Magson watched the pathologist preparing for the internal investigation. She removed one of the two blue latex gloves on her left hand and put on a glove of chainmail so she wouldn't accidentally cut herself. The latex glove went back over and she picked up the scalpel.

Late in the afternoon Magson was back at the mortuary. With him was Daniël Ferreira. Possibly to identify his daughter. Magson would much rather spend all day attending autopsies while the drain was blocked than perform this particular task. They filled in the necessary documentation in a separate room. Magson recalled another waiting room, where he would wait while Emma …

"We're ready."

The pathology officer was standing in the doorway.

"Mr. Ferreira," said Magson.

The man looked at him for a moment, his face pale and drawn. He rose, his hands kneading each other.

The officer led them down the corridor. It was open on the right-hand side, where there was a garden, green and vibrant. In spring it was a sight to behold, when the flowers were in bloom. At the end of the corridor they entered a small room. A washbasin hung on the left wall. The officer held a door open, leading to one of the viewing rooms.

"She is behind the curtain," he said. "When you're ready, you can just let me know and I'll pull it back."

Daniël Ferreira entered and stopped. He looked at the grayish green curtain, rubbing his hands. Against the wall were two benches covered in the same grayish green. Dark Cs curled in a swirling pattern on the fabric. The walls were white.

"Thank you," said Magson softly. "It's all right. I'll wait with Mr. Ferreira."

The officer nodded and followed the corridor back to the reception area.

"Take your time, Mr. Ferreira. Whenever you're ready."

"I don't think I can." His voice was barely above a whisper.

Magson placed his hand on the man's shoulder. Opening that curtain erased all hope.

Daniël Ferreira swallowed. His throat was so dry that Magson heard it. The man reached with one unsteady hand, touched the curtain. The hand hung there. The fingers quivering.

Another dry swallow.

He pulled the curtain.

On the other side of the window the girl was lying on a steel trolley. A white sheet covered her body from toe to chin. Her face was turned towards the window. Her dark blonde hair had been draped on both sides of her head, hiding the ugly furrow in her throat.

Emma had looked peaceful. After everything she had gone through, the physical pain, the emotional struggle, the medication, the … After it had been done, she'd looked peaceful. Beautiful.

The shoulder started shaking beneath Magson's hand.

"It's her. It's Danielle."

All he wanted to do was go home, perhaps get something to eat on the way. But he had told Emma he would try. And so he got out of the Jetta and walked into Pick n Pay. It might be his last opportunity before Thursday's appointment with Doctor Hurter, because Danielle Ferreira's mother and step-father would be arriving from George tomorrow.

The world had slowly, furtively, become plastic. Shopping baskets and trolleys used to be metal. Milk bottles had been made of glass, and there had been the cartons he preferred because the milk had had a creamier taste. Coke and Fanta had come in glass bottles you could return to the café for twenty cents or something. And those cents had had value beyond merely increasing the uncomfortable bulge in your wallet. Toothpaste tubes had been manufactured from a soft metal that had always metamorphosed into a warped mess towards the end. Early in their marriage, Emma had made the executive decision that they would be using separate tubes. This was one instance where plastic was definitely an improvement.

He removed the shopping list from his pocket and started packing strange products into his basket: yellow and red peppers, sage, thyme, cayenne pepper and bay leaves, chicken stock, and a sausage called chorizo, the appearance of which gave him pause. Also a couple of chicken breasts, onions, tomatoes and garlic. He read the list of ingredients in the neat female script once more. There had been a time when it had not been unusual for him to wander through the aisles with just such a list in his hand. Rice was about the only thing he had at home.

He handed the cashier his credit card—even money was plastic—and carried his bag to the Jetta. It had rained again.

As he drove home, the wet streets reflected in the headlights. The blonde girl in her wet clothes returned to him. The drops on her skin. Her mother was the last known person to see her alive, on Friday morning in George. It was suspected that she had run away, presumably to her father in Hout Bay. But that route should not have led through the killer's Bellville-Brackenfell-Durbanville triangle. How had she ended up there?

Magson recalled the shoulder starting to shake beneath his hand. The shattered voice asking …

He shook his head. No. Not tonight. Tonight he was going to cook and not think about death.

At home he pulled the car into the garage, locked the gate and the front door, and took the shopping bag to the kitchen. He locked his pistol in the safe. Next to the revolver. And put on more comfortable clothes.

In the kitchen he unhooked Emma's old violet apron behind the door and tied it around his waist. He poured a glass of KWV, added some water, and read the recipe. Almost everything needed to be diced. That was going to take a while. He'd only really started cooking when Emma had no longer been able to move around easily on her own. Prior to that, he had sometimes helped to peel potatoes and so on, and of course barbecue duties had been his domain, but otherwise his cooking had been confined to breakfast on Emma's birthday and Mother's Day, and when she had had the flu or something.

First, the onion. Then the peppers. The tomatoes were supposed to be skinned and pitted, but he was not entirely sure how—he just knew Emma had put them in boiling water. Well, a tomato's skin and seeds had never bothered him, so he decided to simply dice them. At last all the vegetables were ready. While everything except the tomato was frying, he cut the chicken into smaller pieces and then the chorizo—which he still didn't trust completely—into slices. He'd been too lax with the stirring, and the onions and peppers had burnt a bit. But it wasn't too bad. He added the chicken and chorizo. Hunger had begun to gnaw at his stomach. Water was boiling for the chicken stock. The meat was gaining some color. Herbs and spices. Tomato, tomato purée and stock. And now it had to simmer.

He paused for some brandy. The kitchen had not smelt this good in a long time.

The rice was the final addition. Stir and simmer for twenty minutes.

The hunger was no longer just gnawing.

After twenty minutes he lifted the lid. Still a lot of fluid. He stirred. Studied a spoonful of rice. It didn't look completely cooked yet.

He replaced the lid and gave it another ten minutes.

This time the rice looked much better, but there was still too much fluid. He frowned. Well, too bad. He got a plate. The aroma of the chicken, chorizo and exotic spices went straight to his stomach. For a few moments he just stared at the rising wisps of steam twirling around each other.

At the dining table he glanced at the pastel drawing on

the buffet. He really should make time to have it framed. With closed eyes, he drew the aroma of the hot food deep into his lungs and took his first bite. Needed some salt.

He doubted whether the jambalaya was how it should be, but it was the tastiest plate of food he'd had in a very long time.

May 21, 2014. Wednesday.

"I have a new philosophy in life," announced Menck.

They were in the Corolla, heading to the guesthouse to talk to Danielle Ferreira's mother and stepfather.

"Some days you're the pigeon and some days you're the statue."

"So that's the sentence you recite to yourself as you start your day," said Magson.

"Life is what it is."

"And where did you discover this insight?"

"My sister emailed it to me."

"I am amazed that anyone gets any work done with all these emails they send around all the time."

"They have to make time for Facebook and Twitter, as well."

Magson shook his head.

"We're living in the Information Age, Mags."

Magson preferred the previous one, whatever it had been. "I wouldn't mind having a pigeon day. For once."

Menck looked at him. "Who do you want to go perch on? Or do you want to go on a bombing run?" He turned his hand into an airplane and whistled.

Magson hesitated. "He asked me whether she had suffered. Daniël Ferreira. After he identified his daughter. 'Did he hurt her? Did she suffer?' I wish someone would tell me how you're supposed to answer such a question. Do you tell him a man sodomized his daughter? With so much force that he tore her open? That he burned her with an iron. And then he hanged her and even that wasn't quick. Is that what you should tell him? Or do you lie? So that in a year's time, or whenever the case finally goes to court, he can sit there and find out exactly what the bastard did to her. So he can realize that little bit of comfort he'd clung to was all just a lie."

"What did you tell him?" asked Menck.

Magson grimaced, took a deep breath through his nose, let the air out slowly. "I told him she didn't have an easy time before she died. But no one can hurt her anymore. It's who she was that's important, not what someone did to her."

"That's nice."

It still sounded false, though. And most likely he would have to answer that same question again in a few minutes' time. He parked at the guesthouse. They got out and met Bruno and Ronel Volschenk in their room.

"Mr. and Mrs. Volschenk," said Magson, "we are very sorry about Danielle."

Her mother nodded.

"It's important that we understand the circumstances under which Danielle disappeared. Friday was the last time you saw her?"

"Yes," said her mother. It was from her that Danielle had gotten her dark blonde hair. But not her eyes. "The morning. I took her to school, but she never went to her class. And she must've gone home, because her bag was gone. A backpack. We only realized it a couple of days later."

"Did she say anything that morning?"

"No. She didn't really speak. But Danielle's been moody recently. We didn't … always get along."

"Did you argue?"

"Yes."

"What about?" asked Magson.

"It could have been anything. Small things." She looked down at the brown-speckled carpet. "You just couldn't talk to her anymore. Except Odette, her sister. They got along really well."

"Is Odette here? Did you bring her with you?"

"Yes. The hostess is watching her. Not that she really wants to be away from us since …"

Magson nodded. "Do you have any idea what really bothered Danielle?"

"It was just the normal teenage things," said the stepfather. He had dark hair, almost black, and a moustache crawling halfway over his upper lip.

"It seems like she was on her way to her father."

"They've always had a good relationship," said her mother. "She's had him wrapped around her pinky since she was born."

"So you have no idea why she ran away?"

She shook her head. "No. She really was very moody recently, but I don't know. I thought it was just something at school. It's a difficult time at work, too. I've been very busy." Her eyes grew wet and she looked down, dabbed with a tissue.

"You only reported her as missing on Saturday," said Menck.

"We thought she was at a friend's," said the stepfather. "They're busy with an assignment. We only noticed the next morning that she never came home."

"Her phone was off," her mother elaborated. "We phoned all her friends, but no one knew anything. That was when we realized she was never at school on Friday."

There was a knock on the door. Bruno Volschenk opened it. Daniël Ferreira did not look good. The two men greeted each other with a nod. First names were stiffly exchanged between Danielle's parents. Magson received a handshake, as did Menck when Magson introduced him.

"All right," said Magson. "Now that everyone is here. The thing that bothers me is what Danielle was doing in the Durbanville area. It makes sense that she was heading towards you, Mr. Ferreira, but by whatever means she was traveling—by bus or maybe hitchhiking—the way from George to Hout Bay follows the N2 all the way to the M3 in Cape Town. The alternative is to go along the coast, Mitchells Plain, Muizenberg. But no road goes through Bellville or Durbanville."

"Why did Danielle have to be in Bellville or Durbanville?" asked her father. "Just because he left her there …"

"Danielle wasn't the first victim, Mr. Ferreira."

Her mother made a sound and wrung the tissue in her hands.

"The other girls all disappeared in that area."

"Other girls," said her father. "How many?"

"Three."

"He has murdered *three* girls and you haven't caught him yet?"

"We are doing everything we can, Mr. Ferreira," said Menck. "The problem is he leaves very few clues behind. That's why we need your help."

Daniël Ferreira ran both his hands over his face. "Three girls. And Danielle."

"Did Danielle have any friends in the direction of Durbanville?" asked Magson.

"No," answered her father. "We usually went to Tyger Valley, but Danielle had no friends there. She had one or two in Hout Bay." He looked at Magson. "Why didn't you tell me yesterday that there were more girls?"

"I thought you had enough to handle."

"It was in the paper this morning," said Bruno Volschenk.

"Why didn't you say anything?" asked his wife.

"I didn't want to upset you."

"Do you know of anyone Danielle might have known in the Durbanville area, Mrs. Volschenk?" asked Magson.

"No."

"Would she have hitchhiked?"

"I don't know."

"Has she hitchhiked in the past?"

"Not as far as I know. She wouldn't've. Not easily. She knows it's dangerous."

"I still don't understand why she ran away," said her father. "What happened, Ronel?"

She didn't reply. Merely shook her head. Didn't look at him.

"Come on, Ronel. Something must've happened."

"I don't know, Daniël! Why don't *you* know? You're the perfect parent."

"Why didn't she phone me?" he asked no one in particular. "I would've come and fetched her."

"Typical. She is working on an important assignment, but the White Knight will just rush in and take her away."

"At least I never drove her away."

"I didn't drive her away."

"She ran away. Whose fault is that?"

"This is not—" Bruno Volschenk attempted to step in.

"Oh, yes, of course it's my fault. Because everything is my fault. I was also the one who made you jump into your secretary's bed."

"Ten years ago, Ronel. That has absolutely nothing to do with this."

"You've never been able to say no to Danielle. Whenever she didn't get her way with me, she ran straight to you."

"Danielle is dead and you're badmouthing her? What kind of mother are you?"

"The one who had to do the hard work of raising her. It's easy to point the finger when you're only playing dad two holidays a year."

"I would've taken her any time. Any time."

"Now all of a sudden. Ten years ago you were only too happy to leave her with me."

"And that was a huge mistake."

"That's enough, Daniël," said Bruno Volschenk.

But Daniël Ferreira ignored him. "What did you do, Ronel?"

"Nothing," she said softly.

"You must've done something! Because she ran away from you! And now she's dead! Have you gone to look at her, Ronel? She's lying in a fucking mortuary!"

"Mommy?"

The voice was small and scared behind them. No one had noticed little Odette Volschenk opening the door.

Magson tongued the cavity in his tooth. The thing was less troublesome lately, since he had learned to chew on the right side. It was only drinking fluids, either too hot or cold, that hurt. The sharp edge slit his tongue and he sucked in his breath. He realized that Menck was watching him, shaking his head.

"You are the most stubborn person I know."

"*Ag*, don't start again."

"It's pointless," said Menck and shrugged. He closed the empty KFC packet and took a few swallows of his Coke. "There are none so deaf as those who will not listen."

Magson sighed. "You should rather worry about that Coke you're gulping down."

"What is wrong with Coke?"

"You can use it to remove deposited grime."

"Deposited grime?" asked Menck, smiling, eyebrows raised. "Can't wait to hear."

"If you take a piece of metal with grimy deposits on it and you leave it in a glass of Coke, after an hour or so it's clean and shiny."

"Really?"

"Yes. It even removes rust. Is this the kind of thing you want to have running through your body?"

Menck laughed. "My body could do with some grime removal."

"Then you'll have to start snorting it. Because it's your lungs that need cleaning."

"Warrant Officer Magson, are you advising me to start snorting coke? What the hell kind of policeman are you?"

Magson dropped his head backwards against the seat and exhaled slowly. "Let's go talk to the little girl. I need an intelligent conversation."

Menck laughed and took a big mouthful of Coke, swirling it around.

Magson started the Corolla and drove to the guesthouse. After the morning's drama, they had offered to come back in the afternoon, particularly because they had wanted to talk to Odette, and she had clearly been too upset at that stage. Fortunately, Daniël Ferreira hadn't required much encouragement to leave after witnessing the terrified little face in the doorway.

They knocked on the door and Bruno Volschenk opened it. He came outside, closing the door behind him.

"Look, I understand it's important to ask your questions. And of course we want you to catch Danielle's murderer. It's just that Odette is really upset. The whole thing with Danielle is difficult enough; they were close. It took a hell of a long time to calm her down after Ferreira made that scene this morning."

"We understand, Mr. Volschenk," said Magson.

"So if Odette gets upset in any way, I'm going to ask you to leave."

"That's all right."

"Okay." He glanced at Magson a moment longer, opened the door and the three of them entered the room.

Odette Volschenk was lying on her stomach on the carpet. Two light brown braids trailed down the sides of her face, tied at the ends with bright yellow scrunchies. Her feet swayed in the air while she was drawing in a book.

"Odette," said her mother, "these are policemen. They want to talk to you."

Menck crouched next to the girl. They had decided that he should speak with her.

"Hi, Odette. My name is Colin. What are you drawing?"

She didn't look up and kept on drawing. "It's the Taj Mahal. Daniella said it's the prettiest building in the whole world. Daniella is my big sister, but we have different daddies. She said one day when she had a job, she'd take us to see it. It's in India."

"It's very pretty."

"I'm not finished yet." She placed the thick triangular coloring pencil on the carpet and selected another one. Started coloring again. "A prince built it for his princess when she died. Because he loved her very much. It took twenty years."

"Twenty years! Wow. You're very clever."

"Daniella told me."

"Did Daniella tell you she was going away?" asked Menck.

"No. But Daniella was sad."

"Do you know why?"

"No, she wouldn't say." The pencil's lines were darker, scratchy. "But she got into bed with me and held me and she cried."

"When was this, Odette? Can you remember?"

"The other day." She studied the picture for a while and chose a new color. "I made her less sad. Daniella said so. But I couldn't make her better." She looked up, her brown eyes large and serious in her small round face. "You can't just stick a plaster on your heart to make it better. It's not like when I fall and hurt my knee."

No, thought Magson, and heard Menck echoing him, "No."

She looked back down at the drawing. "I'm sad now, too, because Mommy says Daniella is never coming back."

"I am sorry about that." Menck took one of her braids, letting it slip through his fingers.

"Daniella always told me stories. About princes and princesses and fairies and things. In the evening when I get into bed, then it's Oddie's Story Time." She looked up at Menck. "I'm Oddie." She looked down again. "I liked having a big sister. But now it's just me."

Magson wanted to wrap his arms around her, hold her head against his shoulder and lie to her that everything would be all right. She would believe him, because she was young. She still believed the world was really a good place.

"What do you still have to draw before the picture is done?" asked Menck.

"Daniella and me. She can't take us anymore. But I can take her in my picture." Her face scrunched up. "But I can't do it right."

Someone pounded on the door. Odette's head whipped up, her eyes large. Magson looked around.

"What the hell?" muttered Bruno Volschenk and opened the door.

Daniël Ferreira burst in and grabbed him by the shirt. "You fucking pig! I'm going to kill you!"

Menck was on his feet. Ronel Volschenk screamed at her ex-husband while her current one was trying to fend off the attack on him. Magson moved closer and attempted to separate them. In the scuffle Daniël Ferreira's elbow smashed into his nose. For a moment everything turned black and then the world was swimming behind shimmering bright spots. Warm blood rushed over his mouth.

"Let my daddy go!" screamed Odette. "Let my daddy go!"

The room came back into focus. Menck grabbed Daniël Ferreira from behind and managed to pin one arm against his back.

Bruno Volschenk was breathing hard and started re-arranging his clothes. "What the hell is wrong with you, man?"

"Let me go!" yelled Daniël Ferreira, struggling to free himself from Menck's hold. "Let me go!"

Magson pinched his nose to stem the stream of blood. His mouth was filled with the taste of warm copper.

Ronel Volschenk stared at the men while Odette, crying, clutched at her legs. "Don't hurt my daddy, don't hurt my daddy, don't …"

"Mr. Ferreira! Calm down. Now. You're upsetting the little girl." Menck had succeeded in cuffing his hands behind his back. "Mags, you okay?" He was looking at the blood on Magson's chin and clothes, concerned.

"I'm going to kill you!" snarled Daniël Ferreira at Bruno Volschenk.

"Daniël, what is wrong with you?" asked his ex-wife.

"This scum tried to rape Danielle! That's what's wrong! I'm going to kill you!" Despite the handcuffs, Menck was still grappling with him.

Odette clutched her mother's pants in tight little fists, tears streaming across her cheeks.

"You're off your rocker, man. I would never do such a thing."

"You're lying!"

"Look, I understand you're upset. We all are."

"She wrote a letter, you stupid bastard! Everything's in there! How you came into her room—"

"Okay, that's enough." Menck's voice was loud and decisive. "This is what's going to happen now. Mrs. Volschenk, take Odette outside. Mr. Volschenk, sit on the bed. And Mr. Ferreira, calm down. I'm going to let go and then you will sit down on that chair. Otherwise, I will lock you up in the cells until you calm down."

"But he—"

"One more word, Mr. Ferreira."

Something in Menck's voice caused the man to close his mouth and stop struggling.

"Okay, on the chair."

Menck slowly released him and Daniël Ferreira sat down on the chair. He glared at Bruno Volschenk, but said nothing.

"What are you going to do, Warrant?" asked Ronel Volschenk.

"See whether my partner is okay and then find out what is going on. Please take care of Odette."

The woman seemed uncertain, but she took her daughter outside. Odette looked at her father with shiny, frightened eyes, at Menck and back at her father.

"Don't worry, Odette," said Menck. "I won't let your daddy get hurt."

She looked at him with her large eyes and the door closed behind them.

"Mags. Are you okay?"

"Ja, I'b all right." Magson's voice sounded strange, because he was pinching his nose between thumb and index finger.

"Is it broken?"

"No. But it hurts like a bitch." He went to the bathroom. Tore off a long strip of toilet paper, bunching it together in his right hand.

"What letter are you talking about, Mr. Ferreira?" Menck was asking in the room.

Magson opened the faucet and wiped the blood from his face. The shirt was probably a write-off. His tie was smeared. It was on his jacket, as well.

"It came today," said Daniël Ferreira. "I've got it here. It's in my pocket."

Magson released his nose slowly, but blood instantly tickled inside his nostril. A bright red droplet hit the white porcelain, fine tendrils radiating from the edge. Another droplet. And another.

"You killed her," said Daniël Ferreira somewhere.

The small pool of blood broke and a trickle crawled across the porcelain, glided over the rim onto the silver edge of the drain, mixing with the little water left behind.

"It was *you* Danielle tried to get away from."

Magson watched as more blood dripped, following the same red trickle, finally pushing over the edge, disappearing into the black of the drain.

"Mags." Menck's voice.

Magson blinked. He tore off another strip of toilet paper and rolled plugs for his nose. Checked the mirror to make sure he looked somewhat respectable.

In the room, Menck was holding a piece of paper. "You okay?"

Magson nodded.

"Look at this."

Magson took the sheet. It was about A5 in size, white with black lines. The script was pretty, the words in blue ink that had wept a bit into the paper.

Daddy
I don't know what to do. I just know I can't cope here anymore. I'm coming to you. But I'm afraid I'll chicken out so I'm writing it down and sending this letter. It's so difficult. Something happened Daddy. It's Uncle Bruno. Mom wasn't here because she's always working. He came into the bathroom after I showered and said I'm becoming a lovely girl. He touched me Daddy. And Oddie was in front of the TV! He said if I make a scene she'll hear and what would she think if she sees me seducing her dad. He wanted me to touch him as well but I refused. He said it's okay we can take it slowly. He said I shouldn't bother trying to tell Mom because she would never believe me. And he's right because Mom and I don't get along. She'll think I'm look-ing for attention or something. And poor Oddie. She loves her dad so much. Last night he came into my room. He touched me again and pushed his body against mine. He wanted me to touch him but I wouldn't. He said I'd better start getting over myself because Mom is cold and boring and a man has certain needs and if I don't give it to him there's only one other girl left. Oddie!! I don't know what to do Daddy! I don't know if he would really do something to Oddie but he's completely different when he gets like this. Hopefully I've told you everything already. You'll know what to do. I love you Daddy.
XXX Danielle

Magson looked up at Bruno Volschenk, sitting on the bed with his arms tightly crossed.

"Whatever she's written in that letter," said Danielle's stepfather, "it's not true. I didn't touch her. I'm not like that. Danielle had issues."

"You have nothing to say about my daughter," said Daniël Ferreira.

"She and her mother were constantly fighting. To make up lies about me was probably her plan to go and live with her father."

"You shut up about Danielle!"

"Mr. Ferreira, please," said Menck. "I understand you're upset, but threatening and yelling isn't helping the situation."

"Nothing can help the situation," said Daniël Ferreira, head down. "It's too late. Danielle is dead."

A tear dripped from his chin on to his trousers.

Thirteen

May 22, 2014. Thursday.

Danielle Ferreira was smiling at him. Her light brown eyes were smiling, too. A blonde lock had fallen down the side of her face.

Danielle had loved the ocean, Magson now knew. Sea, sand, sun and her sister. She had found as much pleasure in building sand castles with Odette on the beach as she had surfing. Jeffreys Bay had been her favorite. She hadn't known what she wanted to be yet.

The newspaper report encircling the photo was a request for the public's assistance, in particular anyone who might have given her a lift on Friday, May 16, or seen her aboard a bus.

Magson leafed through the rest of *Die Burger*, listless, scanning the headlines but not reading any of the reports. One of the readers' letters drew his attention. "Concerned" from Brackenfell wanted to know how many more young girls had to be murdered before the "incompetent police" would catch the killer.

Magson closed the newspaper, not even bothering with the sports section.

"Warrant Magson, I just want to say again I'm sorry."

"Long forgotten, Mr. Ferreira." Not entirely, Magson had realized earlier when he'd just scratched his itchy nose.

"And thank you for not laying a charge."

"I don't lay frivolous charges, Mr. Ferreira. Come up to my office."

Daniël Ferreira looked even worse than yesterday. Unshaven, greasy hair, bags under his puffy red eyes. His shirt had a stain and looked as if he'd slept in it, the jacket was crooked. And Magson could smell yesterday's alcohol on him.

The elevator took them to the fifth floor. Magson punched in a code at the security gate and pushed it open. He shut it behind them. The tortured shriek of the hinges echoed along the uncarpeted corridors—and in Daniël Ferreira's head, judging by the contorted expression on his face and the fingers pressing against his temple.

They walked down the corridor.

"What will happen now?"

"We're following up on all the leads we already have. There were reports in most of the Cape and Southern Cape newspapers this morning, requesting the public's help. As the phone calls come in, we'll follow up."

"I meant with Volschenk."

"Oh." Magson motioned for Daniël Ferreira to enter his office. "I passed all the information on to FCS. That's the Family Violence, Child Protection and Sexual Offences Unit. It's their mandate. An investigating officer will contact you soon, but I'll give you their contact details anyway." Magson met the man's eyes. "But I have to tell you, their focus will be on the sister, Odette, to ensure her safety."

"But what about Danielle? That bastard molested her!"

"I'm sorry, Mr. Ferreira, but there simply isn't enough evidence to build a case against him. Such cases are difficult enough with a complainant. Without Danielle's testimony …"

"What about the letter? That's her testimony!"

"I wish it was enough, Mr. Ferreira. FCS will investigate. If they get more evidence against Mr. Volschenk, they may take it further. I just want you to understand that the chances are slim."

"But it's him. It's his fault. He is the reason Danielle is dead. If it weren't for him, she wouldn't have run away. And then she would still have been alive."

How many times had he himself gone down the road of "if." His always started with, *If Emma didn't get sick …* But it changed nothing. "I wish there was something I could do, Mr. Ferreira."

"It's not right. He can't get away with this."

"Mr. Ferreira, I can only try to imagine how you must feel. But I know what it feels like to lose someone. I know how powerless you feel. How angry. You want revenge. I didn't know Danielle, but it's obvious she loved you very much." Magson held the man's eyes with his. "Danielle wouldn't want you to do something stupid."

Daniël Ferreira looked away. "I have to go back to work. But I don't have the energy."

"Let me give you a number. It's a trauma counselor. Go and talk to her, Mr. Ferreira. You need help dealing with this sort of thing. You can't do it on your own."

One of the more promising tips had come from a woman employed at the Buffeljags River BP outside Swellendam. She was convinced that she had sold a cooldrink to Danielle on Friday. The reason she remembered Danielle was because the girl had made an unusual comment about the flowers they used to brighten the washing-up area in the bathroom. According to the woman, Danielle had said it was "nice that there are still people who just want to make something beautiful for someone else." It had made an impact on the woman due to the cynical undertone. The girl had also had a "look," her eyes were dull and "slow;" she hadn't smiled at all. After the report in the paper, she now wondered whether Danielle hadn't been trying to tell her something.

It made sense. That BP was a popular petrol station and resting spot for long-distance travelers. Magson had stopped there for petrol himself, sometimes just to stretch his legs or use the restrooms, on their way to Oudtshoorn to visit Em-

ma's sister. But what really added to the potential of this information was the fact that, unlike the majority of tips, this
one could be verified.

Because petrol stations had security cameras.

Magson looked at the photos of the blonde girl who had
now joined the others on the wall in the operational room. The
same photo that had been in the newspaper—a smiling, vibrant Danielle. And the photo of her body next to the Vissershok Road—a wet, dead Danielle.

Four dead girls now.

Magson typed Ronel Volschenk's number into his cellphone.
He was restless.

"Hello?"

"Mrs. Volschenk. It's Warrant Officer Magson. Have you
decided how long you will be staying yet?"

"No. We'd like to get Odette back at home, try to get things
more normal for her, but we still have to complete the arrangements to take Danielle to George. And the thing with the letter.
I don't understand why she would write such things."

"Mrs. Volschenk, have you considered the possibility that
it might be the truth?"

"No. Bruno is a good man. He's always been a good father
to Danielle. Took care of her as if she were his own. He would
never do such a thing."

"Have you had any contact with her father?"

"Yes, he was here. Fortunately, Bruno had gone to buy a
few things. Daniël wanted to know whether I'd spoken to the
police yet. Whether I would testify against Bruno. He was fu-
rious when I told him I have nothing to say against Bruno."

"Mrs. Volschenk, I think you should consider staying
somewhere else for the remainder of your time here."

"Why?"

"I'm just a bit concerned about Mr. Ferreira."

"Concerned that he might do something to Bruno?"

"Mr. Ferreira is very emotional at the moment."

"I'll talk to Bruno, but he won't want to go and hide."

"There's another reason I phoned, Mrs. Volschenk. We received information that Danielle might have been seen at a

petrol station near Swellendam. The security videos are on the way and I'd like you to have a look and identify Danielle if it's her. And see if you notice anything else."

"Yes. Of course."

He looked at the photo of the girl. Why did so many mothers struggle to believe their daughters when they said that a father or stepfather was molesting them? And Danielle had known her mother would not believe her. How alone she must have felt. Of course it was not impossible that Bruno Volschenk was innocent—it didn't take long for a murder detective to develop a cynical character, and he had been doing this job for far too long. Still, the letter had an authentic feel.

Doctor Michelle Hurter's office was slightly larger than his, but much better furnished. They sat in leather chairs directly opposite each other. The chair was comfortable enough to sleep in and awake without any pain. Magson estimated her somewhere in her late thirties, perhaps early forties. She was wearing a blue knitted polar neck, the sleeves covering half her hands. The thick dark eyebrows immediately drew attention to her dark eyes. Her hair was tied back, except for one lock she kept tucked behind her ear. She didn't wear much make-up, and she didn't need it. Her shoes lay on the carpet in front of her chair, and she was sitting with her right arm on the arm-rest, her legs tucked underneath her, as if she were ready to listen to a friend's story. A juicy story, because she was leaning forward, her attention completely focused on him.

Magson sat with his elbows on his knees. "I'm sorry it took me so long to come back."

"I'm glad you did."

"I started taking the pills." He looked down. "Last week-end."

"Any side-effects?" As if he had been supposed to start then.

"No."

"How are you at the moment?"

"All right. We found another girl on Monday."

"I saw in the paper."

"What the paper doesn't say is that she wrote a letter to

her dad before she ran away to come see him. Because her stepfather had started molesting her. She wrote the letter and posted it in case she didn't have the courage to tell her dad. But then a serial killer crossed her path."

"You see a lot of injustice."

For a moment he looked at her, the dark eyes. "I see only injustice. Do you know why she ran away? Not because her stepfather was molesting her. Because she couldn't talk to her mother. Her mother doesn't believe what she wrote in the letter."

"This girl had no one who listened to her."

"No."

"What about you? Do you have someone who listens to you?"

He looked at her. Then down, at the carpet, at her shoes in front of the chair, the one lying on its side. "I always talked to Emma."

"Emma is another injustice."

"Emma didn't deserve to suffer like that."

"And you?"

He looked at her.

"Did you deserve to suffer along with her?"

He opened his mouth, but didn't answer.

"Emma was the most important person in your life."

He nodded.

"Every day you work with death and heartache and people at their very worst. Emma provided balance."

She had.

"She was your anchor. And now that she's gone, you're just adrift."

That was exactly how it was. And his boat was rusted. With a hole in the hull.

"Tell me about the people in your life."

"Well …" His throat was stuck and he had to clear it. "There is my partner."

"Tell me about him."

"He's younger. He turned forty last year. Wife, two children. Good detective. Good partner."

"Good friend?"

"We're not bosom buddies, but ... ja."

"Who else?"

"Just people at work."

"And your son?"

"He's in England."

"How is your relationship?"

"It's difficult. The distance and ... he works hard."

"What does he do?"

"He's in IT. Doctor Hurter, I don't want to offend you, but I can't see how this is going to help."

She smiled. "Do you know what the most important thing is when you lose your anchor? To look up, out at sea. So you can see where you should row to."

"I see nothing."

"You saw me. Maybe you're right. Maybe I'm just an empty ship. But what if I'm a lighthouse ..."

May 23, 2014. Friday.

As Magson pulled the Jetta into the garage, his thoughts returned to Daniël Ferreira, who still wasn't answering his phone. Was he trying to drink away the pain? The recordings from the security cameras at the Buffeljags BP would arrive tomorrow and he wanted Danielle's father to be there too. It bothered him that the man was not answering.

He locked the gate and walked to the porch. Perhaps he should ask Hout Bay to send a couple of uniforms around to look in on Daniël Ferreira.

"What the hell?"

There was a dog sitting on a blanket, its leash tied to the handrail next to the steps. Magson looked around. Was this Menck's doing? Had he suffered a sudden impulse to clown around again? Magson saw no one and turned back to the small dark-brown creature.

"How did you get in here?"

A bag of dog food leaned against the wall. He looked at the dog and up at the dark sky. He really didn't want to deal with this. If this was Menck's handiwork ...

He took out his phone and selected the number. At the first sound leaving Menck's mouth he set off, "Is this your idea of a joke?"

"You'll have to be more specific, but I am sure I'm innocent."

"The dog."

"What dog?"

"The dog on my porch."

"Is there a dog on your porch?"

"Ja. Did you put it here?"

"Mags, I didn't put a dog on your porch. What kind of dog is it?"

"I don't know. Did you really not do this?"

"No."

Magson rubbed his face. This was worse, because who else would have done such a thing?

"All right. See you tomorrow."

It wouldn't have been the Bradleys. No. It had been too long ago, and besides, these days they maintained an uneasy relationship comprised mostly of nodding.

The dog was watching him. Its long tongue—pink with a bluish purple blemish—moved up and down. It had some seriously long teeth, as well.

"What kind of dog are you, anyway?"

The dog was slightly larger than a Jack Russell, the body perhaps a bit too long. Its fur was dark brown with darker patches, like distorted stripes. There was a kink in its tail.

"Several kinds, by the looks of it."

There was a silver disc on the collar. The owner's details? A telephone number?

"All right." He went down on one knee. "I'm just going to have a look at the disc around your neck."

The dog just sat, watching him, its head cocked to the left.

He reached for the disc, slowly. "Don't bite me. I have a gun."

The dog got up and came closer, sniffing his hand. It looked friendly enough. Magson petted its head. The fur was softer than he expected. He moved his hand down the side of the dog's head and took the disc between his thumb and index finger. ROMMEL.

"Rommel."

The dog barked, its multicolored tongue bobbing up and down.

"All right. So I'm assuming that's your name." Who would name a dog Rommel? Rubbish. He turned the disc over, but there was nothing on the back. Fantastic.

He looked at the dog, the deep brown eyes, the constantly moving eyebrows. He sighed. "I suppose you can stay here tonight. After all, this probably wasn't your idea. But don't get too comfortable. And you stay outside."

He untied the leash and led the dog around to the back garden. It trotted alongside him, happily enough, sniffing here and there. Magson clicked the mechanism to remove the leash and the dog jogged around the small lawn and in the garden, investigating and sniffing everything. It lifted its leg and marked the white stinkwood.

"I said don't get too comfortable."

Magson walked back around the house, took the blanket and food inside. He hunted around the kitchen until he spied the light blue tin plate in one of the cupboards. Hannes's, from when he'd had that friend whose father had been an ex-soldier and had taken them on a couple of camping and fishing trips. After the first one, Hannes had returned to explain to them how to start a fire using flint, before demonstrating all sorts of knots he had learned and describing how you could get fresh water from leaves as the grand finale. He put the plate on the counter. Now he just needed something for water.

At last he settled for the plastic bucket and opened the back door. The evening air touched his face and ran cold fingers down his neck.

The dog rose, wagging its tail.

Magson filled the bucket with water and the tin plate with pellets. As he placed it next to the bucket, the dog licked his hand.

"You're welcome."

The dog started eating with gusto.

Magson watched for a while. He laid out the blanket against the wall.

After he had eaten as well—*boerewors* and mash—he switched on the television and sat down on the sofa. It was chilly and he fetched a jacket. On his way back, there was a bump against the back door. The dog. It was rather cold. And hadn't the paper forecast rain for tonight?

He unlocked the back door. The dog was standing on the mat, tail wagging, eyes staring up at him.

"All right. You can sleep in the kitchen. Just because it's bloody cold and it might rain."

He moved the blanket to the corner of the kitchen. The dog remained on the doorstep.

"Come in." He patted the blanket.

The dog entered and looked at him. He locked the door and unfolded a newspaper, positioning it so one half was upright against the door.

"Listen, because this is very important. This is your spot if you need to do your business. If you lift your leg against the fridge or the food cupboard, I'm burying you in the garden tomorrow."

The dog looked at him with its cocked head, wagging its tail.

Magson felt bad. And ashamed. "That was a horrible thing to say. I'm sorry. But don't lift your leg against the fridge, all right?"

He left the dog there and returned to the sofa. The television programs nowadays left much to be desired, particularly these stupid reality shows. Why these things were so popular, he could not understand. He longed for a good old Jan Scholtz series, like *Die Binnekring* or *Die Vierde Kabinet*. Emma had loved it and he had remained awake until the end of every episode. Then they would discuss it and speculate about what might happen next week.

Something pressed against his foot. The dog was lying on the carpet, its head on his shoe. He reached down, stroking behind its ears, and noticed the white on the sides of the snout.

"Ja, so here we are, hey? Getting old alone, left behind by our people. I just don't understand why they named you Rommel."

The dog raised its eyebrows at the sound of its name, lowered it again.

May 24, 2014. Saturday.

"I wonder where Daniël Ferreira is," said Magson behind the Corolla's steering wheel.

"Some people just want to shut the world out," said Menck.

"I'd feel a lot better if he would just answer his phone."

"Well, we saw the Volschenks this morning, so we know he didn't do something stupid."

Ronel Volschenk had watched the security recording and identified the blonde girl getting out of a kombi, walking to the restroom, entering the shop next to it and pausing at the birdcage before getting back into the kombi as her daughter. There had been three men with her in the kombi. One with short hair and a goatee, one with long braided hair and a full beard, and the third with dreadlocks. They appeared somewhere between twenty and thirty years old. Ronel Volschenk had never seen them before.

The kombi was an older Volkswagen model. Tinted windows on the side. Trailer. But Magson had been much more interested in the licence plate. CY. Bellville.

Music oozed from the flat. Menck knocked louder in order to be heard above the crunchy electric guitars. Eventually, the door opened, revealing a man staring at them. He was wearing only jeans, not properly buttoned. His dreadlocks hung onto his bare shoulders. There was a tattoo on the left side of his chest, a symbol of some kind, and something resembling a thorny rose vine twined around his right forearm. A silver ring curled around the center of his lower lip.

"Kempen Luckhoff?" asked Magson.

"Who are you?"

"Warrant Officer Magson. This is Warrant Officer Menck."

The man had no interest in their identification cards. "What do you want?" He dug his hands deep into his pockets.

"Do you want to go put a shirt on?"

"No. I want to know what you want."

"Do you know this girl?" Magson showed him the photo of Danielle Ferreira.

"No. Is that all?"

"Are you sure, Mr. Luckhoff?"

"Yes, I'm sure."

The music's volume decreased. Inside the flat a girl appeared around a corner. She had long black hair and held the duvet wrapped around her to her chest. Magson looked past Luckhoff's shoulder.

Luckhoff noticed, but didn't look around. "Is that all? Because I'm busy."

"I'm afraid we'll need to clear this matter up first."

"I told you I don't know her. So there. Matter cleared up." He started closing the door.

"Mr. Luckhoff, we have a security video of you getting into your kombi with this girl at the BP outside Swellendam. Last Friday. There were two other men with you."

Luckhoff sighed, looked at Magson and at the photo once more. "Last Friday."

"Yesterday, a week ago," said Magson.

"Me and my band came back from a couple of gigs in Knysna last Friday. We picked up a girl, somewhere outside George, I think. I guess this could be her."

"And what happened to her?"

"I don't know. She got off on Voortrekker."

Magson just looked at him.

"Is that all?"

"Mr. Luckhoff, this girl is dead. She was murdered."

"Oh. Shit." He said it without emotion.

"You don't look shocked."

"Why should I? I didn't know her. To stand here now making a scene would be fake. Life hangs by an ephemeral thread that could be cut at any moment."

"Who are the other two men who were with you?"

"They won't be able to tell you any more."

"We'll have to talk to them anyway."

Luckhoff sighed. "Bertus Malherbe and Hugo Keyser. We're just a rock band."

"What is your band's name?" asked Menck.

"Ystersaag."

Hacksaw.

May 25, 2014. Sunday.

Magson was up to his elbows in suds and dishes when the dog started barking and ran out the back door. Moments later the bell rang. He shook off most of the foam and went to open the front door. Menck waved from the sidewalk. The dog was standing on its hind legs, paws against the gate, barking. Magson enjoyed the scene for a few seconds before walking to the gate.

"Ja, all right now," he told the dog.

"So this is the famous dog-on-the-porch," said Menck. "Looks a bit like a mongrel."

"There's no need to be nasty." He opened the gate.

Menck bent down to stroke the dog's head. "Does he feed you?" And to Magson, "We definitely need to look into this rock band."

"I sincerely hope you didn't come all the way just to tell me that."

"I asked Ben if he knows them. He's seen them live a couple of times."

"Well, given your taste in music, I'm not surprised."

"You know, I see your lips moving, but I can't hear a thing you're saying."

Magson motioned for Menck to enter the house. The dog threaded between their feet.

"Anyway, Ben says they're a post-grunge nu-metal band, whatever the hell that's supposed to mean."

"Coffee? Beer?"

"I won't say no to a beer."

They went to the kitchen and Magson took two Windhoeks from the fridge.

"Thanks." Menck took a good mouthful, swallowed and shivered. "Shit, it's cold."

"Because the bloody fridge's thermostat doesn't work

properly. Now that it's winter, the thing is practically a freezer."

"Must be hell on your tooth."

Magson gave him a look. "If you came here to pester me about my tooth, you can take your beer and go."

Menck laughed and slapped his leg to make the dog jump up against him. He stroked the brown fur and read the name tag. "Rommel." He looked at Magson. "Rubbish or Nazi?"

Magson shook his head. "Didn't your mother teach you the concept of tact?"

"Have you figured out where he came from yet?"

"No. In case you forgot, I'm investigating a series of murders."

"Why don't you just keep him? He looks at home already."

"Didn't Casey want a dog?"

"Casey wants a horse. No other animal will do." Menck placed his hands on both sides of the dog's head, shaking it left and right. The dog had its paws on Menck's wrists, baring its impressive teeth, growling. Menck growled back. "But he sure is cute. Yes, you are."

Magson looked at the muscled body stepping on its hind legs.

Menck pushed the dog away and dug in his jacket's pocket. "Look what I found." The dog jumped back up against his leg. Menck held a CD case in his left hand.

Magson took it and looked at the black-and-white cover. A girl on her knees. She was wearing a simple, shapeless white dress, her long dark hair hanging over her face. A medieval manacle was clamped around her left wrist. She held the chain and tried to free herself with a hacksaw. The saw's red handle was the only color.

"Where did you get this thing?"

Menck swallowed some beer and grinned. "I'm a detective, don't you know."

Magson gave him a look. "I see your point, but these things always have unpleasant covers. For shock value, to draw attention."

"Read the lyrics."

The dog had given up and trotted out the back door. Or maybe it had gone to lift its leg ...

"It fits," said Menck, raising the bottle to his lips. "They live in the right area. They don't have fulltime jobs. And when it comes to picking up teenage girls, what could be easier than being in a rock band?"

Magson nodded. "What about Karlien Pretorius? That was definitely not one of these three." He looked at the photo on the back of the CD. Luckhoff, dreadlocks and black make-up around his eyes, wearing a straitjacket, the other two flanking him further back.

"We've always just suspected it was connected to the others. Maybe our suspicion was wrong."

"Maybe." Magson thought for a while. "One of them, Keyser, did seem a bit uncomfortable."

"He did."

Menck gulped down the last of his beer and placed the empty bottle on the counter. "Listen, I have to go help Casey build the Eiffel Tower. Using nothing but my astounding ingenuity and recyclable materials from around the house."

"Sounds exciting. Is that why you brought me homework as well?"

"We are partners, aren't we?"

Magson saw Menck off, locked the gate and the front door. His beer was still unopened in the kitchen and he returned it to the refrigerator. He finished washing up. Pellets and clean water for the dog.

He took the CD case, opening it on his way to the TV room. He inserted the disc into the hi-fi's tray and pressed PLAY. The first song started serenely and then exploded. Electric guitars and drums. A male voice alternating between singing and screaming. Mostly just noise, thought Magson. He removed the booklet and started reading the lyrics. And saw what Menck had meant. Negative aggression. Dark focus. And all of it directed at a female "you."

freefall

fall through the air

without wings without hope
grope at you at you but you turn away
fall to the ground
without chute without word
call to you to you but you walk away

you take everything
you take everything
you make me nothing nothing nothing

fall through clouds
without wings without hope
search for you for you but it's too late
fall to the ground
without scars without death
spit on you on you on your face

now i take everything
i take everything
i make you nothing nothing nothing

Fourteen

May 26, 2014. Monday.

In the interrogation room, Magson took his seat in the chair. He glanced through the glass table at Kempen Luckhoff's faded jeans, torn open on the knee. Luckhoff's hands lay still in his lap and he leaned back in his chair. He looked bored.

"Mr. Luckhoff, you're not under arrest, but I want to explain your rights to you."

Luckhoff listened without reaction.

"Mr. Luckhoff, do you understand these rights?"

"I think there's a song here."

"Do you understand your rights as I have explained it to you?"

"Yes. I don't have to say anything and I can get someone to come hold my hand if I want. Can we move on? I have things to do and nothing to contribute to your investigation."

"I appreciate your willingness to help, Mr. Luckhoff."

Luckhoff looked around the room again and sighed.

"I'm sorry, but I have to ask," said Menck. "How do you get your hair like that?"

"With a comb, my hands and dread wax."

"Dread wax?"

Luckhoff looked up at the ceiling. "You buy it in a shop."

"Someone told me you dip it in the ocean."

Luckhoff turned to Menck. "Only if you live off the land."

Magson placed a photo of Danielle Ferreira on the table. "So on Friday, May 16, you and Bertus Malherbe and Hugo Keyser picked up this girl by the side of the N2 outside George. Is that correct?"

Luckhoff looked at Magson. "So it is like on TV. You do actually have to say the same thing over and over and over again."

"Is it correct, Mr. Luckhoff?"

"Yes, I think so. I didn't really pay attention. I was driving, after all."

"Mr. Malherbe and Mr. Keyser recognized her."

"Well, then you already have your answer, don't you?"

"And you dropped her off later that same Friday?"

"Yip. And she was very much alive."

"Can you wash it?" asked Menck.

Luckhoff looked at him. "Yes. Can you believe it? You can wash it."

"How?"

"With shampoo and water, twice a week."

Menck was beaming. "That's what I love about this job. I learn something new every day."

"Where did you drop off the girl?" asked Magson.

"Voortrekker Road," said Luckhoff. "In Bellville."

"Where on Voortrekker Road?"

"At the Eskom building."

"At what time?"

"I don't know. I don't wear a watch." Luckhoff pushed up his sleeve to corroborate his claim. "Modern people are way too obsessed with time."

"There's a song," said Menck.

Luckhoff glanced at him, clearly irritated by the remark.

"You must have some idea," said Magson. "Afternoon? Evening?"

"Afternoon."

"It's quite a distance from George to Bellville. What did you talk about?"

"What people usually talk about when they drive a long way. Bullshit. I mostly just listened to the music."

"You must remember something?"

"I can't even remember her name. She stood by the side of the road. We had space in the kombi. I stopped and we gave her a lift. I didn't go on a date with her."

Magson placed a second photograph on the table. Danielle's body at the crime scene. Luckhoff looked at it. He had no discernible reaction.

"Her name was Danielle, Mr. Luckhoff."

Luckhoff looked Magson in the eye. "Each one of us has a number. When it's up, it's up. Car accident. Cancer. Murder."

"Doesn't it bother you?" asked Menck.

"It's part of the human condition. People are born. People die."

"No, man. I'm talking about that ring in your lip."

Luckhoff sighed and rolled his eyes.

"I think it would really irritate me."

"Then it's a good thing you don't have one."

"Hmm. You see, Warrant Magson here is a child of the sixties, but my teen years were spent in the eighties. All the pop stars had earrings those days. I wanted one myself at some stage, but then I joined the police."

"There are less conspicuous places."

"Do you have more? Just don't show me if it's through the nipples."

Luckhoff opened his mouth and stuck out his tongue.

Magson looked at the silver stud and repressed the urge to shake his head.

"You can't tell me that's comfortable," said Menck.

"More comfortable than a tie," said Luckhoff.

"I wonder what my wife would say if I arrive at home with a stud in my tongue."

"Smile. A chick is never the same afterwards." Luckhoff jiggled his tongue. "And you can always get one for her, as well."

Menck stroked his goatee, snapped his fingers and pointed at Luckhoff. "You know, that's not a bad idea. A matching set, his and hers, for our anniversary."

Luckhoff raised his hands, spreading his arms. "Glad I could help. Can I go now?"

"I listened to your music," said Magson.

"Well, I'm impressed. But, no offense, I don't think some-one of your age would really appreciate it. It's not exactly Rina Hugo."

"You're right. It's not really my taste. But it was interest-ing."

Luckhoff smiled, pushing back his dreadlocks. "Something you can't say about Rina Hugo."

Magson slid the CD across the table. Next to the photo of Danielle's body. "What's the story behind the cover?"

"I like a cover with a deeper meaning."

"And what is the meaning here?"

"It depends on who is looking at it. That's what gives a cover meaning. It has to be open to interpretation. It has to have different meanings for different people. Depending on who they are, what shit they've gone through, it changes what they see. It's the same with a good song. When you listen to it, you have to find something in it yourself. Then it becomes your song. Then it means something. Not like this superficial pop crap they're always playing on the radio. That's so fake."

"And your music is what, honest?"

"Yes. Look at these pop chicks. On one hand they're singing about this wonderful love they have for The One. But they're wearing almost nothing and they sell their CDs by advertising sex. In real life they fall around from one relationship to the next. Or they go all out for the slutty image. Like Miley Cyrus. Do you think that's who she is in real life? I doubt it. They're all a bunch of fakes. The boy bands are even worse. Always looking so pretty and wholesome and they sing their love ballads. But half of them are actually gay and the rest fuck every chick they can get their hands on. It's all bullshit."

Magson tapped the CD case. "Your world is very negative, Mr. Luckhoff."

Luckhoff leaned forward, resting his arms on the table, and looked him straight in the eye. "You're a policeman. Are you going to sit there and tell me the world is a happy place? Look at this photo. How many photos like this have you seen? And I'm sure this is one of the better ones. She still has her clothes on. It doesn't even look as if there's any blood."

"Blood isn't necessary for a cruel murder."

"You see? You know what I'm talking about. I can see it in your eyes. They're dull." Luckhoff shook his head, his eyes never leaving Magson's. "I can see you're not happy."

"We're not talking about me, Mr. Luckhoff."

"You spend every day looking at the arsehole of humanity. And then you go home to the same woman you're probably so sick of by now, you wish you had never seen her in the first place."

Magson had to fight the urge to grab Luckhoff, realizing that Menck was aware of him. He looked at the photos of Danielle Ferreira, tried to get Emma's face out of his mind, tried to keep his face expressionless.

"But that's not your world." Menck speaking in his stead, trying to protect him. "I can't imagine that you stay with the same girl for long, so why—"

The rage boiled up too rapidly. "What about her?" Magson asked over Menck, glaring at Luckhoff, tapping his finger on Danielle's photo. "What did you see in her?"

Luckhoff sat back, looked at him and laughed a single note through his nose. "I told you, I didn't really talk to her."

Magson wanted to slap the smug expression from his face, but he snatched the CD instead, snapped it open, yanked out the booklet and tossed the case back on the table. "It says here you write all the lyrics."

Luckhoff seemed amused. "Yes. The music as well. Some-times with Bertus."

Magson turned the pages to one of the songs. "They play in my head," he read. "Dark, dark images. Turn me into a shell, a shell, a shell. But I can't beat it. Don't repeat it. I bleed out. And I scream out. The dark, dark images. Make me blind. Make me blind. Dark, dark images. I can't prevent it. Don't repent it. I yield." Magson turned the booklet around and shoved it into Luckhoff's face. "Your words."

Luckhoff looked back at him. "'A man who has not passed through the inferno of his passions has never overcome them.' Carl Jung."

"Danielle Ferreira was in your kombi. You were the last person to see her alive. She was tortured. Raped. Murdered." Magson shook the booklet. "Are those the dark images you see?"

"I wasn't the last person to see her alive," said Luckhoff, "because I didn't kill her. I use my music to work through my shit. I play my guitar. I scream. I write a song and get it out."

"And that's enough?"

"Maybe you should try it."

"Breaking him won't be easy," said Menck. "We'll have to push the other two."

Magson turned to him. "Don't step in for me again, all right?"

"What?"

"*Ag*, don't act like you don't know. He makes a comment about Emma and you jump in to protect me."

"I just wanted to give you a chance to—"

"I don't need you to give me a chance!"

"Well, I'm glad to see some fire in you at last. It's about time."

"I'm sorry if I took too long to get over my wife's death."

"That's not what I said, Mags."

"Not everyone has your perfect life."

"Oh, my life is perfect, hey?"

"You go home at night and your wife is there waiting for you. Your children …"

"And what? Am I supposed to feel guilty about it? Luckhoff is so full of shit, it practically oozes from his pores, but he is right about one thing: People are born and people die. And all any of us can do is the part in between."

"Luckhoff is not the only one that's full of shit." He paused at Menck's side. "Kathy is still alive, so don't preach to me." He stomped out the door and straight into Captain Kritzinger.

"I have bad news, Mags. They found Daniël Ferreira. Shot dead."

"What?"

"Somewhere near Gugulethu," said Kritzinger. "They found

him on Saturday. No wallet. Don't know how he ended up there."

"What about his car?"

"No sign of it."

Magson sighed and shook his head. Had Daniël Ferreira been busy with something that cost him his life? "Well, I need to go interrogate Malherbe."

"Take a break first."

He looked at Kritzinger. "I don't need—"

"Mags. Take a break."

Magson sat down at the table in the interrogation room again, this time opposite Bertus Malherbe. Malherbe was wearing a black long-sleeved T-shirt, featuring something resembling a fusion between a Rorschach ink blot and a skull, the word STAIND in the eye sockets. He sat with his shoulders hunched forward, his hands pinched between his knees, his face cast downward. His dark brown hair, a long braid, hung down the center of his back. He had a full beard and four or five silver rings in his left ear.

It was just the two of them in the room. Magson didn't know where Menck was and he didn't particularly care.

Malherbe looked up. "I don't know anything else about that girl. She was alive when I last saw her."

Magson took care of the formalities first. "Mr. Malherbe, do you understand these rights as I have explained them to you?"

"Yes."

"Good. Let's go back to Friday, May 16." Magson placed the photograph of Danielle Ferreira on the table. "You and Kempen Luckhoff and Hugo Keyser picked up this girl on the N2 outside George. Is that correct?"

"Yes. She was walking and hiking. Kempen stopped and I asked where she was headed. She said she was going to Cape Town. Kempen said we're going to Bellville, we could give her a lift there, if she wanted. She got in."

"What happened then?"

Malherbe shrugged. "We just drove there."

"What did you talk about?"

"I sat in front next to Kempen. She sat in the back, with Hugo. The music was on. I didn't really talk to her that much. She said her name was Danielle and she was going to her dad. He's in Hout Bay. We talked a bit about the band and so on, but she wasn't all that chatty. She was …"

Magson raised his eyebrows. "Ja?"

"She was preoccupied. As if something was bothering her."

"Did she say what?"

Malherbe shook his head. "No."

"Where did you drop her off?"

"Voortrekker Road in Bellville."

"Where on Voortrekker Road?"

Malherbe's thumb scratched beneath his lower lip. "At the Eskom building. We turned right there."

"How would she get to Hout Bay from there?"

"I don't know." He scratched his beard. "Look, I don't know anything. Can't I go, please?"

"A young girl is dead, Mr. Malherbe. Surely you want her killer to be apprehended?"

"Yes. Obviously."

"Good. Then you won't mind helping us."

"But I don't know anything that could help." He crossed his arms.

Magson looked at him.

Malherbe shifted in his chair and gazed through the glass table top. His eyebrows were bunched together, his lips taut.

Magson kept looking.

Malherbe placed his hands on the table, palms up. "All I want to do is play in a good band. I just want to play my bass in a decent band."

At this point Menck would have said or asked something to take Malherbe on a detour. "Do you think Ystersaag is a 'decent band'?"

"Yes." With conviction. "Kempen has talent. Our fan base is growing and we've even been talking to a record company. We're just looking for a breakthrough."

"So where does this CD come from then?" asked Magson. "If you're not with a record company yet."

"We recorded it on our own. And then we sell it mostly at gigs."

"That must have cost a pretty penny. How did you pay for it?"

"We saved up, everyone chipped in. You have to take that chance, back yourself and take the plunge. Get your music out there. One of these days it will start giving back. Kempen says payback's not a bitch, it's a willing groupie. You just have to be patient and take the punch."

"This picture," said Magson, tapping the CD case, "is this the way you like your 'groupies'?"

"What? No. That's just …"

"What?"

"It's just a cover. Kempen wanted a cover with meaning."

For a few moments Magson just looked at the young man across from him. Unlike Kempen Luckhoff, Malherbe yielded, looking down at the table. Magson slid the photo of Danielle's body next to the other one.

"Shit! Is that …" Malherbe's eyes flitted between the two photos.

Magson added another photo, a close-up of Danielle's face and the furrow around her throat. He wished her eyes were completely open so she could stare at Malherbe.

Malherbe pushed the photos away. "I don't want to see it."

"Why does it bother you so much, Mr. Malherbe? I would think someone who chooses this kind of cover for his CD wouldn't be so sensitive."

"It's not the same. That cover is fake. But she … Just the other day I was talking to her. And now she's just dead. And her neck …"

"It's interesting that you describe your cover as 'fake'. I had a long discussion with Mr. Luckhoff about how he despises 'fake' musicians."

"I didn't …" Malherbe sighed and looked at his lap.

Magson picked up the photo of Danielle and held it in front of Malherbe. "Look here, Mr. Malherbe. I said, look here."

Malherbe raised his head reluctantly and looked at the photo.

"Danielle Ferreira. Young. Full of life. This is how she looked on Friday when she got into that kombi with you, Mr. Luckhoff and Mr. Keyser. I know this because I have a security video that shows it happening. And that was the last time she was seen alive."

Magson took the post-mortem close-up of Danielle in his left hand and held it next to the other one in front of Malherbe's face. Malherbe looked down. "I said, look here!"

Malherbe only raised his head halfway, peeking from underneath his eyebrows.

Magson shook the photo. "This is what she looked like the next time she was seen. Before ..." He shook the photo of the living Danielle "... and after!" The dead Danielle again. "She was fifteen years old. She was tied up. She was tortured. She was hanged. And all of that happened after she got into *your* kombi!"

"No ..."

"Nobody saw her again. And not one of you has a proper alibi."

"I had nothing—"

"Shut up!" Magson jumped to his feet, the chair falling back against the wall. He grabbed the folder and dumped all the scene and autopsy photos onto the table. Malherbe cringed. "Look at her!"

Malherbe stared at the images.

"And look at your CD!" He snatched the case and smacked it down on top of the photos. "It's all rage and revenge. And it's always aimed at a girl."

Malherbe's eyes were large. He raised his hands. "I swear. I swear. I did nothing to her. Nothing. It's all—"

There it was. "It's all—?"

"Shit," said Malherbe, looking down.

Magson leaned across the table, placing his hands on top. "You have one question to answer, Mr. Malherbe. Are you willing to go to prison, for murder—for *murder*—to protect someone else? It's twenty-five years. That's before aggravating circumstances are taken into consideration. You can forget your dreams of making music. This CD is all you'll ever have." He grabbed the CD and hurled it like a frisbee past

Malherbe. It smashed into the wall, shattering onto the floor. "By the time you get out, your life will be over. Or you can decide—now, here—to help yourself."

"I don't know whether he did anything to her," Bertus Malherbe told his lap. "He just told us they had sex."

"Mr. Luckhoff?"

"No. Hugo. Hugo is obsessed with sex. He's always trying to pick up chicks at our gigs." He glanced at the photos, closed his eyes and dropped his forehead into his hand. "He told her he would take her to Hout Bay. But he really just wanted to take her home and f—uhm … have sex with her. We dropped her off at Hugo's."

Magson just looked at him for a moment. Menck would have been proud of his performance; he did enjoy some drama during an interrogation. Menck who seemed to think he could decide how long someone was allowed to mourn his wife, while he had no idea what it felt like. He realized he was glaring at Malherbe. "So what's this story about Voortrekker Road then?"

"Kempen phoned us. He said the police had come to talk to him and we should say we dropped the girl at the Eskom building on Voortrekker. Then all three of us have the same story and you'll move on quicker. Otherwise you'll try to nail Hugo."

"So. You and Mr. Luckhoff dropped Danielle Ferreira off at Hugo Keyser's residence."

"Yes."

"And that was the last time you saw her?"

"Yes."

"You're sure? Don't let me catch you in more lies, Mr. Malherbe."

"I am sure." Malherbe looked up, into Magson's eyes. "That was the last time I saw her. And she was completely okay. I swear it."

"Did Danielle go with Mr. Keyser freely?"

"Yes. She was glad about the lift."

Lambs to the slaughter, thought Magson. "And what did you and Kempen Luckhoff do after you dropped them off?"

"He dropped me at my place."

"And then?"

"Then he left."

"Where did he go?"

"Home. I think he went home."

"When did you see Keyser and Luckhoff again?"

"The next day. We had a band practice and that night we played a gig."

"Did one of them say anything about Danielle?"

"Kempen asked and Hugo said they had sex." Malherbe frowned, his eyes turning to his left. "But …"

"Ja?"

"He didn't go into detail the way he usually does."

"What about Sunday? Did you see them on Sunday?"

"I slept late on Sunday. Had a hangover. And I was just at home the whole day."

"Alone."

Malherbe's head dropped and he nodded.

With Bertus Malherbe's statement at Captain Kritzinger—so that he and Menck could complete the applications for search warrants—Magson was back in the interrogation room. With the third man who had been in the kombi with Danielle Ferreira.

Hugo Keyser had short dark hair, a goatee and a ring in his left eyebrow. His black long-sleeved T-shirt had no design or words on it, but a black string with a silver bullet hung around his neck. He had difficulty keeping his right leg from bobbing up and down while he nodded that he understood his rights.

"Would you say that out loud, please, Mr. Keyser?"

"Ja."

"All right. Friday, May 16. You and Mr. Kempen Luckhoff and Mr. Bertus Malherbe are on your way from Knysna when you pick up this girl outside George." For the third time he placed Danielle Ferreira's smile on the table. "Is that correct?"

"Ja."

"How were you sitting?"

"What?"

"In the kombi. Who sat where?"

"Hmm ... Kempen was driving. Bertus sat next to him. We were in the back."

"What did the girl say?"

"Hmm ... She was going to her dad. She said he lives in Hout Bay."

"Did she say why she was going to him?"

"No."

"It's several hundred kilometers from George to Bellville. Is that all she said?"

Keyser shrugged and scratched his neck. His knee was still bobbing up and down. "I can't remember. We just chatted."

"Where did she get off?"

"Bellville. We dropped her on Voortrekker Road."

"Where on Voortrekker Road?"

"At the Eskom building."

Magson nodded. "And when was this?"

"The afternoon. Probably around three, four."

"What did you do then?"

"Kempen dropped me off. I'm always first, because it's such a mission with my drum kit."

"And what did you do then?"

Keyser looked at the wall, rubbing the underside of his nose. "I hung around. Later the evening I went out for a bit. Why does it matter? By then we'd dropped her off a long time ago."

"So you saw Danielle Ferreira the last time in front of the Eskom building on Voortrekker Road?"

He licked his lips. "Ja."

"Are you sure, Mr. Keyser?"

"Ja." But he didn't sound entirely sure. He didn't look at Magson and his fingers were fiddling with each other.

Magson looked at him a while longer and sighed. "That's a shame."

Keyser looked up. "Why? Why is that a shame?"

"It's a shame, because your friends have changed their story in the meantime."

"What ... what did they say?"

"Why don't you rather tell me what really happened, Mr. Keyser. While you still have a chance to fix things."

The young man hesitated, looked away again. "No. We dropped her at the Eskom building. That's what really happened."

Magson looked at him and shook his head. "No, it's not. You told Danielle Ferreira that you would take her to Hout Bay. She believed you and got out with you at your residence. But taking her to Hout Bay was the last thing on your mind, wasn't it, Mr. Keyser?"

Keyser did not reply, but he was staring straight at Magson. His eyes were larger and his lips pressed tightly together. His fingers did not move. Even his leg had stopped bobbing.

"You had a different plan for her. This pretty, young girl you picked up at the side of the road. Because you like sex. You're always on the hunt. Maybe you would've taken her to Hout Bay. But first …"

Keyser still remained silent, but he didn't seem to be breathing now.

"First you took her inside your flat. And that was the last time Danielle was seen alive."

"No."

Magson stuck his finger in Keyser's face. "You are the last person who saw Danielle alive."

"No …"

"That is your friends' testimony. And this is what Danielle looked like when we found her." Like a card dealer, Magson placed photos in front of Keyser on the table, crime-scene photos, close-ups of Danielle Ferreira's face, wet from the rain.

Keyser looked pale. He swallowed. "I didn't …"

"This happened after she got out with you, after she went into your flat with you, after you closed the door behind you."

Keyser was swaying back and forth. His eyes flitted about the photos, blinking. He shook his head. "No. No, I didn't do anything to her. I swear. I did—I admit it—I did want to … have sex with her. But she didn't want to. I told her it was such a long trip, I just wanted to rest for a while. I chatted with her. Then I made my move. She freaked out. She just completely freaked out. Ran out of the flat. I tried to stop her. I told her I'm sorry; I'll take her to Hout Bay. But she wouldn't listen."

Magson looked at him. Took a deep, slow breath so that Keyser could hear it, sighed it out slowly. "I want to believe you, Mr. Keyser. I do. But now we have a problem. It's never a good idea to lie to the police. Because lies—" he shook his head "—lies have this nasty habit of coming out. And now that I know you lied to me, again and again, even after I gave you the opportunity to tell the truth, it is very difficult for me to believe anything you say."

"It's the truth. I swear it is."

"Just a few minutes ago the truth was that you dropped Danielle off on Voortrekker Road."

"It was Kempen! He said we should all say that."

Magson drummed with his fingers on the glass. He looked at Keyser. "Let me tell you what I think happened. You invited Danielle into your flat, maybe gave her something to drink, talked a bit. Then, when you wanted more, she—like you said—'freaked out'. And suddenly you're trapped in this situation."

Keyser was following every word.

"You tried to stop her. You just wanted to calm her down. But situations like that—it's adrenaline and everything happens so quickly—and here you have her now, and she is pressed against you, and you want her, and before you know it, it's too late."

"No."

"You don't know what to do. You can't just let her go. So you phone Mr. Luckhoff. Because he will know what to do."

"No."

"I don't think you wanted to kill her. I think you were trapped in a situation that got out of hand, and you were afraid. But Mr. Luckhoff said it was the only way."

"No. No. She freaked out and ran out of the flat. I just tried to kiss her, that's all. I didn't do anything else to her."

"Do you want to take this whole thing on you? Because that is what's going to happen. Your friends sat in that chair where you are sitting now and pointed their fingers at you. You are the one who will be put away for this and they will go on with their lives. Is that what you want?"

"But I didn't do anything!" Keyser slapped his hands against his thighs. "I didn't do anything to her!"

"Danielle Ferreira was fifteen years old."

Keyser swallowed. "I don't want to answer any more questions. I want to phone my dad."

Magson nodded. "I hope your dad has a lot of money. Because you are going to need a good lawyer, Mr. Keyser."

Half the afternoon was gone, but they were finally in the Corolla, heading to Kempen Luckhoff's residence. They drove in silence. Menck was staring out the window. Magson was watching the road. The only sound was the Corolla's engine and the tires on the tar.

Magson felt drained after the interrogations, but at the same time there was the adrenaline of a search warrant and solid suspects. His hands were itching to go through Luckhoff's stuff.

He could feel Menck brooding beside him. He who still had everything. Who knew nothing of loss. Who didn't understand how quickly, how deeply it could change you.

Daniël Ferreira had learned that. Was that why he had ended up in Gugulethu? Had he decided to go find justice for Danielle on his own? He'd just been a father who had loved his daughter.

And poor Danielle. Who had tried to get away from one sex offender just to walk straight into another one. Had Kempen Luckhoff's face been the last thing she had seen? His eyes emotionlessly watching her life drain away?

Are you going to sit there and tell me the world is a happy place? Look at this photo. How many photos like this have you seen?

Too many. Far, far too many. And the photos were nothing compared to the crime scenes. A woman, naked and half-eaten by maggots, raped, throat cut. A father who had shot his three children in their beds before botching his suicide. A man who had beaten his girlfriend's one-year-old boy to death with a pan because the child, whose nappy had been soiled, wouldn't stop crying. It had been ten years and he still remembered that terrible smell of blood in the Sizzlers massage parlor.

You know what I'm talking about. I can see it in your eyes. I can see you're not happy.

He had been. Once upon a time. He had been happy. They had been happy.

And then you go home to the same woman you're probably so sick of by now, you wish you had never seen her in the first place.

Magson glanced at his left hand gripping the steering wheel, the gold band on his ring finger. Luckhoff might see a lot, but he saw less than he thought. And the thing with people who thought they were clever was that after a while they started to believe it.

And that was when they fell.

Kempen Luckhoff's home was untidy, but remarkably clean. There were almost no dirty dishes in the kitchen and the entire place looked like it was cleaned often. Magson was not particularly surprised. The bodies had predicted as much. LCRC would go through every room in any case, searching for forensic evidence—vacuum cleaners and cleaning products had their limitations. But Magson was more interested in the victims' missing belongings. The killer kept their underwear and jewelry because the items had personal value for him. He would keep them somewhere, even though he knew how risky it was to do so. All Magson needed was Maryke Retief's gold necklace or Dominique Gould's sports panties marked with her initials.

He looked around. Clothes. CDs. Sheets of paper containing scribbled lyrics. Some guitars and other sound equipment. Hi-fi. Large speakers. Music magazines. PlayStation beneath the TV, controller on the carpet. Several video-game cases. Everything looked relatively new and like products of high quality. Luckhoff had to get money from somewhere.

"All right," said Magson to the LCRC members, "you have the descriptions of the underwear and jewelry. One of the victims' hockey equipment is missing. We're also looking for rope, sex toys, pornography and any weapons. Remember, the victims were held captive for a period of time, and they were hanged, so be on the lookout for any evidence of this. Finally, we're looking for an iron."

Magson nodded and they dispersed. Menck disappeared

into a room. Magson looked at the doorway and touched the nearest LCRC member's shoulder, satisfied that it was sergeant Stacy Faro. "Will you help me search the bedroom?"

"Sure."

Luckhoff had a double bed, unmade in black and gray. It was the only bed in the house and Magson noticed the absence of a head and foot higher than the mattress. No easy way to tie someone to the bed. The rest of the furnishings comprised a closet, a dresser and a table containing another hi-fi, a stack of CDs and miscellaneous items. Another guitar, an acoustic one, leaned against the wall. There was no obvious place to tie a rope in order to hang a person.

He decided to start with the closet and opened the first door. Clothes on the shelves, T-shirts, jerseys, some folded, some stuffed in. A stack of magazines. *Guitarist, Total Guitar, Metal Hammer*. Music, music, music. Looking at the numbers on the CNA price tags, for a moment Magson feared he had developed double vision.

"The man could open a plectrum shop," said Faro.

Magson turned around. "A what?"

"A plectrum shop."

"What the hell is a plectrum?"

"These plastic thingies." Faro wiggled a triangular disc in her latex-covered fingers. "You use it to play guitar." She demonstrated on an air guitar. "My little brother always dreamed of being Lenny Kravitz. Had the whole look and everything. Hair. Ripped jeans. Even the nose ring."

Magson looked at her.

"You don't know who Lenny Kravitz is, hey?"

He shook his head.

"Well, it didn't work out anyway."

He turned back to the closet, resuming his search through the magazines.

"Here's something."

Something more interesting than pieces of plastic, Magson hoped. "What?"

"Panties."

Bingo. Magson joined her at the dresser. A variety of female underwear filled the bottom drawer. A chill slipped through him. "It's a lot more than four."

"There are bras also."

If these were all trophies from victims …

First, Faro took several photographs of the drawer's contents. Then she started documenting the underwear, sealing each item in an evidence bag. In addition to a description of the panties Dominique had typically worn to hockey practice, they had a strong suspicion that Danielle had been wearing black panties, the companion to the black bra she'd had on when they had found her, a set her mother had bought her.

"Somebody kissed this one," said Faro. "Right on the …" She showed Magson the lipstick lips on the white cotton panties. "My brother would've liked this."

Magson frowned. "There was a girl here the first time we came to talk to Luckhoff. Maybe this is hers. Did you find any other women's clothes?"

"No, but I don't think this is one girl's things. They're all in different sizes."

"All right. Look through the black ones first." Magson read the description out loud. "And it would be a medium."

She searched, finally shaking her head. "No. Just a couple of G-strings. What is this tiny thing supposed to cover?"

The "tiny thing" was held up for Magson's inspection. "I don't know. Is there no jewelry or anything?" Of course, they would have seen it already, or at least have heard it scraping as Faro had moved underwear around.

"No. Just panties and bras."

Magson clicked his tongue and returned to the closet. The next two doors revealed clothes on coat hangers, shoes at the bottom. The last door wouldn't open.

"This is interesting. This door is locked." All the keyholes were empty. Where would Luckhoff hide the key?

And why?

"Magson!" someone called.

He left the bedroom, saw Menck entering the kitchen, and followed suit.

"Here."

A door in the kitchen led to the garage. Where the kombi was. As well as a large blue trunk. The lid was open.

"Well," said Magson. "What do we have here? Was this thing locked?"

"No, Warrant. I just lifted the lid."

"So he locks one of his closet doors," mused Magson, mostly to himself, "but a trunk filled with drugs he leaves unlocked."

"What's in the closet?" asked Menck.

"I don't know. Haven't found the key yet."

"Well, let's go find it. I'd like to know what he's hiding in there."

Magson looked on the table, underneath the hi-fi, and started with the dresser again. Behind him, Menck was searching the closet. Plectrums were not the only items Luckhoff had in abundance; he was clearly quite fond of candles, as well. A dresser in a bedroom seemed a strange place to keep such a collection of candles.

"Ta-daa!"

He turned around and saw a key with light gray tufts clinging to the shaft in Menck's blue latex fingers. "Where did you find that?"

Menck shook his head. "Did you never hide stuff when you were at school?"

He walked over to Menck.

"Prestik. A boy's best friend when he needs some privacy." He held the key for Magson. "So. Let's see."

The teeth slid all the way into the keyhole and turned easily. The lock clicked open. Magson grabbed hold of the knob and opened the door.

He gave a step backwards.

He stared at the tall gas cylinder.

Menck crouched in front of the closet. "What do we have here?"

Like the one holding the helium.

"Nitrous oxide. Gas mask. Clothes pegs. Dildo. A woman's ..."

The cylinder had been what Hannes had found. In the cupboard in the garage. Together with the rubber hose and the oven roasting bag and the elastic band. Days later, when Magson finally had gone to get rid of the stuff, he'd noticed that the door had not been properly closed, half of the rubber hose lying on the floor. What had Hannes been looking for? Pliers? An old rag? What did it matter? He had seen the cylinder, the hose and the rest, and he had figured it out. Perhaps not immediately, but Hannes had never been stupid.

"Mags."

"What?"

"Are you still having a look," asked Menck, "or can LCRC do their thing?"

Magson motioned for them to continue and moved out of the way. When had Hannes known? How long had he carried it in silence prior to his mother's funeral?

"Our dentist used laughing gas," said Menck. "When I was at school. Always told me to just breathe naturally and I never listened. We had some good times, Doctor Dave and I."

The inside of the closet flashed repeatedly as the sergeant took photos.

"Do dentists still use nitrous oxide? Not that you'd—" He glanced at Magson and turned back to the closet. "All I get these days are injections. Which results in me chewing half-way through my cheek by the time its effects have subsided. I'm going for a smoke."

Magson stepped closer and really looked at the contents of the closet. A gas mask, a translucent triangle that fit over the nose and mouth, connected to the gas cylinder with a rubber hose. A dildo the shape of a test tube. Ten or more clothes pegs, rather large, made of plastic. A dark gray belt of the same material as a police uniform belt.

Sergeant Faro lifted a black camisole by the straps, studying it. There was lace at the V of the chest area. She sealed it in an evidence bag without comment.

Magson looked at the doorway. He speculated inside his head, but only echoes returned.

It was just after eleven when Magson stopped in front of his gate. Two eyes glimmered in the headlights. He'd completely forgotten about the dog. While he was busy with the lock, the dog stood with its front paws against the gate, tongue out. He pushed the gate and the dog squeezed through the gap as soon as its body was able to fit. Its tail wagged with such fervor that the entire back half of its body was involved in the motion.

Magson smiled. "Did you think I wasn't coming home again?"

The dog barked and panted excitedly.

"You must be hungry. Let me just put the car in the garage, then I'll give you something to eat."

He pulled the Jetta into the garage, still impressed that the dog waited on the side without a word from him, locked the door and walked to the gate. The dog followed and watched as he put on the chain, its tail wagging all the while. He walked to the front door. The dog trotted alongside, looking up at him.

"What do you do here all day while I'm away?"

The dog just panted and looked at him. That spotted brown face looked much too innocent.

He unlocked the front door.

The dog remained outside, watching him, its head cocked to the left.

"Go around to the back door and I'll give you some food."

In the kitchen he grabbed the bag of pellets and opened the back door. The dog came running around the corner of the house. The pellets clattered into the tin plate and the dog started eating. Pellets crunched and the body jerked. The dog devoured each meal as if it were the first one in weeks.

Magson filled the bucket with water. He needed to get around to a shop and buy a decent water bowl.

When he went into the house, he left the door open.

Fifteen

"Look, Mr. Keyser, it is your absolute right not to talk to us, but I have to tell you, things are not looking good for you. We found some damning evidence in Mr. Luckhoff's home. A considerable amount of drugs, which makes it highly unlikely that it is just for recreational use. So we're already looking at drug trafficking. And the fact that we also found drugs in your home, combined with the fact that you and Mr. Luckhoff work so closely together, make it a natural conclusion that you are also involved. Your neighbors told us about frequent drunken parties. There was even an altercation between you and one of your neighbors regarding drug use at one of these parties. But drugs aren't all we discovered in Mr. Luckhoff's residence."

Magson looked at the two men across the table in the interrogation room, Hugo Keyser and his father, an attorney.

"Did you know that there's a closet in Mr. Luckhoff's bedroom that he keeps locked and that he hides the key?"

Hugo Keyser looked at him, at his father, back again. Licked his lips. "No. What about it?"

"We found a number of items in that closet."

"What kind of items?" asked his father.

"Items of an incriminating nature." Magson kept his focus

on Hugo Keyser. "We know you were one of the last people to see Danielle Ferreira alive. We know you planned to have sex with her at your flat. We know Danielle Ferreira was raped before she was murdered. And now we have these items found in Mr. Luckhoff's possession. This boat is sinking, Mr. Keyser. The question you have to ask yourself is whether you're going to go down with it, or whether you're going to jump off and swim."

"Warrant Magson," said the older Keyser, "will you give us a moment, please?"

Magson nodded and rose.

"And turn off the recording equipment?"

"Of course."

Magson waited outside in the corridor. What would the father advise?

His theory was that Luckhoff and Keyser were both involved in the murders, about Malherbe he was not sure yet. Perhaps Keyser would turn on Luckhoff. LCRC would take a while analyzing all the fingerprints. He'd asked them to give priority to those lifted at Luckhoff and Keyser's homes. The gas mask, dildo and other items were currently at the Biology Section for DNA analysis. But that always took weeks, even when a high-profile case received priority.

The door opened. "Warrant?"

Magson entered the interrogation room and took his seat once more.

"Hugo had nothing to do with the girl's death. However, he does have valuable information regarding the drugs."

"Let me be completely honest," said Magson. "I don't really care about the drugs. Organized Crime will want to talk to you about that, but I'm interested in the murder of Danielle Ferreira."

"Hugo has no further information regarding that matter."

"Mr. Keyser, we haven't been able to locate a single person to corroborate your son's version of events. Nobody saw Danielle Ferreira running down the street."

"She did!"

"Hugo," his father silenced him.

"I can tell you about the drugs."

"Hugo. Quiet."

"We get it in Knysna. That's why we're always playing gigs there. They bring it in through the Heads—"

"Hugo," said his father sternly. "Shut. Up."

"I didn't kill her. I didn't do anything to her. I swear."

Kempen Luckhoff did not appear too bothered about the situation. He leaned back in the chair, seemingly comfortable and unperturbed.

"We found your trunk," said Magson. "In the garage."

Luckhoff didn't reply, just looked at Magson.

"It's interesting. Just yesterday you sat in that same chair, telling me how 'fake' all the pop stars are. But you're exactly the same, Mr. Luckhoff. You pretend to be a musician with some kind of message, but in actual fact you're just a drug dealer."

"I'm very disappointed," said Menck.

Luckhoff glanced at him and rolled his eyes.

"Nothing to say?" asked Magson.

"You're a policeman. You look and see crime. That's how you're programmed."

Menck perked up. "So there is another way to look at the trunk? Well, don't keep it to yourself."

"A woman sells her sex on the street. You look and see a whore. But maybe her husband kicked her out and she's trying to feed her kid."

"Oh, I see. It's one of those means-to-an-end kind of situations. You sell drugs so your music may live."

"Like, for example, to finance a CD," said Magson.

"But you don't really want to sell drugs."

"I never said I'm selling drugs," said Luckhoff.

"Surely you don't need a whole military-grade trunk of the stuff for personal use," said Menck.

"I have no use for drugs at all. My music is my drug."

"For you, everything is about your music," said Magson.

Luckhoff nodded.

"All right. So where does this stuff fit in?" He pushed a photo of the closet's contents across the table.

Luckhoff looked at it. Showed no reaction. "Recreation."

"Mr. Luckhoff. We know you did not drop off Danielle

Ferreira on Voortrekker Road as you claimed yesterday. We know you dropped her off with Hugo Keyser at his residence. So that Mr. Keyser could have sex with her."

"And?"

"Danielle Ferreira was raped and sodomized. An object was most likely used. Then she was murdered."

"Oh, I see. And you think I did these things to her because I have an—" Luckhoff formed quotation marks with his fingers "—object in my closet." He shook his head. "You are wasting your time. Yes, I dropped her off at Hugo's. But I never saw her again after that. She was never in my place. And I didn't kill her."

"So why lie to us about where you dropped her off?"

"Because I knew that you would go on a wild goose chase like a bunch of idiots. Because obviously it has to be the rock band who did it."

"All these items are currently at the forensic laboratory," said Magson. "Where it is being tested for DNA."

Luckhoff shook his head and rolled his eyes. "You are never going to catch that girl's killer."

"Is that a challenge?"

Luckhoff slowly turned to him, looking him in the eye. "No. It is the tragic truth. She was never in my place. I did not kill her. You are looking in the wrong place."

"So why lock away a dildo in your closet?" asked Menck. "Why hide a girl's camisole in there when you have a whole drawer filled with bras and panties that isn't locked? Why do you have a bottle of nitrous oxide?"

"For my personal use."

"I thought you don't need drugs. I thought your music is your drug."

Luckhoff looked up at the ceiling. "No wonder crime is so rampant. You're not very bright, are you? I don't use it as a drug. I use it for sex."

"How?" asked Magson.

Luckhoff shook his head. "You would think detectives investigating sex crimes would know more about sex." The brown eyes focused on Magson. "I inhale it. It makes mastur-bation more intense. Just like the pegs and the dildo."

"And the camisole?" asked Menck. "Do you put it on?"

Luckhoff turned to him, leaning forward. "Nitrous oxide is cool, but if you want the ultimate orgasm, you have to tie something around your neck. I like a belt, which I assume you found as well. The camisole goes between the belt and my neck. It prevents bruising. Being close to death makes your body more alive. Everything is more intense. Maybe you should try it. The next time you have your wife on the verge of orgasm, choke her."

"Do you enjoy choking girls?"

"Only if they want it. And once they've had it, they always ask for more."

Magson stared at the wall in the operational room where the photos of the victims and the dump sites were affixed. Lauren Romburgh. Dominique Gould. Maryke Retief. Danielle Ferreira.

"Mags."

He turned around. Captain Kritzinger approached. "I have news about Daniël Ferreira. I thought you'd want to know."

"Ja?"

"Last Friday he withdrew the maximum amount from an ATM in Hout Bay."

"Have they found his car yet?"

Kritzinger shook his head. "Still searching. Volschenk has an alibi for the whole of Friday, so it doesn't look like it was something between them. The theory is that it was a carjacking."

"Maybe. But I can't help thinking he was doing something."

"Something that went wrong."

Magson shook his head, turning back to the wall and the photos. "Kempen Luckhoff looks very good to me, Captain. Almost all his music is about a girl who wronged him in some way and his revenge on her. And now we know he likes throttling. Pain connected to sex."

"He collects female underwear."

"Easy access to teenage girls."

"Vehicle that's convenient for transporting bodies."

"And even if he does only use all that stuff in his closet on himself, serial killers enjoy reliving their murders. I don't doubt it for a second, Captain, he is definitely capable of doing it."

"What about Keyser?" asked Kritzinger.

"I don't know. He is insisting he only knows about the drugs. That is his and his father's story and without something new to push them into a corner with, they'll just stick to it. My gut says he is lying. He and Luckhoff are partners. Malherbe could go either way."

"It is interesting that his flat was clean."

"Hmm. He has to know about the drugs, but in any case, Luckhoff is the one. I went through the profile again and he fits. I would actually really like to talk to that girl who was there on Saturday. Find out what he does with her."

Kritzinger looked at the wall. "What we need is evidence. Something concrete."

"Luckhoff doesn't look concerned at all. As if he knows there is nothing in his home for us to find. He does it someplace else."

"He enjoys torture. He burned Danielle with an iron. She would've screamed."

"And he would've wanted to hear her." Magson looked at the photo of Danielle on the wall. The smile. He turned around. "Where do they practice? They can't do it at one of their homes, because they make a massive amount of noise."

Captain Kritzinger nodded. "They must have someplace to practice. And if it's soundproof…"

"No one would hear a girl screaming."

May 28, 2014. Wednesday.

"Do you play any kind of musical instrument, Mags?"

Magson glanced at Menck and turned his attention back to the road. "No."

They were driving down Modderdam Road, heading towards Parow Industria. It was not far from the SVC office.

"Do you?"

"I can play a bit of piano," said Menck.

"Piano?"

"Yes. What is the reason for that shocked tone?"

"I just wouldn't have thought. What is 'a bit'? 'Chopsticks' with one finger?"

"Well, I haven't tried in years, so I have no idea how it would go if I sat down at a piano now, but I could play with all ten fingers."

"Well, well," said Magson, "I am impressed."

"My mom had me take lessons for a few years in primary school."

"Why did you stop?"

"Because boys tend to think playing the piano is an activity lacking any merit. Then you grow up and you regret it."

They entered the industrial area. Magson started scanning the signs. "You can always start again."

"Yes … The motivation isn't really there, though."

Magson saw the name he was looking for. "There's the place."

Menck held up his hands, studying them. "I don't exactly have piano fingers anyway."

Magson parked the Corolla and they got out. There was a huge triangular sign with the name ROOF TRUSST on the wall above the entrance. The shriek of a saw cutting through wood came from inside. Magson asked one of the workers and was directed towards the owner, Rudolf Nolte.

"Come to my office," said Nolte in a loud voice. "Otherwise we'll have to yell at each other the whole time."

They followed him down a corridor to an office. He closed the door and motioned for them to sit.

"So you're here about Kempen Luckhoff's band?" He had blond hair curling crazily and a matching blond beard, which conspired to make the reddish hue of his face more pronounced. His voice was deep and resonant, someone used to giving loud orders.

"That is right," said Magson.

"Are they in trouble then?"

"It's just something that came up in an investigation. We would like to know more about the room where they practice."

Nolte nodded. "Look, my main business is roof trusses, but my son wanted to be in a band. Obviously, this was a couple of years ago when he was still at school. His mother couldn't stand the noise, and they couldn't find any other place to practice, so I put up a kind of soundproof room here next to the factory where he and his friends could make as much noise as they wanted. Other kids heard about it and so I built another room and started renting it out. Because the kids all want to play in a band and it's electric guitars and drums and everything makes a hell of a racket, so the parents are only too happy to get them out of the house. So now I've got three basics, ideal for the school kids. And then I've got two larger ones, with better soundproofing and a bit more ... let's say luxurious, for the more serious bands. So that's where Kempen and his band always practice."

"And what is your opinion of Mr. Luckhoff?"

"Look, I'm not really a fan of this dreadlocked hair and rings in all sorts of strange places, but I don't have a problem with the guy. He is always courteous. Never any problems with payments. The place is always clean when they leave. You know, some of these people think, because they're in a rock band, they have to bugger the place up. No, this is a band that's always welcome."

"Do they practice in the evenings, too?"

"Not the school kids, because see, we're not here then. But the real bands, let's say, can make arrangements if they want."

"Does Mr. Luckhoff ever make such arrangements?" asked Menck.

"Ja. Look, I've known them for some time now, so it's not an issue to arrange something."

"Do you keep a record of when the rooms are rented out and to whom?"

"Ja. Have to anyway, for the books."

"All right, Mr. Nolte," said Magson. "Can we have a look at the practice rooms?"

The man nodded and rose. They followed him back through the corridor, out of the factory, and around the corner. He unlocked one of the smaller practice rooms, showed them around, and then they moved on to one of the "luxury" rooms. The soundproofing here was definitely of professional quality, making it ideal for torturing someone. But there was no way to hang someone in here.

"All right, thank you, Mr. Nolte. We've seen what we wanted to. If we could just get copies of the records, please?"

"How far back?" Rudolf Nolte led them back to his office.

"How far back do your records go?"

"It's all on the computer. Years."

They each had a takeaway Wimpy coffee, Menck with a cigarette and Rudolf Nolte's printed records, Magson with his notebook. They already knew Ystersaag had practised the Saturday after they'd picked up Danielle.

"All right. Maryke Retief. February 27."

Menck scanned the pages. "February. 26 Ystersaag. 27 Ystersaag. 28 Ystersaag. Then again in March. The fourth."

"All right. Dominique Gould was October 16. That's 2013."

"2013." Menck drew on the cigarette while he turned the pages. "Here. November, October. Sixteenth?"

"Ja."

"Nothing. There's Ystersaag on the tenth. And then only in November again. The fourth. That whole week."

Magson clicked his tongue.

"I'm not convinced they do it there anyway. They can't hang the girls in that room."

"They don't necessarily rape and hang the girls at the same location. The profile says the hanging is important, but what if it's not? Maybe they're only really interested in the sex and torture, and they only kill the girls so they can't be identified. Maybe it is just easier for them to put a rope around a girl's neck and kick her off a chair than strangling her with their hands."

"I feel like a pony on a merry-go-round," said Menck. "Just going up and down, round and round, and I can't get free." He blew a ring of smoke.

Magson watched as the smoke fizzled out and dissipated.

"Why did they have an iron?"

"What?"

"Danielle was burnt with an iron," said Menck. "If she

was tortured at Roof Trusst, why did they have an iron with them?"

His phone rang. "Magson."

"Mags." It was Captain Kritzinger. "We have a problem."

"What?"

"We have now gone through all the flyers found in Luckhoff's residence. They weren't here when Dominique Gould went missing."

"Maybe they printed the flyers, but didn't go?"

"No, Mags, we checked. They were in Knysna, Plettenberg Bay and George that entire week. All three of them."

Magson ended the call, sat for a moment, and hit the steering wheel until he registered the pain in his knuckles.

Menck flicked away his cigarette butt. "I hate bad news."

Magson drove to the University of Cape Town's Medical School. You had to know your way to get to the Falmouth Building. He entered and pressed the button at the security door.

"Yes?" came the voice over the intercom. "May I help you?"

"Afternoon, Mrs. Behrens. It's Warrant Officer Magson for Doctor Killian."

The lock clicked open and he walked down the stairs, turning left. The secretary emerged from her office, an older woman, always smart, always smiling.

"Good afternoon, Warrant. You can come through."

"Thank you."

She knocked on the door before opening it. Beneath Doctor Killian's name was a picture of Garfield, his claws extended: *Don't upset me—I'm running out of places to hide the bodies.*

He smiled and entered. The pathologist closed a file she'd been busy with. "Sit. Coffee?"

"No, thank you, Doc. I just wanted to get your opinion on something."

"Okay."

"Our suspects have a strong alibi for Dominique Gould. Is it possible that Dominique and Maryke were murdered by one person and Danielle Ferreira by someone else? Maybe someone who read about Dominique and Maryke in the papers and copied it?"

Doctor Killian considered it, but the scepticism was apparent on her face. "It's highly unlikely. The similarities between all three victims are just too great. And it's not as if the papers published that many details."

Magson nodded. "That's my feeling, too."

"There are dissimilarities with each victim, but nothing that is inconsistent. The same abrasions on their wrists. The sodomy corresponds, but it escalates. And it's not just that they were hanged, it is also the manner in which they were hanged. Apart from this case, when it comes to hanging we only really see suicides, and the knot appears in different places. In most cases though, it's on the side. By contrast, all three of your victims were hanged with the knot at the back, basically in the center. They were hanged with great precision. In every instance, the rope is the same thickness, the same thread. And of course the panties being kept every time." The pathologist shook her head. "It's the same person's work. It's like a good artist. Once you've studied his work, you recognize his style."

He took a deep, slow breath. "Ja. I knew it really. These suspects are just such a good fit for Danielle's murder. So many pieces fit."

"It's difficult to let go."

He nodded. Especially Kempen Luckhoff. He would love to look into those eyes as he arrested him. The drug-related charges were not good enough.

"How strong is the alibi?"

"Better than dammit."

She looked at him. "How are you?"

"All right." He shrugged. "I just wish we could get a breakthrough. I really don't want to stick another girl's photo to the wall."

Doctor Killian looked at something on her desk. "These cases are different. Because you know the killer won't stop on his own."

"No." On the shelf behind her was a photo of a blond boy

looking at the camera from beneath his eyebrows, a shy smile tugging at his lips. "How old is he?"

She turned to the photo. "Four."

"He's cute. What's his name?"

"Marius. Like my dad. He is a handful. Also like my dad."

"Then he is normal and healthy. Your dad probably too."

She looked at him and smiled.

To the right of the photo were books with titles like *Forensic Pathology*, *Post-mortem Procedures* and *Practical Aspects of Rape Investigation*. "Can I ask you something, Doc?"

She nodded.

"What do you tell him you do—for a job?"

She pulled a face. "So far I'm getting away with, 'I'm a doctor, but I help the police.' But the other day he asked me why policemen get sick so often that they need their own doctor. 'Is it because they have to catch the crooks at night?'"

He laughed.

She shook her head. "I'm still figuring it out. Can you imagine him standing up at the nursery school, saying, 'My mommy cuts up dead people'?"

Rommel was waiting for him at the gate, all teeth and runaway tail, when Magson stopped and got out. He opened the gate and couldn't help but smile at the wiggling body. "Hello, Rommel." He stroked the brown head. "Are you happy to see me?"

The dog barked and panted excitedly, as if he understood.

"Well, I have good news. You had your last drink from a bucket. Now you have your own dish for water, and another one for food."

Walking to the front door, he noticed how tall the grass had actually grown—Rommel had literally run a number of pathways through it, tunnels really. There was a sound at the Koertzen house, and the dog dashed off with a bark, a stirring through the grass with a brown head and ears emerging every now and again. He leapt against the wall, uttering several indignant barks, before looking back. To see if Magson was watching. The performance was for his benefit, then. He smiled.

"Come, Rommel!"

In the kitchen he filled one of the shiny new dishes with pellets, the other with water, and set it down against the wall outside. For a while he watched Rommel eating and then took Hannes's old tin plate inside.

For himself he had bought a packet of pork chops to put in the oven tonight. With some stir fry. Pellets crunched outside. Rommel would enjoy the bone, something to keep that set of teeth busy.

May 29, 2014. Thursday.

"How was your week?"

Doctor Hurter had kicked off her shoes and folded herself into a comfortable position in her chair. She tucked the loose lock of hair behind her left ear. Her eyebrows stole his attention every time—it was seldom that you came across a woman where they were naturally this prominent, or at least left that way. Emma used to make hers darker with make-up, usually while expressing her desire that she had been born with them that way.

"It started well. We had a few strong suspects, but in the end it wasn't them. Otherwise, it was all right."

"Are you still taking the pills?"

"Every day." Even though he disliked the idea. He still found it hard to believe that he was on chronic medication for psychological problems. "I think it's beginning to work."

She nodded. "Do you feel different?"

"I feel … more." He disliked this conversation as well. "With the interrogations, for instance. It's been like I am sitting there and …" He didn't really know how to talk about this. "It's like driving. You do all the right things that you're supposed to do, but you're not completely there."

"You ask the right questions, but you're not really involved. Not on an emotional level. You're just going through the motions."

"Ja. But this week it was different. I even had a fight with my partner."

"What about?"

"*Ag*, he is actually a good guy, but sometimes he talks out of turn. And it came out that he thinks I should've been over Emma by now. Moving on with my life. But what does he know? He's married to a good woman. There are no real problems there. His children are at home, one in primary school, one in high school. So what does he know? He hasn't lost his family yet, so what gives him the right to judge?"

"He still has what you have lost, and then he thinks he can tell you how you should feel."

"He has no idea what that illness takes from you. It didn't just take Emma. It took the rest of our life together. It took a piece of me. It took my son."

"He doesn't realize how much you have lost."

"No. He still has everything and I had to watch Emma get so weak and have so much pain that she would rather—" He stopped on the very edge of the precipice and realized at the same time how loud his voice had become—his words still hung in the air.

"Emma would rather go."

"She wasn't the kind to give up, but she couldn't—" he had to swallow "—she couldn't take it anymore. She was so weak. And the pain …"

"Emma couldn't do it alone."

He shook his head. He couldn't look at her. "She asked …" Now his voice was barely above a whisper.

"And that is what is holding you back. That you helped her."

"She was my wife. And I …"

"… loved her very much."

He nodded. "I do."

"That is why you could help her. When she needed you the most, you took this burden on yourself. But you don't have to carry it for the rest of your life. It's okay to let it go."

The psychiatrist doubled and the two images shifted across each other through the tears in his eyes. "How? I don't know."

"The first step is to accept that it is okay. Is it what Emma would want for you?"

He shook his head. "The last thing she said to me was 'I am sorry.'"

"You have carried this thing long enough. What you did for Emma was an act of love. You released her from her suffering. Freed her."

Emma *had* been free. After the last of her life had left her, she'd looked peaceful. Beautiful. She had been Emma again.

"Now it is time for you to be free, too. I will help you."

May 31, 2014. Saturday.

It was Saturday morning. Magson stood outside his house, looking up at the sky. The weather forecast had been accurate. The sun might not be shining with wild abandon, but the rays were trying to bring the color out of the world.

Rommel stood beside him. Doctor Hurter hadn't said anything. Magson neither, but he had begun to suspect her, although he hadn't figured out how the psychiatrist would have entered the yard to leave the dog and his food here.

"All right. Let's fix things up a bit around here."

He unlocked the garage and pushed the lawnmower outside. Rommel followed him every step of the way. Magson uncoiled the electric cord and connected it to the power. For a moment he just stared at the lawn. When had the grass grown so extremely long?

It was going to require two runs, the first one with the lawnmower set to its highest position and without the cuttings bin. Rommel ran from side to side in front of the lawnmower, barking at its roar. When he was finished, Magson started raking the grass into heaps. It didn't take long before he had to stop for a while, to straighten his back.

Rommel watched him with a protruding tongue.

"Raking grass and an old man's back are not friends."

Eventually, he had raked several heaps and he stuffed the grass into an old burlap bag.

"It's looking a lot better already, hey, Rommel?"

Rommel just wagged his tail.

"Hey, Rommel!" He clapped his hands against his thighs.

The dog barked, jumping up against his legs.

"All right. Phase two." He attached the bin and set the lawn-mower lower. The second cut went much quicker and easier, despite Rommel's continued efforts to intimidate the lawn-mower.

After everything was put away, he stood and observed the fruit of his labor. He was rather tired and his back ached, but he felt a sense of satisfaction. The winter sun. The smell of freshly cut grass. The layer of sweat from physical exertion.

Rommel went on reconnaissance expeditions, returning to Magson between missions.

"All right. Now you don't have to fight your way through the grass anymore."

Sixteen

June 12, 2014. Thursday.

He would never have believed it, but he could not deny looking forward to his session with Doctor Hurter. Last week they had only spoken about Emma, his favorite memories, her little habits. Later he had realized it had been the first time he'd really talked to someone about her since her death.

He took his seat and gave her a short summary of his week.

She smiled. She had a dark sea-blue scarf around her neck, contrasting against her skin, and then the dark brown eyes and eyebrows. "Is there anything in particular that you want to talk about today?"

He shook his head.

"Then I think we should talk about the cancer."

"All right."

"The sicker Emma got, the more everything revolved around her. Because it was her body that was under attack, it was she who needed care. Your body was healthy, but the cancer was yours, too."

He nodded.

"But you pushed your experience away, what you were going through, because she was the one who was ill."

She nodded, got up and left the sitting room.

"Teenage girl," said Menck under his breath. "Walking alone in the afternoon. Sounds familiar so far."

"If the dog had the leash on, that means the girl could have disappeared anywhere between here and the park. If the times are correct, probably on the way back."

"The dog must have made a hell of a racket."

"Ja." Magson looked at the Jack Russell still eyeing him with distrust. "But these dogs are so small, they don't mean much more than an alarm system."

"Could still be helpful if someone heard something. Saw a car drive away maybe."

"Unless the dog knew him, of course." Magson glanced at the dog again, clicking his tongue. "If only you could talk."

Lizl Uys returned, giving Magson a photo. He looked at the girl. Pretty, delicate features. Dark brown eyes smiling along with her mouth. Dark brown hair tied back, perhaps in a bun, or a sort of braid against her head. He showed the photo to Menck and their eyes met.

"Did Sarisha have a boyfriend?" asked Magson.

"No," replied her mother.

"Did she say anything recently that might be important? Like a stranger who approached her. Maybe a car following her. Someone watching her at the park. Anything you can think of."

"No. Things were just the way they always are."

The phone rang and she started, jumped up and ran out of the room, bumping a small table as she went.

The table toppled and Magson got up to fix it. Lizl Uys's part of the conversation drifted in from the next room, "Hello? ... No. You? ... The police are here. Two other detectives ... I don't know ... Werner, it's dark and someone has our daughter. How are we going to get her back? ... I'm trying ... Okay." There was the sound of the phone being replaced in its cradle. Followed by sobbing.

Menck met Magson's eyes momentarily before turning to the carpet.

Magson walked to the kitchen. Lizl Uys was standing with her back to him, her upper body shaking. At first she shrank away when he placed his hand on her shoulder, but then she turned around, pressing her hands and face against his chest.

He hesitated, but put his arms around her.

"Where can she be?" she asked into his jacket. "Who's got her? And what does he want with her? What if he ... She's a good girl. She's only sixteen."

"We will do everything we can to find her." He felt so ham-fisted, the words empty.

"We argued," she sobbed softly, her face still pressed against his chest. "She left here angry. What if that was our last conversation?"

He didn't know what to say.

"Please find her. Please. I would give anything to get her back."

Captain Kritzinger placed the street guide on the Corolla's bonnet, directing his flashlight's beam to the page, pointing with his finger. The group of detectives huddled closer. "Okay. So Sarisha would've followed this route as she walked home. Uniforms will be going door to door around the park. We'll start here and work our way to her house."

"It happened around four o'clock," said Magson, "but take that only as a guideline. And remember the dog was most probably with her and would have barked."

"I don't need to tell you what is at stake here. If it is the same killer, she's got maybe two days if we're lucky, but you know what the girls look like when we find them. Be thorough, but don't waste time. She is sixteen and her name is Sarisha. She is afraid. She is alone. Let's get her back alive."

They started knocking on front doors, ringing doorbells and pressing intercom buttons. It was going to be a long night.

It was just before four in the morning. Magson was drinking black coffee, too strong, too sweet. Menck had bought ten cigarettes from a uniform when his pack had been depleted. He drew on one while massaging his eyes. The street interviews had failed to produce anything of significance. A woman had heard a dog barking, but thought it had been a larger kind and she hadn't bothered to go outside and look, anyway. A primary-school boy had seen Lady running alone, leash dragging behind, which at least helped to narrow down the area where Sarisha had been abducted. Finally, there was a woman watering her garden who had seen Sarisha and Lady jogging in the park's direction. The uniforms had fared no better. Either people had not been at home during the afternoon, or they hadn't see anything. And how would they? Everyone was entrenching themselves behind high walls and security gates.

Magson took another sip of coffee, swallowing it with a grimace.

We argued. She left here angry. What if that was our last conversation?

He severed the thought.

He despised stranger crimes. Often the victim's history and personal life led you to the guilty party—a spouse, lover, family member, partner. You could dig and chances were somewhere in the victim's life you'd unearth someone with a motive. But not when it was a stranger crime. Particularly when the crime had been the first contact with the victim. Success in solving a case was too dependent on mistakes by the offender. Or luck.

What if that was our last conversation?

He shook his head violently to shut the voice out and poured more coffee. Here he stood, drinking vile coffee, wishing for luck, while Sarisha Uys was possibly being tortured somewhere. Where was she at this moment? In a room, bound, alone, afraid? While *he* was sleeping? Was she awake, or had the fear and emotional exhaustion overwhelmed her? She was trying to free her hands, but the ropes were too strong, the knots too tight. She only managed to chafe more of her skin off. She jumped at every sound in the strange house. Opened her eyes wide in a vain attempt to see in the dark. Wondering if the sound was *him* returning. To do more things to her. She was still sore from earlier.

He would have been busy with her till late. Young. Pretty. Fresh. His to use as he pleased.

He would wake up early. Excited. So much to do …

June 13, 2014. Friday.

The sun was up. It was Friday morning. Magson looked around the park. It could be divided into several generous properties and bordered on three streets. The grass had been mown sometime during the last month. The few trees looked as if they'd been handed out for free, growing at an angle with twisted branches. A trail cut diagonally across the width, probably the result of many years of domestic and garden workers coming and going. There was a jungle gym in the shape of a dive bomber, with a slide at the tail, and two swings fashioned from tires. The bright colors remained, but the paint was losing its footing in several places.

There were houses all the way around. A high-risk area. Had he noticed her here and followed her home?

Menck was leaning against the Corolla, smoking from a new pack already threatening to be closer to empty than full. The other detectives were elsewhere, engaged in aspects of the search, but Captain Kritzinger had stayed. Now that there was sunlight, the scene could be properly searched. Magson watched the members of the Local Criminal Record Center as they prepared their equipment. They would cover the park first, before following the streets Sarisha Uys would have walked home.

Almost two hours in, the search was well underway. There had been a couple of used condoms and a wrapper at the slide, which LCRC had collected. At one of the trees they had found several cigarette butts and shattered beer bottles that had obviously been there for quite some time. The rest of the area covered so far had yielded the usual litter: potato chips packets, sweet wrappers, cooldrink cans, cigarette packs and a plastic Spider-Man presumably missed by a little boy somewhere. Everything, including the lost superhero, looked rather sun bleached and weathered.

The media had arrived piecemeal. Fortunately, it was not Magson's responsibility to talk to them. Of course, some journalists did try to get a sound bite or two from the detectives, particularly one young reporter from the *Cape Times* who had already earned herself a bit of a reputation as a bulldog.

Several bystanders had accumulated to observe the police activity. Magson studied them unobtrusively. An elderly man in walking attire. A woman with her dog. Three workers in overalls. Two boys in exercise clothes. A few women from the surrounding houses, speculating about what had happened. Where had they been yesterday afternoon, wondered Magson, his eyes returning to the young man. He was standing on his own next to a tree on the corner, a red beanie on his head, his hands stuck deep into the marsupial pocket of his tracksuit top. Something about his demeanor, the way he was watching the proceedings …

Magson walked over to Menck.

"Don't draw attention, but have a look at the bystanders."

"Anyone in particular?" asked Menck, pretending to watch the LCRC members.

"Red beanie."

Menck observed him for a while. "Hmm. Seems a bit nervous. Shifty."

"Maybe he came to see if we find anything."

"Or he wants to get a kick out of the show he's set in motion."

Magson thought for a moment. "All right. If it's a show he wants, let's give him one."

He walked around the outside of the park, leisurely, trying to look preoccupied while he was actually watching the man in the red beanie from the corner of his eye. The man was shifting his weight from one foot to the other.

"Captain!" called one the LCRC members, raising his left hand.

A ripple of excitement washed through the media. Photographers raised their cameras, while uniformed officers tried to prevent them.

LCRC's performance was now in full swing, the members looking extremely excited about their discovery. Magson's attention was already back at the man with the red beanie. He was swaying now, appearing uncomfortable, looking around.

He saw Magson.

For a moment their eyes locked.

The man turned and ran. Magson started running after him, but he was probably a hundred meters away. His old man's legs would never chase down the younger man.

"Stop! Police!" yelled Menck, running down the row of walls forming the borders of the adjacent properties. It had no effect.

Magson swore inside his head. If only they had come closer before he'd noticed.

A boy ran past Magson, one of the high-school boys who had stood watching the search. He ran at an impressive pace, with the ease of an athlete. The other boy came past as well, running after his friend. Magson's body began protesting, his left knee threatening to give way. He had to jog slower. The first boy was past Menck, gaining on the man with the red beanie. What if the man was armed? At the end of the block, the man turned left into a side street and Magson couldn't see him any longer. The boy followed. And then Menck.

When he finally came around the corner, Magson saw Menck handcuffing the man with the beanie. The second boy was congratulating his friend.

"You should've seen it, partner," said Menck once Magson joined them. "It was beautiful. A tackle any Springbok would've been proud of."

"Dries is our first team's wing," said the second boy. "No one outruns him."

"If it weren't against the law," said Menck, "I would buy you a beer."

"Thank you," said Magson, still catching his breath, and shook Dries's hand.

"It's a pleasure, *Oom*. We're all sick of the crime. One of our friends was carjacked with his dad."

"Gun against the head and everything," said Dries's friend.

"And they broke in at my aunt's house in Bloemfontein and beat her for no reason. She had to go to the hospital."

"I'm sorry to hear that," said Magson. "Is she all right?"

"Ja, *Oom*, but she had to move, because she couldn't stay there on her own anymore."

Magson thought of Karlien Pretorius.

He looked at the man with the beanie. Close up he looked

disheveled, his hair sticking out in tufts underneath the beanie, his beard uneven, his clothes a size too large. His eyes never stopped moving.

"No weapons, no identification," said Menck.

"What is your name?" asked Magson.

The man's face was turned downwards. He shook his head. "You're not going to do it," he muttered, "not going to do it, not going to do it, not going …"

Magson glanced at Menck. "Let the three of us go back to the office. We have a lot to talk about."

They took the man to the seventh floor of the SVC office, where they turned right, unlocked the security gate and followed the corridor. The man had not said anything meaningful, only muttered a few phrases. Magson unlocked the interrogation room and motioned the man inside.

He only gave a couple of steps into the room, looked around and stopped. "No! No! No-no-no! You're not going to! You're not going to!"

"Calm down, sir," said Magson, "and please sit down."

The man was getting increasingly agitated and animated. "No! I won't be like that! I'm not! You're not going to make me! No! You're—"

"Sir, please, calm down."

"—not going to! I don't want to! I don't want to—"

"We just want to talk."

"—be like that! No!"

Magson and Menck each grabbed hold of an upper arm and tried to subdue him. He struggled and fought and Magson was relieved his hands were cuffed.

"Sir, please calm down. We're not going to do anything to you."

"Let me go! Let me go! I know what you want to do! Let me go! Let me go!" He had become like a wild thing.

"We'll have to take him back to the cells," said Menck.

The man seemed to settle down a little once they had him back in the elevator. However, his eyes never stopped moving and his breathing was hard and rapid.

On the ground floor they escorted him to the holding cells

and locked the door behind him. Contrary to Magson's expectations, the man offered no real resistance, entering the cell rather calmly.

"What is your name?" Magson tried again.

No reply.

They left him and went to the operational room.

"You think this is the start of some or other insanity defense?" asked Menck.

"I don't know." Magson paced up and down along the wall of dead girls.

"Well, either he's putting up an act, or he's got other issues. Our murders are much too organized to be the work of some loon."

"No, he is smart. Smart enough to have a plan in case we catch him."

"Hmm. Interesting how it was at the interrogation room where he started to really freak out."

"Well, either it's him or it's not. Whatever the case, Sarisha Uys is still out there and she can't afford us standing around here, wondering what's what."

"She also can't afford us being rash and doing something stupid."

Magson thought of Lizl Uys pleading with him through her tears. "Well, we have to do something."

"I know. All I'm saying is we have to be calm and think things through. As you said, he is smart. That means we have to be smarter."

"I'm not dragging him to Valkenberg. You know how long those psychiatric evaluations take."

Menck shook out a cigarette, stamping it against the pack. He pushed it back inside. "I have an idea."

A little more than forty minutes later, Magson and Menck dragged Patrick Theko to the holding cells. He didn't make it easy, but they managed to get him into the cell with the man still wearing the red beanie, and locked the door.

"We'll come get you when we're ready," said Menck.

Theko raised his right arm and smacked his left fist into the crook of his elbow.

They turned and left.

"White dogs!" the black man yelled after them.

Magson and Menck remained just outside the door, heads cocked to listen.

"Nothing against you," they heard Theko saying. "Because you are white. You are not a dog!" This last was presumably hurled in their direction, followed by a kick or something against the bars.

Silence.

"So why did they put you in here?"

Silence.

"Why don't you speak? Are you one of them? Hey, is this one of your dogs!"

"Shh, you mustn't talk so loud," came the muted voice of Theko's cell mate.

Magson had to concentrate to hear what he was saying. Fortunately, the bare walls of the cells assisted in carrying the sound.

"I don't care if they hear me," Theko replied loudly.

"You must! You must!" Hushed, but desperate. "Otherwise they will mute you. They take your thoughts. They take them away so you can't hear yourself. Or ..."

"Or what?"

"Worse."

"What do you mean?"

"They will only mute you, so you can't think. But they know about me. They found out."

"What did they find out?" asked Theko.

"They know I know. They know about my plan."

"What plan?"

"I can't tell you! No. No-no-no, I have to save them." So softly that Magson could barely make it out. "Only I can. I have to save them, have to save them, have to save them, have to—"

"Who do you have to save?"

"But they got to me. How did they know? How did they know?"

"Maybe I can help you," offered Theko.

"No, I must do it. My plan. Mine! Only I can do it. Only I. Only I."

"Maybe I can help you get out of here."

"How?"

"They will come get me soon. They didn't search me properly."

Silence.

"But then I want to know. Tell me your plan, or I leave you for the dogs when I go."

Silence. "They take the souls." Barely audible. "They throw the bodies away, because they're going to build new ones. They only take the souls. I know. I have a plan, but it's not complete yet, not ready. Need more time. They have eyes everywhere. Watch you. I was so careful, but now they know. How do they know? That's why I am here. There is a room at the top. A machine. That's where they take the souls. I saw it. They had me in the room. The soul is the most important part, the most important part."

Magson and Menck went back in.

"Ah, the white dogs return," said Theko.

"We'll have to teach you some respect for the police," said Menck, while Magson unlocked the cell door.

They escorted Theko to the operational room. "I don't know," he said. "If it's an act, he is very good."

"You weren't bad, either," said Menck.

"It's in his eyes. The man is not well."

"Souls being taken and bodies thrown away," muttered Magson. "Where does he get this shit from?"

"I don't know," said Theko, "but I think he believes it."

As the elevator slowly descended, Magson looked at his watch. Lunch had come and gone. The search had moved on to the route Sarisha Uys would have walked home. None of the possible evidence found thus far would assist them in tracing the girl's whereabouts. Captain Kritzinger had informed him that someone was asking about a missing man—one resembling the man with the red beanie. Uniforms had brought the woman to the SVC office. Furthermore, media reports that had appeared this morning had not yielded anything of assistance, either. There had been a number of phone calls with potential, but further investigation led to dead ends.

We argued …

Magson pressed his thumb and index finger against his eyelids. The lack of sleep was beginning to catch up to him. His head had systematically progressed from a dull to a proper ache. One of those insidious headaches that started at the back, slowly extending tendrils until finally overwhelming your entire brain.

What if that …

The elevator's doors stuttered open and he walked to the reception area, where the woman was waiting. "Mrs. Lamprecht. I'm Warrant Officer Magson."

"Where is my brother?" She was probably around thirty, her light brown hair neatly tied back to fit with her clothes, dark pants, white blouse and black jacket. Her face, however, had creases in several places and her eyes focused sharply on him.

"We had to put him in a holding cell, Mrs. Lamprecht. He got a bit violent."

"Violent …" She pressed her fingers against her lips. "Did he hurt someone?"

"No. No. Maybe 'violent' isn't the right word. He was upset."

"Oh. It's the pills." Her shoulders sagged. "He doesn't want to take his pills, because he says they're stealing his thoughts. I don't know what to do with him. I can't afford to put him somewhere he will be taken care of. My brother is schizophrenic, Warrant Officer. If he would just take his pills, he'd be okay, most of the time. But I have to work; I can't look after him the whole time."

"I'm sorry, Mrs. Lamprecht."

"I'm not married." She shrugged. "I have to take care of him. He's my little brother and there is no one else. Psychiatric institutions are so expensive. And the government won't take care of him anymore. They say he is functional as long as he is on medication." She dropped her head, looked back up. "Where is he, Officer?"

Magson led her to the holding cells.

"Danie? Oh, Danie, what did you do?"

"You, too?" He tapped with his fingers against his teeth. "No, no, no. Betta. How did they get you?"

"No one got me, Danie. I came to take you home."

"You can't trust them, Betta. They know." Two fingers tapped his head. "They know!"

"This is the police, Danie. They are the good guys."

"No. No!" He paced up and down in the cramped area, shaking his hands at his sides. "They have a machine, Betta. They have one of the machines!" He slammed up against the bars. "They wanted to take my soul," he whispered.

His sister folded her hands over his around the bars. "No, Danie. That is not what the machine does. This machine makes sure that you still have your soul. They wanted to make sure that you are okay."

"Really?"

"Would I lie to you, Danie?"

"They didn't want to take my soul?" His eyes stopped moving for the first time, large like a child watching his dad promising him that the thing that had tried to grab him when he wanted to get out of bed was only the towel he had left on the floor.

"No."

"Okay. I want to go home, Betta. I'm so tired."

"Miss Lamprecht," said Magson. "Can we talk for a moment, please?"

"I'm coming back soon, Danie," she said and followed Magson.

"Miss Lamprecht, do you know where Danie was yesterday afternoon?"

"At home."

"Were you with him?"

"No, I was at work. Why?"

"A girl disappeared yesterday afternoon."

Her eyes narrowed, her face hardening. "And now you're thinking it was Danie? Because he has problems?"

"Miss Lamprecht, a schoolgirl is missing. I wouldn't be doing my job if I don't make sure."

"Well, it wasn't Danie. He would never hurt someone."

"How can you be so sure, Miss Lamprecht?"

"Because he has this whole elaborate plan to save people whose souls he believes will be stolen. His entire room is filled with little pieces of paper and things as he works out his great plan. I try, Officer. I try to keep him on his pills, but I have to work and take care of us and do everything. It's not easy, but I promise you, Danie did not hurt anyone. When I got home yesterday, he was in his room. He was calm."

Magson arrived back at the SVC office just before half past five, parked and entered the building. The headache was like a clamp inside his skull. He pressed his fingers against the back of his head, groaning, while he went into the operational room.

Captain Kritzinger was there. He looked exhausted. "Where were you?"

"I took the Lamprecht girl and her brother home. Asked if I could look around."

"And?"

"She didn't mind. Simple little house. It used to be the parents' house. They are both deceased. I had a look at Lamprecht's room, in particular." Magson shook his head. "The whole place is filled with scraps of paper with notes and pictures and scratchings. It wasn't done overnight. Even the walls. The sister says she has thrown everything away before, but he just starts again. Apparently, it keeps him calm."

"Why isn't the man in an institution?"

"She can't afford it. State thinks medication is good enough."

Kritzinger shook his head. "And then we have to mop up the mess when he unhinges."

"There is nothing of the victims. No underwear, no jewelry, nothing. Nor any weapons other than kitchen knives. The sister says her father had a pistol, but she claims she handed it in to the police after his death. In any case, I don't think it's necessary to look at him any further. The man is cuckoo. I can't believe he would be capable of committing these types of murders. Not so neat and sophisticated. Plus, he doesn't have access to a vehicle."

Kritzinger clicked his tongue. "Back where we started."

"Ja." Magson pressed against his head, grimacing.

"Headache?"

"Ja."

"Listen. Go home. Get some sleep."

"I can't go and sleep now."

"You can and you must. Take something for your head. Sleep a few hours. I'm already rotating some of the others. It's your turn."

"And if something happens?"

"I'll call you immediately. Now go."

At home he fed and watered Rommel, and took his burger and chips from KFC to the dining table. Despite his hunger, he ate listlessly. Too little sleep. Too much throbbing inside his skull. Too much stress about a missing girl. Too many thoughts.

We argued. She left here angry. What if that was our last conversation?

Sarisha Uys and her mother kept milling about inside his head. Her shoulder beneath his hand. Her face against his chest.

I would give anything to get her back.

All these parents—the Romburghs, Claire Gould, the Retiefs, Ronel Volschenk and poor Daniël Ferreira, and now Werner and Lizl Uys—how many times had each of them had that thought, said it, offered it during negotiations with a Higher Power? There was still hope for Sarisha Uys. For the others it was forever too late.

And here he was. Jan Magson. His son was alive. He knew where he was.

What would those parents not sacrifice to be in his situation?

I would give anything …

Rommel came into the room, carrying the hoof Magson had bought a couple of days ago. He lay down next to the chair and began chewing on it.

What if that afternoon after Emma's funeral had been their last moment together?

His chest tightened and he had to swallow and open his mouth to gasp for oxygen.

Paws on his thigh. He looked down. Rommel's head rested on his paws, his mouth closed, his eyebrows moving above the dark eyes watching Magson intently. He stroked the brown head.

"It can't ..."

He got up. Walked to the phone. He didn't want to think, because then he would put the phone down before it started ringing. He wanted this panic to drive him to go through with it. More than anything, he wanted things to be fixed.

His finger automatically found the right buttons. Each digit emitted a beep closer to his son. Like a timer on a bomb, ticking. He took the phone away. Rommel sat motionless on the floor, watching him. The same way Doctor Hurter did. He pressed the receiver back against his ear. And kept it there. This time he would not defuse it.

It rang.

"Hello?"

His mouth wouldn't move. His whole body was trapped in a spasm. Only his heart was thumping. Rommel's eyes did not leave his for a second. "Hannes?" His voice cracked in the middle.

"... Dad?"

The only voice that could call him that. "Ja, it's me."

Silence on the other end.

"I ..." His heart thudded with such intensity that he heard the echo in the receiver. But he only looked at Rommel. "Hannes ... I am sorry. About your mom. It was the most difficult thing I've ever had to do."

Still only silence. The voice had been so close when he'd answered, as if he were just in the next room, but now it felt even further away than England.

"I don't want to go on like this any longer, son."

He couldn't even hear Hannes breathing on the other end.

"I want to fix things between us. But I don't know how."

What if Hannes didn't say anything? But he hadn't put down the phone yet.

"Help me. Please."

It remained silent. Perhaps he was not listening. "It's not that easy. I know Mum was very ill. I know she would never have been healthy again. But you killed her." His voice was very soft.

"Your mom was the bravest person I've known. She fought as hard as she could. But she had so much pain. The whole time. She was constantly on medication. She could do so little for herself. She just couldn't anymore."

"But it still didn't give you the right."

"Do you think I wanted to, Hannes?" Tears burned in his eyes and he struggled to get his voice out of his throat. "I miss your mom every day. Every day. She asked me to help her, because her body was done fighting."

"But you told me nothing. You send me shopping as if it were just … And when I get back, it's done."

"We didn't want to involve you."

"I wasn't a child anymore, Dad!"

The pain in Hannes's voice cut through him. Why was he so inept with his own son? There had always been this space between them, a distance, a step that remained even when he tried to take it. Even before Hannes had gone to high school. "I didn't know how."

"So you just sent me away as if everything were fine. As if there were more time."

The realization hit Magson.

"I didn't have the opportunity to properly say goodbye. Because I thought I still had more time."

Emma would've known what to say. All he could say, was, "I am sorry." About a lot of things. "I tried to do the best I could."

The silence had turned into a finely woven spider's web, pulling, pulling …

Magson heard a female voice calling something. Christine.

"I have to go. We have a thing."

Magson didn't know what he was feeling. He heard himself say, "All right." It was barely above a whisper.

Hannes had not hung up yet.

He swallowed to try to open his throat. Just enough to ask, "Are you well?"

"Yes. I got a raise a few weeks ago."

He tried to say he was glad, but all that came out was a strangled sound.

"I really have to go."

Magson gripped the receiver tightly, pressing it so hard against his ear that it hurt. He didn't want to lose this connection. He wanted it to continue for as long as possible before the dead tone came, like a heart monitor after—

"Perhaps you can ring again."

He couldn't keep the tears at bay any longer, even if he wanted to. They were the five most beautiful words he had heard in a very long time.

Rommel pressed his muzzle against Magson's leg. He bent down and stroked him.

The telephone rang. The sound dragged him out of the darkness. He reached, feeling for the phone and finally found it. He brought it to his ear while he inhaled deeply, rubbing his face with the other hand.

"Magson." He kept his free hand over his eyes, resting his head.

"Mags. There's another one."

"What?"

"Another girl is missing."

Seventeen

It was just after ten. A section of the street was cordoned off with glimmering yellow police tape. Blue lights flashed and reflected off the dark, wet tar. Police officers moved around, their breath creating wisps of vapor. Magson showed his identification card to gain access to the scene and walked over to Captain Kritzinger.

"… pain in the arse," he heard the captain of LCRC saying, "but we'll do what we can."

"Thanks," said Captain Kritzinger, and nodded to Magson. "Nanette Reid. Sixteen." He pointed with a finger. "That's her *poegie*."

Magson looked at the scooter. An LCRC member was examining it with a flashlight.

"The taillight is broken," said Kritzinger. "Bumper is damaged. Looks like someone hit her from behind. Not hard. Doesn't look like she fell. No sign of blood."

"Did anyone see anything?" asked Magson, scanning the surrounding area.

"Not as far as we know. I've sent a couple of uniforms on a recon, but nothing yet."

Magson sighed. How was it that there was never anyone around to see anything?

"She went to buy pizza. Parents got worried. Dad went looking and found the *poegie*. He is here on the scene."

"Did someone phone the hospitals? Just because there isn't blood, doesn't mean she wasn't hurt."

"Parents did. And she has a cellphone. Which is off." Like the other girls who'd had phones with them.

"All right. Where is the father?"

Magson followed Kritzinger to a man standing with a cell-phone against his ear. He was wearing dark chino trousers, a shirt with a collar and a thick jacket zipped up. "… taking so long … Listen, the police want to talk to me … Yes, I'll phone again later. Bye." He ended the phone call.

"Mr. Reid," said Captain Kritzinger, "this is Warrant Officer Jan Magson. He is the investigating officer."

"Warrant Officer," said the man, extending his hand. "Nor-man Reid."

"Mr. Reid." The man had a firm handshake. "I would like to go through the details with you." Magson took out his note-book.

The man nodded. There was a deep crease between the angular eyebrows. He looked worried, but in control. "Nanette said she was in the mood for pizza." His voice was strong. "She offered to go to Debonairs. She left around seven, just before the News. When she still wasn't back by quarter to eight, my wife got worried."

"How far is Debonairs from your house?"

"Ten minutes. Maybe fifteen if there's traffic. My wife tried to phone Nanette on her cell. It rang and then went to voice-mail. I told her Nanette was probably on her way back, that's why she didn't answer. But by eight o'clock she still wasn't back. My wife phoned again. This time Nanette's phone was off. It went straight to voicemail. Her phone is never off. Es-pecially when she goes out. It's a rule. I phoned Debonairs and they said she'd left there long before. That's when I got in the car and came looking for her. And found her scooter. A dog was eating pizza from the box when I got here. Growled and barked at me."

"All right," said Magson, "so then it happened on the way back."

"I saw there was damage to the scooter. I thought some-one had hit her. Maybe she got hurt and the person took her to a hospital. My wife phoned all the hospitals and clinics in the area. I asked at the houses here, then drove around the area. But nothing. And then I phoned the police."

"Does Nanette have a boyfriend, Mr. Reid?"

"Yes. We phoned him, but he doesn't know anything, either."

"How is their relationship? Do you know if they argued recently?"

"No, there are no problems. Anyway, he is also sixteen and can't drive. His mother brought him to our house so he doesn't have to phone every five minutes."

"Was there any indication that something was bothering Nanette? Did she mention anything?"

"No. She's happy."

"Can you think of anyone who would want to hurt Nanette, or who might have a grudge against you?"

Norman Reid shook his head. "No. Nanette is popular, and I get along well with my colleagues."

"If there is anything, Mr. Reid."

"There isn't."

"Do you have a photo of Nanette?"

"Not on me." He looked away, as if embarrassed about it.

"All right. I would like to stop by your house later to get one. What was she wearing?"

"I didn't really notice. My wife says jeans and she thinks a light top. And a windbreaker for the scooter. A light violet one. And of course her crash helmet."

"That wasn't here? The helmet?"

"No."

"I just want to look around a bit and hear if they've found anything, then I'd like to go home with you and get a photo of Nanette."

"I'll go and get one."

"Oh. Good. That would be very helpful."

Norman Reid looked at him for a moment. "Please, Warrant Magson."

Magson looked into the eyes, the same desperation as Sarisha Uys's mother, and nodded. Norman Reid turned and walked off. Magson returned to the scooter, where an LCRC member was showing Menck something at the broken tail-light.

"Did you find something?" asked Magson.

"Looks as if there are two different colors paint," said Menck.

"It's difficult to see by flashlight." The LCRC member pointed. "One is darker and the other lighter, metallic. Gold or silver, most likely."

"Silver," said Magson.

"But sprayed a darker color," said Menck.

"Interesting. What else?"

"No blood," said the LCRC member. "Pieces of the taillight on the road over there." He directed the flashlight's beam to a marker some distance away. "So it happened here. And the key is still in the ignition."

"So he follows her," speculated Menck, "hits her from behind so that she stops, and forces her into his car."

"All right. We'll assume it's the same guy until we find out differently," said Magson. "Why two girls in two days?"

"They were both in his area. Sarisha Uys in Bellville. Now Durbanville. And the same type of victim, white teenage girls."

"But why two so quickly, one after the other?"

"Perhaps something went wrong. Maybe he had to kill Sarisha, but he still wanted his kick. This reminds me a lot of the Romburgh girl. Perhaps Nanette Reid was also a victim of opportunity."

"Both at night." Magson nodded. "So he's driving around, sees a girl on a scooter and follows her. Sees an opportunity and grabs it. Spur of the moment."

"Or …" Menck's eyes narrowed and he looked at Magson. "Or he saw her at the pizza place."

"Maybe because he was there for pizza, too."

Magson and Menck were discussing their theory with Captain Kritzinger when Norman Reid returned with a photo of Nanette.

Blonde hair in a ponytail, one lock hanging down her cheek. Round face. Eyes apart. Wide smile with shiny teeth. A pretty girl.

"Thank you, Mr. Reid," said Magson.

"This morning's paper," said Norman Reid. "There was something about another girl who's missing. Bellville, I think. Have you found her yet?"

"No."

"They say it might be the same man who murdered the other girls. The girls who were hanged."

"It is only a possibility at this stage. We don't know."

"Do you think …" It was the first time his voice faltered. "Do you think it was him? Do you think he's the one who took Nanette?"

"It's still too early to say, Mr. Reid," said Kritzinger.

"What does he do to them?"

"We should focus on getting Nanette back."

Norman Reid nodded. "You're right."

"We will do everything we can to get her back safely, Mr. Reid," said Magson. "The Debonairs where Nanette went, where exactly is it?"

The man explained. Magson thanked him again, and walked to the Corolla, Menck in tow.

Menck studied the photo. "Have you noticed that missing and murdered girls always leave behind pretty photos? Smiling. Happy. Healthy."

Magson started the engine and drove down the street, turning at the bottom.

Debonairs was located in the Palm Grove Center, on the corner of Main Road and Church Street. It was closed for the night.

Loud music and a red glow poured from Stones on the top floor. A club directly above, and on a Friday evening as well. Fantastic.

It required several phone calls, but eventually he reached the manager of Debonairs and convinced him to come.

While they waited, he replayed his conversation with Hannes. And his chest tightened again, because he couldn't remember whether it had actually happened. The few hours prior to Captain Kritzinger's phone call had been the first he'd really slept since Sarisha Uys had disappeared. And he had taken two Adco-dols for his head. Had he dreamed it? He didn't know, and it made him feel cold inside. And claustro-phobic.

Menck wandered off, saying something about cameras.

Magson had left his private cellphone at home, otherwise he could've checked the call history. He tried to remember. Tried to recall everything Hannes had said.

"Mags. Are you listening?"

He looked up and saw Menck watching him. A cigarette glowed between his fingers. "What?"

"There are two cameras," said Menck. "One there, above Steers—" he pointed to the takeaway restaurant on the left of Debonairs "—and one over there."

Had he phoned Hannes?

"Real cameras, hopefully," said Menck. He joined Magson against the Corolla. Dragged on his cigarette. "He might have sat right here, waiting for her to leave, and then followed her. Maybe luck is on our side for once."

He had phoned Hannes. It was a feeling that convinced him. Hope. Because Hannes had said he could phone again.

"And if he had come out of Stones and seen her," said Menck, "the cameras would've caught him, as well."

A metallic red Golf rounded the corner at the pharmacy and stopped in front of Debonairs. A man got out and walked towards them. Probably in his late thirties, neatly dressed in a thick brown jacket. Highlights in his hair. "Brent Pollard. I'm the manager of Debonairs."

Magson and Menck introduced themselves and shook his hand.

"Who is this girl you're looking for?"

"Nanette Reid," said Magson, showing him the photo.

"Reid, yes. They order quite often. What happened?"

"We found her scooter about halfway between here and her home. We suspect someone may have followed her from here."

"And she's just gone?"

Magson nodded. "Do you have any form of record of the people who bought pizzas from you this evening?"

"Shit." He looked up. "Well, we take the surname and number of the customers who order over the phone. Write it down. I can get that info for you. But customers who just come in and order ..." He shook his head. "Come, let me open up."

The restaurant was rather small, perhaps two meters between the door and the counter stretching across its width.

"We'll also need the names and contact details of everyone who was on duty tonight," said Magson.

Pollard nodded. "But there is a Steers next door. Stones above us."

June 14, 2014. Saturday.

"Hey! I'm talking to you and you're sleeping."

Menck's head moved slightly against the car window. "I'm tired. I don't function well with too little sleep. You're supposed to know this by now."

"Ja, well, the sun is up," said Magson, wondering how he was still awake. "Time for sleep is over."

"Man, it's like being in school again."

"I said, we need to contact panel beaters. For silver BMWs sprayed metallic red."

Menck gave a drawn-out yawn, not bothering to cover his mouth with his hand. "Five minutes. To rest my weary head. Hmm? You could've told me this when we get there."

"And any metallic red car that comes in for damage to the front bumper."

"You don't even need me to have this conversation."

"He'll probably go to a backyard mechanic or someone who won't tell us. But we can always hope."

On the security camera recordings from the Palm Grove Center, they had seen Nanette Reid leaving on her scooter. Two cars had left shortly after her and they had managed to trace both. One was a matric boy with a learner's licence who had come with his mother in a metallic blue Opel Astra, the other a family with two children of primary-school age in a gold C-Class Mercedes. Neither vehicle had any damage. And none of the occupants had seen anything of note.

Nanette's cellphone had disappeared off the air shortly after her mother's first phone call. At that stage, it had still been in Durbanville. But there the trail ended.

Magson parked in front of the apartment building and nudged Menck's shoulder, not bothering with any finesse.

They got out, found the correct apartment number and knocked on the door. A girl opened. She looked at them. "You must have the wrong flat."

"I'm Warrant Officer Magson. This is Warrant Officer Menck. Are you Wendy Slabbert?"

"No."

"But this is Wendy Slabbert's address?"

"Wendy is my flatmate. Why are you looking for her?"

"Miss Slabbert may be able to help us with an investigation. Is she here?"

"She's sleeping." The girl looked from Magson to Menck and back at Magson. "I'll go tell her you're here." She shut the door.

Magson glanced at Menck. "What happened to those days when people still invited the police inside? When we were the good guys and they wanted to help us?"

Menck leaned against the wall. "Long gone. These days we're only welcome if they really need us." He closed his eyes.

The door opened a while later. A girl of student age regarded them with worried eyes. Her blonde hair looked finger-combed and her clothes picked up off the floor.

"Wendy Slabbert?"

She crossed her arms. "Yes?"

"Warrant Officer Magson. This is Warrant Officer Menck. You were working at Debonairs last night, is that correct?"

"Yes?"

"Did you see this girl there?" Magson showed her the photo. "Her name is Nanette Reid."

"Yes. She was there. The Reids order quite often."

"Was she alone?"

She pushed her fringe to the side, frowning. "I think so. Someone phoned and she came to get the pizzas. If I remember correctly. We're quite busy on Friday evenings."

"Did you notice anyone talking to her, or watching her?"

"Except Bernoldus?"

"Bernoldus?"

"The manager." She rolled her eyes. "He tells everyone his name is Brent, but actually he's Bernoldus."

"Did Mr. Pollard—"

"Wait. Did something happen to her, or what?"

"She is missing."

"Oh. I don't think Brent had anything to do with that. I mean, he is a bit icky, and touchy, but ..."

"Was Mr. Pollard there the whole evening?"

"Yes. Until closing time and a bit later. He always locks up."

"At what time did you leave?"

"We close at ten, but on weekends it sometimes goes a bit later. Somewhere between ten past and half past."

"And then?"

"What do you mean, 'and then'?"

"We were here last night and there was no answer," said Magson.

She frowned and crossed her arms again. "I was out. At a club."

"Was there anyone else who stood out for some reason?"

Her forehead remained creased. "I can't think of anyone. But Friday evenings are busy."

"Thank you, Miss Slabbert. Here's my card. If you think of anything ..."

"Okay."

They walked back to the Corolla. "I had a look at Pollard's Golf last night," said Menck. "More or less the right color, but no damage."

"He would've had to drive right after Nanette and the cameras show he didn't."

"Yes. That, too." Menck yawned, but didn't let it prevent him from speaking further. "So that was the last of the personnel. Who's next?"

"We have Van Zyl and Rheeder."

"I went out with a Van Zijl at school. Spelt with an I-J. Rienke van Zijl. Quiet girl. Decent. Excellent kisser."

"Interesting what things your brain thinks of when you're tired."

"She had beautiful eyes. She *looked* at you, as if she really saw you."

"So what happened?" asked Magson.

"Her dad was not impressed that a half *soutie* was hanging out with his pure-bred Afrikaner daughter."

"Well, I wouldn't have trusted you with my daughter, either."

"Ah," said Menck, reaching behind his back, "another knife for my collection."

Magson opened the Corolla's door and got in. "I keep waiting for the phone call."

"Which one?"

"The one saying they have found Sarisha Uys's body."

"Now this is the kind of house I like," said Menck. "White and modern and angular. But I want large windows."

"Which you'd have to bolt shut with steel bars."

"And on the beach."

They got out and walked to the black gate.

"I want a cottage on the West Coast," Magson surprised himself. He hadn't thought of that in a long time.

"I remember. Mags wanting to spend his golden years pulling his supper straight from the ocean."

"That was our plan. Emma and I. When we retire. A cottage on the West Coast. Far away from murder."

Menck pressed the intercom button. "My dad would've liked you. Now there was a man who loved the sea. I wish I had gone fishing with him more often. But at the time I thought it was boring." He shook his head. "You're so bloody stupid when you're a child."

"Ja?" answered a female voice, a combination of tin and plastic.

"Mrs. Rheeder?" asked Magson.

"Yes?"

"It's the police. May we speak with you, please?"

"What about?"

"It won't take long, Mrs. Rheeder."

"Okay. But I'm not dressed yet."

"We'll wait."

"Do you think you'll miss it?" asked Menck. "The job?"

Magson shook his head slowly. "No. It's just too much nowadays. People kill too easily. Just because."

"A person's life is the only thing that gets cheaper in South Africa."

"I think Rommel would like the beach."

Menck was watching him, but the front door opened and a young woman approached. She was wearing jeans and a loose black jersey with sleeves covering her hands. She stopped on her side of the gate, crossing her arms. Magson introduced them.

"What do you want?" asked the woman.

"Did you buy pizzas at Debonairs last night?"

"Yes. Why?"

"Did you see this girl while you were there?" Magson showed her the photo.

"My husband went to collect the pizzas."

"Oh. Is he here?"

The wind whipped her hair into her face and she tucked a blonde lock behind her ear. "Yes."

"May we speak with him, please?"

"I'll go call him." She turned around and walked back to the house.

"And once again we are not invited inside," said Menck. "I'd really like to sit."

"You'll just fall asleep again," said Magson.

"When we're done here, we have to stop somewhere for coffee. And cigarettes."

A while later a man exited the house. He was wearing blue jeans, a shirt and a brown jacket reaching halfway down his thigh. At the gate he adjusted his dark hair before opening it and nodding. "I'm Frans Rheeder. How can I help?" He was probably in his early thirties.

Magson shook the firm hand, introducing them. "You bought pizzas at Debonairs last night?"

"That's right. Come in."

Menck glanced at Magson, nodding with raised eyebrows.

They walked to the front door and into the house. Again the man fixed his hair and turned to them.

"Did you see this girl while you were at Debonairs?"

The man took the photo from Magson and studied it. He nodded. "Yes. She was there. Why? Did she do something wrong?"

"She is missing."

"Oh."

"Did she come in before or after you?"

"After. We order over the phone, but I like my pizza fresh and hot, so I go early. She came in while I was waiting."

"Was she alone?"

"I think so."

"Did you notice anyone talking to her or watching her?"

"Hmm." He scratched his head and tidied his short dark brown hair with his fingers. "You know, there was a guy who was checking her out."

Magson took out his notebook. "Can you describe him?"

"Well, not really. I just remember he stared at her arse. It was obvious he would rather have her arse in his pizza box. But I didn't really look at him, you know. I think he had brown hair."

"Long? Short?"

"Shortish, I think. Not as short as your partner's." He pointed in Menck's direction.

"Age?"

"Twenties, maybe?"

"What about his build? Tall? Short? Thin? Muscled?"

He raised his hands and dropped them. "I don't know. Not short, not fat. Just average."

"Did anything about him stand out? A scar or a tattoo or anything unusual?"

He shook his head. "Nothing I noticed."

"What about his clothes?"

"Listen, I really didn't notice. I just went to fetch the pizza. And a man doesn't really check out other men, you know?"

"Mr. Rheeder, this girl is missing. Anything you remember might help."

"I wish I could describe him in more detail." He raised and dropped his hands once again.

"Was the girl still there when you left?"

He nodded. "Yes."

"And the man?"

"Think so. Listen, wasn't there another one in the newspaper yesterday morning?"

"One what, Mr. Rheeder?"

"A missing girl."

"We don't know whether the two incidents are connected."

"The paper said it might be that serial killer, the one who hangs the schoolgirls."

"Journalists like to write front-page stories," said Magson. "Sometimes they're a bit too enthusiastic. Do you follow the story, Mr. Rheeder?"

"Well, every time it happens, it's in the paper for weeks afterwards. It's hard not to follow it. Do you have any idea who it is? The serial killer?"

"The investigation is still ongoing."

"Yes, I suppose you can't really talk about it. It's a pity—I like the cop shows."

"What do you do, Mr. Rheeder? Your occupation."

"I'm in marketing."

Magson nodded. "Oh. Before I forget. May I also ask what kind of car you drive? We're trying to eliminate the vehicles seen by witnesses."

"An Audi A4. Blue one. But last night I took my wife's car. It's a white Renault Mégane."

"Thank you for your time, Mr. Rheeder."

"Yes. I wish I could do more. They're still so young. I'll walk you out."

He escorted them to the gate.

"Do you think they're still alive? The girls."

"We're hopeful," said Magson.

"Yes. Well, good luck. I hope you find them. Would be nice to see a happy story on the front page for a change."

Back in the Corolla, Magson turned the key and pulled away. "I want to take another look at the parking area."

"Good idea. We can get coffee there, as well."

They drove in silence. Magson turned onto Main Road.

Menck looked around. "You know, when you look at the CBD, you wouldn't think Durbanville is a rich man's suburb. Doesn't look much different from Kuils River."

"I wouldn't walk around here proclaiming that opinion, if I were you."

Menck shrugged. "It's true."

Magson turned into the entrance to the Palm Grove Center, followed the narrow road to the parking area.

"Stop here. I'll go get coffee."

Last night Nanette Reid had walked out of that door, hungry and excited by the garlic and oregano and cheese rising from the hot pizza box in her hands, without an inkling that her life would be in danger only minutes later.

Perhaps you can ring again. Hannes's voice offering a sliver of hope.

He wanted to get her back. Sarisha Uys, as well. Perhaps then he would deserve another chance with his son.

The door opened and Menck got in. He held one of the paper cups beneath Magson's nose. The steam slipped seductively across his cheeks.

Magson took the cup, closed his eyes and breathed in the aroma. He took a mouthful, scorching every taste bud on his tongue, and had to pant with an open mouth.

Menck watched him, blowing on his own coffee. He shook his head, grinning.

The exit of the parking area was next to Tong Lok, another takeaway restaurant to the right of Debonairs. Magson drove up the rise into the street behind the center, and stepped hard on the brake pedal.

Menck's coffee spilled in his lap. "What the hell, man!" He tugged at his trousers. "You did that on purpose."

Magson grinned.

"Okay. Okay. Laugh, bastard. We'll see who gets the last laugh."

Now Magson *was* laughing.

A Volvo was parked diagonally across the street, next to the sidewalk. The laugh died in his throat.

"He could have sat right there, waiting for her."

Menck looked as well. "Yes. If we're right about the Debonairs connection. Perhaps he saw the cameras and drove here to wait for her to leave."

"Like a predator."

June 16, 2014. Monday.

The alarm clock began its monotonous beep and Magson smacked the button on top. He swung his legs out from under the blankets, inhaling deeply, and rubbed his face. Outside, in the dark, it was raining. Monday. It was Monday. The weekend was over. If the man who had taken Sarisha Uys or Nanette Reid, or both, was the same man who'd killed Lauren Romburgh, Dominique Gould, Maryke Retief and Danielle Ferreira, they were dead now. They were probably lying somewhere with furrows around their necks, clothed but without panties and jewelry.

He sat with his elbows on his knees, head hanging.

They had driven all over last night. Magson and Menck, the other detectives, dozens of *klagtebakkies*. Driven around the areas surrounding Durbanville and Bellville. Looking for cars parked by the side of the road. Hoping they would catch him while he was dumping the body or bodies.

Rommel entered the room, wagging his tail, excited about the day ahead. Magson wished he could get a smidgen of the dog's energy. But it had been too long since he had really slept.

He sighed and got up. His old body was stiff and sore and tired. It took longer and longer to get his spine loose. Rommel accompanied him to go and fetch the paper.

Back inside Magson removed the newspaper from the bag and unrolled it.

"Missing girl's father offers reward"

He closed his eyes.

The moment Magson entered the SVC building, he received a message to go straight to the unit commander's office. He knocked, heard the "In!" and opened the door.

Lieutenant Colonel John Hattingh had the phone against his ear and the conversation was serious. It was not the first time Magson was glad this office did not belong to him.

Hattingh replaced the receiver in its cradle. He lifted *Die Burger* off his desk. "You've seen this?"

"I have, Colonel."

"You know." He tossed the paper onto the desk. "I have sympathy with the parents, but sometimes the family is just a pain in the arse. Especially if they have money." He sighed. "Look at my ashtray. You and I have to go and talk to the man. See if we can somehow salvage the situation."

Magson stared out the windows while they were driving. Streets, cars, people.

Hattingh parked next to the sidewalk in front of the Reids' home. They got out. The high wall was bright white, bearing no sign of the weekend's rain. Hattingh pressed the button next to the pitch-black gate and identified himself and Magson.

Norman Reid came to the gate. "Colonel. Warrant Officer. I thought you would want to talk to me, although I was expecting a phone call. But come in. My attorney is here, as well."

"Thanks, Mr. Reid," said Hattingh.

Again Magson couldn't help looking at the house. It had to have been an impressive amount of money that had been spent here, on the building and the interior decorating, and of course the garden. There had been some speculation that Nanette might have been kidnapped for ransom, but any experienced South African detective knew that such kidnappings almost never occurred in this country. Unlike sex crimes, which flourished. Besides, a kidnapper would probably have made contact by now.

Norman Reid led them to his study. A man was waiting there. He introduced himself as Max Kleinguenther, Norman Reid's attorney. His suit was shiny and looked as if it had been tailored specifically for him. The black leather of his shoes had a luster, as well. He had small eyes, too close together, and a long, thin nose.

"Mr. Reid," said Hattingh, "I have no objection to the presence of your attorney, but I want to talk to you directly. We want the same thing, after all, getting your daughter back safely."

"But it's not the same, Colonel," said Norman Reid. "Because it's your job. But Nanette is my daughter."

"Of course. But it is the police's duty to apprehend offenders, to arrest them and collect the necessary evidence to prove their guilt in court. To offer a reward without at least consulting us, and then hiring private investigators to manage it all, makes our work very difficult."

"I have respect for the police. I understand you have a thankless job. I also understand that you are completely overwhelmed with cases."

"We have a team of detectives that is currently only working on this case."

"That's good, but I only care about one thing—getting Nanette back safely. Anything else is of minor importance. I am more than prepared to pay the person who has my daughter, and even see him go free, if that means she sleeps in her own bed tonight."

"Mr. Reid, I have children of my own. Believe me, I understand what you are doing. But the manner in which you are doing it is interfering with a police investigation. It amounts to obstruction of justice. I don't want to go down that road."

"All relevant information will be passed on to the police, Colonel," said the attorney.

"And who decides what information is relevant?"

"Colonel Hattingh, view it as a helping hand. A team of highly qualified investigators assisting in your investigation, at no cost to you. Time is a critical factor. Nanette has been missing for three days and we are not aware of any progress in your investigation. Rest assured that detailed records will be kept on our side."

"Mr. Reid, I ask you to please reconsider and work with us."

"Mr. Reid's decision regarding this matter is final, Colonel," said Kleinguenther.

Hattingh sighed. "That is a pity."

On their way back to the office, Hattingh was practically foaming at the mouth. Magson opted for a strategy of listening in silence.

"Fucking rich people. A 'team of highly qualified investigators'. Who the hell does he think he is? Oh, but they will provide us with all 'relevant information'. They'll keep 'detailed records' of all the information their crack team of Sherlocks uncovers. Fucking lawyers. We'll see what the court has to say."

They drove a block or two in silence. At the speed the unit commander was maintaining, it passed in no time.

"Now we have to waste our time on this shit. While we have two missing girls to find."

Another block slipped past in silence.

"And if we find that girl's body and catch the killer with information someone phoned in to *them* and the court throws it out and the bastard walks, who will get the blame? The police. Then we are the ones who fucked up the investigation."

They had almost made it back to Bishop Lavis when Hattingh's cellphone rang. He answered.

At first Magson didn't follow the unit commander's words, but then realized what the conversation was about.

"But, General, they are directly interfering in our investigation. How are we supposed to make progress?" Hattingh pulled onto the side of the road.

From the corner of his eye Magson saw Hattingh's taut face reddening.

"But, General, with respect …" Hattingh's face grew even redder.

Magson turned his head to look out the window.

"Yes, General."

It was silent for a moment.

"You know what the problem is with cellphones? You can't slam the fucking things down." Hattingh was glaring at the phone and finally sent it sliding across the dashboard, all the way to Magson's corner. "Lieutenant General Zalu is ordering us not to interfere in Norman Reid's private investigation. He has complete confidence that they will collect the information in a professional and transparent manner." Hattingh pulled away and did not say another word until they reached the SVC office.

Menck looked up from behind his desk, grinning. "Did you have a nice outing?"

"Oh yes," said Magson, dropping into the chair. "And the general has taken our hands and tied them neatly behind our back."

Menck raised his eyebrows.

"We are not to disturb Norman Reid's private investigators. But they will let us know if they find anything."

"Must be nice to have money and know the right people."

"Ja."

"So. Two hundred and fifty thousand rand for information that assists in getting his daughter back. More if the person who has her returns her safely."

"Good idea. Except, if our suspicion is correct, nobody will see Nanette again. If anyone saw anything, it would have been on Friday evening. There where she was abducted."

Menck took out his pack of cigarettes, sniffed deeply and returned it to his pocket. "Well, at least we're not the ones who have to listen to all the shit stories the masses will be phoning in. Because with that amount on offer, you know *everyone* saw something."

Magson shook his head. "I can't blame Norman Reid. It's not as if we have anything."

"I suppose we can always hope he loves money. She might still be alive. I just don't know what condition she'll be in."

Magson sat up and smacked his right fist in his other hand's palm. "I want the fucker. I want to cuff his hands and read him his rights. I don't want him making some kind of deal with Norman Reid and disappearing into the sunset. He has to die in prison."

Once again Magson went through the security recordings of the evening Nanette Reid had disappeared. He watched her parking her scooter, getting off and walking to Debonairs. He watched her tying three pizza boxes to the scooter, getting on and exiting the parking area. The matric boy got into the Opel Astra. Magson knew his mother was waiting for him in the car.

The matric boy …

Magson paged through his notebook. Here. One of the witnesses had mentioned a young man in his twenties looking at Nanette. The matric boy barely looked old enough to be in Grade 12. Who was this young man? He scanned the statements and his notes. No one else they'd spoken with had mentioned him.

Magson rewound the recording and watched again. He saw nobody fitting that description leaving Debonairs during the period Nanette entered and exited again, not even during the twenty minutes that followed. Only the matric boy and a couple of men, and even on the recording Magson could clearly see they were much older.

He rewound again. Studied the footage closely. There was Frans Rheeder, the one who had mentioned the young man. Nanette was still inside. The matric boy was still inside. Magson frowned. Nanette exited. He hadn't seen Frans Rheeder leaving the parking area. Rewind. Frans Rheeder walked out of Debonairs, carrying a couple of pizza boxes and disappeared off the screen. Magson scanned his notebook. Rheeder had said he drove a blue Audi A4, but he'd fetched the pizzas with his wife's white Renault Mégane. Nanette exited and no Mégane, or any white car, had left.

Magson switched to the second camera's footage. Finally he located Frans Rheeder. His car was not clearly visible on the screen and it was far from the camera, but it was definitely not white. Nor was it a Renault Mégane. Rheeder pulled out of the parking space. Magson squinted, pressing his face almost against the screen. It was no Audi, either. Rheeder disappeared from sight, leaving via the other, narrow exit.

In a BMW.

Eighteen

Frans Rheeder. Magson thought back. Rheeder had been the one with the house Menck had fancied. Who'd invited them in. After his wife had come to the gate. His wife …

Magson took out his cellphone and selected Menck's number. "Do you remember Frans Rheeder?"

"I remember when people said 'hello' when they phoned and asked after you well-being."

"Man, this is important. Do you remember him? He was with Nanette at Debonairs. You liked his house."

"Yes. What about him?"

"Do you remember his wife?" asked Magson.

"Hmm, yes. She wasn't so friendly. But pretty. Why?"

"What color was her hair?"

"Blonde, I think. What have you found?"

"Rheeder said he drives an Audi, but he went to fetch the pizzas with his wife's Renault. I've now got him on camera. On the one side. In a BMW."

"Well, well," said Menck. "It's not metallic red, by any chance?"

"It's definitely not white like he said it was."

"And a blonde woman. You're thinking of the couple who visited Lola."

"That too, but mostly the hair on Maryke's clothes."

A few hours later the group of detectives had assembled in the operational room. They hadn't been able to obtain a lot of information on Frans Rheeder. Magson had already checked over the weekend whether he had a criminal record, which he did not. But neither did he have a permanent job. His wife's record was clean, as well. She was employed at a dentist's office. Did she support the household while he was out hunting for schoolgirls?

Azhar Najeer shook his head. "No magistrate will sign anything based on this."

"The wife is the key," said Menck. "We have to work through her."

"Jeanine Rheeder." Captain Kritzinger stood in front of the wall, looking at the photos. "The question is, how exactly is she involved?"

"If she's helping Rheeder because they're a killer couple, we could provide her with an opportunity to help herself by turning on him. And if she is afraid of him, or if he's coercing her in some way, we can offer her a means of escaping the situation."

"The problem," said Najeer, "is that we have basically nothing. The only thing you can frighten her with is that they are suspects."

"The girls may still be alive," said Patrick Theko. "If there is a chance, we must take it."

"Not even a lawyer who scraped through on crib notes would be concerned about what we have."

Menck hopped off the table. "The way I see it, we don't really have that much to lose. She can think about it and decide to give him up. Or she can tell him. We can keep an eye on him and see how he reacts. I think the chances of one of the girls still being alive are slim, but he might still have to dump the bodies, and then we could grab him there."

"And if he knows we're watching him," said Theko, "he may wait a while before he goes looking for a victim again."

"Colin and I can go talk to her, Captain," said Magson. "Get her at work, away from her husband."

Captain Kritzinger was still looking at the murder mosaic. He scratched his chin, nodded and turned around. "Go. We'll follow up further. And let you know if we find anything."

The waiting room had that smell that all dentist's waiting rooms seemed to have, presumably some kind of disinfectant. On the sofa, a young woman was massaging her cheek. A small boy was creating chaos on the floor with the available toys. Another woman was sitting in a chair, reading a magazine.

Magson walked to the counter and showed his identification card. "We're looking for Jeanine Rheeder."

"Jeanine?" asked the receptionist. "Is there a problem?"

"Mrs. Rheeder might be able to help us with an investigation. Is she here?"

"She's with a patient." The receptionist glanced at the clock. "But she should be done any moment now. Just a few minutes."

It was indeed just a few minutes. A door opened somewhere deeper inside the practice and a man entered the waiting room.

"I'll go tell her you're here," said the receptionist.

"We'll come along," said Magson.

She opened the first door in the corridor. A plaque read ORAL HYGIENIST.

"Jeanine, there are police detectives here who want to talk to you."

Jeanine Rheeder looked up. She was pretty, as Menck mentioned, but not exceptionally so. Her blonde hair was tied back, with one lock hanging down each side of her face. Dark blue eyes and a pointed chin. Average height. A body that probably often jumped around in aerobic classes.

"Mrs. Rheeder. Can we speak a moment in private?"

"Thanks," said Menck to the receptionist, closing the door.

"I told you on the weekend already that my husband went to get the pizzas. I don't know anything else."

Magson nodded. "We still haven't found the girl, Mrs. Rheeder. And we've gone through all the information again and found some discrepancies."

She said nothing, but looked at him.

"We just want to get our facts straight. We would really appreciate your help."

She tucked one of the loose locks behind her ear.

"With which car did your husband drive to Debonairs?"

"I don't know."

"He told us that he took your car, a Renault Mégane."

"Then that's probably what he did. I didn't notice."

"You see, we went over the footage from the security cameras again and there was no white Mégane in the parking lot. So maybe he was mistaken and he actually took his own car?"

"Like I said, I don't know."

"What kind of car does your husband drive, Mrs. Rheeder?"

"Why don't you rather talk to him?"

"We don't have Mr. Rheeder's cell number, and the girl is still missing, so we don't want to waste time unnecessarily. You understand, don't you?"

She nodded, looking at the floor.

"What kind of car does your husband drive?" asked Magson again.

"A BMW."

"BMW? Your husband told us he drives an Audi."

"Yes. It's an Audi. I always get confused."

"I don't understand why he would lie about that," said Menck, addressing Magson.

"I just said I made a mistake."

"No, Mrs. Rheeder," said Magson, "you were correct. We have your husband on camera in his BMW."

"Unless he's got something to hide," said Menck.

"It must be a misunderstanding," said Jeanine Rheeder.

Magson looked at her for a moment. "A misunderstanding?"

"I've never met a man who doesn't know what kind of car he drives," said Menck.

"Here are the facts, Mrs. Rheeder. We know the person who abducted Nanette Reid drove a BMW. We know this person followed her from Debonairs. We know your husband was with Nanette Reid in Debonairs. We now know he drives a BMW. And we know he lied about it."

She looked at him and then turned her eyes away. "Frans went to collect the pizzas and came back home. That's all I know."

"You don't have children?"

"No."

"Did you have guests on Friday evening?"

"No."

"But you ordered three pizzas," remarked Magson.

"We always order an extra one for the next day."

"How long was Mr. Rheeder away while he went to fetch the pizzas?"

"Not long and I think it is absurd that you would come in here and accuse my husband of abducting some girl! Just because he drives a BMW and we like pizza. I have patients waiting and I'm not going to answer any more of your questions. I want you to leave now."

"Do you have a contact number for your husband?"

"No. His cellphone fell into water and he hasn't got a new one yet."

"Here's my contact card. You can phone me any time." He looked her in the eyes while he said it, keeping his voice softer. She didn't take the card, and Magson placed it on a cabinet. "Any time, Mrs. Rheeder."

Magson and Menck walked past the receptionist, who clearly could not wait to ask Jeanine Rheeder what the police had wanted to talk to her about.

In the parking area, Magson rubbed his face. "Too subtle?"

"I don't think so," said Menck. "The seed has been sown without shoving anything down her throat. Without the gag reflex, the chances are much better that she might consider it."

"I hate it that we can't just go into his house."

"I think that receptionist can hear Jeanine Rheeder's brain working all the way from her counter."

They got into the Corolla. Magson stared out the windshield. "If it is Rheeder ... Colin, we were inside his house. We stood there and chatted to him while at least Nanette was still alive."

"I know," said Menck quietly.

"We know he killed Danielle two days after he took her. Dominique's estimate is about the same. Almost all the girls disappeared on a Thursday or Friday."

"Weekend fun."

"Weekend fun," repeated Magson. "The weekend is over."

It was a little before six when Magson and Menck entered Durbanville. They drove past the Palm Grove Center and Debonairs, left the town center behind and entered a residential area. Houses, driveways, walls. Magson parked behind the white Mazda some distance to the right of Frans and Jeanine Rheeder's house.

Patrick Theko got out of the Mazda and walked over to inform them that the woman had already come home in a white Mégane. No one else had arrived since their conversation with Jeanine Rheeder.

Three quarters of an hour later no other vehicle had stopped at the Rheeder residence. The only visible activity had been a light or two being switched on or off. It had become quite dark.

"So. How is your housemate doing?" asked Menck.

"Too well. He is so at home, I'm beginning to feel as if I'm the one staying with him."

Menck grinned. "My housemate has decided we have to go to a hydro."

"What's a hydro?"

"It's like a spa, but they have all sorts of well-being treatments. Like skin treatments, massages, detox, these weird Eastern techniques."

"Sounds unChristian."

Menck laughed. "That's not a bad point. If only I was more devote, I might've been able to use it."

Headlights turned into the street. Approached. Continued on.

"So I take it you don't want to go with her."

Menck sighed. "No. Not particularly."

"So why doesn't Kathy take a friend? It sounds more like the kind of thing meant for women, anyway."

"Because the friend has already gone, dragged her husband along, and has returned to poison Kathy's mind with wild tales of how wonderful and healthy they both feel. Their stress has simply evaporated and they are effervescent with renewed energy. They're practically two walking Energade bottles. With fizz."

"I wouldn't mind feeling like a bottle of Energade."

"Yes, well, I have no desire to have my face painted with cucumber, or to have needles poked into me, or to have my equilibrium calibrated with a handful of magical stones. Besides, I'm a smoker. It's like going to hell."

"Ah. Here we arrive at the truth. He doesn't want to betray old JR."

"If only that was all. They have this disturbing thing called hydrotherapy, where they basically rinse out your colon. It is a critical part of the detox."

Another car approached, but Magson could tell it was a four-by-four. It drove past. "So people go to this place to get enemas?"

"I'm assuming it's a bit more sophisticated than that, but yes."

Magson shook his head. "Rather you than me. I have enough fun with my bloody prostate exams." Another thing he probably should get around to at some stage. At least the dentist had been crossed off the list last week.

"It's just unnatural. And don't think Kathy has any sympathy. She simply reminds me of what she had to go through to bring my—*my*—children into this world. I might accept responsibility for Ben, but I distinctly remember her telling me how much she wanted another baby. Sliding up against me with Ben's baby album, telling me how cute the little fingers and toes were, and just look at that little mouth laughing."

"I suppose just telling her you don't want to go is not an option."

Menck raised his hands. "It's too late. She has decided."

Magson grinned. "So when is the big day?"

"I don't know. It takes almost an entire day and the worst of it is that I have to pay for this torture. And I don't want to think how much, because anything that claims to be good for your health is more expensive. As if they're really trying to convince you not to lead a healthy lifestyle."

"That's true."

"Except of course for cigarettes. Doesn't matter how bad that is for you, it's the first place the tax budget hits you every time."

"Which is a good reason to stop."

"I need it, okay? With all the shit we have to deal with every day, I need something."

"And rather cigarettes than alcohol," conceded Magson.

"Precisely."

A new set of headlights reached up the street. The beams approached and turned in at the Rheeders' house.

"It's him," said Magson, watching a man getting out of the car to unlock the chain on the gate.

"Well, it is a BMW," said Menck. "Pity we couldn't see the bumper properly."

The man pushed the gate open, got back into his car and drove in. He returned to close the gate and lock it.

By the time Youth Day was over, the house was dark.

There was no further activity.

June 17, 2014. Tuesday.

Despite the winter's best windy effort outside, Magson was overcome with a desire for a glass of ice-cold milk. The result of the sandwich with apricot jam he'd had for lunch. His tongue was still digging out the remains between his molars when his cellphone rang. It was an unknown number. "Magson."

"Warrant Officer Magson, my name is Jakob Mouton. I'm an attorney. I have a client with information about Nanette Reid, as well as a couple of other cases I understand are unsolved."

Magson's heart quickened. "What sort of information?"

"Information of quite an incriminating nature."

"Then I would very much like to talk to your client, Mr. Mouton."

"Yes. This is, however, a rather unique case with extraordinary circumstances."

"What do you mean?"

"Well, Warrant, the person who is responsible for these acts is known to my client. She is, however, severely traumatized and fears for her life."

"We can protect her, Mr. Mouton."

"I'm afraid the situation is somewhat more complicated. My client is married to this particular person."

Magson's heart picked up more pace. "We can place her in protective custody if she has nowhere else to go."

"Warrant, her husband has abused her over an extended period of time. Broke her down psychologically and emotionally."

"I am sure we can get her the help she needs. Is she afraid to testify against her husband?"

"It's more than that, Warrant. My client was forced by her husband to be complicit in his crimes."

"I see. Well, Mr. Mouton, I'm not a law expert, but if her husband abused her, that has to qualify as mitigating circumstances. And if she shares her information with us, it would certainly count in her favor."

"Yes. I just want you to understand her circumstances. I am well aware of the importance of the situation and my client wishes to give her full cooperation. But as her attorney it is my duty to prioritize her interests."

"I understand. And if your client helps us to arrest her husband, I will do what I can to help her. I give you my word."

"Thank you, Warrant. We would like to meet with you as soon as possible."

"I'm available any time."

"Good. I think my client would be less uncomfortable if you could come to my office?"

"All right."

"She is here now." He gave Magson the address.

"Then I'll see you soon, Mr. Mouton."

"There is just one more thing, Warrant. The girl who went missing the day before Nanette Reid's disappearance ..."

"Sarisha Uys?"

"Yes. My client's husband was responsible. I am afraid she is dead."

Magson closed his eyes, recalling the weight of her mother's head against his chest.

"But Nanette Reid is still alive."

He drove entirely too fast, but the adrenaline had kicked in. Perhaps they could remove one girl's photo from that wall without adding one of her body.

He parked across two spaces in front of the building in Durbanville and they got out, jogging up the stairs to the entrance. They identified themselves via the intercom and waited an age to be granted access. Halfway towards the receptionist, he saw a man coming down the stairs, walking directly towards them.

The man extended his hand. "Jakob Mouton." His hair and beard were gray, but his eyebrows and moustache were still mostly black. He was not particularly tall and his stomach was testing the thread holding his jacket button in place.

Magson shook his hand, flashed his identification card and introduced them.

"Please come to my office."

They followed the attorney up the stairs. He opened a door and waited for them to enter.

There was a large table in the center with six chairs. Jeanine Rheeder was sitting on one of them, her hands in her lap. Like yesterday, her blonde hair was tied back. Like yesterday, she didn't look "severely traumatized." But Magson had learned that human beings had a remarkable ability to adapt and live with all sorts of things.

And to put on masks when they opened the front door.

"Mrs. Rheeder."

She met his eyes, but said nothing.

The attorney shut the door and took his seat next to his client. Magson and Menck sat across from them.

"Thank you for deciding to come forward, Mrs. Rheeder. We would like to talk to you later in detail, but right now we just want to concentrate on one thing. Mr. Mouton said that Nanette Reid is still alive."

She nodded.

"Where is she?"

"She was at our house, but I don't know where she is now. Frans took her."

"What is he going to do to her?" Magson asked quickly. "Is he going to kill her?"

"No. He wants the reward. It was in the newspaper yesterday."

"So he wants to return her to her dad?" asked Menck.

She nodded. "But he won't phone the number that was in the newspaper. He said that would just be stupid. He is going to contact her father directly."

"How?" asked Magson.

"I don't know." She had strange eyes. One moment it seemed she was peering straight into him, and now it was as if the eyes had turned a light blue and stared right through him.

"Do you know when?"

"I just know it's today. But Frans will phone me when it's over. He hasn't phoned yet."

"All right. So we still have some time. What is his number?"

She read it off her phone and Magson jotted it down in his notebook.

"Does your husband have a firearm?" He didn't have a licensed one, but …

"He has a pistol. And several knives."

"Thank you, Mrs. Rheeder. Mr. Mouton, I will contact you."

"There is something else," said Jeanine Rheeder. "Frans has a wig and a couple of false beards. He won't look like when you saw him."

While descending the stairs, Magson dialed Norman Reid's cellphone.

No answer.

They exited the building and got into the Corolla. Magson drove to Norman Reid's house, again entirely too fast. Meanwhile, Menck was on the phone.

"It is Rheeder, Captain … Yes. His wife confirmed that Nanette is still alive. Rheeder is apparently planning to return her for the ransom … Yes … Today … She doesn't know, Captain, but according to her, it still has to happen. We're on our way to Norman Reid's house as we speak … Yes … Yes … As soon as we know anything." He ended the phone call.

Magson had to stop at a red traffic light. He watched the

green light for the cross traffic, annoyed, tapping on the steering wheel until it turned orange.

Menck reached for the mouthpiece and tuned the police radio to an open channel. "Azhar and Theko are on their way. And we have a chopper ready to take off. The captain has already begun arranging potential roadblocks."

At last the traffic light turned green.

"This thing bothers me," said Magson. "I can't believe that Rheeder would just let her go. He wasn't wearing a wig or anything in Debonairs. And I doubt whether he would bother with wigs and beards once he has them at home, because he knows he's going to hang them. He can't afford to let her go—she knows what he looks like."

"The question is, will Reid just leave the money somewhere, or will they meet for the exchange?"

"I think Norman Reid is the type of man who would demand an exchange. It's his only chance to get Nanette back."

"Parents don't think clearly when their children are in danger." Menck slipped a cigarette between his lips. "But if he goes to meet Rheeder alone, things can turn really ugly."

"I think that is precisely Rheeder's plan."

Magson parked in front of the Reids' house. They got out and he pressed the button at the large iron gate.

"Ja?"

"Mrs. Reid?"

"Yes?"

"It's Warrant Officer Magson. May we speak with you, please?"

Silence from the speaker. "I'll open the gate."

The gate slid to the left and as soon as the gap was wide enough, Magson squeezed through and jogged to the front door. It opened when he was a few steps away.

Mariëtte Reid did not look good. The dark bags beneath her puffy eyes were prominent in her pale face. Her hair had most likely just been combed with her fingers. Her shoulders sagged.

"Mrs. Reid, time is a factor, so I'll get straight to the point. Do you know where your husband is?"

She hesitated. "I'm not sure."

"We have reason to believe that the man who abducted Nanette contacted your husband today."

She looked away.

"Where is your husband, Mrs. Reid?"

Her eyebrows drew together and her lips grew thin.

"Mrs. Reid?"

She looked up at him, her eyes wet. "We just want her back."

"I understand."

"She's alive, Warrant! My husband spoke to her." She looked so desperate.

"I can't imagine the hell you must be going through. But, Mrs. Reid, this man is not someone who leaves loose ends. If your husband meets with him on his own, I doubt whether you'll see him or your daughter alive again."

"He said if he sees any sign of the police, he'll shoot—" she had to swallow "—shoot Nanette dead right there."

"Mrs. Reid, this man is not a kidnapper, he's a murderer. He is now exploiting a situation he couldn't foresee. Nanette can identify him. She may even know where his house is. He can't afford to let her live."

She made a sound, covered her mouth with her hand and closed her eyes. Magson didn't enjoy being so tactless, but he was fighting for Nanette's life and every minute he had to spend arguing with her mother was one less to find her father.

"Mrs. Reid, your only chance to get Nanette back is to help us to talk to your husband. If he tries to do this alone …"

"He is at the bank," she said. "He came to get all the money in the safe and he's at the bank to get more. We just want her back!"

"Will you phone him? Please. I have tried, but he doesn't answer."

"Norman told me not to. The line has to be open."

"Try. Please. You *have* to convince him to include us."

"Norman said—"

"He is going to kill Norman as soon as he has the money. He is going to hang Nanette. Help us. Help your family."

She turned around and fumbled for her cellphone on a

small table in the foyer. Pressed the phone against her ear. Her knuckles were white. "I know, but the police are here ... They already knew. They say you can't trust him." She shut her eyes. "But Norman—Norman? Norman!" She looked at Magson, shaking her head. "The line is dead." Her face was pale, too pale.

She sank to the floor. Magson reached for her, grabbing an elbow and arm. The cellphone clattered onto the tiles. She was like a ragdoll. He lowered her to the floor, propping her against the wall.

"Mrs. Reid! Mrs. Reid!"

The whites of her eyes were showing. He patted her cheek and kept calling her name. He needed to know which bank her husband had gone to.

Menck splashed water from a vase onto her face. Her eyelids fluttered and she looked around, startled and confused.

"Apologies, Mrs. Reid," said Menck, "but we have no time."

Water dripped from her face, hair clinging to her forehead. Her eyes rolled slowly in her sockets.

"Mrs. Reid." Magson took hold of her face and turned it towards him. "Look at me. Which bank did your husband go to?"

"Standard."

"The branch here in Durbanville?"

"No. Bellville. Norman knows the manager." Her eyes regained focus. "Well."

"How long ago did he leave?"

"Maybe twenty minutes before you came."

"We'll do everything we can."

He didn't like leaving Mariëtte Reid in this condition, but her life was not in danger. Menck pressed the button on the intercom to open the gate and they ran to the car.

Magson took out his phone. "Captain, Norman Reid went to the Bellville Standard Bank to draw money. We're on our way there."

"I'll let Azhar know," said Captain Kritzinger. "They are closer."

"All right."

Magson pushed the Corolla out of Durbanville towards

Bellville. After the lanes rejoined on the other side of the N1, the police radio crackled, "Call sign Magson, come in."

Menck grabbed the mouthpiece. "This is Menck. Send."

"We've found the vehicle outside the bank," said Theko. "We think Reid is still inside."

"Copy. Where are you?"

"In Kruskal Avenue. Just before the circle."

"Copy. Give me a description of the vehicle?"

"Mercedes CLK500. Gold. Licence plate November-Golf-Romeo-five-zero-zero-Whiskey-Papa."

"Copy."

"What do you want us to do when Reid comes out?"

Menck looked at Magson with raised eyebrows, holding the mouthpiece to his lips.

"Just follow him," said Magson. "Don't lose him. We're almost in Voortrekker."

"Copy," said Theko.

Of course every traffic light was red. At least the next street was Voortrekker Road. Magson tapped the steering wheel.

The radio crackled. "Menck, come in?"

"This is Menck. Send."

"Reid just came out," said Theko. "He has a briefcase with him."

Magson tapped harder on the steering wheel, tried to stare the traffic light green.

"He's in his car. We are following."

"Copy," said Menck.

At last the traffic light changed and the cars began pulling away. Slowly. The traffic was bumper to bumper.

"Reid is turning right into Durban Road," said Theko.

That meant Norman Reid was now approaching from ahead. They were heading towards the same crossing, from opposite directions. The traffic bunched up quickly and there were at least ten cars between the Corolla and the traffic light where Durban and Voortrekker roads intersected.

"Reid is turning left into Voortrekker. He's going in the direction of Parow. We are following."

"Copy," said Menck. "We're at the same intersection. Traffic is bad."

"Copy," said Theko.

They inched forward, but the traffic light changed too quickly. "*Ag, donner*, man!" Magson hit the steering wheel with his palm. At least he was in the correct lane to turn right. Two cars ahead.

The light remained red.

"Come on, come on." He was now rapping his knuckles on the steering wheel.

Menck exhaled loudly.

The light turned green. "Finally," said Magson.

They were halfway into the intersection when the radio crackled again. "Menck, come in?"

"Send."

"Reid is past the M16, entering Parow."

"Copy."

"He's far ahead," said Magson. But they were moving in the same direction now. "Just look at this bloody traffic. On a Thursday afternoon."

Except for the blood-red Alfa Romeo that turned off in front of him, Magson could not make any headway. The traffic couldn't flow, because there was one traffic light after the next. Almost every one was red and then there were the pedestrian crossings to contend with as well.

"Nobody is ever on the side they want to be on."

"The opposite side always looks better," said Menck. "Until you get there and see that the dogs over there—"

"Menck, come in?"

"—shit just as much. Send."

"Reid turned off at Parow Center," said Theko over the radio. It took Magson a moment to process, because in his mind the shopping center still remained the Sanlam Center.

"Going to the center itself?"

"Yes."

The Corolla passed the M16 and the railway tracks.

"Okay, copy," said Menck. "Is he parking, or what?"

"He turned in at the parkade."

"Surely the meeting isn't here?" asked Magson. Norman Reid might have wanted a public area, but surely Rheeder would have refused.

"He's parking," said Theko.

Again Magson had to stop at a traffic light.

"Is there any sign of Rheeder or his car?" asked Menck into the mouthpiece.

"No. Reid is getting out. He's doing something in the boot."

"What?"

"Can't see. But he made sure no one was nearby."

"Copy. We're here now. Where are you?"

"On the second level."

Magson drove around the left side of the shopping center.

"Reid is now sitting in his car," said Theko.

"What's he doing?" asked Menck.

"Nothing. He's just sitting."

"Copy. Any sign of Rheeder?"

"No. Wait. Reid is talking on his phone."

Magson turned at the entrance to the parkade. There was no boom or a machine spitting out tickets, because parking was free.

"Reid is pulling out," said Theko. "He's leaving."

"What?" asked Magson, stepping on the brake and putting the Corolla into reverse.

"Copy," said Menck. "We're down at the entrance. We're waiting for him."

"Copy," said Theko.

There was a small Shell petrol station next to the entrance and Magson drove in there. "So why did he come here? Waiting for a phone call?"

"Perhaps Rheeder is playing *The Amazing Race*." Menck nodded. "Gold CLK. There he is." He raised the radio to his mouth. "Theko, come in."

"Send."

"We have him."

"Copy."

Magson waited a while before following the Mercedes. Out of the parking area. Left to Voortrekker Road, then right, back in Bellville's direction. It went well until they reached the M16, with only a dark gray Peugeot 308 between them and Norman Reid, but here the traffic light turned orange.

The CLK slipped through the intersection, but the Peugeot's brake lights glowed.

"*Fok!*" spat Magson, forced to bring the Corolla to a stop. He glared at the red light, tapping the steering wheel.

And the M16 was a wide, busy road. The cross traffic went on and on. Some turned into Voortrekker Road—yet more cars between him and Norman Reid. The gold CLK had disappeared. And still the light remained red.

Menck informed Theko and Najeer of the situation. They had traffic problems of their own.

The light turned green.

"*Ag*, drive, man!" yelled Magson at the Peugeot, pulling away slowly.

The *bakkie* in the right lane stopped to turn and Magson seized the gap, cut right past the Peugeot and accelerated.

"Where the hell is that CLK?"

They were stuck behind one of those large four-by-fours that simply refused to go out of fashion, and he couldn't see anything ahead. There was a gap on the right. He floored the petrol pedal and passed the four-by-four.

"There, there, there!" called Menck, pointing with his left hand. "He's going to turn left."

Magson flicked on the indicator and pushed in front of the four-by-four, behind a Ford Fiesta. He received a hoot and raised his hand in apology, mainly to get the driver to stop drawing attention.

The CLK turned, the Fiesta turned, and Magson turned. He breathed a sigh of relief.

Menck updated Theko and Najeer. They had been caught out by several traffic lights and were currently trapped at the M16.

"Looks like we're heading back to Durbanville," said Menck. "Or perhaps we're going to all the shopping centers."

Norman Reid did not turn off at Tyger Valley, but continued on to Durbanville and, except for a moment's delay due to a Golden Arrow bus, they followed without incident. At Eversdal Road he turned right. Up to this point, they had been following roads with two or three lanes, but Eversdal Road was a narrow, single-lane affair, and Magson maintained a greater distance between the Corolla and Reid's Mercedes.

"Where the hell are we going?" asked Menck.

"Brackenfell?" offered Magson.

"Into the heart of the murder zone."

At the first large intersection, the CLK turned left. Magson followed. On the right was open veld, to the left, houses with tall walls and trees. And then a construction site. Norman Reid stopped in front of the gate and Magson slowed. It looked like a new extension still in development. The site was fenced off with metal sheets. Magson could only see the higher floors of the partially completed buildings reaching towards the sky. There was no sign of any workers or activity.

Norman Reid got out, opened the gate and drove into the site. He stopped and closed the gate. His cellphone was against his ear.

"Probably talking to Rheeder," said Menck.

"Ja. But where is Rheeder? Is he here? Is he inside there somewhere?"

"Darrington Village," read Menck from the large sign on the corner. "New modern spacious duplexes in secure complex. Coming soon. Darrington Village … Why does that sound familiar?"

While Menck brought Theko and Najeer up to date, Magson phoned Captain Kritzinger, even though he was listening to the radio in the unit commander's office.

"What's going on, Mags?"

"We followed Reid to a construction site in Durbanville. He entered the site."

"Any sign of Rheeder?"

"No. But he could be inside."

"What site is it?"

"Darrington Village. Half-built duplexes. But I don't see any construction workers."

"You won't," said Kritzinger. "That's the site with the financial problems and the money that disappeared. Doesn't matter. What's your take on the situation?"

"Difficult to say, Captain. We'll have to go in to see. I don't want to waste time."

"Okay. Be safe."

Magson switched his phone to silent and parked in the side street. He got out, closing the door quietly. Menck grabbed the bulletproof vests and they put them on while jogging across the street. Next to the fence was only dirt, dark brown and uneven. It was quite muddy in places. Magson took up position at the corner of the fence and peeked at the gate. He couldn't see much from this vantage point.

He heard the soft snap of fingers and looked over his shoulder. Menck beckoned, pointing at a hole in the sheets of metal.

He peered through the hole. Stacks of building materials. Heaps of rubble. The skeletons of several double-storey duplexes. And on the opposite side, Norman Reid's gold CLK. It wasn't possible to see whether Reid was inside the car. He couldn't see any other vehicle from here.

"I can see Reid's car," whispered Magson. "No sign of Rheeder. Let's go around this way. See if we can get over."

They followed the fence, until they reached the nearest duplex. Magson studied the fence. It was higher than he was tall.

"Come," said Menck, interlocking his fingers. "Old men first."

Magson stepped and Menck boosted him up. He scanned the area, saw no one and pushed himself high enough to get his right leg up. The toe part of his shoe caught on the fence and he struggled to get it high enough. He yanked, a muscle pulling, but his foot was over. The action disturbed his balance and he started falling. The only option was to sit, one leg on each side of the fence, and take the pain. He tried to muffle the groan and swung his left leg over, dropping on the other side. There was no grace left in his body, he thought, but the paralyzing ache drowned that thought out as well. He pressed his hands where the pain was, bending over.

It had not been as quiet as he hoped, but Menck made even more noise as he manhandled himself over the fence. Why did they have to use metal sheets anyway?

"Both still intact?" asked Menck, grinning.

"Too much pain to care."

"Remind me to tell you a story later," said Menck. He looked down at the streaks of mud on his hands and rubbed his palms together.

"Come."

They jogged to the nearest duplex. Each step hurt. Magson moved down to the corner, peeking around it. There was the CLK. And Norman Reid was at the car.

He retreated behind the wall. Menck had drawn his pistol and covered the other corner.

"See something?" whispered Magson.

Menck shook his head.

"Reid is next to his car, but he's just standing there. Unless he's waiting for Rheeder to phone, it doesn't look like he's supposed to leave the money here. We have to get closer."

"Well, we can work our way around here, between the buildings." Menck pointed. "There is a good amount of cover."

Magson nodded. He drew his pistol, flicked off the safety and moved around the corner and along the wall. Looked left and right, saw no one, and jogged across the narrow tarred road to the partially completed duplex on the other side. Slowly, he followed the wall to the corner on the right and took a peek. No one. The road forked and the next duplex was along the other road, the one where Norman Reid's car was parked. Magson couldn't see it from here, but he knew it was at least two more duplexes further on.

He jogged to the next building. The muddy ground made squelchy sounds with each step, extremely loud. This time he went to the left corner. Took a peek. Followed the wall to the corner, ensured it was clear and jogged to the next duplex.

Voices.

He looked over his shoulder at Menck, indicated that someone was talking. He moved forward. Slowly. Each duplex had two openings for back doors and he peered into the first, slipped inside and tried to step lightly on the cement floor to muffle the echoes of his footsteps. The mud sticking to his shoes made it more difficult and he grimaced at every crunch and scrape. There was a partially built wall, presumably to partition off the kitchen, which he used as cover to ensure the area further on was clear.

The voices were coming from outside—there was no echo. And it sounded like the one was angry. "What is *this*?"

The sound of his footsteps on the cement floor caused him to gnash his teeth. He pressed his shoulder against the inside of the outer wall, next to the opening for a window. He peeked towards the left.

Two men were standing at the CLK, about three metres apart. One was Norman Reid. The one on the left had dark hair hanging onto his shoulders, a faded blue-gray cap on his head. He was wearing jeans and a camouflage jacket. It could be Rheeder. Wearing a wig. It was difficult to say from this angle, as Magson was seeing him from the back and side.

The second man aimed a pistol at Norman Reid. "Do you think this is a fucking game? Don't you want your daughter back?"

The CLK's boot was open. Was whatever Norman Reid had done in the parkade at Parow Center the cause of the second man's dissatisfaction?

"The money is there." Norman Reid sounded calm. "As soon as I have Nanette, I'll give you the code. I don't care about the money, I just want my daughter back."

"Then give me the money!"

"Not until I have Nanette."

"You're not in a position to make demands. Either you open the safe, or I go and shoot your blonde bitch in the head! Do you understand what I'm saying?"

"Then you won't get the money. The safe is tamperproof. You won't be able to open it without the code." He looked the man with the pistol in the eye.

Magson admired his composure. How many parents would be capable of such?

"Maybe I should shoot you and screw the money. We can still have lots of fun together, me and the bitch."

Magson wondered if Nanette was here at all. Whether she was still alive. Or whether he had hanged her after she'd spoken with her father on the phone.

"With this money, you can disappear," said Norman Reid. "Before the police apprehend you."

He snorted. "The police can't find their own arseholes, man. They're like hamsters running in their little wheel."

"How certain are you? The investigating officer phoned me earlier today and said an eyewitness came forward and they're on the verge of making an arrest."

If only Norman Reid realized how close to the truth his lie actually was.

"What eyewitness?"

"I don't know, because they refuse to give me any detail. But he was very sure of himself."

The man with the pistol—it had to be Rheeder—was silent for a while. "Where's your phone?"

Norman Reid pulled it from his pocket.

"Throw it over to me. On the ground."

The phone landed with a sharp cracking sound, sending a couple of shards flying. The man stomped on it, twisting his heel while the plastic crunched. He kicked it away. "Lie down on your stomach."

"Why?"

"Do you want to see the bitch or not?"

Norman Reid dropped down onto his knees and lay face-down on the damp tar.

"Spread your arms and your legs."

Norman Reid obeyed.

"Put your forehead on the road."

The pistol aimed down at the man lying spreadeagled on the tar.

Magson suffered a fresh burst of adrenaline, like a sliver of ice, his heart beating faster. Was Rheeder going to pull the trigger? Should he intervene now?

The pistol whipped up in silence, like a boy imitating the recoil with a toy gun. "When I come back, if you're not lying exactly like this, I'll shoot her dead right here."

Did that mean she *was* here? wondered Magson, breathing again. The new hope energized him.

He looked around at Menck, nodded, moved through the duplex and out the back door. Along the wall to the corner. The man had walked in the opposite direction from where they'd scaled the fence, but could be anywhere by now. Magson peeked around the corner. The gold nose of the CLK was visible, but nothing more. He jogged over to the next duplex, pistol at the ready. All along the wall to the furthest corner.

There was one more duplex on this side of the road. No activity there. Then there was a duplex across the road, the last one on that side. He looked at Menck, indicating that he should go around the left. Menck nodded. Magson ran across the road to the wall. Peeked around the corner. Nothing. Moved around and followed the wall.

"Get out, bitch."

Magson peeked around the corner. The man was pulling a girl, presumably Nanette Reid, from the boot of the metallic red BMW. The car was closer to the furthest side of the duplex. There was another gate here, probably a temporary one for the construction vehicles, because there was no tarred road like the one coming from the front entrance, only wide muddy tracks. The gate was open.

The man had the girl out of the boot now. He tugged her. She didn't fight him. She seemed lethargic.

Magson raised his pistol. "Frans Rheeder! You're under arrest! Drop your weapon and let the girl go!"

For a moment they looked into each other's eyes. A shot exploded. Magson jerked backwards, hearing the bullet cutting through the air very close to him.

"Drop the weapon, Rheeder!" yelled Menck from the other side.

Rheeder looked around and yanked the girl into the duplex.

Magson rushed after him, while Menck went around the building to the other side. He stopped at the back door. Looked around the corner.

"Stop, Rheeder!" yelled Menck from the other side.

Rheeder shot in Menck's direction and dragged the girl up the stairs to the second storey. She stumbled and fell to her knees, but he yanked her back up and around the hundred-and-eighty-degree turn halfway up the stairs.

Magson followed, pistol raised.

"Nanette!"

He whipped around and saw Norman Reid approaching

at pace. Menck grabbed him, but it quickly escalated into a scuffle.

"Where is Nanette? Is she okay? Who was shot?"

Menck tried to calm him.

Magson moved further up the stairs, looking around the corner. Like the other duplexes, this one had no roof yet, and he saw gray sky. Slowly, he moved up to the top, ignoring the words behind him.

Rheeder was standing near the edge of the building, Nanette in front of him. His left hand gripped her throat. The pistol was pressed against her right temple. The outer walls had not been finished and there was nothing behind Rheeder.

"There is nowhere to go," said Magson. "It's over, Rheeder. Let her go."

Rheeder said nothing, but he seemed calm. Nanette was looking down. She appeared to have difficulty focusing, as if not completely aware of what was happening.

Had he given her something?

"Let her go. No one has to get hurt today."

Rheeder stared at him. No indication of panic. That was good.

"Put down the pistol."

"You put down your pistol," said Rheeder.

"I can't do that."

"Oh. So your plan is to get me to drop my pistol and then you can shoot me right here?"

"No. I don't want anyone to get shot. I want all three of us to walk out of here."

"So you can be the hero all of a sudden? So you can say you saved this bitch? Get your name in the paper? What a joke. After you were with me in my home on Saturday, chatting while she was just down the hallway."

Rheeder was smiling now.

"She was in the next room. Ten steps from where you stood. And you had no clue. And I sat there and I couldn't share the joke with you."

"Let her go."

"You probably wouldn't have got it anyway. You don't

really look like someone with a sense of humor." The smile disappeared as if a switch were flicked. "Okay, Magson, here is your chance to be the hero. Drop your pistol, or watch me blow this bitch's brains out right in front of you."

Magson didn't look away from Rheeder's eyes for a second, but he noticed that Nanette had no reaction to the threat made against her. What had he given her? "Don't make things worse."

"Doesn't look like you want to save her."

Rheeder pulled the hammer back with his thumb. But that was not what convinced Magson that he was not bluffing. It was his eyes. Staring at him. There was nothing in them. He knew Rheeder would do it, regardless of the consequences. And what was the alternative? Even if he trusted his own ability more than it deserved and he took the chance of shooting Rheeder, he would fall backwards, taking Nanette with him, two stories to the ground below.

"Say bye, Nanette." The index finger started to curl.

"All right." Magson raised the pistol and his left hand. "All right." He lowered the pistol.

"On the ground."

He pressed the safety back on and dropped the weapon.

It clattered on the screed.

"All right, Rheeder. I've done what you asked. Now let her go."

Rheeder removed the pistol from Nanette's temple.

And aimed it at Magson.

"This is not the road you want to take."

"How do you know which road I want to take, Magson?"

The shot erupted. Magson saw the flash. Felt the violence smashing into him. Fell backwards on the hard floor. It was cold. Damp. He smelled the cement. He stared up at the sky. Gray clouds. Winter. And silent. Everything was silent. His life seeped from him onto the cold cement.

He saw it all in his mind and thought of Hannes. *Perhaps you can ring again.* A month ago he would have begged the bullet to come to him. But not today. Not here.

Magson closed his eyes and opened them, returning to reality.

Frans Rheeder was smiling behind the dark hole of the pistol's barrel. How much time before he actually pulled the trigger?

Nanette moved backwards. Rheeder had to take a step back and his foot was on the edge of the building. He lost his balance and started falling. His left hand still gripped Nanette's throat. Her face was like wax. She was still pushing backwards, as Rheeder's right arm waved wildly in an attempt to regain his balance.

Magson rushed forward, grabbing Rheeder's arm with both his hands. His right hand was around Rheeder's wrist, but the left had only gotten the jacket's sleeve. He pulled, and for a moment there was equilibrium between Rheeder and Nanette falling backwards and Magson trying to prevent it. The sleeve slipped and the balance shifted. The faded blue-gray cap tumbled to the ground.

"Take my arm!" yelled Magson.

But Rheeder was still clutching the pistol. He looked into Magson's eyes.

Magson pulled. His front foot was scraping across the cement, but he tugged harder. Rheeder's fingers gripped his wrist. Magson felt the power in the man's arm and had to bolster his stance, but they started coming, more, and more, and then too much and he lost his balance. His head hit the cement, hard, and Nanette and Rheeder collapsed on top of him. Fingers curled around his throat, strong fingers that squeezed, and he couldn't breathe. His right arm was trapped under the weight of the bodies. He managed to wrench his left arm free, but a second hand was now around his throat. He couldn't breathe. He tried to get the hand away, clutching at the fingers, but with only one hand he didn't have enough strength. His lungs were burning. He needed oxygen. He clawed desperately with his left hand, scratching off skin, but got no traction.

The fingers loosened around his throat and he sucked the cold winter air into his lungs in scraping gasps. It was at once painful and wonderful. A man's voice was yelling.

Magson saw Menck pulling Rheeder off him, pistol against his head. Rheeder's face was contorted with rage, but even that found no reflection in his eyes.

"Are you okay, Mags?" asked Menck.

"Ja." His voice lacked power. He pressed against his aching throat. Najeer and Theko were also at the top of the stairs, but Magson was looking at the girl.

Norman Reid hugged her to him and touched her face. He studied her as if he wanted to make sure that it really was his daughter. He talked to her, but she did not respond. Again he folded his arms around her and clutched her close to him. Her face was turned towards Magson. She was crying. Without a sound. Without any emotion on her face.

Menck cuffed Rheeder's hands behind his back.

Magson got up.

There was movement on the right. Norman Reid had a pistol in his right hand, aimed at Rheeder. With his left he was keeping his daughter behind him.

"What the hell did you do to her?" he screamed.

"No, Mr. Reid," said Menck. "Don't do this."

"Look at her!" There were two wet trails down his cheeks.

"Mr. Reid," said Magson. It hurt to talk with any volume and the hoarse voice remained low. "Norman. He deserves it. But Nanette doesn't. She will need you. If you pull that trigger now, you won't be able to give her the care and love she needs."

"Look at her," he said again, his voice broken.

"I know. I know. That's why you must not do this. She will need you now more than ever."

Norman Reid's hand quivered. His face was shattered and tears flowed freely from his eyes.

"Come, Mr. Reid." Magson placed his hand around the pistol and removed it from Norman Reid's. "Nanette is all that is important now."

"She will never forget all the things the two of us did together," said Rheeder.

Magson stepped forward and punched him. "Shut up!"

Rheeder raised his head. His face was twisted and he licked at the blood at the corner of his mouth. His cold eyes glared at Magson.

Magson thought of photos against a wall in a police building. Three girls with dark brown hair—one with a shy smile, one with a slightly mischievous expression, one with exceptional eyes. A blonde girl with a lock of hair hanging down the side of her face. Another brunette with delicate features. And a sixth one, wide smile and blonde ponytail draped over her shoulder. All of them young. All of them pretty. All of them smiling, with dreams for the future. All of them taken and used for this man's pleasure, and discarded once he was finished. Only one had survived, but how long would it take her to smile again?

"Frans Rheeder, you are under arrest for the abduction of Nanette Reid."

Rheeder just stared at him.

"You have the right to remain silent. Anything you say or do will be placed on record. You have the right to hire an attorney of your choice. If you can't afford a private attorney, you can apply to the court for a legal aid attorney. Do you understand these rights?"

Rheeder said nothing.

Nineteen

Magson left the house. The night air was chilly against his face. It smelled of smoke and something thick and heavy. He looked up at the gray clouds, the dark spaces between. Here, at the back of the house, it was quiet. At the front there were cameras and reporters and neighbors and uniforms. He walked over to the Vibracrete wall and peered over the top. Squares of light in the house next door. The light reflected dimly on the black ripples in the swimming pool. Nobody had had any idea what was going on inside this house. The Trellidoor at one of the bedrooms. The additional burglar bars in front of the window. The next room containing the large double bed and the mirrors on the walls. The closet. Dildos of various sizes on one shelf. A collection of rope in neat coils. Panties and jewelry. And two metal rings on the ceiling, a pulley system on the wall.

After you were with me in my home on Saturday, chatting while she was just down the hallway.

Every time he thought of Nanette Reid, his chest closed and he struggled to breathe.

Ten steps from where you stood.

In the study they'd found several notebooks. Some were written in some kind of code. Others were filled with sketches and descriptions of fantasies, activities Rheeder had undoubtedly performed on the girls.

Ten steps from where you stood.

They had been there and they had walked out of the house and left her there. Three days. He couldn't get that image of her against her father's shoulder out of his head. The emotionless tears. The dead eyes.

He gripped the top of the wall, pressed his forehead against the cold cement.

And thus far all they had been able to determine regarding Sarisha Uys was that she was not here.

Her face like wax. Dull eyes without expression. Tears flowing silently.

Look at her!

He had been so close; how could he not have noticed something?

She will never forget all the things the two of us did together.

"Mags!" Menck's voice.

He let go of the wall and walked back to the house. His hands were cold. It was only in the light that he noticed the blood on them.

June 18, 2014. Wednesday.

The young blonde woman sat with her legs pressed together and her hands neatly in her lap. Outwardly, she was handling the situation extremely well. She was dressed plainly but nicely, in gray trousers and a dark-blue jersey stretching down below her middle, the sleeves hanging over her hands. Her hair was tied back neatly. She was wearing make-up. She looked like a young woman on her way to buy groceries at Checkers or Woolworths. Perhaps it was because she knew she was free.

"The date is June 18, 2014. The time is thirteen minutes past nine A.M., at the Serious Violent Crimes Unit in Bishop Lavis. Present are Warrant Officer Jan Magson, Mrs. Jeanine Rheeder and her attorney, Mr. Jakob Mouton. Mrs. Rheeder, I want to thank you for coming forward. Yesterday we arrested your husband, Frans Rheeder, for the abduction of Nanette Reid. You claim he was also responsible for the disappearance of Sarisha Uys on June 12, 2014. Is that correct?"

She nodded. "Yes."

"And that is the girl in this photograph?" Magson slid the photo across the glass table.

She looked down at it. "Yes."

"Do you know where Sarisha Uys is now?"

Her head tilted to the right and she looked up at him. "No. Frans took her away after she was dead."

"Do you know for a fact that she is dead?"

"Yes."

"How do you know this?"

"I was there."

"You have no idea what Mr. Rheeder did with the body?"

"My client never went with her husband when he disposed of the bodies," said Jakob Mouton.

"Were there other girls besides Sarisha Uys and Nanette Reid?" asked Magson.

Jeanine Rheeder nodded. "Yes."

"How many girls were there?"

"Five or six. I'm not sure."

"I have more photos. Would you identify those you recognize?"

She nodded.

Magson started placing the photos on the table. Lauren Romburgh.

"Yes. She was the first. I remember her well."

"What happened?"

"Frans brought her home one evening. She was completely freaked out. Frans kept her blindfolded the entire time. She didn't have a lot of sexual experience. And Frans is very specific with what he wants. I had to help her to do some of the things."

"This is a photo of Lauren Romburgh. She disappeared on April 26, 2013. Did your husband kill her?"

She nodded. "Yes. I wasn't there, but I know he strangled her with rope."

"How do you know this?"

"Frans told me. And I saw her. After."

Magson placed the next photo on the table. Dominique Gould.

"Frans selected her. He came and told me about her. He wanted me to help him to get her."

"Did you? Help him?"

"I couldn't say 'no' to Frans."

"Frans Rheeder abused my client physically, sexually and emotionally," said the attorney. "If she failed to comply with his wishes, he punished her. And after he murdered the first girl, her worst fear became a reality: she knew Frans Rheeder could kill her at any time he wished."

"This is Dominique Gould," said Magson. "She was last seen on October 16, 2013, at hockey practice."

"Yes," said Jeanine Rheeder. "She was wearing a hockey uniform. There was a massive bruise on her hip where a ball had hit her."

"Tell me what happened."

"Frans stopped by the side of the road. I had to get out and ask her something. Frans walked around the back of the car and forced her inside with a knife. She was English. Very quiet. Said very little. This one—" she tapped Lauren Romburgh's photo "—kept asking when we would let her go, when we would let her go. But she—" her index finger pushed Dominique Gould's photo about a centimeter towards Magson "—was just quiet. Frans didn't blindfold her. He knew it didn't matter that she saw us."

"Did your husband kill her?" asked Magson.

"Yes. He hanged her."

"Why did he choose this method?"

Jeanine Rheeder looked at him, then at the knobbly gray foam on the wall. "He said he'd rather just watch. Frans often 'hanged' me. He would tie me up and put the noose around my neck. Pull me up until only my toes touched the floor. Frans has a thing for rope. He's always tying me up. In different ways. Them, too." She nodded towards the photos in front of her.

"What about her?" asked Magson, placing a photo of Maryke Retief on the table.

"Yes. We did the same thing to get her."

"As with Dominique Gould?" Magson also pointed to the photo.

She nodded.

"Maryke Retief. February 27, 2014. Did Mr. Rheeder select her, too?"

"No. He was just looking for a new 'bitch'—that's what he calls them. I had to drive with him. Frans saw her walking and stopped. She really tried to do everything he wanted. Right until the end she still believed he would let her go."

She sat very still while she was speaking. Sometimes she turned her head away but, except when she'd been pointing to the photos, her hands remained motionless in her lap. Her voice was normal, as if describing a work project.

Magson didn't know what to make of this woman.

"Frans has this whole speech when they get to the house. She's here now and she can't get away and he's going to do what he wants and she can't stop him, but if she cooperates, it will be easier on her, and in a few days' time, he'll let her go. Before he hangs them, he lets them take a bath. He tells her he wants to let her go now, but first she has to be completely clean, so there's no evidence. He puts her clothes on the bed, because they are naked the whole time they're there. They scrub until they're red. Frans does an inspection. Then he tells her he just wants to take one last photo to remember her by, and then he's going to blindfold her and drop her off somewhere. This one still believed he would let her go as he put the noose around her neck."

He slid the next photo across the table. Danielle Ferreira.

"Danielle." The left corner of Jeanine Rheeder's mouth turned into a half-smile. "Frans picked her up. She was hiking or something. I was surprised, because Frans always wants a brunette—he says it looks good with my blonde hair. I liked her—she had spunk. Frans was hard on her, because she refused to cooperate. Frans has these things he wants you to say, and she wouldn't say them. He would tell her to do something, and she just refused. It didn't stop him. But he had to take everything—she gave him nothing."

"Danielle Ferreira, May 16, 2014. Before we get to Sarisha Uys and Nanette Reid, were there any other girls?"

"I know of one. Frans tried to take a girl—I think it was before Danielle. I wasn't with him. She got away. Frans was so angry. Went on and on about how she almost broke his foot.

He brought her school bag home. Found out where she lived. He was planning to go back to get her …"

"Ja?"

"I managed to talk him out of it. I said the police were obviously watching her, because they knew he had her bag. I had to pretend I was the girl who got away. Finally, he let it go. Frans likes role play."

"All right," said Magson. "Sarisha Uys." He placed her photo next to Danielle's.

"Frans chose her. He drives around in the afternoons. Sometimes he'd see a girl and watch her for a while. She often took her dog to a park to play. I talked to her. I told her I wanted to get a dog and how cute her dog was and we played with it a while. Then I asked her if we could show the dog to my husband, to convince him. When we got there, Frans forced her into the car."

"How did he do it?"

"At first he talked to her about the dog, asked if it fetched the ball when she threw it. When the dog ran after the ball, he took out his knife. He got in with her, on the backseat, and I had to drive."

"Couldn't you keep Sarisha Uys from going to the car?"

"Frans doesn't like it when you don't do what he says. Do you know what he did to Danielle? In the beginning he only raped her and used the bottle. But by Sunday he was so pissed, he couldn't perform anymore. So he tied her up and got the iron and told her she was going to beg to be his bitch. He wanted to hear her scream until her voice was gone. He stuffed a rag into her mouth so the neighbors wouldn't hear and burned her on the back with the iron. She did scream. He got stiff and raped her and hanged her. She didn't bathe. While he hanged her, he spat on her and cursed her. I had to clean her afterwards."

"My client was in constant fear for her life, Warrant," said the attorney. "Her life was a living hell of abuse and murder she could not escape from."

"I understand," said Magson. "I just want to get all the facts. Let's talk about Nanette Reid. Was Sarisha Uys still alive on Friday evening?"

"Yes," said Jeanine Rheeder.

He tried not to show the cold spreading through his chest. "Why did Mr. Rheeder want another girl if he already had Sarisha Uys?"

"Because he could. Frans doesn't need a reason. He went to get pizzas on Friday evening and came back with Nanette."

"Where was Sarisha Uys while Mr. Rheeder went to fetch the pizzas?"

"In the house."

"With you?"

"Yes."

"Did Mr. Rheeder often leave you alone with the girls?"

"Warrant Magson," interjected Jakob Mouton, "it takes a lot of courage for my client to talk about these events. She is traumatized enough without these kinds of questions aimed at incriminating her."

Was there anything more annoying than an attorney? "I am not trying to incriminate Mrs. Rheeder. I just want to be sure of the facts."

"The facts are that Frans Rheeder gradually pulled my client into his perverse world, cut her off from her family and friends, broke her down emotionally and morally, and ultimately involved her in abduction, rape and murder. She did not want to be a part of these activities. She did not want these innocent girls to be murdered. But she knew better than anyone what Frans Rheeder was capable of. He frequently told her he would kill her if she ever turned against him and described to her in detail how he would do it. And there was no one she could turn to for help."

"But you were not held captive," said Magson. "You have a job, your own car. Why did you never go to the police?"

"Because Frans knows people in the police," said Jeanine Rheeder. "They've been at our house. If I went to the police, they would know and tell him."

"Who are these policemen?"

"I don't know their names. Frans brought them and said, 'There's the slut. Take her away.' They handcuffed me and read me my rights and put me in the back of their car. We drove around for a while and then they asked me if I had a criminal record or whether this was my first offence. Then they said I had a choice. Either they would take me in and I would get a record for prostitution and lose my job, or I could pay a fine and go home. The fine was not money. When they were done with me, they took me home. Frans thought it was a huge joke. After they left, he told me what would happen if I ever decided to go to the police."

"Would you be able to recognize these policemen?"

Jeanine Rheeder looked down, shrugging. "They weren't the only men Frans brought home."

As she recounted the things she'd gone through, she revealed little evidence of the "traumatized" woman her attorney was so fond of describing. But people, those who learned to survive in extreme circumstances, developed a hardness. Like street children, or prostitutes who had spent years on street corners. Emotion was suppressed, dulled, often with drugs or alcohol but also naturally. Jeanine Rheeder didn't look as if she was on anything strong, perhaps a mild sedative. And one thing Magson had learned about women over the years: they had an inner strength that enabled them to survive unimaginable circumstances.

"What made you decide to contact me?" asked Magson.

"Hope. There was something in your eyes. When you gave me your card. I could see you'd been hurt. I thought you would understand."

"I am trying."

Jeanine Rheeder stood up. She turned her back to Magson and pulled up her jersey, above her shoulder blades. She was not wearing a bra. Her back had bruises in several places and marks caused by some kind of long, thin cylindrical object. The blue discolorations looked as if they had bled out of the dark-blue jersey. She turned around. More welts from lashes across her stomach and one across her left breast going straight through the nipple.

She stared at him. "Do I have to take off the rest of my clothes so you can see it all? It's okay, I'm used to it."

Magson looked away. "That won't be necessary, Mrs. Rheeder. Please sit down."

She pulled her jersey back down and took her seat again.

"Mrs. Rheeder came forward of her own volition, in order to help stop a dangerous serial killer," said the attorney, "not to be further victimized. Warrant, surely I don't have to remind you that it is largely thanks to my client that Frans Rheeder is currently behind bars."

"And I appreciate it," said Magson. "All right. I'd like to go back to the events of the past weekend. When did Mr. Rheeder kill Sarisha Uys?"

"Frans didn't kill her."

He looked at her. "What was that? What do you mean, Mrs. Rheeder? You said before that he killed Sarisha Uys."

"No. I said she is dead. I didn't say Frans did it."

"So who then …" He turned to the attorney.

"Frans decided to play a 'game' with Nanette and Sarisha on Saturday," she said. "That was after you left."

It was as if everything in his body ground to a halt. And then his heart started beating with such ferocity that he could feel it thudding against his ribs, the sound in his ears.

Jeanine Rheeder looked him in the eyes. For a moment she reminded him of her husband, on top of the partially built duplex, as he'd removed the pistol from Nanette's temple and turned it on Magson instead.

He blinked and saw Jeanine Rheeder looking at the photos on the table.

"He showed them the newspaper reports of Rykie and Danielle. He told them that's what happens to bitches who upset him. Then he put the noose around each's neck and pulled it tight until they were standing on their toes. He said he was going to tell them what to do and give them points depending on how well they do it. And the one who lost he was going to hang that evening."

Magson swallowed. "What did they have to do?"

"All kinds of sex things. With each other, with themselves, with me, with Frans. It went on the whole day. Frans wrote down the score so they could see it. They tried really hard. Then he wiped it out and said he was giving them one final challenge and the one who lost would hang right after."

He didn't want to, but he had to ask. "What was the challenge?"

"They each had to think of something and do it and the one Frans liked best, would win."

"Who won?"

"Nanette. Sarisha cried. Begged. Frans took both of them to the rope. He tied Sarisha up. Then he told Nanette to hang her. She wouldn't do it. She begged him to let them go, they had done everything he asked, they wouldn't tell anyone. They all say that. 'I won't say anything.' But Frans doesn't let anyone go. And he likes it when they beg. Frans grabbed Nanette and said then he's hanging her and put the noose around her neck and started pulling her up. Eventually she did it. After that she wasn't the same again. She was like a zombie. I thought Frans would hang her on Sunday, but he kept her longer. He was very proud of what he had achieved with her."

Magson stared past the woman, to the recording equipment, the TV screen. He tried to find a place inside him where he didn't feel, because that was for later. For now he just had to be a detective and obtain the information. He looked at the knobbly gray foam on the wall that aided with the acoustics. He took a breath.

Jeanine Rheeder was watching him.

"Did Mr. Rheeder ever tell you to hang one of the girls?"

"No."

"So the girls were held captive in the house for a couple of days. Where were they kept?"

"When Frans wasn't busy with them?"

"Yes."

"Frans has a huge sexual appetite. He ties them up in different ways, takes photos and m—"

"And?"

"And movies. He makes them do things. Me, too. Frans likes watching and likes doing. And he doesn't get tired. But when we sleep, there is a room with a Trellidor. Frans ties them up and locks them in there when he's not using them."

"Where did the sex acts take place?"

"Mostly in our room."

"Where were they hanged?"

"Also in our room. There is a pulley on the wall. He pulls them up with that."

"You mentioned photos and videos. Where are these items kept?"

"In the study."

"Where in the study?"

"There is a computer. And DVDs."

The computer had been collected for analysis, but there had been no DVDs. Only the suspicious gap on the shelf. "Where are the DVDs kept?" asked Magson.

"On the bookshelf."

"There were no DVDs on the bookshelf."

"Oh." She shrugged. "That's where they've always been."

"All right. I think that's enough for now. But we will have to go through everything again, in detail, so we can compile a complete statement."

Jakob Mouton nodded. "My client wishes to give her full cooperation."

Sarisha Uys had been alive.

She had still been alive.

Menck and he had walked out of the house—*Thank you for your time, Mr. Rheeder*—and left the two girls there.

He went into the bathroom.

How could he have stood right inside the man's house and not notice anything?

"Thank you for your time, Mr. Rheeder." His voice choked on the words and he hit the wall with his fist.

Had the girls known they were there? Had they thought they were being rescued, only to hear …

"Thank you for your time, Mr. Rheeder!"

He kicked the door of the nearest stall and it crashed into the wall. He kicked it again. "Thank you for your fucking—" he hit the door as hard as he could "—time!" Another punch. And another. There was a dent in the door and the top hinge had been ripped from the wood.

He turned around and placed his hands on the wash-basin, dropped his head, breathing hard.

Sarisha Uys was dead. They didn't even know where her body was.

He glimpsed himself in the mirror, wanted to smash it, but he didn't deserve to.

And Nanette Reid was hiding somewhere inside herself. How long would it take before she emerged again?

He should have put a bullet in Frans Rheeder's head on top of that building. Kept on pulling the trigger until the magazine was empty.

Menck was smoking an illicit cigarette out the window while waiting for the percolator to utter its final gurgle. "I'm brewing fresh coffee. I'm sure you could do with a mug."

"Ja." Magson's hand was aching. Afterwards, when he had become aware of the pain, he'd wonder whether he might have broken something. He would have to replace the door.

"You okay?"

"Everything Jeanine Rheeder has said so far corresponds with the evidence. She hasn't tried to hide anything. I think her attorney's plan is to milk her 'complete cooperation' for a plea bargain."

"It is an interesting tactic to provide cooperation without trying to get something in return."

"I think he's trying to present her as someone who wants to do the right thing, regardless."

Menck nodded. "It's not a bad idea. Refreshing, to say the least."

"She says Rheeder made videos. They're supposed to be in the study."

"So that's the weird gap on the bookshelf."

Magson nodded. "But where are they now? And that's not all. I phoned. The computer's hard drive was removed."

Menck frowned and forgot to blow the smoke out the window. "So Rheeder hides his movies somewhere, but leaves the victims' belongings in the closet? Why?"

Magson shrugged and leaned against the counter. He held his right hand.

"Did you get anything about Sarisha?"

"No. The woman says she never went with Rheeder when he dumped them." He pressed his thumb and index finger against his eyes. "She was still alive, Colin. She was there."

Menck did not reply.

"And everyone is congratulating us on getting him." A laugh escaped Magson's mouth, ugly and devoid of any humor. "The SAPS is *proud* of us."

It was not often that Menck had no response.

Magson took a deep breath, exhaling slowly. "Nanette still hasn't said a word. She just wants to sit outside the whole day. At night she sleeps with her mother."

"The one positive thing is that her parents have the money to get her the treatment and counseling she needs."

"It's our fault. Ours."

Menck shook his head. "No, Mags. It's Frans Rheeder's fault."

"We should've known. We should've done something."

"We hadn't slept in two days, Mags. We talked to so many people. By the time we knocked on Frans Rheeder's door … And even if we did suspect something, unless we actually saw or heard one of the girls, we would not have been able to search his house. It's easy now, in hindsight." He sighed. "The two of us will carry this. Because yes, we could've stopped it. But it's not our fault. The guilt is all on Frans Rheeder."

It didn't change how Magson felt.

The percolator sputtered and hissed. Menck poured two mugs.

"Do you think she will ever be normal again?" asked Magson.

"Nanette is a survivor. It's going to take time, therapy, support, but she will recover."

"She killed Sarisha."

"What?"

He told Menck about the "game."

"Shit like Rheeder should just be taken outside and shot. And dumped somewhere in a deep fucking hole."

"I would just really like to be able to return Sarisha to her mother."

"Yes," said Menck softly.

Behind his desk Magson looked at the cactus. The crown looked greener—getting some water on a weekly basis was having an effect. The brown thorns seemed a little redder as well.

He looked up the number in his notebook, picked up his phone and dialed.

"Warrant Officer Magson!" The pleasure in her voice touched him.

"Hello, Karlien. How did you know it was me?"

"It says so on my screen."

His name and number were saved on her phone, he realized. Still. It made him smile. "How are you?"

"Okay. I'm at home today, studying."

Of course. It was June. "How are the exams going?"

"Okay. Math was a slasher movie, but the rest wasn't too bad."

"The new school?"

She hesitated. "I miss my friends. It's just Gerhard who still puts in the effort. But there's a girl here who was in a car accident on Easter weekend. Her leg was broken and her older brother was in hospital for a long time. We clicked. The Lucky Escape Club." The last sentence contained a note of sadness, hinting at something that had been lost forever.

"We got him, Karlien."

Silence.

"He will never be able to come near you again."

There was a small, shrill sound, followed by a sob.

"You don't have to be afraid that he'll come back anymore."

"I heard you arrested the man who hanged those girls." Her voice was just a whisper. "Was it him?"

"Ja. He will be locked away for the rest of his life."

For a while she just cried. The girl with the long brown hair, thought Magson. The one who got away.

"I'm sorry," she said finally.

"You have nothing to be sorry about, Karlien."

"The girl, the one who was rescued, is she okay?"

Once again he saw Nanette Reid's head against her father's shoulder, the silent tears. "Physically there is no permanent damage. But she is very traumatized. She will require a lot of therapy."

"Were you there?"

"Ja."

"I knew you would catch him, Warrant Officer Magson. Now I am safe."

Frans Rheeder stared at him. The gray-blue eyes were relentless. They never turned away.

Magson looked at the man sitting across him in the interrogation room. Neat brown hair. Cleanly shaven. This was clearly a man who spent time on his appearance.

There was no emotion in his eyes. Rheeder's stare made Magson uncomfortable, but he refused to show it.

"Who?"

"Sarisha Uys."

"I don't know who that is."

"It's the girl you forced into your car on Thursday afternoon at a park in Bellville." Magson held the photo in front of Rheeder's face.

"Are you going to try to dump every missing girl on me now? I have never seen her in my life."

"Mr. Rheeder, we know you killed the girls. Lauren Romburgh. Dominique Gould. Maryke Retief. Danielle Ferreira. And Sarisha Uys. We found their underwear in your house. Their jewelry. The sex objects you used on them. The rope you used to tie them up. The noose you hanged them with."

"If any of those things are in my house, you planted them there." He smiled. "Except the sex toys."

"What did you do with Sarisha Uys's body?"

"Have you ever used a sex toy, Magson?"

"What did you do with Sarisha Uys's body?"

"There are few things as fun as shoving a large dildo up a bitch's arsehole. It always impresses me how large you can get their holes to go if you just put in a little effort."

Magson pressed against his damaged knuckles. Frans Rheeder was the reason why the death penalty was necessary. Some people simply had to be removed from society. Permanently. He pressed harder. Rheeder wanted him to lose control, perhaps only for his enjoyment, perhaps in the hope that Magson might do something stupid. Magson focused on the pain.

"Mr. Rheeder, you are going to be locked up in prison for a very, very long time. Maybe, if you tell us where Sarisha Uys's body is, the judge will accept it as mitigating circumstances when passing sentence."

"The best part is if you can watch her face as you shove it all the way in."

The Jack Russell started barking while Magson was still walking up the path to the front door. He pressed the doorbell. The dog's nails were scratching against the wood. The lock clicked and the front door opened. The dog hurled itself against the security gate.

"Lady!"

"Evening, Mrs. Uys."

"Have you found anything, Warrant?"

"May I come in, please?"

"Yes." She began unlocking the gate. Her hands were shaking.

The dog kept on barking.

"Lady!" Lizl Uys scolded again. "Please excuse her, Warrant. This dog has been acting so strangely since Sarisha … she sits in front of the door all day long and …" She finally managed to open the gate. "I'm sorry—I can't—I have to know, is she …?" Her eyes were pleading.

"We haven't found Sarisha yet, Mrs. Uys, but we are convinced that the man we have arrested is the man who abducted her."

"But what about Sarisha? Where is she?"

"We don't know."

Lizl Uys's eyes closed and her hands found her mouth. She leaned against the wall.

"I am sorry, Mrs. Uys. We searched the suspect's house and found these items." He opened the box. Inside were evidence bags containing a pair of panties, a necklace, two earrings and a watch.

She looked at it, her hands covering her face as she cried.

That raw sound of a mother who knew her child was never coming home.

There was movement deeper inside the house. He was sure it was Sarisha's brother who'd disappeared behind the door frame. Simon, Magson recalled.

Lizl Uys looked at him. Her cheeks shimmered in the light at the front door. "Where's the rest of her clothes?"

He recognized the hope in her eyes and looked away.

"If they weren't there," she said, "then she could still be alive. She could still be somewhere out there."

"I'm sorry, Mrs. Uys. The person who came forward—"

"I don't care! She could still be alive!"

He just stood there, the box with Sarisha's things in his hands.

"You don't know ..."

"We also found the other girls' underwear and jewelry. Girls that we know ..."

She made another sound. "Who is it? Who did this to my child?"

"I'm sorry, but I can't give out details at this stage. We have a lot of evidence against him. He won't get away."

"Why?" The tears and emotion had made her voice raw. "Why did he do it?"

"I don't know, Mrs. Uys." His voice was just a whisper.

She looked up, red, wet eyes. "Didn't he say anything?"

"He doesn't want to talk to us."

Her face distorted again. "But where is she, Warrant? Is she lying out there?"

He couldn't look at her. "I am very sorry." His voice was gone.

She took his hand. "Thank you, Warrant."

June 20, 2014. Friday.

Magson was sitting on the sofa, Rommel lying with his head against his thigh. Magson stroked the lush fur above the dog's shoulder.

He looked at Karlien's drawing. Since it had been framed,

it was even more striking. Before, he had never understood how much you could see in art if you only spent time looking.

Beside him, Rommel gave a contented sigh.

His time as a murder detective was over. It wasn't a decision. It was a realization.

He would not leave the SAPS like so many other ex-detectives. The police was all he knew. But his final years in the Service had to be in a different role. Perhaps the Police Academy in Paarl.

In Karlien's drawing, the sun poked its phantom fingers through the trees, caressing the yellow flowers, the bruised leaves where someone had passed through.

Sometimes he saw it as Emma's trail, the one she'd left behind when she'd gone. Sometimes he saw signs Doctor Hurter had left for him to follow.

He picked up the phone next to him and pressed the numbers to reach Hannes. Perhaps later he would simply select his son's name from the list, but he still had to earn that convenience. For now, he had to treat each phone call with the gentlest of care, the way Hannes had treated his hamster. Kasper. Magson smiled, as his son's phone started ringing in England. The hamster's name had been Kasper.

Perhaps it was neither Emma nor Doctor Hurter who had walked through the flowers.

"Hello?"

"Hello, Hannes."

"Hello, Dad."

Perhaps he was really looking back at his own path as he was walking out of the forest.

Author's Note

I strive for realism, as much as is possible, but there always has to be an exception. In this case, it is SVC. The Western Cape Serious Violent Crimes Unit in Bishop Lavis no longer exists. The SVC Units were disbanded some years ago, the detectives transferred to police stations. Some later joined the Directorate for Priority Crime Investigation, also known as the Hawks. The name explains why I decided to have SVC live on in my books: my interest lies in serious violent crimes and their investigation. SVC mainly investigated murder, bank and transit robberies, kidnappings and attacks on police officers. I like this focus, in contrast to the Hawks, a unit that is tasked also with the investigation of organized crime and corruption. And I like the old hostel they used for their office in Bishop Lavis.

Thank you

I only began reading in earnest when I was in high school. It wasn't long after I discovered Stephen King that I started writing. Since then my vision of my future self was always in front of a word processor flickering on a computer screen. It was a long and winding road. At times it was barely discernable. At times it was barred. And then, finally, I found the place I've been looking for for so long. The following helped me to stay the course:

God, who decided to give me a love of words and stories;

My parents, Pieter and Marietjie, who laid a solid foundation and always supported my dream;

Stephen King, because *The Dark Half* was where it all started;

Tania, my first "fan," who made me believe this was possible;

Wilna Adriaanse, who molded my writing at the South African Writers' College, offered advice and never stopped believing in Mags and his story;

Cecilia Britz, who made my dream a reality by saying yes and who makes it so easy to feel at home at LAPA;

Chanette Paul, who identified troubling areas in the manuscript and gave me a cherished compliment;

Karin Schimke, who took my words and sentences, made some repairs and added some polish;

Sean Fraser, who cast a sharp eye during proof-reading;

Charlene Hougaard and Esmé Smith, who made sure everything came together in book form;

Flame Design, who created a deliciously sinister cover; and

Shantelle Visser, who not only knows how to capture a moment on film, but also how to let it unfold.

In my quest for realism I rely on the assistance of people who actually do the jobs I write about. I was constantly surprised by the generosity with which they shared their time, knowledge and experience with me.

Lieutenant Colonel Michael Barkhuizen, erstwhile unit commander of the Serious Violent Crimes Unit in Bishop Lavis;

Lieutenant Colonel Johan Kock of the Biology Section, Forensic Science Laboratory, Western Cape;

Professor Lorna Martin, Doctor Gavin Kirk and Doctor Linda Liebenberg of the University of Cape Town and the Salt River Forensic Pathology Services;

Mark Myburgh of the Salt River Forensic Pathology Services;

Lieutenant Colonel Neville de Beer of the Somerset West Detective Branch; and

Lieutenant Colonel Kokkie de Kock and Warrant Officer Lilian Davids of the Local Criminal Record Center, Somerset West.

There are too many books to mention, but the following authors had a definite influence on the story: John Douglas, Robert Ressler, Roy Hazelwood, Gregg McCrary, Robert Hare and Vernon Geberth.

And, finally, to you, who picked this book and began reading it, because without readers a story is merely words on paper.

m.s.

www.martinsteyn.com